CHASING SHADOWS

Sharon Collins

authorᴴ

AuthorHouse™
1663 Liberty Drive, Suite 200
Bloomington, IN 47403
www.authorhouse.com
Phone: 1-800-839-8640

First published by AuthorHouse 8/27/2008

ISBN: 978-1-4389-0214-2 (sc)

Printed in the United States of America
Bloomington, Indiana

This book is printed on acid-free paper.

And for the best mother and brother in the world
Margaret and Alan Collins
And my beautiful talented little boy
Dylan Thomas
"God only knows what I'd be without you"

And finally, for everyone that lived in the Dublin of the early
90's, all the girls and guys I danced with in Mc Gonagles
and drank with in Bruxelles. Who have since mourned the
passing of "Bartley Dunnes"and who still think Packie Bonner
walks on water!
To **Murray, Eddie, Sinead and Helen**
Natalie Jones and Paul O'Rowe
To **Phil Lynott**, the first, and best of the real Irish rockers
Thom Mc Ginty, the soul of the city
And **Rory Gallagher**, proof that only the good die young
This one is absolutely, definitely, for you.
XXX

Prologue

The last five minutes always seem like an eternity.

Trying to look as though you're busy in case Christina, the hawk eyed manageress saw you dawdling near the changing room and collared you to sort something in the stockroom that would keep you over time.

The shop was almost empty, a last couple of student types, looking at the incense and perfume oils, and the buskers outside on the street playing their last songs of the day.

And then salvation. Six o'clock.

Home time.

The bells of the church up the street begin to peal and finally we grab bags and run.

Mrs. Chandra barely looks up from the till as the long z-reading comes spewing out, and she counts the small change in the drawer with her manicured nails and only says a cursory goodbye as we run out the door.

We three, Nancy, Becky and me, Carrie.

Like synchronized dancers we stop, about four steps out in the street and light up, and then start walking down the street towards the Molly Malone statue.

"Thank God it's Friday" Nancy exhales a stream of smoke and sighs.

Any other evening we would have turned right leaving the shop and went in for one drink in Bruxelles and then headed home when the heat of the evening had faded and the crowds on the street had gone. There's something gorgeous about Dublin on a summer evening. And twilight is my favorite time of the day.

But on Friday nights, it's different. No matter if your tongue was stuck to the roof of your mouth and you were on your hands and knees dying for a pint, on Friday night you sped home like the hammers and hounds of hell were chasing you!

At one minute past midnight our wages went into the bank and sat there all day Friday, gathering interest, until we hit the cash machine later in the day.

On Friday night we all go home and get glammed up in our best and meet at nine in Bruxelles Bar and go on to McGonagles. On Friday, every girl is Stevie Nicks or Lita Ford, and every guy is dressed in his best Axl Rose outfit and is, most importantly, a prospective Saturday date.

Friday night is rockers night and it's not to be missed. Tommy from the Sound Cellar does DJ and he plays the best music around. The air of the nightclub heaves with condensation and pulsates with good, hard, rock music. Tommy has never played the likes of Europe or Bon Jovi, because he said that any man that wore more lipstick than a woman should be shot, "with balls of his own excrement", never mind be a rock star. The smell of leather jackets from "Unique" and "American Classic" in Temple Bar, mingles with the overwhelming hum of "Lynx" shower gel and aftershave. And as for the girls, they are doused in patchouli and dewberry oils from the Body Shop and wearing all sorts of Indian frippery from "Chandra's" and "Damascus".

The aim of the night is to get a "court" or a "wear", Dublinese for a snog, down the side of Trinity College and bag a date for

Saturday night when no one wants to sit at home counting the stipples on the ceiling.

We push through the hordes of Spanish students, sitting and standing on the pavement outside Mc Donald's and give the Dice Man a wave as he begins his last turn and trip up the street of the evening.

"G'night Thom" Nancy smiles and he gives her his slow careful wink and stays in character.

The daytime buskers are packing up, the guys from Australia who do the Beatles covers are singing "Love me do" in harmony and they wave as we walk by, blonde hair shining in the sun. Sometimes, when it's very hot, Mrs. Chandra sends out for ice cream and we get to stand out in the street and listen to them for a while.

The sound of their singing follows us till we get to the junction of Nassau Street and cross at the lights, and then the traffic noise drowns it out and they are gone.

The sun is beaming down still, we all have sunglasses on, mine are the little round blue ones, John Lennon's they're called, bought for a fiver off the stalls on the bridge.

The people are like a wave, all moving toward O'Connell Bridge, and we get swept along, barely talking, all lost in our own thoughts.

"What are you wearing tonight?" Becky asks.

"Dunno, I'll find something clean" I say, not being one who thinks too much about clothes, and not having the time or the money to invest in my appearance anyhow.

Becky is different, she comes from a better house than mine, and can actually afford some of the clothes in Chandra's before they get to the bargain rail. She gets to keep all her wages, as her family don't take "keep" off the girls till they are earning over a hundred pounds a week. It's a good deal, and since our take home pay is eighty pounds a week, she's quid's in.

"Wear that shirt you got last week, the patchwork one, that suits you" She stubs her butt out on the wall of the bridge and we keep going.

"Maybe"

I'm already trying to calculate my budget for the week ahead.

Mam takes thirty of my eighty pounds off me, I have to buy my clothes and lunches and bus pass myself, and save with what I have left.   And its not as if I can borrow clothes off the other girls, I'm taller and broader than both of them put together.

We come to the junction of Abbey and O'Connell Street and it's like a different world.   The designer clothes and hippy dresses are replaced by shiny tracksuits and cricket jumpers and white trainers. Me and the girls look like creatures from another planet judging by the stares we get.

"Right, I'm off, I'll have three pints on the bar at nine, be there" Nancy stops, shifts her handbag onto her shoulder and starts walking towards Dorset Street, her steel tipped heels clacking on the pavement, while me and Becky turn for the bus on Middle Abbey Street.

"Jesus I thought this day would never end, I was so tired I thought I would die" I sigh, lighting another smoke.

"Who are you telling, Christine was on my ass all day, do this do that, had me ironing in that heat for fucking hours, I can't wait till that bitch goes to India, and gives me a break" Becky didn't get on with Christine, the poker faced manageress, who was thankfully about to take a career break and go to India.

She had left the shop once in the years she was working there, when she was supposed to be marrying this guy from America. She met him on a spiritual retreat of some description and had gotten engaged in a matter of weeks. But he jilted her at the altar and she ended up back behind the till in Chandra's and devoted her life to making ours miserable.

"Career break my arse, she's working there nearly twenty years and she's earning the same as us" Nancy snorted, when we heard she was going.

"Think she'll be back?" I ask.

"Hopefully not, I am praying that she gets trampled by a herd of sacred cows when she gets off the plane and has to stay there forever" Becky grimaced-

"Look at that fucking queue!"

The 39 bus stop was crowded, hordes of workers going home. There was nothing for it but to shove our way to the top of the queue and hope for the best. We're women on a mission, Bruxelles is calling, and we can't afford to stand waiting on the next bus to come.

By half past six we're on the bus pulling out of the city, and the traffic on the quays isn't too bad for once. By seven, we're cruising along Millionaires Row in Castleknock and Becky is getting ready to hop off the bus-

"See you in there later, yeah?"

"Cool, see ya" I slip my walkman out of my bag and put it on as she goes downstairs.

Castleknock looks cool and leafy in the evenings; you can just see the roof of her house from the road, not quite one of the mansions on the "row" but a fancy enough place as it is. Tucked into a cul de sac and exclusive. Her neighbors in "The Pines" are doctors and teachers and one low grade politician.

Over the hump back bridge and into the village and then, the bus stops at Macari's, and looking out the window, I groan.

"Oh nooo..." Under my breath.

Anto Kelly is at the stop, his bus pass in hand, and he looks up to see am I on board and seconds later bounds up the stairs.

"Carrie" He plunks himself into the seat and slips his arm along the back of the headrest. He leans to kiss me and I pull away-

"Anto" I say my voice as bored as I feel.

"Have you made up your mind yet?"

"About what?"

"What we were talking about last night?"

"I dunno what *were* we talking about last night? I forget" I'm playing for time here and he knows it. I slide my headphones off my ears and turn off the tape.

Last night, we met in our usual spot, at the tunnel, and I had made my mind up that this was going to be our last meeting. I got enough shit at home without adding fuel to the fire.

But Anto wasn't listening.

His whole conversation had been two topics, two things that he repeated and repeated ad nauseum until finally I lost it and went home.

"Fucks sake Carrie, the debs, and... and the other thing" He says.

"Oh, that" my voice is flat.

Put simply, Anto and I were snogging buddies, and no matter how hard he tried to make it into a proper relationship, I wasn't interested. He wanted to come to my Debs with me, seeing as he was out of school himself, working in a kitchen design company for the past two years, and this might be his only chance to get dressed in a tux and travel in something other than a squad car or on a bus for the rest of his life.

"I haven't had time to think about it Anto" I muttered, looking out the window. The village was packed with traffic and I willed the cars to part like the red sea so that the bus would move on and I could get out of the seat away from him.

I supposed that I would ask him to the debs, but only if no better opportunity presented itself. Skinny, scrawny, baldy headed Anto wasn't quite what I saw myself with dressed in a debs dress. I know it sounds shallow, but I was hoping for something better by then.

"Okay, and what about....the *other thing*" He at least had the grace to blush, his face puce, right up to the bleached blonde fringe on his skinhead haircut.

The thing he referred to was me and him, going all the way.

He'd told me the night before that he had a free house the following weekend and that his parents were going to be away for the whole weekend, down in Courtown at a darts tournament.

"What did I say last night?" I snapped, staring out at the bank and the row of phone boxes.

"Ah Carrie, come on" He tried to grab my hand.

"Anto, I told you, that's all finished, I told you that straight, I can't help it if you can't accept it" I pulled my hand away and the bus began to inch forward.

He got the huff and he sat back in the chair and folded his arms.

"So that's that is it?" he grunted.

"Yep" I was still looking out the window.

"You won't get a better offer you know?"

"Really, well, I guess I'll just have to live with that, won't I?"

Silence. But not for long. What is it with fellas? They think that when a woman says no to them, that it's an affront to their manhood! Could it not be that we have a bit of respect for ourselves and just don't bloody want to? A man in front of us tittered and I could see he was really enjoying our exchange.

I suppose it livened up the ride home. For him anyway.

"You know what you are?"

"No Anto, I don't, but I'm sure you'll tell me" I'm tired of this conversation, not even listening if the truth be told.

"A prick tease, that's what you are" he muttered.

"Yeah? Glad you think so" I yawned. Sorry I'd asked.

"Prick teasing, that's about all you do" He muttered and I shifted in the seat.

"Ever since you went working in Grafton Street in that bleedin' shop, you have fuck all time for me, I was all right to go out with when you were on the dole but not now, that you have your posh mates from work" He was furious but I couldn't help smiling.

"Posh mates? Like who?"

"Like, like that, ah Carrie I don't know, but you've changed a lot lately, you know, I don't know where I am with yeh any more"

"Where you are with me is precisely where you were last night, a friend and nothing more..." I said, but he interrupted me-

"But we had something special, you know we did, I thought we had something more than friendship, I mean, we've nearly done it loads of times, what about all that?" He wasn't making any effort to lower his voice and I was cringing in the seat.

Someone in the seat behind us roared-

"Ah love, will yeh ever give the poor lad his hole, he's mad about you"

Anto turned in the seat and grinned-

"Women, they're all the same aren't they? Always on the look out for a better catch"

Now I was mad!

"Anto, fuck off, I'm not listening to this shite from you, I told you no, in fact, if I was a virgin about to die wondering I wouldn't go to bed with you, and if you can't take that then tough, now, get out of my way, I'm getting out at the next stop" I literally walked over him and towards the stairs. My face was burning with shame and I knew that half the bus was listening to our row now.

"You'll be sorry Carrie, you won't ever meet anyone like me again, there's no man will put up with you teasing the way you do" He shouted from the seat, not caring if half the bus was turned around and laughing.

I shook my head-

"Meet anyone like you? I'm only sorry I laid eyes on you in the first place, and as far as being a prick tease, well if you had one worth teasing, instead of that sorry little acorn of yours, I might have paid it more attention" I went down the stairs. The upstairs of the bus erupted into cheers and cat calls.

"You'll be sorry" he shouted again, above the din.

And then, when I finally shove my way to the door and get off, just as my foot hits the pavement, there's a piercing whistle-

"Carrie, hey, Carrie"

I look up at the window-

"What?"

"You going to Mac's tonight?" I can't believe he has the cheek to ask.

"Where else would I be on a Friday night Anto?"

He grins-

"See you there so"

So much for me being a prick tease, eh?

When the bus pulls away I start to walk the half mile or so to the house.

Hey, I don't want anyone to think that Anto was a bad bloke, because he isn't, it's just me and him have been mates for years and the snogging thing happened by accident one night after the local disco. We sort of fell into a relationship or something, convenience really, if truth be told, because neither of us had the confidence to go out there and look for something better and it was easier to plod along and hope that our feelings might change some day.

I didn't feel anything like what I should feel for him. In fact, one of my recurring nightmares was that I was being walked down the aisle to marry him. I mean, most girls long for the day they slap on the meringue dress and do the wedding march, but not me, and definitely NOT if it was Anthony Kelly at the other end of the aisle.

I knew I didn't love Anto and I never would. And you might as well talk to the wall as tell him that. And according to Ma I was mad, a lad with a trade was always a good thing, she said, times being what they are.

I just wish I could feel different about it all. Close off the part of my mind that wanted so much more than this.

But then again, lately it had been difficult to know what I felt about anything any more.

The only way to describe it was a feeling of loneliness, and a feeling that this life I was living wasn't it, that there had to be more to it all, an aching emptiness inside me that tore me apart sometimes when it caught me unawares.

I suppose I had felt like that for years only now, as an adult, I could articulate it and make some sort of sense of it all.

I cut across the park and walked down Edgeworth Lawn, passing the so called posh houses, the little oasis of purchased homes that made up the more affluent section of the bad end of Blanchardstown. Where the burnt out cars and used condoms are removed a bit quicker by the council cleaning squad because these people actually pay taxes and mortgages and subsequently, their wages!

I was beginning to feel like the square peg in the round hole, not knowing any more what or who I was. But did I ever know?

Anto was part of a phase and that phase was over now, there had to be a better way to live.

I came to the gap in the shrubbery fence.

Back when the estate was built and families were being shifted out of the inner city into the houses, they were sold a dream of the better life for the kiddies, clean air and green spaces to play in.

And they took the bait, moved into the houses, and then reality struck, and they realized that while the council could build upwards of five thousand houses in the space of a year, they took five years to build a church and another three on top of that to build something approaching a shopping centre.

The old joke in the primary school, where the school yard faced the building site for the shopping centre, and we would sit watching the slow progress of the builders every day, drinking our little cartons of free milk, the saying there was-

"Blanchardstown, where they only lay a bri-ick a day"

Sung to the theme of the Mars bar advertisement.

And so the council planted, at the end of every row a couple of shrubs and left it at that.   A couple of conifers and a bit of box hedging and hey ho, we were supposed to believe that we were living in paradise. But with all the endless people taking short cuts, the ground was compacted and half the shrubs were dead.

Some wag had put a notice on the battered down fence-

"Abandon hope all ye who enter here, unless you're a junkie looking for gear"

Never was there written a truer word.

The sense of hopelessness was palpable. The sunlight didn't seem to make the place look any better, not even on bright summer mornings. And when the needle exchange at the end of the road opened at three in the afternoon, the zombies would surface, anemic looking babies in prams, clutching bags of Chickatees in dirty little fists while their mothers went in and got a little something to keep them alive for another day without having to shoplift or rob handbags.

Who needed Steven Spielberg to write horror movies when there was one unfolding day in and day out in front of our eyes? With permanently closed curtains and permanently vacant eyes, they lived and sometimes died, right on our street and no one seemed to care. As long as the health board handed out the physeptone and methadone they weren't that inclined to climb in someone's bathroom window at four in the morning, and rob rings round them.

"I'm all right jack; I'm looking after number one"

Don't think Bob Geldof wrote a truer word, ever!

Not that free methadone stopped them thieving. Hell no, listen; if it wasn't nailed down in our estate, it was robbed. And if you couldn't nail it down, you sat on it!

For years my Ma took the video recorder up to bed with her at night, hiding it in the wardrobe.

Rumour had it that Mrs. Staunton's false teeth were robbed out of her handbag at the bingo. What they were doing in her bag was a source of amazement to me, though Mam said that she was eating a mint imperial at the time.

As if that excuses being gummy in public!

Our shrubbery was the shortcut from the lawn in to the estate without the long walk round and I clambered up and hopped up on the wall. I sat and lit a smoke.

Home sweet home.

My house was right facing me, the sunshine turning the windows into mirrors of glaring white light.

It didn't matter what type of weather we had, the estate was relentlessly grey, and depressing. We had the highest instance of suicide in the city; we had the highest rate of people taking antidepressants. And, surprise!-

The lowest rate of third level students.

The local school had never sent anyone to college. Bet you'd never have guessed!

The chicken factory, the fish factory, or the local supermarket were the highest ambition for any girl that didn't get pregnant before her sixteenth birthday candles stopped smoking, and as for the boys, the army or a career in cat burglary was about it.

So by the time you were seventeen, if you weren't in uniform you were in handcuffs.

I didn't know what I wanted to be, but I knew one thing was crystal clear-

Someday soon, I was going to leave all this behind me, and fly far away.

I was going to be the type of person I always thought I could be and have music and wonderful literature and poetry in my home.

I was going to be somebody.

All the nights I spent dreaming in my stuffy, pink bedroom and trying to sleep on nights when the weather was so muggy there wasn't a breath of air, they weren't going to go to waste.

Because I knew that there was more to life than what we see, and even the things we see aren't all they look.

There are two sides to every story, the part we know and the bit that's in shadow.

And sooner or later it all comes into the light.

Just lately it seemed like my shadows were starting to overtake me and I didn't know what to do any more. I didn't feel like I belonged anywhere. I didn't know who I was and it was bothering me. I didn't have any mates in the estate because I went to what they termed a posh school in the city, and so had little in common with them. If only they knew that my school was right next to the fish markets and the girls were all inner city with accents you could cut with a blunt shovel, never mind a knife!

Sometimes I wanted to die, because I felt so alone.

I just felt that I was chasing a hopeless dream and I should give up.

But giving up meant staying here and marrying someone like Anto and living in a concrete box like these houses and eventually dying there. I couldn't do that, not ever.

I slipped off the wall and went into the house to get ready for my night out.

Maybe tonight would be the night that the lights went on and I'd begin to see again.

And over the next couple of years, I would remember that day, that trip home on the

bus, the row with Anto Kelly and the time I spent sitting on the wall looking at what was my home, and I would think, even though life seemed hard, then, it wasn't.

I couldn't have known what was to come, and what shadows would loom and threaten, and virtually destroy me.

Never again would life be that simple, where I knew who my friends were and most importantly, who my enemies were too.

By the end of that night I would have changed.

And so would my life.

So much so, that by the end of that weekend, I could never go back home again.

Part One
1990-1992

1

Carrie

Maybe there's a God above
But the only thing I learnt from love
Is how to shoot somebody who'd out drew ya
And it's not a cry you hear at night
It's not someone who's seen the light
It's a cold and it's a broken Hallelujah
©Leonard Cohen "Hallelujah"

Mc Gonagles.

Dark as the pit of hell and smelling like the bottom of a biker's rucksack. Or as Nance put it-
"The leather clad side of a hells angel's liathroidis"
That's his balls, to anyone who doesn't speak Irish!
Always had a way with words did our Nancy.
Every Saturday morning I woke up with a splitting hangover and a sore neck from head banging to the Ram Jam band and I swore that I was never going to neck another glass of that piss water they called wine, for as long as I lived.

Until Friday came around again and after a night of snakebite and "T'in Lizzie" in Bruxelles, we would stomp en masse across the road and into the dark hallway, trying to walk straight and hide our inside legs from the bouncers, because that was where we hid the naggins of vodka tied up under surgical stockings.

It was the music really. There wasn't anywhere else where a girl could go and hear Motorhead at its intended rate of decibels. Everywhere else was full of Stock Aiken and Waterman freaks in tracksuits, who's life ambition was to dance beside the guy in the pink fright wig and white Speedo's on the "Hit Man and her", and, of course it was more than your life was worth to venture into the Apartments or Rumours.

Not that you'd want to. Natch.

I had spent the last five years in school with girls who thought Bon Jovi were trash metal and whose style icon of the moment was a bird called Felly (short for fellatio, I thought) who sang a song called "Pump up the jam" in a German accent. She was the reason the Pound Shop sold out of neon "bum bags" in three hours. Nasty plastic things that were strapped round your waist and did away with the need to put your bag on the floor when you were dancing to Black Box or Dollar.

God only knew what Felly did for the sale of cycling shorts and vests; it certainly wasn't Steven Roche that had half of Dublin togged out as if they were doing the Tour de France. I mean, is there anything, this side of hell, more hideous than a size 18 arse in Lycra with a belly hanging over a bum bag, and a very visible camel toe, up on the floor dancing to acid house?

Didn't think so.

My nightmares were vivid enough without going looking for them in a nightclub, so I stayed well clear of the "Felly Brigade" and went south side to Mc Gonagles.

Best thing about heavy metal, I thought was that you didn't have to move your feet, but shook from the neck up. If you were like me, born without rhythm, it was heaven sent!

And heres the thing about head banging-

Listen to the drumbeat. Bang to that. Do not, I repeat, do not, bang to the guitar solo. Because if you do, one verse of "Ace of Spades" will fuck you up, big time, and land you in the hospital with a brain hemorrhage. You have been warned!

I had long since ripped the A-ha posters off the wall, and replaced them with Metallica and Motorhead, and a particularly vile picture of a strung out Sid Vicious with faux blood stains on it. I thought that it was profound.

Dorrie, my Ma, thought I was doing drugs.

But then again, she also thought I was shagging every lad in the estate, and I had caught her checking my drawer for unopened boxes of Tampax.

And condoms. Or as they are called in Dublin- rubber Johnnies.

Although back then, the rigmarole you went through to buy a pack of Johnnies was so ridiculous, that any lust you might be harboring would be well and truly evaporated by the time you had your box of twelve, extra strength, Durex in your shaking mitts.

Condoms were illegal in Ireland all through the eighties, bought on prescription only. And most doctors would only prescribe them to people who were married. Then the AIDS thing happened and the government stopped burying their heads in the sand and realized that people were having sex anyhow, and allowed them to be sold in pharmacies and other places. Including the Virgin Mega-store on the Quays. Apt, eh?

It was around this time that paper toilet seat covers started to appear in the toilets in town. Talk about paranoia! "Don't die of ignorance" the adverts on the telly said. It seemed to me that the government was the most ignorant of us all.

Most guys carried a single condom, the same condom their "mad cousin"-usually an unmarried bloke of a certain vintage with the look of a seventies corner boy about him- brought back from "Sin City"- otherwise known as Belfast- along with illicit magazines, tales of loose Protestant schoolgirls in short uniforms, blank cassette tapes and illegal boxes of Spangles in 1979. This cousin was also the one who promised the lads, a job lot of fake identity cards for a trip into the Lower Deck bar in Rathmines, to see a woman by the name of "Toni" who danced in her chain store, black lace, underwear and whose pendulous breasts and very visible stretch marks adorned the Sunday World paper week in week out. Apparently bus loads of oul lads from the back end of nowhere sat watching her week in and week out, and at the time it was the nearest thing to "String fellows" you got in Ireland. Nancy called it "String Vest Fellows".

I know Anto carried his Johnnie in a wallet, the same wallet he got the day he made his confirmation, with a faded gold dove on the cracked navy leatherette, the condom stuffed in behind the miraculous medal his Granny brought back from Knock Shrine the same year.

There was something not quite right about that, I thought. It was like wrapping rosary beads round a bottle of KY jelly or something.

Ma must have thought I was braver than I was, because there was no way I would walk into our local chemist, under the eye of Mr. Cousin's, the geriatric pharmacist and ask for any such thing. If I did, I honestly think the poor man would have keeled over and died, right there and then, among the antique home perms and the dust covered bottles of Vaseline tonic on the poky shelves.

His was the type of chemist where they wrapped a packet of sanitary towels in four layers of newspaper before they put it into a paper bag and then into a plastic one. God forbid that a woman could be so brazen that she would carry them home in a Super Quinn bag for the entire world to see!

He sold one type of Johnnie and one type only. The super duper, h'extra strong, rubber so thick you could fix a puncture on a Honda fifty with it, that covered the willy, and the balls and half the thighs in a layer of rubber so thick that your genitals could have been bombarded with a power hose and a shower of plastic bullets and still emerge unscathed. And with them, by special request only, a bottle of ice cold, tongue numbing, lubricant, the colour and consistency of the Gloy Gum the kids in the local primary school used to make Christmas cards! But you had to get a prescription for that. It was so viscous that you could have hung wallpaper with it, and I am almost sure that Mam did, once, when she hung the border on the hall wall. Nothing else worked on Super Fresco wallpaper, especially when you were hanging the "fleur de lis" border over painted woodchip that had been up since the year dot, and when it was dry a blowtorch wouldn't have shifted the thing!

In Mr. Cousin's world, the only hair colours were the ones that sounded more like paint stain for the front door, Mahogany and Burgundy and the ubiquitous Plum. All right if you wanted your head to glow in the dark, but not okay for me!

So anything I needed, I went into town and bought it in the more anonymous chemists on the Quays. Otherwise, the whole estate would know you had a facial hair problem, when you needed your roots doing, or when you had your period, or more importantly, when you didn't!

Ma's lightening raids on the bedroom brought her no joy. I told her I wouldn't be caught dead with any of the acne-fied, tracksuit wearing how-a-ya's in my estate and that she should calm the fuck down.

I said that I wanted love, real, proper, passionate love. Though not if it meant going out with some goon who's entire life revolved around Kylie and Jason "are they or aren't they?" and the next "now that's what I call music" compilation.

Not if I was to die wondering would I give my self and my virginity to some eejit who spent the night propping up a gable wall with a can of supermarket brand cider in one hand and a John Player Blue in the other, talking to equally inebriated gobshite's about wether or not Debbie Kelly, the local "femme fatale" was wearing a bra under her denim shirt last Sunday at mass.

Incidentally, she *never* wore a bra! Subsequently, she had three kids by the time she was twenty, and her tits were so saggy they hung, one under each arm, like deflated balloons.

Brings a brand new meaning to "lift and separate" I suppose.

At which point, in the conversation with Mam, the holy water and the pictures of Padre Pio came out of the handbag and I was doused and blessed till she calmed herself. I suppose the religious mania was a relief from the drinking binges she used to go on when I was younger. It amazed me sometimes that social services didn't come and whip me out of her care years ago.

Ma adopted me when she was still with her hubby, who had buggered off years ago when it became apparent that she was breeding prolifically with someone other than him. The first baby he took as his own, but by number three his patience was wearing thin.

I remember sitting on the lino in the hall and listening to them rowing.

"It's yours I swear Peter, honest to God it is" she screamed

"I'm firing' blanks all me life, I went to the doctor you lying cow" He roared and then the door opened and he came tearing out, and was gone.

I sat there for ages in my little flannelette nightie and waited to see would he come home, finally nodding off with my head against the banister rail, my knees tucked up under the skirt of my nightdress and my feet freezing cold.

Most nights when Daddy went out he came home smelling of the cold air and beer and the sharp smell of vinegar from the brown bag under his arm, and would bring me into the warm kitchen and me and him had supper, as he called it, together.

Chip sandwiches and Irel coffee in a mug, with a ton of sugar, and we would chat softly so we didn't wake Ma.

But he didn't come home. And I will never forget being shaken awake that night, in the small hours by Ma, no smell of vinegar, no comforting heft into Daddy's arms and the warmth of the coffee to defrost my feet. Only the stale smell of cigarettes and a curt-

"Carol Anne, go to bed" before she shut the kitchen door again.

He came back sometimes, for a bit. Then the gaps got longer and longer and by the time I was making my confirmation he was only a memory. And the way memories do, even that faded, till all I had were a couple of old photos. I couldn't remember the sound of his laughter, or his voice. It was as if he was dead. And to me he might as well be.

So time went on and Ma got in with the other deserted wives and went drinking after the bingo and then it was fuck the bingo and to the pub with them. By the time I was fifteen things were woeful at home.

Until one night the priest came to the house and sat in the chilly living room drinking out of the one unchipped mug we had and talked to her and asked her to come to the women's meeting in the church.

I don't know what he said to the women but it was out with the gin bottles and in with the Lourdes water and nightly rosary. Maybe old Father Green was more charismatic than we thought.

If I thought life was crap with an Alco it was worse with a religious nut.

I had to hide my tapes after the time I came home to the smell of burning plastic in the house and her on her knees in front of the kitchen fire the charred remains of Led Zeppelin IV in a heap in the grate.

It had been Daddy's and I loved it.

"What the fuck are you doing?" I screamed.

"Devil music, it says so in the paper" she rocked back and forth on her heels rosary in hand, and open copy of the Sunday world newspaper on the floor with the firelighters.

Seemingly some kid in America committed suicide after listening to Led Zeppelin backwards, or some such bullshit, and so his parents were urging people to destroy the albums and send the children to boot camp to get the influence of this filth out of their heads.

Alice Cooper was next for the pyre and I grabbed it from her and screamed-

"Ma, for fucks sake, his dad is a vicar"

"I'm calling Father Green down to you, you're a devil worshipper" she got up and scooted out the back door.

About an hour later I heard her in the kitchen her voice monotonous and a deeper one answering. I snuck down and listened outside and realized that it wasn't Father Green but his curate "Razor" or Father Ray.

I knew I would be all right; Razor had a fondness for U2 and roll ups. He strummed his guitar in the youth club and taught us Bob Dylan songs in four part harmonies.

When Ray went, there was a rake of soggy roll up butts in the ashtray and there was a calmer Ma. She stayed out of my room. I never came home to a funeral pyre again.

When I was in third year she took up with a new fella. He was someone she knew for a while and the three little brothers were the image of him. He shacked up with her the week after the letter came from England with a decree absolute and a note telling her to be happy. Peter, Daddy, never even asked how I was. I knew that at one time in the past I had been his everything and he had brought me everywhere with him, out onto the building sites and all. Showing off his little princess. But it came down to nothing when he went away. And from then on I stopped thinking of him as Daddy and called him Peter.

And then I stopped thinking about him at all. After all, he must have stopped thinking of me from the night he walked out, so, why should I bother?

Noel, the boyfriend, was a bollocks I thought. Bone lazy like, and a sleeveen. He was always finding an excuse to thump me or "put manners on me". He came from some god forsaken part of the midlands, the kind of dump with nothing in it bar the four roads out of it. He had been a horse trainer, he said, and though he was dogged looking now, there was something in him that told me that he wasn't always like that.

You kind of know when someone has been handsome or gorgeous; they carry themselves differently to the rest of the normal drones. I always think it must be the hardest thing in the world to have been like, say someone like Grace Kelly, or Marilyn Monroe, and imagine being that gorgeous and getting old and seeing it all falling apart! I thanked God every day that I was just passably good looking, nothing special or anything, just ok.

The story was that the Ma and he were friends and he and she were having an affair for years and that's why Peter walked. I tried in the beginning to find out where he got his money, and what he worked at, but he was like a clam in a shell when I questioned him.

He called me the little cuckoo from day one, and even Ma thought it was a term of affection. I knew better. It was in the way he looked at me, sometimes with cold furious hatred in his face. I stayed out of his way as much as possible as I began to grow up, because my very existence in the house was like a red rag to a bull.

He cleaned the house and kept the three young ones under control while Ma went out cleaning houses and the local pub. He seemed to be a bit of a control nut but she adored him. Everything she did was for him or about him. He was like a scruffy looking sultan with one wench in his harem dancing attendance on him day and night. A look from him was enough to make her shiver with fear, or, horrible thought this, desire.

I wouldn't dance to his tune, I never did, and he hated it.

He didn't say too much to me of late, but once or twice I felt there was a big bang coming and he was only biding his time. There was no reason for Ma to stick up for me now anyhow, I turned eighteen in June and she wasn't getting the cheque from America for me anymore.

I saw that cheque once, and it was for a lot of money. I never saw any of it. I knew people, Becky Whelan's Mam, in fact, who fostered kids, and she loved doing it but from what Becky told me, it was no where near what Ma got for me.

"You were adopted privately" was all she said and I had to leave it. There were so many things I wanted to ask but never seemed to get the right moment to sit down and get the answers I needed. Noel was always skulking around, or the kids were running riot and Ma always seemed to be up to her eyeballs in washing and ironing, and then I would forget and get caught up in studying or something, and let it go again.

In hindsight, I should have made it my business to ask. Life could have been so much easier had I known the truth about myself, back then.

The Leaving Cert was over and I knew I wouldn't get too high a pass in it. I had serious problems with Math and without it you were doomed. I had plans to hit America as soon as I could and was saving a few pound a week from my job in the Indian shop in town. Probably not as much as I could have saved when you considered that I was out three nights a week at the pub and McGonagles drinking pints that could have been better spent on my first weeks rent in the Bronx.

But hey, life was for living and God knew I needed a break.

Tonight was a weird one. Something had happened in the past few weeks that made me realize that I had to shift out as soon as I could. Sooner, even.

World Cup Mania had hit Ireland. It was all Italia '90 everywhere you looked, and the sale in counterfeit jerseys was unreal. I was heading in to town for a few drinks to celebrate the Ireland-Romania match that day, when I realized that Noel was on the landing. That was another thing about him, he sneaked around so you never knew where he might appear next, and unfortunately for me, it was all too often at the door to my bedroom when I wasn't fully dressed. I never knew what he had seen, on nights like this when I had showered and changed to go out, and it made me sick to my stomach.

"Off out" he asked, barring my way across the landing.

"Yeah, meeting the girls" I was looking for my pan stick in my bag.

"Sure it's not a fella" he hissed.

He was so near me I could see the yellow tint on his teeth.

"None of your business if it was, but its not, its Becky and Nancy actually" I tried to shove past but he held onto me.

"I saw yeh, in the lane with that young fella, I saw yeh, are you a virgin still after that?" He leaned in and for a horrible moment I thought he was going to kiss me. I swear if he did I would vomit on him, my stomach was churning so much. Squeezing past meant I would have to brush right up against him and I couldn't bear that either.

I racked my brains to think of who he meant. Who he might have seen me with. Then I realized that he must mean Anto, the guy I was kind of seeing for the past couple of years. We had a deal if neither of us pulled at the end of the night then we got it on. He wasn't a bad kisser and he was better than walking the Corduff Lane alone in the pitch dark. It was a well known, local courting spot, the local skin heads broke the lights every time they were fixed by the council and they had finally given up fixing them. Anto lived in the hope that I might give in and drop my knickers in the tunnel one night, but I wanted it to be better than that, with someone better than him, the first time, and so, we hadn't progressed beyond the odd fumble and I wasn't going to either.

He held it over me that there were "other girls" who would when I wouldn't but my answer to him was that he could go off and find one and leave me in peace.

He never did. He hung round me like a bad smell and now, I was regretting the day I laid eyes on him for giving Noel fuel for his fire.

"I see what you're up to, you're a tramp so you are, maybe you do it with everyone" Noel grinned, and my stomach turned over again.

I had to say something to get him away from me, there was something I couldn't take going on here, something dirty. Something filthy, that I could nearly smell in the air around me. Unfortunately I had to fight fire with fire and lower myself to his level-

"Must be hard for yeh, living with me Ma, only getting it once a year, and only then if she can do her rosary at the same time Noely, but I tell yeh, you won't be getting it off me, now are you getting out of me way or do I start screaming?" I tried to keep my voice cold and didn't shout, but a little tremble in it gave me away and he won.

I could hear Ma in the kitchen and I knew one roar would bring her running.

He grinned. I could see the spit in the corner of his mouth, a white scum on the inside of his lips. Oh God, I would kill myself if he kissed me.

"You're not my daughter, it wouldn't be a sin at all, you're not my blood, remember that" he ran one finger down my arm, brushing the outside of my breast. I shivered with revulsion and he laughed.

"Listen here Noel, you touch me again and I'm going to scream blue murder and you can explain why" I hissed.

He stepped away smirking and I pushed past him and ran for the stairs on shaking legs.

"I'll sort you later you little whore, you wait and see" he snapped.

I'd just run out of the house, and went into town.

For weeks I tried really hard to stay out of his way and never be in his company alone. But it was getting harder to do and I didn't know what I was going to do if he did corner me. It would be my word against his, the pillar of the local church and fine upstanding citizen. Who would believe me?

And now tonight, I was trying to be the life and soul of the party and it was falling apart on me. I'd heard of this type of thing before, before we knew where we were he'd be coming into my room at night and I didn't think I would fight him off so easily if he was on top of me.

I hadn't enough saved to even pay for a bed-sit, but that would change. Very soon I would be out of that house, and free.

∾

Looking back, it seems to me that I hadn't a clue, and if I had an inkling about how my life was going to change, right there in the black painted pit of McGonagles, I might have run for the hills and then swam for America that night.

I'd spent an hour fending off the drunken advances of Anto, who hadn't pulled, and who thought he wouldn't by twelve o clock and who thought I was it for the night. But somehow I didn't want him that night. I was feeling restless and antsy and wanting to be out of it, so drunk that I couldn't remember my name, so that I didn't have to think too much. The girls were all either dancing or getting stuck into the fellas in shady corners. I began to wonder what the point of it all was.

I'll have one more drink and if nothing happens I'm out of here.

I went to the back corner of the bar where it was dark and slipped the half empty naggin bottle of vodka out of my boot and filled the coke can I was carrying. I'd been drinking steadily since nine o clock that evening and was still cold sober. The can was filled with almost neat vodka now, that should do the trick.

I had just got the vodka bottle back into my boot, and my jeans pulled down over it, when a voice in the shadows said-

"Neat trick, are you always your own barmaid?"

Oh shit, a bouncer

Although it was well accepted that people brought their own spirits into the club, it wasn't really allowed, though the bouncers were usually good about turning a blind eye, unless, like tonight, there was a fight and lads thrown out in the road, and consequently, a little more Garda attention outside, then they were like Gestapo officers in monkey suits.

I decided to brazen it out and turned round with a smile.

And my heart literally stopped. He was beautiful. In the way that men can be beautiful. Even in the near dark I could see his skin was perfect, and he had lips that were made for kissing, in any other man they would have been girly, but on him they were perfect. But then I saw his eyes and they were the palest blue, like glass, glinting. He had long, dark, jet black, hair, a colour I had to use a dye to get. He was sitting there alone with a bottle of the wine they sold on the ledge in front of him.

"Hey" he smiled. And his teeth were perfect, his eyes crinkled as he smiled.

He looked grown up, finished, complete. In the way that none of the other guys I knew did. They still had the acne scars and the gaucheness that marked them as teenagers. This guy looked like he'd never had a bad day in his life. He wore the "uniform" like he'd been born in them, jeans and leather jacket with a shirt under it.

"Hi" I said.

And then he stood up and he took my hand and pulled me over to his chair.

"I've wanted to talk to you for ages, sit down"

So I did.

I sat there and we talked and somehow I felt like I knew him, but couldn't figure out how. It was weird, I was sitting there trying to be normal and cool and together, and all I could think about was touching him. I had to stop myself getting up and biting him. And the way he looked at me, I really think he felt the same.

We talked about the music, the club, and the people, the usual stuff you talk about when you meet someone you like and yet you're dying with shyness, in case you say something dumb.

"When did you see me before?" I asked.

"Here, I've come here for the past five weeks, watching you" he smiled.

"Really? Why didn't you..." I stopped.

The reason he didn't was standing a few feet away glaring at me like I'd killed a kitten in front of him, cooked it and made mittens from the fur.

Anto.

I prayed he wouldn't do anything stupid like lurch across to me and take me away from this Adonis. It was just the type of territorial bullshit he would go on with.

"He's not anyone, just a buddy, you know?" I stammered.

"Have you told him?" He jerked his head in Anto's direction, and I watched Anto scowl and stomp off towards the bar.

He knows for Gods sake! Surely he wasn't expecting happily ever after from me?

15

I nodded and stayed quiet. Happily ever after wouldn't be a bit of trouble if this guy wanted it. Not one bit of trouble at all.

And it happened.

You know the way you know when you meet someone that this is someone you can see yourself with? You know? The long haul, forever?

Dumb as I thought it was, I was experiencing feelings the likes of which I never felt before. And before you ask, not all of them were in the knicker department. I'd never gone there before, I was a fully paid up, card carrying virgin, mainly because I'd never met anyone who provoked a reaction in me, certainly not enough of a reaction to throw my caution and undies to the wind!

I knew, I prayed that when this night was over he would take me home.

But till he asked me for it, as dating etiquette dictated, I couldn't even give him my address or work number. I thought that I had to play it cool.

So we left McGonagles and turned onto Grafton Street, hands not even touching. I fell silent, wondering if it was just me in turmoil. All I could think of was kissing him, but I kept myself in check as I walked along beside him in the humid night air and we fell silent. In the dark club it had been easy to ask questions and tell him a little bit about my own life. We had a lot in common really, our tastes were similar.

He lived with his father, his mother was dead, he had come back from England when he was young, about nine years ago, and had gone to a private school, so this was his first real foray into the nightlife of the city.

"You're a late developer so" I teased. And he just smiled that smile that lit me up like fireworks.

I'd been out dancing for three years already, drinking for two and a half, Jesus you had to have something to keep you sane in the madhouse I lived in, even if it was ancient vermouth and gin from the cabinet in the living room. To this day I never taste vermouth without getting the smell of my Ma's freezing cold living room with its plastic covered sofa and chairs and the gluey smell of the MDF cabinet filled with discolored decanters, china statues, and plastic souvenirs from Courtown.

I wondered would I ever be able to tell him the half of it. He'd think I was nuts if I started to tell him now. I stayed quiet and looked at him now and then, a sideways flick of the eyes, so he wouldn't catch me.

God he was tall. At least six feet, three inches tall. More maybe. He had long hair and that rangy look about him. He wore a leather jacket like he'd invented it. His hands were gorgeous, artistic looking, Jesus; even the guy's nose was perfect!

If he looked like anyone, it would have to be a better looking, younger, not drug addled, Jim Morrison.

Going down the street he got the come on from at least ten women who in turn gave me dirty looks, but either he was used to it or a bit thick, because he didn't seem to see them, never mind acknowledge them. Seriously, not even when a skinny blonde, who had more than a touch of Stevie Nicks about her, spike heeled boots and carefully tousled blonde hair, falling artistically over her leather clad shoulders, walked right into Brown Thomas's window while she gawped at him like a goldfish out of its bowl. You could hear the thump of her head hitting plate glass for a hundred yards and it didn't even register with him.

She landed on her arse on the cobbles and her handbag went all over the street and he kept on walking along, oblivious to it all. I couldn't help thinking that it was usually me who did dumb things like that. And I thanked God that it wasn't me tonight, and kept on walking along, afraid to speak in case I made a fool of myself.

But he kept throwing glances at me, and smiling as if he wanted to say something but couldn't.

I had to say something; the silence was too loaded, to heavy with something, something I could not put my finger on. It was as though the air had turned into treacle and I couldn't breathe properly.

"How old are you?" I asked. Muggins thinking on her feet again!

"Twenty one, you?"

"Eighteen"

We got to the bottom of Grafton Street and he stopped-

"Look, the taxis are over there and I have no problem putting you into one and saying goodnight now, but I don't want tonight to end, I'd like you to stay with me and maybe talk some more, that's all, just talk" He was turning pink with embarrassment.

I thought that was sweet. Because in fairness, nobody gets to twenty one a virgin, at least I hoped not!

"Talk?" I smiled

He looked like he was going to die of shyness all of a sudden.

"On one condition" I said

"Name it"

"You tell me your name and where you live so I can tell the girls where I am, in case you are an axe murderer or something"

"I live in Blanchardstown, my name is Steven"

"Nice to meet you, my name is Carrie, Carol Anne actually, but I prefer Carrie"

"Carrie, come here to me" he murmured. And then he pulled me to him and kissed me and I swear to God I thought all my birthdays had arrived at once. My God could this guy kiss! He didn't do what every other guy did, try to feel you up in public, the second your lips met theirs, so that at times you felt like you were snogging an octopus, but kept his hands around my waist, and occasionally just stroked my back. It was pure, unadulterated, heaven.

For ages, oh it had to be at least ten minutes, we stood there leaning against the wall of the bank and just kissed like a pair of nympho's on death row. Eventually we broke apart, for air more than anything, and I let him lead me, on legs made of jelly to the taxi rank and we got in the queue.

When the girls arrived, a sullen and silent Anto in tow, I told them where I was heading and a little later, me and Steven were alone again.

So we talked.

Back to his place which was a little self contained unit like a cabin or a mobile, down the end of a garden which was his fathers.

"Why don't you live in the house?" I asked, as he led me to the gate.

"We got this when we were doing the place up and I used to use it for playing computer games, and hanging out with my mates, so when we moved out of it and back into the house, I asked Dad could I keep it for myself" he was rooting for keys.

"We eat together in the house, but I have my own space when I want it"

"Oh, right" I said.

He laughed-

"Don't be afraid little darlin' I'm not a beast or anything, I just like my own space" He stroked my face.

"It's just I..." I didn't know what to say.

He kissed me again and pulled me close to him-

"Carrie love, I wouldn't hurt you for anything, I promise you, you can stay as long as you like or you can go home when you want to, I want you to be comfortable with me, okay?"

"Okay" I breathed, my voice muffled in his jacket.

19

"Come on in to the *passion palace* then" he stood back to let me in.

I was busy wondering if he was a lothario who used the cabin as his own private knocking shop, and I wondered how many of the girls he had chatted up in McGonagles and brought back here for a "chat". And I was sure of one thing, if this was a knocking shop he was going to be sorely disappointed when he didn't get his jollies from me.

And, the part of me that had literally eaten the face off him in the taxi, well that part, was going to be sorely disappointed if he didn't at least try!

We got inside and it was amazing. He had candles all over the place and incense had been burning earlier as the smell had stayed in the room. There were chimes and big throws on the sofa and beanbags. The stereo took pride of place in the living room with a pile of vinyl three foot high, all the greats, Lizzy, Zeppelin, Cohen, and The Doors.

Deadly!

Altogether the ideal crash pad for my sort of people. Those who were hippies twenty five years too late, that is.

I couldn't help going into the bathroom to see was there any clue to past female occupancy, but there was zilch, zip, nada. Not even a hairclip or a bobbin.

Happy days.

So then, he asked me did I want a beer or a coffee and I took beer, and he asked my opinion on what type of music I wanted and I chose The Doors, and we sat on the sofa under the window, and we, we talked.

And I could feel something building up inside of me so that I felt like I was going to explode. He was sitting opposite me on the chair that was built in around the wall and the lights were low. There was a beautiful smell in the air from all the candles and the incense and I was feeling more than a little bit mellow from all the drink early in the night. I was putting the slow burn inside me down to the half bottle of vodka on an empty stomach. No wonder the nuns wanted us all to take the pledge, if alcohol made you feel this comfortable with a strange man!

I was listening to him talking about his work with his father and asking me about my writing, I kind of dabbled in a bit of writing when I was in school, and was hoping one day to pen a bestseller or something.

"If you're good, my dad might publish you" He said, and I laughed.

"I'm a long way from that let me tell you, I need a bit of life experience first"

"Like what?"

I sat up and hugged my knees and sighed.

"Oh I dunno, I suppose I'd like to travel, see the world, and do things, maybe fall in love and have the kind of grand passion that you read about in books all the time, you know, that kind of thing"

He smiled- "Grand Passion eh? Carrie...?" He looked straight at me, with those unnervingly beautiful eyes.

"What?"

"Haven't you ever been in love then?"

"Me? With who?" I nearly choked on a mouthful of beer. Didn't he know the kind of cultural wasteland we were living in? Most guys around here wouldn't know the first thing about music, or books or anything I liked. They thought the height of style was pristine white runners under their shiny tracksuit and the only thing they read was the auto supplement with the Saturday paper! Not my cup of tea at all.

And I presumed that the women wouldn't be his idea of fabulous, with Lycra tube skirts in a range of day glo colours teamed with corned beef legs and Sunshimmer tan from the Pound Shop, bum bags and high permed ponytails completing the look... at least I hoped they wouldn't be his idea of fabulous!

Then again, if that was what he was into, he wouldn't have a picture of Led Zeppelin on the living room wall, Motorhead over the little sink in the kitchen, and a record collection that John Peel would spit bullets to own!

And he definitely wouldn't be here with me, with my patchwork shirt and faded flares and Docs.

Would he?

I was the girl who got cat called when I walked down the street to the village, by the bloody adults! But like I said, wearing an Indian skirt and beads and subsequently being told to go home and "Give your Ma back the curtains" was character building!

At least it looked as if this guy knew his cahoona's from his Kerouac anyhow! I leant back and waited to see what he would say or do next.

"Who would I love? I mean have you seen what's out there" I said, more to break the silence than anything else.

And then he reached forward and touched the side of my face, his fingers twining into my hair, his touch sending shivers through me.

"I dunno, maybe some of the guys you hang out with, you must have been someone's girlfriend, maybe you were in love once before?" he kept stroking behind my ear and I closed my eyes.

No one I knew made me literally shiver with a touch. There was no one among all the people I hung out with, that danced with me in various discos and clubs in the city, made me feel the way this guy did.

I gulped another mouthful of beer and tried to move away a little so that I could get it together and actually talk to him properly. He smiled again and sat back, and funny, I missed his hand touching me and felt sad all of a sudden.

"No, I've not been in love, not till… not yet, I mean" I said.

"Neither have I, till now, I mean"

And you see that was what really freaked me. All along I felt I had to be cool as ice with men, and not let them know what I was feeling and what they meant to me. And up to now, dealing with the Anto's of this world, it had worked.

But convent education or not, morals or not, I felt something for this lad that I had never in my life felt before.

Desire.

It was bubbling under my skin like lemonade in a well shaken bottle. Ready to explode all over the place...if I let it.

I think the closest I ever felt before this, was the night I went to see Ian Astbury perform with his band The Cult, when Nancy and I had front row passes, and I nearly keeled over with excitement when he looked at me.

I felt like I shouldn't be here, in this place with him alone, because I knew that I couldn't trust myself not to sleep with him. And I was terrified that if I did he wouldn't want to be with me again. So I figured that I ought to leave while I was still ahead.

But I also knew that I would feel an unbelievable wrench when I left him.

"I should go, it's late" I said, putting my beer bottle on the floor.

"Do you want to go?"

"I..." I couldn't speak. He came closer to me again and stroked my neck, and I sighed and moved closer to him, my hands wrapping around him feeling his muscles moving under his shirt. I was dying to slip my hands under and feel his skin, but I couldn't summon the courage to do it. I knew if I did I'd lose myself in him and never go home again.

"Because I want you to stay, I don't want you to go, but if you have to then I'll walk you home, but I wish you wouldn't leave, not yet" He stroked my back and I could feel my skin literally tingling. Oh, it felt so nice to be touched like that.

"I shouldn't stay, I only know you a few hours and...." He stopped me with a kiss that took all my breath, his hands moved

23

up to the skin on the back of my neck and I sighed against his lips.

Damn he was good.

"Carrie, listen to me, you don't have to do anything you don't want to do, but I want you to know something, I love you, I loved you the minute I set eyes on you weeks ago and I can't believe that I have you here now with me, and…"

"You love me?" I gasped.

"Yes, I do, and I want you, I want to make love with you, because you, you're beautiful, you're fucking gorgeous" he kissed me again and I held him tight my head reeling with delight.

He thought I was beautiful, he thought I was gorgeous. He wanted to make love, not have a ride, or shag, he wanted to make love. And he loved me. I felt so fucking good it was like my birthday and Christmas had come on the same day as Ireland won the world cup and the Dubs beat the daylights out of Meath in the all Ireland football *and* hurling final! Highly unlikely but a wonderful thought just the same.

"But… you don't know me Steven, how can you love me already?" I whispered.

"I know what I see, the moment I saw you I knew you were the one, and I want to know more, I want to know every bit of you, you don't know how lovely you are, you really don't…" he touched the side of my neck with his tongue and I got goose bumps all over.

"Have you ever? Did you? I haven't done it before you see and…" I was pink with embarrassment   I didn't want him to think I was totally inept.

I'd a few near misses in my time and a fair bit of slap and tickle in the lane when Anto was walking me home, but the actual deed remained undone and I was scared to death that I would be crap at it and he wouldn't like me.

He nodded-

"A couple of times, when I was younger, but not like this"

"Oh" he kissed my eyes and along one side of my cheek and then down my neck, his tongue tracing a line to my collarbone.

"Carrie, I won't make you do anything you don't want to do, just tell me you don't want to and that's okay" he whispered, opening the buttons on my shirt and slipping it back so my shoulders were exposed.

I wished I was wearing a nicer bra. I wasn't exactly dressed for a night of seduction in a plain bra that had seen too many turns in the washing machine and was now a fetching "used chewing gum" colour, and my knickers were the polka dotty ones you get in Penney's, five pairs for three quid, but he didn't seem to mind that.

And after a while I didn't mind either. Not when I was lying back on the sofa, my shirt and bra on the floor, tangled up in his shirt, and the stubble on his face rubbing against the skin of my breasts. I wanted to inhale him, I wanted to be so tangled up in him that I wouldn't know where I began and he ended. I wanted him to be this close to me forever. I never in my life felt anything as erotic as when his bare skin touched mine for the first time. It absolutely blew my mind.

He smelt fabulous, a clean sort of soapy smell, so far from the usual smell of Lynx that most guys doused them self in when they were going out for the night.

Nancy used to say you needed three pints of beer to acclimatize to the assault on your nostrils when you walked into Bruxelles because all the guys were wearing it and the place stank like a whore's handbag!

Why did they think chemical smells were attractive? This was a million times better.

His hand reached down and opened the buckle of my belt-

"You okay?" he whispered, and I nodded.

He popped the button open on my jeans and slid the zipper down, and then slipped his hand inside, and started stroking me really softly, till I could feel myself getting warmer all over. I was wet and it would have been embarrassing with anyone else but him. I kissed him again and then moved my own hand to the zipper on his jeans.

"Have you got...something?" I asked. He stopped and looked at me.

"Yeah, do you want to go into the bedroom?"

"Yes" I smiled.

He kissed me again and then pulled his jeans up over his hips, I couldn't help looking at him and saw that he was hard, but at the same time I was mortified with embarrassment. I hadn't seen one before you see, and I thought it was fascinating.

He saw me looking and knelt down in front of me.

"You sure your okay?" he barely touched me and I felt his breath on my face as he whispered into my ear.

I reached out and slipped my hand into his jeans again and felt him, skin like velvet and yet warm and hard at the same time. He groaned softly and I moved my fingers around him and felt him stiffen all over.

"Bedroom" he whispered, his voice catching.

I grinned and took my hand away and went into his bedroom.

I kicked my jeans and boots off and slipped under the Indian bedspread on the bed. A huge poster of Metallica hung over the bed, and one of Jimmy Page at the wardrobe.

It was chilly enough in the bedroom and when he came and finally lay beside me in bed it was nice to have someone to heat me up.

And heat me up he did!

I thought, from all the stories I heard from other girls, that it was all a bit quick and none of them seemed to get much from the actual act of having sex. But then, they weren't with Steven and they weren't me. There was a lot more to it than the "putting it in" every guy seemed to ask for when you were snogging them, there was so much more to it than that, and I was loving it.

This beat the hell out of a quick deflowering in the lane on the way home from the disco, with a guy that reeked of garlic from the kebab he ate after the dance closed. No wonder the other girls hadn't liked it so much, in lanes and on park benches and in fields down by the canal. It was a million times nicer in a bed, with music playing and candles lighting.

He was gentle and slow with me. He didn't rush it, and he didn't go inside me till he was sure I was ready and he had a condom ready to go. It did sting a tiny bit but nothing to what I thought it would be and it was amazing to know that there was actually another human being joined to me like this. It was the most intimate thing I had ever done and I wanted it to go on forever.

"Carrie, you're amazing, you feel amazing, you're beautiful" he whispered in the dark and I felt goose bumps on my skin with every word. He looked like he was carved out of marble, his skin was so pale and perfect, and his hands were beautiful, his fingers moving all over me, his mouth following them, and then, just when I thought it couldn't get any better than this, I felt myself getting warm, and a wave of pleasure came rushing from my feet to the top of my head, and I held him tighter and felt him go into me harder than before.

I cried out and he kissed me hard and then I felt his body stiffening up, and he buried his face in my shoulder and called my name so many times I couldn't count. I was seeing stars myself and could only imagine what he could see and feel.

And then we were quiet, no sound only the faint scratch of a branch against the roof of the mobile and our breathing in the darkness.

He was still lying on me, and I didn't want him to move. He shifted his weight a little and looked down at me, his outline in the dimness like an Indian warrior, his hair falling around his face and brushing against me.

I touched his cheek and he smiled-

"Was it okay?" He asked.

"It was amazing, I loved it, and I love you" I whispered.

Even in the dark I could see his face light up. He kissed me again-

"You're amazing, I love you too, and I swear to God, I'll never let you down, not ever"

And then he had to move, he slipped out of bed and got rid of the condom in the bathroom and I heard water running for a second, and I just lay there all lazy and sleepy and thinking that I finally knew what all the fuss was about.

He came back to bed, and we lay there whispering in the dark, until I felt something move against me in bed and he kissed me really slowly and for ages, his mouth went everywhere, all over me, till I thought my fingernails were going to be embedded in the mattress and my lips were raw from biting back the cries of pleasure.

He leaned away for a second and rooted in the drawer beside the bed and took another condom out.

"Are we going to do it again?" I asked.

He looked up-

"Well yeah, if you'd like to, you're not too sore or anything are you?"

"No, not at all, I just didn't think, you...that you could do it more than once is all" I was scarlet and glad that it was still pretty dark. His laughter was lovely though-

"Oh you can, you can do it all night if you like, oh Carrie, we're going to have such a good time me and you" He hugged me tight and I smiled.

"You think so?"

"Yeah, I do, that's what love feels like, a damn good time, this is going to be brilliant!"

And I believed that. I walked home, next morning, down the Corduff lane in a daze. The sun beaming down and me still in the clothes I wore last night.

I didn't give a damn.

People were walking by me, heading to the village for the shopping, but I smiled and kept going. For the first time in my whole life I was doing the walk of shame, I was ruined, a dirty stop out, and I loved it! I couldn't have cared less if the old rumour was true and you could tell when a girl has "done it" for the first time.

Though come to think of it, I was probably glowing, even if the hickeys were well hidden under my clothes. Oh, it was obvious something had happened to me. I wanted to sing my head off, I wanted to dance. I was so happy I thought that the world should know it, and I figured that this is what being in love really meant.

Every inch of my body, the body I had hated till about three hours ago, the body I avoided looking at in the mirror and covered in outsize shirts and baggy sweaters, every little bit of it was tingling from his touch and his kisses. I had stubble rash where I wouldn't show a doctor and I was literally ready to fly with happiness and delight.

I had been paranoid about the little roll of flesh round my stomach and had been holding it in all night, especially when his mouth was traveling down, kissing a trail from my breasts across my stomach and lower still. I held my breath as he reached my navel and he stopped-

"Carrie, breathe for heavens sake, you'll pass out!" he laughed.

"It's just…my stomach…it's…" I gasped, letting out the breath I was holding for ages.

"Its warm, and its soft and its lovely, so stop worrying, I think it's lovely" he grinned.

So after that I didn't care a bit.

He'd left me to the tunnel in the lane, about three quarters of the way home, and we'd stood there kissing in the early morning for over an hour, till I finally told him to go home and get a sleep.

"Don't want to, like it here" he'd said and I'd laughed.

"Well, I need to have a shower and a sleep and change these clothes, and much as I would love to have round four with you, up against the wall in the lane with all the shoppers ready to walk past us to the village, well baby that ain't my idea of erotic" I said, still laughing.

"Oh I dunno a bit of scandal is what this town needs" He said, biting softly on the side of my neck till I squirmed out of his arms.

"Stoppit now, go on, home with you and have a shower and be all nice and fresh for tonight, I need my beauty sleep, I didn't get any last night" I was backing away and he followed.

"And you ain't getting any tonight either Carrie, I promise you that" he kissed me hard and went, leaving me tingling with desire again and facing the last little bit of the walk alone.

I called it love; I felt it really was love. It was like living in one of them Disney films where the birds sing and everyone breaks into song at the drop of a dime.

I was Doris Day in tie dye and jeans and I practically skipped up the path, rooting in my bag for my key-

Bang!

The door crashed back against the wall and I was punched. Hard.

I hit the wall with my shoulder and cried out with pain. A rain of blows came down, till I didn't know was it a fist or a boot that hit me but something was, again and again and again, till all I could see was the dark patch of lino on the floor beneath my face where I lay.

"Noel, NOEL, stop it, for Gods sake you'll kill her"

There was no let up-

"What harm if I do kill her, the fucking slut" he was gasping, maybe it took a bit more out of him than he thought it would.

"Noel, stop, the neighbors will hear you. NOEL" she screamed as he raised his foot again.

And he stopped. I lay on the floor still as a mouse. Afraid to even breathe.

He grabbed my hair and he pulled my face up so I was looking at him, and he turned my face to the side, where I knew by the look on his face, the abject disgust in his expression that there must have been a hickey on my neck.

"One fella not enough for yeh, ya tramp, I know where you were all night, and it ends now, do you hear me?" he slapped me right across the face and my eye burned.

I had no idea as to how he found out, but he had. And now like everything else in my life so far, it was going to be ruined and made dirty.

He had gone away and I was left sitting on the floor with my eye throbbing and tears falling down skin that was burning and raw.

Ma wasn't the motherly type at all, but this time she knew that Noel had overstepped the mark and had done wrong and so she brought a face cloth out to me to wipe away the tears and try to take down the swelling on my face.

"How did he know where I was Ma?" I asked.

She sighed.

"He met Anthony Kelly in the chipper, he was annoyed with you for going off with that fella. Who was he by the way?" she asked.

"Just a guy I met, he's nice, really nice Ma, a keeper" I winced, my lip stung like mad.

"Did you sleep with him?" she asked.

How could I tell her that? How could she *ask?*

31

I lied and said no, but that we had spent the night talking and time had flown away on us. She knew I was lying and I knew that she knew.

"Where's he from?"

"The village, the houses behind the supermarket" with every word my lip throbbed.

"What's his name?"

"Steven"

"Steven what?" She asked, holding her hand out to me to help me up.

I realized with a start that I didn't remember if he had told me that last night. I knew why Ma was asking, she had lived in Blanchardstown for so long now that she knew practically everyone in the place.

Well, practically anyone that lived in one of the five council estates that is.

Back then there was a definite divide in the town, between the people who lived in the likes of Corduff, Whitechapel and Fortlawn, like we did, and the people who lived in the more affluent end of the town like those in Castleknock. I'd only met Becky because she happened to go to the same school as I did, because otherwise, a family in Castleknock wouldn't allow their daughter to venture into the estates alone. Even at that, her Da used to sit in the Merc outside with the engine running when he was collecting her from mine, afraid, I suppose, that the wheels wouldn't be left on when he came out, if he chanced it and left it there.

It wasn't a bit strange to me that I had lived in the same town as Steven for over nine years and we had never met before now, I was "wrong side of the lane" after all, and he was absolutely, definitely, from the good side.

Back in the eighties, poverty was rife in the estates, and crime and drug abuse, and it was no surprise that he hadn't ventured into them. I wondered how he might feel when he knew that my mother was on first name terms with the local relieving officer and used the butter vouchers to buy her smokes rather than butter. It wasn't a big deal on our street, everyone had ways to fiddle the system, and cut the corners so that they survived, but to him, not brought up to that sort of life, it would be a revelation.

The Veggie Man sold runners, the Egg Man sold clothes, the Coalman gave the coal on tick till the Christmas bonus came in, and from the age of seven I knew how to fiddle the electricity meter with magnets so that the wheel turned slower and we could use the immersion. But not for too long. I think my mother was more afraid of the immersion than she was of dying, or anything else, for that matter.

You know what? I think I was in my twenties the first time I had a proper, scalding hot, deep bath. When I was a child, three inches of lukewarm water with a squirt of Fairy Liquid was your lot! And even then, you probably were second or third in.

Mam used to say that once one house had a loaf and another had a drop of milk, then no one on our street would ever go hungry. And that was true enough. I wondered what Steven would say if he knew that sometimes, a pot of stew fed four households on waiting day, and that the main meal in some houses on the day before the dole cheque came through was boiled rice and a scraping of jam from the pot bought last week. We didn't think of it, because it was just the way things were back then. We shared everything, from food to shoes and communion dresses. If you had it you gave it, and if you didn't you didn't.

Going to work in Grafton street had been like flying off somewhere in the tardis with Dr.Who because I saw people day in and day out, spending the whole of my weeks wages on a skirt in Chandra's that would fall apart after one turn in the washing machine, and wearing shoes, the price of which would feed us for a month. I couldn't get over it, not then and not now, the whole class divide, the insanity of it all, freaked me out.

"And we're supposed to be living in a republic" Nancy used to mutter when another spoilt rich bitch slapped her daddy's credit card on the counter for the pile of tat she might only wear once and throw into the Oxfam shop.

Mam was still sitting on the bottom step-

"Carol Anne?"

"Mam, I'm really tired, I need to go to bed, can we talk later on?" I grabbed her hand and tried to heave myself up. Jesus I ached all over. It was agony moving.

I got up off the floor in three stages and literally crawled up the stairs and into bed.

My whole body was in pain and I had promised Steven that I would meet him later for a drink in the Greyhound Bar. I needed to sleep and get myself together somehow. It took me a while to drop off, and I listened to the sound of the telly blaring and world war three raging in the kitchen below me.

I looked up at the frayed edges of the posters on the walls and the faded wallpaper with cabbage roses in sickly pink and wondered how I could even think of bringing someone like Steven here to meet my mother?

How could I bring someone who was obviously from a lovely home with nice manners and a good upbringing, to this lunatic asylum, with Noel like a lion in a cage ready to spring at a moments notice and Ma pandering to his whims like a Stepford wife?

I knew his mother was dead, but his dad lived with him and I could imagine him as a nice man with nice manners like his son. Cultured... that's what I thought he might be.

How would he feel when he realized that the girl his son said he loved, came from a run down council estate and a house that smelt of strong tea and cigarettes, with the odour of Dettol seeping down from the boys room, because all three were chronic bed wetters and the mattresses were scoured daily, and which had lino on all the floors and a mother who cleaned pub toilets for a living?

The hammering from Noel had spun me into a ferocious depression and I don't mind telling you I wept a little and felt very sorry for myself lying there in my bed with the duvet that was too short and too thin and only got to sleep when the music for Grandstand blared up through the floor. My last thought before sleeping was that the memory of that lovely night would have to last me a while, because when Steven realized the lunatic family he was getting involved with, he'd run a fucking mile away from me and that would be that.

I hated Noel for all the things he did on me for the past couple of years, but I despised him now with a passion, and a ferocity that actually scared me! I fantasized about killing him, slowly and painfully and watching him die.

Because he had taken the light and the happiness and joy out of something that was beautiful, and he had ruined it.

And I knew for sure that I would never be able to forgive him for it. But the bastard wasn't worth a life in prison for it.

I slept fitfully for the afternoon and when I got up and saw my self in the mirror, I couldn't believe what I was seeing.

My face was in bits, lip cracked and a beauty of a shiner on my eye. I was literally black and blue all over.

I had had beatings off Noel in the past when I got a bit lippy but nothing compared with the rage and hatred he had unleashed on me earlier. I couldn't even put the comb through my hair it hurt so much.

I did the best I could with a ragged looking ponytail and a good measure of Pan Stick on the face, but I was a wreck. I sneaked out of the house while the family was at their tea and walked as quickly as possible out of the estate and down to the lane.

I almost believed that he wouldn't be in the bar waiting, that the whole thing would be a memory and that maybe I was imagining all the things he had whispered to me and the muttered talking we had done in the dawn. Maybe it was all the lectures from Ma over the years, or the convent training, but the fear was there, that he wouldn't be.

"Men don't respect a girl who gives in before she gets married" Ma used to say. I wondered what she might think if she knew that I had "given in" after four hours of knowing him. And Noel used to call me a slut anyhow, as a matter of course. This whole episode copper-fastened his diabolical opinion of me. I had heard him roaring in the kitchen about me "bringin' aids and scabs and dirt" into his house! I'd wept with shame when I heard that, wept at the thought of something so right and so lovely being so wrong in his eyes. I'd heard Ma saying that he might be a nice fella and to give him and me a chance, and then Noel said, probably aware that I could hear him-

"That one, no decent lad would be bothered with a whore like her, she'd have to be with a dirt bag, she's so desperate for a boyfriend"

I'd buried my head in the pillow but the words still stung. And the memory was there, even as I walked down the street to the bar.

Even with all those horrible things Noel said, rushing in my brain like a whirl wind, and my face in the mess it was in and my insides still sore from the night before and the kicking round the hall in the morning, I still got a tingle up my spine every time I thought of him. And I blushed scarlet when I thought of the brazen things I had done! I composed myself and walked into the bar, full sure he would not be there.

But he was there and he lit up when I came in the door and then the smile died on his face and he grabbed my arm and brought our drinks to the table in the corner.

"What the hell happened? Carrie, your face, its all red, fucking hell, your eye! What happened?" he asked

And it felt like a dam burst in me and the tears started to fall and I wept and wept there in the pub like I never had before.

I couldn't tell him what happened, I was choking on the tears, and so he grabbed my bag and took my hand and we left the pub, and walked to his place.

I was shivering sobs by that stage and finally he managed to get out of me what had happened and he stared at me-

"I'll kill that bastard Anto, and as for Noel, the fucker" he stood there, fists clenched.

"And what good will that fucking do?" I sniffed.

"It'll stop him ever doing that to you again, its not the first time he hit you is it?"

"Never this bad though" I gulped. I was lying, he had hit me before and it was always painful. But you know what? I didn't think about it, once the pain went away. It was the run of the mill in my house and it wasn't something I could tell anyone. I suppose it's only when you see your family through a, well, a strangers eyes that you realize how fucked up it really is.

I knew Steven for maybe fifteen hours. I'd lived with Ma for the past eighteen years and I knew that our house wasn't the only one with secrets hidden behind the closed doors and net curtains in the estate. And my house wasn't the worst. But Steve was appalled that I could be living in a situation like that.

Comes from having a cushy life, I supposed.

As I said, I didn't know him too long and didn't know the half of it then.

He was still brooding, still standing in the middle of the room, fists clenched and fuming-

"That's not the point Carrie; you should be able to live your own life by now"

"And look where it gets me"

"Oh Jesus, I can't believe he did this to you, my poor Carrie"

"He's mad, he always hated me, I dunno what I did to have him hate me so much" I winced, everything I did hurt, even talking. I was so tired inside I could have laid down on the floor and slept.

"He has to be fucking crazy, Jesus what kind of man hits a woman like that?"

I couldn't bring myself to tell him the rest, the terrible filthy things Noel had said about him and me. I felt dirty even thinking about them and couldn't tell him, I felt like puking when I thought of them, from pure shame.

"You can't go back there, not now, not ever...." He began.

The door creaked and I jumped about three feet in the air.

"I thought you were going out son"

In the late sunshine he stood framed in the doorway. A man less like his son would be hard to imagine. Hazel eyed and hair the colour of a chestnut, stocky built and tanned. No more than five foot seven. Where had his tall dark handsome son come from? He must be a throwback to a previous generation, I thought.

He stared at me, and I realized I must look a fright, and I tried to clean my face with a tissue.

"What's going on son? What's happened?" He came in and perched on the sofa opposite me.

So we told him. Obviously not what had happened the previous night, I guess there's a limit to what *anyone* can tell their father. But about my home and what happened when I went there earlier on.

He just sat and listened.

"You look like a decent girl Carrie, and I would like to get to know you better, so why don't we go into the house and have a stiff drink and a think and we will see what we can do about this" he held out his hand and I took it.

"Thanks Mr., eh?" I looked at Steven and he smiled.

"Williams, But its David, I'd rather you called me David" he grinned.

And he led me into the house.

Two drinks later and it was settled.

I wasn't going back to Ma's house that night while Noel was there. I was to wait till the following day, Sunday, while she was out at Mass with the kids and Noel, and sneak up with David in his car and take my stuff. I could live there in the mobile till I got sorted out. I was seen by David's doctor, who gave me a cert for work for a couple of weeks till my face calmed down a bit and then I could think what I wanted to do.

He'd also asked me did I want to report the assault, and for a moment I thought about it, but then thought about what it would do to Ma if the police came to her door and how upset the kids would be seeing Noel being taken out, and shook my head-

"No, its okay" I said.

And when I rang Nancy in the flat to tell her that I wouldn't be in work and she offered the services of a few of her mates to go up and kick the bollocks out of Noel for me, I declined that too. I just wanted to be left alone and in peace.

Two vodkas on top of all that emotional stuff and the fact that I hadn't slept a lot in two days meant I was ready to drop. I yawned.

"Come on you, its time you were in bed" Steven pulled me up to my feet, and I sighed. I was so tired I could have slept on the sofa!

I was barely in bed before I was out cold. I didn't even know if Steven stayed with me or left. Until much later, when I opened my eyes for a second, I saw him sitting there in the dark, smoking and listening to music on a Walkman. I felt safer than I had in ages, and I slipped into sleep again. I was going to be all right.

Of course, the next day I was rattling with nerves. It's all easier said than done, but effectively what I was doing was walking out of my home, the only home that I had ever had. Okay it wasn't ideal and it wasn't the safest place to be lately, but it was all I had. But Steven wasn't having any of it; I was getting out of there. He was moving into the house for the time being, to give me space, although it was him I needed more than anything. Somehow I felt that once he was with me I was anchored. And then there was David. He felt like a father to me. I had never had that, not since Peter went away, and I loved the whole "I'll look after you" lark.

We got into the car and drove in silence up to the house. It looked quieter than it had been for a while. Then I remembered it was Sunday and most of the people on the road would be either sleeping off a hangover or in church praying. I slipped in and nipped up the stairs, and into my room.

Of course my room was thrashed, bed up against the wall and things thrown all around the place. I took down the rucksack that lived on top of my wardrobe and stuffed my few clothes in, and threw in my make up on top of that. I was stuffing my tapes into a super Quinn bag when I heard something behind me.

"What are you doing Carol-Anne?" Ma was quieter than usual.

I stared at her. She looked old this morning. She hadn't put her face on yet.

"I thought you'd be at Mass" I whispered.

She sighed-

"I stayed here; I knew you'd be back, thinking we would be out"

She must have seen the way I looked out on the landing, thinking that Noel was lurking there.

"He's out, I pretended to have a migraine so I stayed here, I didn't sleep last night waiting on you to come in" she lit up a cigarette.

"I couldn't stay here Ma, you know that" I felt tears welling up. She looked so forlorn there in her house coat.

"Where will you stay?"

I explained a little about the mobile in the garden and who I was staying with, being careful not to give the full address. The last thing David needed was Noel in full steam mode roaring and bawling in the front yard at three a.m.

I was ready to go, and I swung the rucksack on my shoulder, and she took the bag of cassettes.

"I'll bring them down for you" she walked ahead of me in her old slippers, and I felt so sad for her. She must have felt I'd let her down. Or she'd let me down, one way or the other, this wasn't an easy parting.

We got to the gate and Steven got out of the car and grabbed the bags.

"She'll be okay with us, I'll mind her" he said, and threw the bags into the boot. I stood there, unsure of what to say or do next. I tried to think of something, but then I realized that she wasn't even looking at me, but was staring in the window at David.

"I know you from somewhere" she whispered.

David rolled down the window.

"I'm sorry?"

"I said, I, I know you from somewhere, let me think" she closed her eyes and stood still for a second.

"Maybe you saw me around the village, I run a small company there, the publishers, Round tower, that's where you saw me" he was still smiling but what was that glint in his eye, like he was afraid.

"We have to be moving on Carrie, come on, hop in" he said. I could see the people beginning to come back from Mass and I knew Noel was probably one of them.

"Yeah Ma, listen, I'll be in touch with you, okay" I said, jumping into the car real quick.

We were moving then and she still stood there thinking.

"Where would she know *you* from Dad?" Steven asked.

"I've no idea son, no idea at all" he laughed "Now, how about breakfast somewhere nice?"

I smiled along with them, but somewhere inside me fear flickered, and I knew that the idyllic life I imagined wasn't going to be as easy as I thought.

2

Of course it was easy enough to plod along and fall into a routine.

I went back into work and had Nancy and Becky's eyes nearly popping out of their heads when I told them of the previous week's drama. They couldn't believe that I was living with the guy from the taxi queue and they were dying to see the little place that was fast becoming mine.

We were upstairs, ironing the clothes that came into the shop in big black bags. Mrs. Chandra gave us the pricing gun and we had to iron and put on hangers every stitch that Jan, the stockroom boy, brought around to the shop. It was a hit and miss affair and there was a whole heap of chatting and smoking going on at the same time.

"Is he the one then?" Nancy asked, tapping her ash into the Buddha statue that served ten years worth of shop assistants as an ashtray. At some stage someone had discovered that the head was loose and had slipped it a little to the side so that there was a gap big enough to hide the ash and the butts. We all wore so much patchouli and burnt so much incense that no one could smell anything else so Mrs. Chandra was none the wiser.

"I think so Nan, I really do"

"Wow, your sorted, its amazing" she sighed. Nancy was a really funny girl but you could tell at times that she wished she could find her soul mate. There was no shortage of men in her life, no shortage of them wanting to go home to her little flat, but she never seemed to be with them any longer than a night or two.

In fact, since she ended it with Paul, the roadie, she seemed to be on a, as Becky called it, a shag fest through Irish rock. Her black book was sight to behold.

"You know, you'd make a fortune if you sold your memoirs to the Sunday paper" Becky said. We were out one night having a beer.

"Yeh think? Jaysus I haven't done that much" Nancy laughed, and male heads turned from every corner of the bar. Even over the music her voice was like a bell.

"Will you go way out of that? Who was it last weekend? Gary Kenner? I mean Jaysus Nancy, he's worth a fortune" I giggled. Gary was a new boy on the block, part of a rock outfit from up north, newly signed and gagging for it, if she was to be believed.

"Yeah, worth a few bob but, not worth round two, if you get me" She crooked her little finger and we spluttered.

"Tiny" she whispered.

"God, who'd have thought it?" I breathed. The band were being marketed as the bad boys of rock and roll, sort of the Irish answer to Guns n' Roses, with a ballad at number three in the charts and rumors of drug taking, rampant whoring and whiskey drinking adding spice to an already explosive mixture. Gary was the pretty boy in the leather, up front, giving it socks to the girlies. He'd fallen for Nancy big time, by the sound of him. She had come out tonight because he was making a pest of himself, ringing the flat and asking her out again and she didn't want to go.

"He's good looking an' all that, but he has the tiniest mickey ever and no technique at all" Nancy giggled.

"Flippin' heck, who'd have known that? In his posters he looks....bigger" Becky finished lamely.

He did too. In the promo posters that seemed to be in every record shop, he looked as though he was hung like a donkey. Tight leather trousers left very little to the imagination.

"So, what? Is he airbrushed or something?" Becky asked.

Nancy gulped a mouthful of beer-

"Banana's..." She said coughing as the beer went down the wrong way.

"What?" I asked.

"Or courgettes, they shove them into their trousers, you know?"

I couldn't believe it.

"You mean to tell me that, even, someone like Axl Rose might do that? Go 'way out of that, you're having me on!"

"They all do it, makes it look good, you know, bigger for the photos... pain in the arse though when they fall out on the bedroom floor and you forget about them till next morning and you nearly break your neck on the way to the toilet"

We exploded into laughter.

"You'd never know who you'd find tied up in her flat if you called unexpected" Murray said. We hadn't realized he was listening. Murray had long been trying and Nancy wouldn't have a bar of him. She reckoned that there were plenty of men to be had without lowering yourself to the level of a waster like him and she wasn't going there for any money.

"Well it won't be you Murray so stop worrying! Anyway, you smoke so much weed lately it'd take rigor mortis to make you get a stiffy" Nancy raised her glass and grinned at him.

"Aw, you break my heart kid, you know I love you, and I'd suffer anything to get you into me bed, rigor mortis and all, that's love Nancy" He sighed.

"Ain't no such thing as love baby" She smiled back.

I knew I was probably being a pain in the arse, but I really believed that I had found the one, my soul mate. I sighed.

"He's just, he's perfect" I smiled, and listened for the answering snort from Nancy.

It came, on cue-

"There's none of the fuckers perfect chicken, don't put all your eggs in one basket till your sure, I know he's gorgeous and all that, but, just be careful, okay?" She came over and put her arm round me.

"Your such a softie Carrie, don't let him hurt you"

"I won't, he won't Nancy, don't worry"

Becky slipped yet another fringed skirt over the ironing board, and grinned-

"Well, I have a bit of news myself; I'm off to London next week"

"LONDON! How come?" we shrieked.

"Shuddup will yeh? It's a secret, well sort of" she glanced over the spiral stairs to see if anyone was coming up.

"I'm going to work as a model, I went over for a weekend there before the exams and brought round my photos and there was this one agency that signed me but I wanted to do the leaving first, it wouldn't have been fair to leave my parents up the creek like that" she sat on the edge of the banister rail.

Becky came from what I thought was the ultimate family.

Seven kids, five boys and two girls. Her dad was a doctor, her mum a psychiatric nurse. Both of them worked like crazy to make sure the kids had a great home and everything they needed. When it became apparent that the convent school me and Becky attended up to third year wasn't going to cut the mustard at leaving cert level, they took her out and put her in one of those new fifth form colleges so that she would get a good result in the exam. And she did, and I knew they had set their heart on making a doctor out of her. She certainly had the brains.

"But what do your Mam and Dad say?" I asked.

"Oh, they went mad for a bit, but Serena sat them down and told them a few home truths, you know, like, that a good leaving will always be a good leaving, and that I am technically taking a year off studying and seeing a bit of life, and that med school is a long hard slog and that I deserve a bit of craic" Serena, Becky's older sister, trainee solicitor and head of sense when it came to getting round your parents. She had sorted it and Becky was off to London for a year.

"But if I have my way I'm not going to be a doctor, I'm going to be a supermodel" she giggled.

Supermodels were the new breed of highly paid clotheshorses. And there was no doubt that she could do that job. Becky was tall, as tall as me, but with the size eight body that I would have made two of and her long auburn hair was straight. In some lights she was a ringer for Kate Moss, the new model on the scene.

Her father, trying to curb her enthusiasm a little, had signed the lease on the London flat for one year, hoping that she would have her little fling and get it out of her system. But I'd known Becky a long time, and I knew once she set her heart and mind on something, she would do it, no matter what the cost.

"You're both so lucky you know, Carrie is in love and Becky going off to London, poor old Nancy is being left here on her own some" Nancy put on a pout and we laughed.

Becky slipped her arm round her-

"Come on our Nancy, can't you go out to the love shack in Blanch and see if that sex god of Carrie's has any good looking pals we can set you up with? Or, if that doesn't work, you could come over to London to me and I'll get you off with Mickey Rourke or someone like that, cos I'm bound to be on the A-list soon, you mark my words"

"I might just do that, I wouldn't mind getting a snog from him" Nancy laughed again and we got on with our work, before Mrs. Chandra came up snooping.

Steven worked hard too. He did a bit in his fathers business but there wasn't enough to justify paying someone full time so he did a little here and there and also worked in a pub in town pulling pints on alternate nights. But it was an easy summer, easy going and with lots of time to discover one another and be together.

We drove one weekend to a place in Connemara, he had borrowed the car from David and we pitched a tent near a little beach and lay under the stars, listening to wave's crash onto the sand. I'd never been happier. I'd never felt freer and more at ease with myself. I hadn't been back to Corduff, it just seemed like I was growing away from them. I could hardly imagine that I was once living there, and having to answer to Noel Holliman.

"Its like magic, isn't it?" I stared up at the sky, at the stars twinkling.

"Yeah, since I met you it is" he whispered.

"Isn't it strange though, Steven, the way I know you so well, I feel like I knew you before?"

"Maybe we were married in a past life or something" he was drowsy; I could hear it in his voice.

"Maybe I'm psychic or something" I smiled.

"Maybe"

There were things that happened that were too freaky to be true. Like how I just knew things about him without being told. Like how we seemed to have the same taste in music and the same jokes made us laugh, and how we both had a very sore spot round the family subject. He didn't talk about his mother at all, and it was strange to me because he had her up till when he was eight or nine, in fact, he didn't talk about anything that came before he landed in Ireland.

And he seemed to be a loner, no close friends, just mates that would call up now and then for a game of pool or something. I'd wondered about that, wondered who he had talked to and confided in and went out with when he was younger, but he just shrugged and told me he preferred his own company most of the time as a kid. It seemed that very quickly I was his whole world and though that might sound overwhelming to some women, it suited me right down to the ground. I had lived most of my life being a nothing and having no body who really and truly cared about me, since Peter went away anyhow, and to have someone who wanted to be with me all the time, and who cared what I thought and listened to what I said, it was like being reborn.

Because, I did feel like I was with my soul mate when I was with him, no doubt about it. Maybe this is what happens when you meet the one you're meant to be with forever.

Three fantastic days we were in Connemara, and four magical nights.

Every evening we would walk the mile or so over the rocks and the beach and to the local pub. There was one that had traditional music, and one that had more up to date stuff going on. And one that had the best Guinness in the world, we were told. We would usually sit in a corner and talk, oh, about anything and everything.

"You know what?"

"What?" I asked.

"I don't ever want us to be like, well, like *that*." He nodded over at a couple, in their thirties who were sitting, dressed in their best clothes, obviously on a weekly night out. She was staring at the beer mat on the table and playing with a gold chain she was wearing, eyes glazed with boredom, and he, beer belly straining his jacket buttons to the max, was looking longingly at a crowd of men at the bar, laughing and joking, obviously his cronies. They hadn't exchanged two words in as many hours.

"Oh, we wouldn't be like that Steve, not you and me!" I smiled.

He nodded.

"I think I'll always have something to say to you, and I'll always like talking to you and listening to you, your so *bright* Carrie, you don't realize how bright you are, and how funny, even my dad says it" he drank the last of his beer and took a fiver out of his pocket.

"Will you get them in, I need to get smokes and go the loo" he rubbed my head as he passed and I went up to the bar.

I was standing there, waiting for the pints to settle, and was making idle conversation with the barman. Yes we were only here one more night, yes it was lovely, the beach was gorgeous, yes we'd be back, yeah, Dublin, from Blanchardstown.

You know the sort of thing?

I swear to God, I didn't see the guy coming.

He was one of the drunks at the bar, the silent guy's cronies? I was just putting the change into my purse and putting my bag onto my shoulder, when the next thing I know he has me in a clinch and I had his tongue down my neck. He had me pinned to the bar and I tried to push him off, but in fairness, I couldn't do much, I was penned in and my hands were pinned to my sides. I could smell the whiskey off his breath and it was the vilest thing I had ever experienced. I hated the smell of whiskey, Noel drank it, and the smell off his breath turned my stomach all the time.

I raised my foot and stamped, hard.

Now anyone who ever got a kick from a pair of Doc Martens will testify, it fucking hurts. He howled with pain-

"You fucking whore" He screamed.

He let me go and then backhanded me in the face.

Then all hell broke loose.

Steven must have been coming back and saw me in a clinch and flipped, he was head, neck and ears into a fight with two of the guys mates.

The barmen eventually restored order and we were separated from the other lot.

The guy who had kissed me was in his late thirties and was smirking-

"You want to watch that woman, she's a hot one, was chatting us all up the minute your back was turned" Steven said nothing and I was too sick to argue.

We left the pub, and walked silently along the cliff path down to the beach.

For the very first time since we met, he didn't automatically take my hand the minute we left the pub. I was still shaking from the, well, the violation of it all, Jesus all I was doing was making small talk, from where did that clown get the idea that I....?

And I remembered something that Nancy said once, when a close encounter with a roadie left her thoroughly shaken and vowing celibacy for life-

"You don't need to do fucking anything, when that type of man gets it into his head he wants sex, then sex is what he is going to have, wether he rapes you or stays on the more acceptable side of aggression, it doesn't fucking matter, they never need an excuse and they certainly don't need a come on or a reason, you could be sitting there knitting contraceptives out of bicycle tyres, dressed in a suit of armour, with so much hair under your arms it looked like you had Tina Turner in a headlock, and it still wouldn't matter a fuck to them"

The guy in question hadn't taken no for an answer and had punched her in the face, giving her a shiner that lasted two weeks, or about as long as her vow of celibacy.

And then there were the men who couldn't bear to see a woman happy and contented and at peace, men like Noel, who raised hell every chance he got.

I was really frightened now. Mostly by Steven's silence. He most probably thought that I was leading that guy on, but why he would think that I could want a fat oul git like that when I could have someone like him was totally beyond me. I always thought we were secure, or he was anyhow. I never thought that he would doubt me, or that he would think I might stray. But, surely he realized, if I was going to stray, I'd pick someone better than that old soak in the bar!

We walked along in silence.

Something had changed. I was afraid, really afraid. Surely this wouldn't finish us? Surely he had to see that it wasn't me? I had to say something, he was just too quiet, and he had the start of a beautiful shiner on his left eye, I could see it, even though it was quite dark and cloudy now. Our stars had gone. I could hear our breathing and the crunch of our footsteps on the shingle.

"Is your eye sore?" I asked, my voice sounding small enough to be blown away by the breeze. It was picking up and no mistake. I didn't like to think of the rain pelting down on our little tent. As it was, Steve was too tall for it; his feet stuck out somewhere all the time! I called him a giraffe, or Big Bird, like the one on Sesame Street.

No answer.

"Steven? For fucks sake talk to me" I snapped.

He stomped on for a while longer and just as we came to the beach, at the gaps in the rocks, he turned and grabbed my shoulders-

"Carrie, I...."

And as if God himself planned it, the heavens opened, and it fucking *poured* down.

Ten seconds and we were drenched. It was the kind of rain that hits the ground so hard that it bounces. It had been quite warm in the evenings, I thought that it wouldn't rain till during the week, but then I thought that heat brings lightening, and sure enough, a huge bang and a flash and the beach lit up.

Normally I loved electrical storms, found them exhilarating. But I was too leaden inside to enjoy this one-

He laughed as the rain battered down on us for a second-

"*C'mon*, run Carrie" he grabbed my hand and we ran, over the sand, my dress sodden and clinging to my legs. He couldn't be serious? Surely we would be half dead by the time we got to the tent if we ran like this all the way? Well…I would be anyhow. Running for a bus was about my limit, the four minute mile was way beyond me. Especially in a long dress and Doc Marten boots that were half full of sand and water and weighed a ton! But he dragged me along with him, and I tried to keep up with him.

And then I saw what he saw.

That day, earlier on, we had walked down and watched two old men caulking a boat, a currach, and they had left it to dry in the sunshine. It was still there, upended on the rocks, the rim leaning on a rock about four feet high.

He lifted the end of the boat-

"Get under there, quick" I slipped under and the sand was dry as bone, and funny, still warm. I was shivering, my dress was light, and it was stuck to me with the wet. My feet were frozen and soaked too. I leaned up and took my boots off, unlacing them, and stuck my bare feet into the warm sand.

My hair was sticking to my face and I rooted for a bobbin or something to tie it back.

All this time, he said nothing and the silence was loaded, with what I couldn't tell, not yet.

He was drenched too; the shirt he was wearing was clinging like skin, and his jeans so soaked that I could see the muscles in his legs as he sat there.

The lightening flashed every couple of minutes.

"It's a bad one" he said.

"Yeah"

I gave up looking for the bobbin; I shoved my bag down into the crevice between the rocks, and sighed. The rain hammered on the boat but we were out of it, and I leaned back against the rocks and listened. I bit my lip and looked at him under my eyelashes.

I wanted to tell him that I was sorry for whatever I had done. I wanted him to know I loved him more than anyone on earth. I took a deep breath and yet couldn't form the words and couldn't say what I wanted to say. I don't know what was stopping me, but I just couldn't tell him what he meant to me.

I felt the tears coming to my eyes and I willed them back.

I pulled the front of my dress away from my skin, and the cold air made me shiver. I looked at him and for a second, I saw something, a look in his eyes as he met my gaze and it was like nothing I had ever seen before.

It was as if they were lit from within.

Fire.

It could have been the rain or the smell of the sea, but we suddenly felt like the last two people on earth, and I wanted him. I wanted that fire to be inside me too.

It was more than the way I felt before now, it was better and worse and stronger than any feeling I'd ever known.

Since we'd met, he'd been the one who took the lead. He initiated sex most of the time, because most of the time I was too shy in the light, too shy to let go, to let him really see me.

But tonight, it was dark, I couldn't see him till the lightening came, but still I knew where he was and I suddenly felt that I wanted to do all the things that had been too intimate till now.

And for that split second in the lightening, I had seen the answer to a million questions in his eyes and I knew what I was to him.

If this was our last time, then by Christ he was going to remember it, and me, for the rest of his life.

54

In the dark, confined little space, smelling of tar and the sea, I knelt up. I could hear him moving; I thought he was trying to get somewhere that was a bit more comfortable for him to sit. And sure enough when the next flash came he was pushing his hair back off his face. I smiled to myself, and slipped the straps of my dress off my shoulders.

I felt like a siren, one of those mystical sea women who lured men to their death. Oh but, this, this had nothing to do with dying, I was alive, and every cell in my body knew it!

Rain still drumming, I got out of my clothes and crept the couple of feet to where he sat. In the dark, I started to find the buttons of his shirt and got it open, and then my fingers reached his belt, and I slid it out of the loops and opened the top button of his jeans.

Looking up, I could see him looking at me, his face mostly shadow, but still I knew he was there. His breath was on my face, and I saw him lean forward to kiss me, but I held him off with my hand flat on his chest-

"Wait" I whispered, thrilled to feel his heart pounding against my palm.

"Carrie?"

"Sssh"

He fell back against the rock and waited. I kept going; I got the other buttons open on the jeans and slipped them down a little, not enough so that he was out of them, but enough so that the line of dark hair from his stomach down was visible.

I ran my nails softly across his stomach and he moaned-

"Jesus Carrie, oh God, what...?" he slid down a little in the sand so I was across his knees, my head was bent under the boat, and I could see the outline of my breasts in the dark, and if I could then so could he.

Sure enough he touched me, really softly, stroking down the side of one breast to the nipple. It was hard anyway, but I felt something like lightening shoot through me and I shivered. But

I didn't want him taking the lead yet. So I took his hand and held it, and put it down on the sand.

"Wait" I murmured.

"I can't" he moaned, but he was laughing too, but I knew that it wasn't the kind of laugh that made me feel foolish; it was his way of trying to diffuse the situation and hold on.

But that wasn't what I wanted right now; I wanted to show him what I could do, that the person he had been with all this time wasn't the whole me, that I was capable of everything and more. That when it came to him, I would give him my very soul, if that's what he asked for. Hell, he'd had it from the minute I laid eyes on him. He didn't need to ask me for it.

I laughed softly and leaned down and traced a line, with my tongue and my lips, down his chest to his stomach, and then stopped, he arched his back and I could feel his hardness pressing into me through the damp jeans that just about covered him still.

"I want you Carrie, I want you now" his voice was hoarse, his breathing ragged.

A surge of power rushed through me as I scratched him lightly again.

"Wait" was all I'd say.

Rain still drumming on the roof, I slid the jeans off, and he kicked them away from his feet in a crumpled heap. I still didn't let him move, just waited for him to be still again, dying for him but still holding on, and amazed at my own temerity.

They didn't teach us *this* in the convent!

But then again, they couldn't have known that men like this still existed, I hadn't thought so. And if they did, I never in a million thought that he would be half naked under a boat in Connemara with me, about to do the boldest thing I had ever done.

I didn't touch him with my hands, I leant down and took him in my mouth, and he took a shuddering breath, which I could feel under my hand on his stomach. His fingers twined into my hair and he pushed my head down.

I could smell the sea on him, and the salty air, and there was another smell, of him, his smell, one that wasn't in a spray can in the bathroom or a bottle on the shelf. Without even realizing it I found the way and began to move my tongue and my mouth over him and on him in a strange sort of rhythm. But every time I felt him getting harder I would pull away and stop, kissing up higher, on his stomach or on the hip bone that was jutting out and where my hands rested.

"Carrie, for fucks sake, your driving me crazy, please..." His hands were buried in the sand, his fingers desperately trying to find something to grip.

"Stop?" I whispered, before bending down again.

He groaned-

"No, don't stop, *don't*"

I could feel him tensing up his muscles and I grinned to myself.

I touched him once with my tongue and he shivered, and then grabbed me, pulling me up so that I was half lying and half kneeling across him, he gripped my hips and pushed me down, and was in me, and I felt heat spread through me like electricity. His hand spread across my hip and onto my stomach, his thumb down, he found me and started to touch me, slowly first, then harder, his fingers wet and slippery.

I couldn't kneel up fully so my elbows were somewhere near his, my hair falling over my face, and when I kissed him, his mouth was dry and hot. He struggled out of the damp shirt that was still clinging to him and half leaned up against the rock,

I couldn't bend down enough to kiss him again, and anyway, I could feel myself getting dizzy, he was kissing my breasts, his tongue on my nipples one at a time, and the feeling of his stubble against my skin was amazing. I leant on the rock behind him and without thinking, shifted my body so that he was able to move deeper into me.

Still his fingers stroked and moved and he still thrust into me while I came again and again, till finally I felt I couldn't stand anymore, and he moved faster till at last he gripped me so tightly I thought his fingers would go through to my hipbones, and he came.

The silence was profound afterwards. The rain had stopped and the sound of the breeze and the waves was all around us with the sound of our breathing.

His voice came from below me, his forehead leaning against my collar bone, his mouth still on the crevice between my breasts. I could feel him still in me, and every couple of seconds, a tremor would run through me there, like aftershocks. I wanted to be like this forever, still, listening to the sound of him breathing and with my heart pounding in my chest.

"Carrie, oh God Carrie" he kept saying, and I stroked his hair, because at last I knew, I knew it all.

He shifted his weight and put me onto my side, where he had been lying became my place now, my hair in the sand, and my arm under my head. I felt like I could happily drift away now, but he had other ideas, and moved me so that I was lying on my back and he was straddling my hips.

The light was changing, the short summer night coming to an end, and I could see the crack of light getting brighter under the boats edge, and I could see him outlined more clearly leaning forward, just looking at me. He was so beautiful, my throat caught when ever I looked at him. I kept looking, his eyes half closed, and I reached out and stroked his chest with one finger, and he sighed. He took my hand and twined his fingers into mine.

"Wait" he whispered, and smiled.

I could feel the sand under me and the roughness of the hair on his legs around my hips, and he holding my hand so that I couldn't grab him or touch him again. I laid my hand in the sand and nodded, so he knew that I knew.

He half smiled again and kissed me, and then moved across to my shoulder, and slowly downwards.

"My turn" he whispered.

I closed my eyes tightly, and listened to the singing of the birds as once more, I was turned inside out.

This time it was quieter, and when I looked back on it later, I thought that night was the time our souls actually fused together. How on earth could we ever find this again if it wasn't with each other?

I knew him now as well as I knew myself. Knew his taste and his smell and we truly were the same soul now. How could I feel anything other than joy in him? There wasn't any fear, and any shame? Well, that was washed away with the sound of the waves and his breathing in my ear.

That night I felt truly that I was born again, and he told me, oh, much later that he felt the same.

"Like we were two halves of the same person" he said.

I knew just what he meant too!

When we eventually got dressed and were walking up the beach to the tent, he told me why he was so angry earlier.

"It wasn't you I was pissed at, it was them, they were just like Noel, taking advantage and hurting you, and you've had enough of that Carrie, that's all"

I was still in a dream world, floating along like I was on air.

"Doesn't matter any more, does it babe?" I yawned.

"Nope, not now"

He pulled me closer into him, his shirt crumpled and still damp and laughed-

"Hey Carrie, look" he squeezed my arm.

Walking up the beach were the two old men, nets and rope in hand and a black and white sheepdog running in the waves, barking at the seagulls.

"Morning" one of them smiled at us.

"Yeah, good morning" Steven had the grace to blush.

I couldn't do anything but smile. If only they knew eh?

&

Summer passed and the autumn came.

September was well in by the time Becky wrote from London with her first magazine spread photocopied in the letter. It was a small article about a teeny new bikini and she was beautiful in it. She was pictured with a couple of other models but they faded into the background where she was. She looked so lovely, but apparently the photographer said she ought to slim a little bit, because she would get more work that way, more high profile stuff.

So I've been slimming like mad and you won't know me when I come home for the debs, I have a gorgeous dress and I want an even more gorgeous escort for the night. I want to hear all the news.

I had a dress too, and though I had agonized about inviting Ma to the house for the pre debs drinks David had said it was the right thing to do and that she would enjoy it. He was asking in some of the neighbors and it would be a nice opportunity for her to see that I was living in a nice place with decent people around me.

"She did rear you Carrie, be nice to her eh?"

But when I went up one day and asked her she went very quiet and refused to come-

"Why Ma? It'll be nice" I didn't want to beg her. But she had been my mum for most of my life, and I wanted her to share in my life.

I mean, I was happy now; couldn't she be happy for me too?

"I have my reasons Carol-Anne; please don't push me on this"

"But, Mam, for heavens sake, what's the problem? You can't say you have your reasons and then not explain them, I mean, that's wrong"

And then she stared at me, really cool and calm and said-

"You can think what you like, but the only ones who are in the wrong are you and that Steven, and his father for encouraging you in what you're doing"

"I haven't the foggiest notion what you mean Ma! What? Just because we haven't got married you think it's all a big sin, come on, that went out with the Indians, get real! It's the 1990's" But she stood there staring at me and then she smiled-

"You don't know, do you? You haven't a clue what a terrible mess you've walked into, your sleeping with him and you just don't have a notion what your doing, but his father knows and he's letting it happen, under his roof, he's a...."

I was really mad. I snapped-

"I'm not in half as big a mess as the one I walked out of Ma, and that's saying something, and what me and my partner do is nothing to do with you, not now and not ever, I left here because Noel was making my life hell, and if you had any sense you'd be gone long ago, and that is exactly what I'm going to do now, leave!" I grabbed my bag and headed for the door.

I turned at the door and tried once more-

"Why do you want me to be so unhappy Ma? Why do you hate me so much? I mean if you didn't want me then why did you adopt me at all? Can you not be happy for me? I found someone that I can really love, he makes me happy, please Ma, try to be happy for me"

She sighed-

"It has nothing to do with loving you or not Carol, it's everything to do with what's right and what's wrong, and what you're doing is wrong, but you can't see it, and there is nothing I can do for you but pray, and hope that one day you see sense"

"*See sense about what*" I yelled.

"Ask his father what I mean"

"No, you tell me!"

But she wouldn't answer and I stormed out of the house in a foul temper. Stomping down the lane to the village in a high old mood. I was still in the horrors when Steven came in from work and only after much cajoling on his part did I tell him what she said-

"Well, she's your Ma, she's bound to be upset that your shacked up, particularly when your not married" he was sitting on the couch in the mobile, his legs out in front of him and his shirt half out of his waistband, so I could just see his stomach. What was it about his stomach that I couldn't think of anything other than biting it when I saw it? I dragged myself back to the conversation and tried to think. But he had seen, and he was smiling that half smile that made my stomach flip over every time-

"You worry too much my darlin" he was stroking the side of my neck and down to my collar bone knowing of course the effect it would have. I wriggled away from him, pretending to be cross-

"But there's more to it Steve, she's hiding something" Hands were replaced by lips and I gasped, eyes shut tight-

"You're too bold! How am I ever going to have a decent conversation with you when you carry on like this?" I could barely make my lips form the words. He laughed, and it sounded like a growl-

"Do you want me to stop?" He paused and looked down at me.

I shook my head-

"You are joking! Right?"

He smiled-

"Thought so, now listen to me until she actually tells you there's no way of knowing, what bee is up her arse, so forget it for now, bring yourself into my bedroom and we'll do something a bit more relaxing than thinking of religion and morals and mammies all evening" he pulled me up off the sofa and we went to bed.

After that I had more or less made up my mind to forget about her and my past. After all she had made it clear that she was objecting to the way I lived now and I thought that it was all a load of crap. I mean, just because she was in church night and day, she probably had this queer notion that I was living in sin or something, and that she couldn't condone it. I mean it was 1990, there was nothing wrong with what I was doing, was there? And we were careful. We saw all the AIDS stuff on the telly and though he told me that he was never into the promiscuous thing, we used condoms, most of the time, and were very aware that it was an issue.

I'd actually gone up to Father Ray one day for a chat to see what the best thing to do was with the way Ma was going on and he had made me tea and we'd sat in the vestry talking. He was really approachable and I thanked my lucky stars that it wasn't Father Green that was there, he would be preaching hell fire and damnation to me for sure.

"Father its just that she seems so dead set against us, and you know, she isn't married to Noel herself, and I thought she would be more, I don't know, understanding, I suppose" I sighed. Ray sat on the edge of the table and shook his head-

"Look Carrie, I thank God that this isn't old Ireland, things have changed, and for the better in some ways, at least now a girl doesn't get packed off to the nuns for what ever she does, but its hard for some of them, the older ones, to think that in this day and age, sex is part of love, and that you might do it with a number of partners before you marry, even if you marry at all" He was rolling another cigarette as he spoke.

"Carrie, what's the situation with you and him, your mother seems concerned that it got intense very quickly, that seems to be the size of it" he blew out a stream of smoke.

"I dunno Ray, its just.." I stopped.

How could I explain to him the way I felt? I looked at Steven and my heart literally turned over inside me. I loved him with every fiber of my being, and he only had to smile for me to light up inside. When I was with him I felt that my insides finally matched my outsides. I was a whole person. And as for the sex, there were no words to describe what that made me feel! Certainly none that I could say to a priest, not even on as enlightened as Ray.

Even in my letters to Becky, I had found it hard, telling her. It cheapened it somehow, telling her about the time we spent together. Father Ray seemed to understand-

"You love this guy?"

"Yes, I really do" I smiled.

"And, do you see yourself staying with him, long term?"

"God I hope so"

"So the question of marriage will most likely arise soon enough?"

"I think so, maybe in a year or two, I'm still only eighteen like, and he's twenty one, we're a bit young for it yet" I blushed.

"Well then, I'll try and talk to her, tell her that it will work out all right in the long run, I think that young love and young desire were always with us, and its just you lot have a bit more freedom to express it than your Ma's lot had, and sure, one of these days you'll be up calling the banns and there'll be celebrating all round!" he grinned.

"I'll even do the wedding myself"

"That's a deal!" I laughed and we clinked our mugs together.

And he was as good as his word and there was less of a frostiness when I called up to the house. Though she still refused to come to the house on the deb's night.

By the time the debs rolled around, I had other things on my mind.

Becky had come home, and true to her word, she had been slimming. I asked her what diet she was on and she had laughed, telling me she lived on fruit and black coffee. No more kebabs on the way home from the pub. That shocked me, because she used to eat like a horse especially after a night out. She spent a couple of nights with me and I was shocked by how thin she had become in the two months she had been away. Her ribs actually stuck out. Her hip bones were like razor blades under her skin. I told her I was concerned and she promised to eat normally for the couple of weeks she was home, and she seemed to do it too. I didn't notice she had become a bit moody, I thought it was just her family giving her a bit of stick. David noticed something in her though and he asked me was she on anything-

"Like what?" I asked.

"Slimming pills, something to keep her buzzing, suppress the appetite?"

"I haven't seen her take anything"

"She's a bit hyper, maybe you should check her bag" he said.

But if she had anything, it was hidden where I would be unlikely to find it. She made a lot of phone calls to her agent in London and always seemed happy enough when she came out of the phone box.

"He says I'm going to be big time when I go back, to enjoy the break now because he has something huge lined up for me when I go home" She *was* a touch hyperactive all right.

"Becky, you wouldn't take anything like drugs, would you?"

"What makes you ask that?"

"Ah, I dunno, you seem a bit *out of it* or something"

She pulled up her sleeves-

"Look, I model swimwear and underwear and short sleeves; if there was any marks on my body they wouldn't use me for that, I'm not a junkie Carrie, for fucks sake, get a grip"

"I never said you were a junkie, drugs don't begin and end with needles, I just wondered were you on something"

She hummed and hawed a bit, and then she told me that Jacko the photographer, had given her something to help her get some energy for the long days she was putting in, they were harmless, she said, and anyhow, she hadn't taken them regular since she came home for the debs.

"*You* wouldn't understand Carrie, it's the *life*, its fourteen hour days and then out for cocktails at some club for another six or seven hours, six days a week, I have to have something"

"But its speed, Becky, that's hard drugs, I mean, can't you have the night off sometimes? Do you have to fucking go out every single night?"

"I have to be in all the top places and be seen by the right people, Jacko says so"

"Well if you ask me, Jacko sounds like a prick, and you're going to end up in bits, its all a bit too much Mothers little helper to me!"

"What the hell would *you* know?"

This was a different Becky to the one I had been friends with all through school, this Becky was brittle and bitchy and hard nosed and not a bit like the girl I used to mime Madonna songs with in the bathroom mirror. It was as if there was a resentment, a jealousy, seeping through the fabric of our friendship, and it wasn't on my part, I swear, I wanted her to do well, get to the top if that's what she wanted, but not at the cost of losing her health and her looks through drug use.

She was seething with temper, nothing like her usual good natured self. And I was pissed off at her thinking I was a wide eyed innocent, I'd seen what drugs did at first hand, much more than she ever would, for heavens sake, they sold deals of heroin outside the youth club for years till Razor ran the dealers out of it, and then there was one man used to put the wraps of gear into the bottom of ice cream cones, winter and summer he would have a row of zombies, like the living dead, waiting to buy 99's and screwballs, even when the snow was thick on the ground. And she thought I knew nothing?

"What do ya mean by that? What would I know? Let me tell you Becky Whelan, I know what drugs are and what they do, I grew up in the estate remember?" I couldn't believe we were fighting. She had been my best friend for ever.

"Well, you have nothing only a shop job and a caravan to sleep in, what do you know about ambition or anything?"

"Is that what you think? That its ambition that's turning you into an asshole? You're a fucking fool Becky if that's what you think, I'd rather stay in a damned shop with my caravan to sleep in than fuck myself up on drugs, your turning into a different person Becky, and I don't like it one bit"

"Huh. You don't like me? *I'm an asshole?* Well that's tough, you haven't been anything like yourself since you got with Steven, everything you do and everything you say comes from him, and you won't get anything career wise if you stay working in a shop and living there, that's all you'll ever be is someone's wife, and someone's mother, and your going to be sorry" Her hands shook as she lit her cigarette.

"You're jealous" I whispered.

"I am not" she snapped.

But she was. I could see it written all over her and it scared me. This was my best friend, the girl I had envied all my life, for her family and her security and the peace in her home. She was jealous of me. What the hell was happening to us?

"Why Becky? Why? You know all I ever wanted was to find someone nice and settle down, I never wanted to be a high flyer and have a big career, you were the one was going to do that, not me, I'm happy that you have got what you wanted, and I'm not jealous that your going to be famous, so why are you being like this with me now?"

She ground her butt out on the wall beside her-

"Listen here, the only reason that guy is with you is because I knocked him back three weeks earlier, oh yeah, he didn't tell you that, did he?"

"That's not true" I gasped. I could feel myself choking.

"Ask him, and see what he says, go on, I dare ya, and see what lies he tells you then"

"You're a fucking liar"

I remembered them meeting, properly meeting, that is. Becky had been busy getting ready to go away when me and Steven met and I hadn't been out much because of the state of my face at the time. By the time I was ready to go out socializing again she was gone to London.

I'd introduced them a couple of days earlier and I knew in my heart that he was not interested in her as a woman, just as my mate. Of course I knew he would be either stupid, blind or gay if he didn't see how beautiful she was, but he didn't seem to fancy her, not in the slightest, and I remember thinking that he didn't talk to her too much, that their conversation was stilted.

Was that a ruse? Was it to hide the fact that he fancied her?

"Am I a liar Carrie? Well, you just remember this, Miss Perfect, I could take him off you in five seconds flat if I wanted to, maybe he might like someone on the up, rather than someone like you going nowhere fast" She smiled and at that moment I hated her so much I could have killed her.

"Fucking try it Becky Whelan, and I'll kill you"

I was shaking, I remember getting away from her, running off towards the house, and hearing her venomous voice in my head for hours.

I wasn't in the mood to go to the debs now, but I had the frock and the man and I thought I might as well. I could worry about my lack of ambition and Becky's lies later.

But it stung. All I wanted was to be happy, and I *was happy*. But the people who loved me couldn't see that. I was worried about Becky, because she wasn't the same person I knew for years anymore. Maybe I would chat to her later when she had calmed down. She would see sense. I was sure of it.

And it was a lie about Steven. I was sure of that too.

Becky

Becky stormed off through the village and out into the park. She walked for about an hour, finally sitting on a bench when the anger had simmered down to less than boiling point and she could think straight.

"The cheek of that Carrie one! The nerve!" she ground her teeth in temper.

They just didn't know what it was like! You get over to London and literally within a couple of days you're in there, fighting for jobs, fighting for pole position among younger, slimmer and prettier girls. If you had the look, you got the work. Simple. And the look today was thin, stick thin. Being a size eight was considered fat in the high fashion market, and Becky couldn't comprehend being a house model for the catalogs.

"Do the catalogs and your left with them, you'll never do runway or haute couture when you've modeled for Family Album, it's the kiss of death for your career, you may as well model for knitting patterns and get it over with baby" Jacko said, and Jacko knew everything there was to know about the business.

Jacko befriended her the week she arrived, and was putting her straight on lots of things. He was well up with all the photographers for the glossies and the supplements and he told her that she had a chance to make the big time, if she minded what he said and did what he told her to do.

And for all that she had known the scene in Dublin, it was small fry compared to London.

It was so big for a start, and so confusing. She spent three days trying to make sense of the Tube map, looking at the twisting lines in rainbow colours that seemed to spread out like a triffid, or some kind of mutant growth all over London.

And she was hungry, bloody starving, in fact, all the time. She was dying for a proper meal, but all anyone seemed to do was eat ice cubes and drink cocktails and nowadays, instead of dreaming about being locked in a lift with Izzy Stradlin from Guns n'Roses she fantasized about a Sunday dinner in her mothers.

Cup a Soup's, Pot Noodles, herbal tea and dry toast were no substitutes for her mother's roasties and gravy. She'd always had a healthy appetite and that dream was enough to make her cry sometimes, when she would wake up with the scent of her mothers cooking in her nostrils and realize that she had nothing in the house only a stale half loaf of wholemeal bread and a decaying jar of Marmite.

And boy was she lonely!

None of the other models wanted to go out shopping or go for a coffee when the days work was done, none of them wanted to chat when they were standing around between shots. They would look at her like she had landed from another planet if she suggested a ramble down town to Top Shop or Selfridges, and give her the cold shoulder.

There was no girl talk, no gossip, and no fun.

It was all competition and jealousy.

She ached for a good chat, a good chinwag with the girls. Millions of times she wanted to pick up the phone and even ring her sister Serena, and tell her that it was crap over there and that she was lonely and sad and wanted to come home, that she was ready to give up.

But then the side of her that fought like a tiger for the chance to do this, to follow her star to London, that side of her tore her out of the phone booth and into the nearest bar, where Jacko would be waiting with a strong drink and a pep talk or three.

She was tired too, she knew it. When she lived at home she might have three late nights a week and one of them would be a Friday or a Saturday when she could sleep late next day, but London was nuts. You could be out till three at an event- nothing was ever a party or a gig, they were all events- and home and then expected on a shoot or worse, a casting for a shoot, at six with full make up and hair done, portfolio in hand.

She seemed to live on double shot coffee, wired to the moon on caffeine, her stomach growling with emptiness. She had to get skinnier, she had to be, otherwise it was Littlewoods, or worse, knitting patterns, for her, and that was all she'd ever get! All she would ever be. It just didn't bear thinking about. She didn't come all this way to model fucking cardigans!

When Jacko saw her drinking another large coffee he had shaken his head at her-

"Honey, that will retain water on you, you shouldn't be drinking it" His big brown eyes stern in his beautiful face. His father was Jamaican, his mother French, and his real name was Jacques. He knew everyone who was everyone, had started taking photos when he was seventeen, and now, in his late thirties, was well regarded, although, he didn't have the name of someone like Bailey, he did all right.

He was achingly hip and with it.

He had a loft apartment long before they were fashionable and was on the VIP list of all the main nightclubs in the city, and never went out without at least three models on his arm. He had been engaged once, she was told, to a girl who became a top supermodel, and who dumped him when she hit the big time, and so he wasn't into relationships. He wasn't bitter, he said, he just didn't want his heart broken again. Becky could understand that.

He smiled down on her now, and she sighed-

"Jesus Jacko, I'm bollocked tired, I can't stand up with the tiredness" Her shoulders sagged and she longed for bed, to curl up and sleep for hours.

"You're only starting out kid, you need to look your best, top dollar, and you're already on the heavy side for vogue shoots..."

"On the heavy side? Jesus Jacko, this is a size six and its hanging off me! Any more slimming and I'll be buying me clothes in the kids department!" Becky pulled at her tee shirt. Her stomach was concave, her ribs like the keys on a piano-

"Look, me ribs are sticking out and me hipbones are like razor blades! Any more of this lark and I'll be in hospital being drip fed"

And Jacko laughed-

"You want to work catwalk dontcha? You have to be size four for that baby, if you want it, the coffee has to go" he spilled it onto the grass.

"You don't see Naomi or Christie drinking that, they be modeling maternity clothes if they did, make the belly stick out" He stuck his hips out and patted his belly. She was too sick and tired to smile-

"Ah, Jacko, what will I do now?" Size four, how in the name of God could she get to a size four? Did they even make adult clothes that small? To hear him talk you'd think she was obese or something.

She ate once a day, she walked as much as possible, when she wasn't too tired to think straight, and she drank lots of water. Lately, walking was becoming painful; her legs ached all the time, her shins felt like they would snap through her skin. But then a photographer told her she had "glass ankles" and it made it all worthwhile.

Even if she hadn't landed the job itself. That one, for a glossy magazine, went to a black girl who looked like she lived on the leaves from a privet hedge and water. Her eyes and lips were the biggest part of her.

"I'm six foot tall Jacko, size four is too thin for me, I don't think I can do it" She sighed. She hadn't any more fat to lose. She just *hadn't*.

"I mean it, the only way I'm gonna lose more weight is to amputate a fucking limb" She snapped, wishing she could go home.

He stared at her for a minute and then sighed-

"Okay, I don't do this for everyone, but see, I know your getting the swimwear job, well your up on the shortlist for the job, so look, I'll give you something to keep you going and you won't need the coffee, right?"

He shook out a couple of yellow pills into his hand-

"Here, try them; you won't know the energy you'll have in a few minutes"

Becky shook her head-

"What are they? I'm a doctors daughter you know, I can't be arsed with drugs"

"They aren't drugs, not really, just energy pills, on prescription, you could get them yourself if you went to the GP" He held them out and she took them, and sure enough, a couple hours later she was jumping around the set full of the joys of spring. Her hunger and fatigue were gone. She felt fantastic all day.

And all night, she was awake till the dawn broke, up dancing and carrying on in the night club while Jacko looked on, laughing.

And then, she went to the doctor Jacko recommended, there seemed to be nothing he didn't know about the fashion industry and the people who lived off it. There were doctors who would sign a stick thin anorectic fit for work, even when one girl, Neenah, was surviving on a diet of diet coke and TOILET PAPER, and who ended up hemorrhaging all over the "white Christmas" set in a ski suit by Versace! Needless to say she wasn't paid for the job and the suit was destroyed! Her career was ruined; she was currently in hospital trying to get her stomach sewn back together, all in the name of fashion.

Jacko dismissed her with a shrug-

"Stupid Cow, she didn't take the good advice offered her"

Becky took it to mean he had tried to help her too. And toilet paper diet or not, Neenah had been thinner than her, a size two, it was rumored, but Becky drew the line at eating Andrex for supper!

Jacko knew the right clubs and places to be seen.

"You should be living a bit nearer the action babe" he said one morning when she arrived at her shoot, already buzzing on her third dose of uppers.

"Sure I can get cabs or bus it to anywhere" she grinned

"Yeah, but you know, I have a room in my place free and it would be better for you in the long run, you'd be on hand for anything that came up, you could work with me all the time, you know, like partners?"

So she took him at his word and cancelled the lease on the flat and moved in with him just before the trip home for the debs. He was great, she told him that she would be incredibly busy all the time and he told her to make sure she had enough little energizers to keep her sweet for the time she was away. He was concentrating on her work now, out a lot with agents and people in the know, and she knew that when she went back she was going to be in the fast lane to the big time. And then she would show Carrie!

The fucking nerve! Wait till this debs tonight! She'd show her!

She unzipped the sleeve pocket of her anorak and took out a pill and stuck it under her tongue. No one who didn't live in fashion could possibly know the pressure!

Not even Nancy knew what was going on with her. In fact, she'd given Nancy a very wide berth on this trip home, not wanting the lecture from her about the perils of pills and potions, or the peril of trusting a man like Jacko, which was rich coming from her, the poor mans Pamela De Barres! If it could play three chords and had a pulse, Nancy would shag it.

No, it was miles better to take the advice of the people in the know, people like Jacko that knew the system and knew how to milk it, and one day, when she was a star as big as Cindy Crawford, then she would be so clean living and good, no one would believe it!

She'd learn yoga and meditate, and live in a big apartment with huge windows overlooking Central Park in New York and all her furniture would be clean and white and simple. Yes, that's what she would do! Wait and see!

Until then she'd do what she had to do to make it. She would work through the pain and the hunger and tiredness and would get by on whatever means she had to.

The pill was dissolving on her tongue and she felt the familiar warm little tingle, and smiled. Her eye was caught by a couple of lads walking through the park, with the clumpy slow gait of the addict, their clothes dirty and their eyes glazing.

She hopped off the bench and grabbed her bag-

She wasn't like them, she wasn't. She had a job and a life, and friends, and she wasn't going to end up like that!

The pills helped, that's all.

And when she got where she wanted to be she would quit, and that would be that.

Carrie

I guess when I thought about the debs, I always thought it would be a happier event than it turned out to be. It was warm for October, and the dress I was wearing was lovely, and it was nice that I didn't need to bring a coat. And Steven looked amazing in his suit. I had bought a dress in a second hand shop and spent hours sewing sequins and glass beads onto it so that it shimmered like the stars had in Connemara. I wore my hair up and carried a little silver bag I had found on a stall in Georges Street Arcade one lunch time.

I looked great, and David told me I was beautiful and slipped some money into my bag.

"Running away money, in case it gets too much for you" he whispered.

I laughed-

"Whatever you think is going to happen to me tonight, you can be sure that I won't be running from it, meet it head on I say"

"Just remember its there honey" he patted my hand.

Admittedly I had come home from the row with Becky in such a mood that I wasn't fit to throw a word to a dog for about an hour. David wasn't one bit surprised when I told him what she was at and he told me he had seen it all before and knew the signs only too well.

And Steven was in a weird humour, not saying much but was drinking steadily in the house before we left, and smiling very little.

In the hotel, and through the meal, he was almost sullen. I tried talking to him and he wouldn't respond to me at all and I was contemplating doing that runner after all. I got up and went into the bathroom before the dancing started, and redid my make up, all the while thinking and wondering what the hell was going on.

Becky had completely blanked me in the hotel. She had come to the debs alone, her partner had cried off earlier in the day with a sore throat. She looked amazing. He hair was glimmering like spun gold, in curls down her back, and she wore a dress that looked like it was made out of cobwebs. When I walked into the ball room she was up dancing alone on the floor, and almost every male head was turned to her. Watching.

But not Steven.

He was at the bar, back turned to the floor and looking drunk all ready-

"You okay babe?" I asked.

"Yeah, I'm okay, what do *you think?*" he snapped.

I bit my lip and thought about it for a second. This wasn't the time or the place to bring this up, but he was like a demon with me anyhow and I was tired and fed up, that this night of all nights should be ruined by him.

"Look, I don't know what's wrong with ya but will you snap out of it, your ruining my night and if you won't tell me what's wrong, how can I help?"

He looked lost. I could see it in his eyes. I put my hand out and touched him and felt his arm go stiff and then he slumped a little.

"I'm sorry Carrie, really I am, it's just... Oh, I want to tell you but I don't know how to start" He sighed.

"We could get out of here, go for a walk or something, talk there, and maybe come back later when you feel better?"

"Yes, that would be good" he leaned over and kissed me on the forehead.

"Give me two seconds and I'll grab my wrap and we'll go, okay?"

And I ran out into the foyer and got my shawl and was stuffing my purse into the little silver bag, and I heard a giggle and turned around, and saw Becky, wrapped around someone in the alcove by the ball room door. I went to walk past when I saw the ring on his finger was the same one I had given Steven a couple of weeks previously, with our two initials entwined. I don't know if I said anything, all I know is I found myself speeding away in a taxi, heading for home, and not having the faintest clue what I would do once I got there.

3

David

I always liked music. Particularly when it had meaningful lyrics, and a good tune. I was pleased when Steven grew up and liked it too. Though he was prone to playing some of that trash metal a little too much for my taste and it was a relief that he took his stereo out to the mobile home when he turned 19.

Lately though, he had taken to playing more melodic stuff, particularly since Carrie had arrived on the scene. I remember the first night he brought her home, poor thing, and I went up to my room, and through the open window could hear Leonard Cohen singing Hallelujah in the dark.

I remembered feeling like that about someone once and I prayed so hard that night that his love story would have a happier ending than mine.

Carrie is such a lovely girl. She seems to have come through so much in her life and come through it shining. Steve needs someone like her. He is so lost sometimes. I wonder how much of his early life he really remembers. Does he even remember Elizabeth?

They say that children have a great propensity for adapting, for moving on and getting over things the way an adult couldn't. They don't brood and wonder what if?

I wish I could do that. Because I know I have made a hell of a lot of mistakes in my time. I know one of the biggest ones I made was sheltering my son from the outside world far too much.

But I was afraid, I was terrified of *them* coming and taking him, before he was of age and had a mind of his own. People round here think it's great that we went everywhere together but they don't know why?

I drove him to school, I Made sure he didn't go to the local comprehensive, afraid of whom he might be in contact with, and that someone might take him from the gates one day and I would never know. I broke myself paying for private schooling and was there at the door to take him home, right up to his Leaving Cert.

He never ever questioned it. He must remember more than I thought he ever did.

He never had many friends, he had nothing in common apart from his gender with most of the boys round here that kicked ball on the green areas and whistled at the young ones passing by. He would sit for hours writing in a big black diary and listening to music and daydreaming. He had two lads that he palled with for a summer or two, Eddie and Fran, a pair of brothers, wide boys, whose family was large and loving, with a mother like a woman in a storybook, who insisted on him going on holiday with them to a caravan in Courtown for a week.

"He's eighteen, let him come with us, he'll be fine" Mrs. O'Carroll said, and I let him go, though I sweated bullets all the time he was away.

He came home, with a new confidence, probably because he'd been out and had a few beers with the boys in the evenings, and chased a few girls, and most likely got more than he bargained for in the dunes when the disco closed. Though I never asked him. I wouldn't ask. Some things are best left private.

He got a job in a bar and I picked him up after work and made sure he was okay, and he would go out with the two O'Carroll boys for a pint or three in the local on Friday nights. Both of them would court women from the area, but Steven wasn't bothered about chasing anyone here. Oh, there was the odd night, when he was out late, but nothing to make me lose sleep.

I stopped worrying so much about him and relaxed a bit, and then Eddie got engaged to Sandra who was a stylist in the local hair salon and stopped going out so much with the lads, and then Fran went to Australia, having gotten his qualifications as an electrician, and Steven was left alone again.

He took to going into town, I suppose searching for people like him. He must have felt like a misfit for a long time. And he came home one night and I knew he had found something he liked and asked him-

"It's just a club, but the music is wicked, it's brilliant"

"Oh, right so" I held my peace and prayed he would be okay.

And that's what happened, he'd go in there on Fridays and come home at all hours and then, about six weeks into that he met Carrie and brought her home too.

And she fills the void for him, fills the big empty space his mother left behind her. Oh God, I wonder does Liz ever realize

the damage she did to us all. If there is a God and a heaven, is she up there looking down? Is she sorry?

All I know is that I loved her, the moment I first set my eyes on her and it hadn't changed. Not then and definitely not now. But how long was the pain going to carry on?

She had destroyed me, taken five or more years out of my life, she had hurt me beyond reason. And still she was the one I loved. She was gone for so long now; it was nothing more than a ghost I could feel in the night. Even in life, she was gone from me before I ever really had her at all.

They say that she used me. I accept that. They say that she never loved me at all. How would they know? I saw the real her, the tangle of dark curls and the sadness in her eyes, the bruises on her skin and the panic. I saw it all and tried to be a stable place for her to come and be at peace. But it only worked for a little while. Every now and then she would get restless and run away again. Of the seven years we were married I had her for maybe two of them. And in those two years she was perfect, a wonderful mother and wife. Until the pull of the city, the lure of the bright lights took her away again.

And so it went.

We never should have met really. I was a young ruffian from the inner city of Dublin, reared in a flat in Sheriff Street that in its entirety would have been as big as the living room in her family home, Baird Hall. My mother gave me the greatest gift of all, a love of reading. I devoured books from the time I was a child, and though I knew I wasn't going to make it as a writer, I wanted to be involved in the making of books in some way.

When I was fifteen I hit the boat to England and was lucky enough to get a job in a print works in Birmingham. They printed school books and texts for colleges and in my spare time I learnt a lot about history and literature, because I read the off cut books that weren't suitable for selling to the schools. I showed initiative, they said, and before I knew where I was, at nineteen, I was out on the road selling for them, in a battered old car and seeing parts of England I never knew existed. I did well, I made money. That was all I wanted to do. And that was how I met Elizabeth Bard.

James Bard, her father was one of the big shots in publishing. He had a list of authors as long as your arm and made a mint of money from it too. They lived in a manor house with a huge estate round it, and when I met him at an exhibition, he took a shine to me and asked me to come up for a days shooting in the autumn.

I'd never been near a gun, never. The only gun I ever saw in my life was in the St Patrick's Day parade in Dublin in the hands of the soldiers marching along. But I thought that maybe they would have some notion of where my career could go, progress maybe, and I thought it could be a good idea to go and see.

So up to Scotland I went. On the train with my battered little suitcase and was met by a Daimler at the station. The chauffeur was better dressed than I was, in my three button mohair suit that looked the business at all the hops round London, but looked shiny and cheap here.

My bag was taken up to my room and I was left standing in the hall with my two arms the one length, with no clue what to do next. I remember looking at pictures that must have been Old Masters, dark and gloomy and a bit intimidating, and then the sound of a gong ringing in the distance for tea, and having to walk in there in my shiny suit, mortified with embarrassment.

I was sitting on a sofa with a delicate china cup in my hand, praying that I wouldn't spill the tea in it and trying to make conversation with some woman who had been to Dublin once and was asking had I ever stayed in the Shelburne hotel?

It was on the tip of my tongue to say-

"Only so long as the porter didn't spot me"

But, she was a nice old dear and so, I refrained and muttered something about the Gresham being more my cup of tea. And then it happened. The door crashed open and this girl walked in. I stared, openmouthed at her. She had curly hair with the sheen of black silk, it was falling out from under her hat, and she wore a white blouse and a riding habit skirt.

She looked around her and sighed-

"I forgot about this weekend, how awful"

She flopped down on the sofa opposite me and groaned.

"Such a bore, all those business people and their awful wives and husbands and not a decent one among them, how can Daddy stand it?"

She grabbed a sandwich from a tray and ate it. I was sitting with my tea going cold in my hand and she suddenly stared right at me-

"Things *are* looking up, who are you?"

I stammered out *something* and she grinned. Her teeth were perfect and she looked so lovely when she smiled.

"And is your wife here David?"

And when she said my name, I felt a shiver in my back and I shook like a leaf.

"No miss, I'm not married:

"Well well, who would have thought it, a nice Irish boy like you? You're a Catholic I suppose? And *probably* an IRA man too, How wicked! What can Daddy be thinking of?" she smiled. Her eyes were like pale blue water.

"No, no, I'm not in the IRA, but I am a Catholic"

"Elizabeth, stop that! This is Mr. Williams, he's from Browne and Stokes of Birmingham, he's here for the shooting, not to be tormented by you!"

James Bard was smiling but I could see his jaw was tense and he was annoyed with her. I felt even then that it was more than her teasing me had bothered him.

"Where were you all day Elizabeth, you knew we had company and I thought you'd at least have changed out of your riding clothes"

"I was out on Shadow, since Hollis left there's no one to ride her so I thought she needed a good gallop, honestly- its madness"

She glanced around the room-

"*We* get the best groom in the country and just because he was a little indiscreet in his private affairs Daddy here has to let him go, what a spoilsport you are Daddy"

"Daddy" looked more than a bit annoyed and I saw him closing his eyes and his fist clenched.

Maybe Elizabeth knew she had pushed him far enough and decided to leave it. Either way, she left, soon afterwards, and I went back to my cup of freezing tea and wondering would I get some time alone with her. Soon.

"She's a wild one you know, such a pity really, her father adores her" my companion whispered as we broke up to dress for dinner.

"Is she? Wild, I mean?"

And she looked me straight in the face then said-

"Yes, and you dear, you'd be biting off more than you can safely chew with that lassie, so don't even think of it, for your own sake, stick to the nice girls back home in Ireland, that's what you need to do"

But the fool in me didn't listen and I waited for the next time we met. It couldn't come soon enough for me.

She didn't appear till dinner was over. She came down the stairs in a white dress with tiny little mirrors sewn into it, and sandals that looked like they were made out of silver threads. She had brushed her hair and was wearing very little make up. She stood on the staircase and looked around the room and spotted me standing with a couple of young men who worked for James Bard.

"Its you again" she said, coming over and taking my hand.

"Hello Miss" I smiled.

"Miss! Am I a teacher or something? Call me Elizabeth for heavens sake, although, it might not be a bad idea to educate you someday, would you like that?" she grinned wickedly.

"I, I read a lot myself, so maybe I'll educate you" I tried to match her and failed, because she threw back her head and laughed loudly-

"I wasn't talking about books David"

It dawned on me then what she had meant and I blushed.

"So shy! Come on; let's go for a walk and a *nice chat about books* then, give you time to cool off a bit"

We went out into the night and walked about the gardens. I can't tell you how it began, and how we ended up in the stables and how she climbed up into the loft and called to me. But I went, and ended up making love for the first time in my life.

I forgot about everything. About the girl I had been seeing in London, a nurse, and who had been working this weekend, otherwise she would have come with me and I would never ever have found myself in this amazing, fantastic position. I had been talking about engagement to my girlfriend and marriage, she had been looking for a job in Birmingham to be near to me, and now this had happened.

I remember lying there on the straw thinking that I had never dreamed of such a girl. I thought it would be a local lass I married from back home even, not someone this beautiful. Even now, words cannot do justice to her, she was stunning, so stunning that I was totally blinded by her and wanted to be with her forever, right there and then.

She was very quiet, and I touched her shoulder-

"You all right? Is everything all right?"

She nodded, and lay there with her hair fanned out on the straw and her cheek on the crook of her elbow.

"You're beautiful Elizabeth, really beautiful"

Her eyes filled with tears and she shook her head-

"Oh Darling, I'm not, I'm so not"

Two months later it was different.

I had gone back to my job and my flat and my girlfriend, working in Birmingham and heading to London to see Mary at weekends, having been told by Elizabeth that what had transpired between us meant little or nothing to her and I should forget her and it and go back to my life like she had never existed. So I went back and tried to put the bits back together, but it was hard. You cannot have something like that and just forget it in an instant. I tried and failed over the next few months.

It was like being taken to the top of the world and seeing what it was, knowing that there was real beauty and then, being brought back to earth with a thud and told that you couldn't have any of it.

I tried to forget her, but I couldn't. It was too hard to do.

And then one Monday morning I was getting out of the car at the works and there she was. In a rain coat, soaked to the skin with sleet, shivering.

"Elizabeth! What are you doing here?"

"I c-came to see y-you" she shivered.

I saw the lights of the café opposite and I pulled her through the rain to its door.

"Tea, and then you can tell me all about it" I steered her through the tables to the back of the shop and we sat down.

Two cups later she had stopped shaking and she told me-

"I'm pregnant"

I felt the room spinning and I tried to focus on the stained cover on the table.

"Are you sure?"

"Yes"

"How long?" I stopped. Should I ask this question?

"Two months or so, I don't know really"

"Jesus, what did your father say?"

"He wants me to give it away" Her hands were shaking as she lifted her cup and my heart went out to her.

This was every girl's worst nightmare. Falling for a baby before she was married. Back home, couples in this predicament would get married quickly. If not, the girls were sent away to the nuns. And I wasn't going to let that happen to her. She was too beautiful for that.

"You are not, you're giving no child away, not my child, and you're going to marry me" I sounded more confident than I was.

"What?" she stared at me for the longest time.

"Marry me?" I said.

"You'd do that? Because of this? Marry me?" she gasped.

"Well, sure, we have to get married, it's the thing to do, I mean, the baby, we *have* to" I could feel my voice shaking and my stomach felt like it was full of ice water. But still and all, I couldn't think of anything other than marriage, where I come from, if you had your fun and a child came from that... then... you did the decent thing and put a ring on the girl's finger, the alternatives weren't even discussed. There were no alternatives. Not back then!

Back home, the church would open at seven on a Wednesday morning, winter and summer, and the priest would marry maybe three couples on the side altar, quietly, discreetly, and without celebration, the only people there maybe a stern faced father and a weeping mother, the bride in maybe a suit and a hat, instead of the usual head square.

"It's my baby, we have to get married, and I have to give it my name" I said.

A girl like her could have expected a huge wedding, with a white dress and bridesmaids and all the pomp and ceremony of the wealthy, maybe a Rolls Royce to bring her to the church and a beautiful engagement ring to show off. I had barely enough money for a wedding band.

"That's if you want to, marry me, I mean"

She stared at me for a second, as if she was weighing me up and trying to see what kind of husband I would be. Finally, she smiled-

"Okay, let's do it then" she said.

"Really? When?"

"As soon as possible, now if we could" she smiled again and my heart leapt. This gorgeous, beautiful creature was going to be my wife. I felt like I had won the pools.

"Oh Elizabeth, I love you so much" I jumped up and grabbed her, and kissed her soundly to cheers from the other people in the café.

"I know you do David, and...I... I'm going to try and be a good wife to you" She hugged me tight. I didn't realize it then, but she never said anything about loving me too. Not that I cared.

"That's all I want you to do Liz, that's all I need from you" I whispered into her hair.

I didn't expect her to love me yet, but hoped against all hope that it would grow in time. I was certain that it would, when she realized that I would look after her, and not let her down.

So I ran over to the works and told them that I needed a couple of days off and we went to my flat where I wrote a letter to Mary at the hospital, and then we caught the train up to Gretna Green and that was that. We got married.

And then we went to her father and told him what we had done and he asked me to come into his office and have a chat, and so I stood before his big oak desk and he questioned me about me and Elizabeth and why the suddenness of the marriage-

"But, sir, you are aware that she is pregnant?" I said

"Well aware, but I was not aware that the child was yours" he snapped.

"It is sir, as far as I know" I said.

"You seem to fall a little short in this case David, how many times did you and my daughter sleep together? And when? The only time I know it may have happened is in September and..." he stared at me then. I felt his anger, and then he seemed to deflate in front of me.

"So, this child will be given your name? And your faith? What of that?" he asked.

"Sir, if my faith mattered that much to me, then I wouldn't have made love to Elizabeth in the first place" I thought that was strange, Elizabeth told me she was Catholic too. Faith shouldn't come into this!

He nodded.

"All right, you win, this time, but I would like her to be near home, so would you consider coming to work with me? Here, as an agent, you would be well paid..."

"Mr. Bard, I don't need a payoff for marrying her, I love Elizabeth and I will happily go on working to provide a home for her if that's what I need to do, But I am happy to have married her, I love her very much" I said.

And if it's possible to age in front of someone's eyes, I think he did. He sagged in the chair and looked so tired that I pitied him.

"All right then, come work with me on your own merits, and you are welcome, because I have heard great things about you. But be warned, Elizabeth is my daughter, and you have married her, and I pity you now, for it's up to you to control her" He lit a cigar and sighed.

I went out and up the stairs to the bedroom and sat in the window seat looking at the snow falling. Elizabeth was asleep, and as I looked down at her, I thought how lucky I was and how wrong they all were about her.

They would see how wrong they were.

This was nothing to do with anyone only us. And that night, looking at her in bed, thinking I was married to the nearest thing to an angel outside of heaven; I couldn't see the road ahead being paved with anything other than happiness.

Our son, Stephen Patrick Williams was born in 1969, on a bright morning at the end of May.   I sent everyone pictures of the new baby who looked nothing like me and everything like his gorgeous mother.   Little Stevie and I bonded immediately and I looked forward to spending time with him in the evenings and on weekends when I was off work.

James had given me the new authors list. People who hadn't been published before and to be honest, it was less demanding on me than some of the divas that were on the second or third book. Most first timers just wanted the book printed!

We had a little cottage in the grounds of the mansion and it was lovely. We had it decorated and painted and I grew stuff in the garden, roses and daffodils and a small patch of vegetables. Elizabeth said it was the Irish Farmer in me coming out. I just laughed it off.

But by the end of 1970, there were things happening that I couldn't laugh off.

In 1970, Stevie was one year old, and Elizabeth decided to head down to see an old friend of hers in London. She left on the Friday and came back, not on the Monday as she had arranged, but the following Thursday. When questioned as to why she hadn't come back as promised she told me that I wasn't her jailer and to get lost. And then about a week later I came home early from an overnight trip, and found Stevie sobbing in the bedroom soaked through, filthy, and so hungry that he had tried to eat the stuffing from a toy, while she was lying on the bed listening to records and stoned out of her mind on marijuana. The sickly smell all over the room, and the child trying to wake his Mammy.

That day she begged and pleaded and told me it was never going to happen again. But by that stage I wondered how long it had been happening before I caught her. I figured that she was bored in the house all day so I asked her father if it was possible that I take over the London offices, and therefore she could be near her friends and the social life she said she was missing. Maybe if she could be out and about and not so isolated she might feel a little better.

We moved to London that November and all was fine for a while. She was the model wife and mother for a bit, going shopping in Carnaby Street with her girlfriends and then coming home to model what she bought for me. I took her to dinner and dancing, anything she wanted.

We hired a nanny, Breda, who came from Dublin herself and we got on well. And she idolized Stevie.

It was Breda who filled me in on Stevie and his progress.

And then she told me about the people that were hanging out in my house during the day.

She told me that she and the child were locked into the top floor nursery during the day, that there were God only knew how many people using my house as a crash pad when I went to work, and the one time I had been away for the weekend at a conference, there had been mayhem, and Breda had gotten Stevie out of the house and round to her sister Doris, who was living in Clapham at the time.

"They smoke that stuff, and some of them take pills and inject themselves" she said, and my blood ran cold. What if the baby picked up something? A pill maybe and ate it, what would happen then.

So I waited one morning and saw it for myself, people coming out of the woodwork whistling up for the keys, and others, having a key already, letting themselves in. I waited till after the last of them were in and then I went to a phone box and dialed 999. The police were there in seconds and I waited till they had cleared the house and went in-

Elizabeth was sitting on the stairs, her hair hanging over her face, wrapped in a bath towel.

"Here he is! David, darling tell them how silly this is! They think this is a drug den" she shrieked. I could see that she had taken something and that the police had made quite a haul of drug paraphernalia. Bottles, syringes and pills in plastic bags.

I walked into the kitchen and my stomach heaved, the draining board was covered in dirty needles and blood splattered the tiles over the sink. What the fuck was going on here? And how long was it happening before anyone saw fit to tell me?

"David? Tell them darling, tell them it's a mistake" She begged.

I wanted to be sick. I stood there and waited till the police left and then I hit the roof.

She cried and cried and told me she was sorry and that it would never happen again and that she *wasn't* taking drugs herself and that her friends had bullied her into it, please believe me, please, she kept saying.

So I did, I forgave her, but I couldn't help but watch her and maybe that was what drove her out of the house so much. Many times in 1971 she was brought home incoherent and sick and left with me to fix and sober her up. That's what they did back then, your spouse sorted you out. I hadn't a clue what to do, I had no experience of anything other than alcohol, and the worst a person could be in Dublin back then was drunk, Drugs didn't come into the equation.

I couldn't figure out where the money came from for her lifestyle, until I remembered that her father was still paying an allowance into the bank for her. Truth be told, she spent that and more in a week on the stuff she was doing, I didn't want to think what else she might be doing to subsidize herself and her habits.

In November 1971 she told me she was pregnant again and I went to see her father. There was no earthly way this child was mine and I now thought that Stevie wasn't either. Hollis, the groom that had been fired was his father, and she had known she was pregnant when she slept with me. I found this out one night when she wanted to go out at three am to see friends and I barred the door, worried for her safety in the street at that hour of the morning.

"Fuck you, I'll leave you, and I'll take Steven and go where you won't find us" She screeched.

"Like hell you will, take my child to some squat, you will not" I'd said.

"He isn't your child you asshole, he's mine, I was pregnant when I had you, you stupid fool" She'd laughed.

I'd been totally devastated, but I knew I had to stay tough. In them days, having your name was enough, Steven wouldn't be allowed go into such a horrific environment by any court she chose to go to.

Steven, oh he was my son in all the important ways. I bathed him and told him stories and sang to him. I played football in the garden with him and made sure he brushed his teeth. He was a solemn eyed little thing, as dark as his mother was with her amazing blue eyes.

So next day I took him north so that I could see his grandfather.

Stevie was borne off to the kitchen in Baird hall, to be spoilt by the cook and the maids, and given enough biscuits to fill an elephant. I went up to the old mans office.

"So, you've figured out the whore you married then?" he asked.

"Did you know?" I asked

"I knew, and I thought you did too, and now, I hear she is gone crazy altogether in London and you can't cope with her" he smiled.

"I have tried" I said.

"Trying was never going to be enough David, she's wild, and she's a whore, and you took her on" He tutted and shook his head.

"What do you want David?" he smiled.

"Get her into drug treatment, something, save her, she's pregnant again and I know its not mine, but she needs help, get her sober, and then, I can think of what to do then" I said.

"Divorce her I suppose?" he was still smiling, that snaky smile, like a cat watching a mouse hole.

Divorce had entered my head, only because I was so tired, so wretchedly exhausted that I couldn't think straight anymore. I couldn't second guess her any more; I couldn't stay ahead of her any more. I wanted to go home to Ireland with Stevie and live like a normal person. Marriage wasn't something I could do again anyhow, there was no divorce in Ireland and so no one would want to live with me, a divorcee. But if I was home, there would be people there to help, to lift this burden off me for a little while. That's all I needed was a rest.

"I truly do not know Sir, divorce wasn't on the agenda because of my religion, but I am worried about her, honest to God I am"

"I'll do something to help, I know of a clinic that might do something for her, but I cannot say whether it will work for her" and that was it, he picked up the telephone and dialed, and later that evening she was in a bed in a very expensive clinic and we thought that this would be the end of the matter.

But like we all know nowadays, it takes more than a detox in a fancy clinic to wean someone off the hard stuff, and by now, there was no escaping the issue, Elizabeth was a junkie. She broke out of the clinic and ran away four times, coming back in a dreadful state, dirty and bedraggled and with open sores on her skin. She was pitifully thin, her pregnancy all the more pronounced. People looked at me with pity as I walked with her up and down the corridors of the clinic, when I went to see her.

Sometimes she was sweet; she remembered Steven and asked about him and how we were getting along without her. She always planned to be home one day, to be with us again, and that's how I know she really loved me too.

"You're determined to save me David, aren't you?" she asked one day.

I stared at her, lying on the bleached white bed in her nightdress, her hair damp from the bath and I knew that I still wanted and loved her, but that it was hopeless, that she would not stop till she was destroyed.

"I love you Elizabeth, I want to help you because I love you"

"Poor fool, I'm beyond helping David, save *you*" she said "I don't want to be saved anymore; I just want it to be over"

I sat there that day and tried to build her life again, telling her all the things we could do together as a family when she was better. We could travel; see places like India and Morocco if she wanted. I would have done anything to will life back into her. But to me, she had already made up her mind. Whether it happened now or later was immaterial.

She ran away again from the clinic and they wouldn't have her back again and all we could do was sign her into a hospital, when we found her. She was due the baby any day now; it was summer time again, June 1972.

We found her unconscious in a squat in Kilburn, and brought her by ambulance to a hospital. When they had pumped her out and made her stable, her father hired a private nurse and ambulance to bring her to a hospital in Glasgow for her confinement. I knew she was there and I went in once to see her, before she had the baby, and then I went back to London to my son.

She gave birth to a baby daughter in the second week of June 1972. She called her Amber. I waited till she was home in Baird hall and went to see them. I dreaded to think what the poor baby must have gone through, and was pleasantly surprised to see that the child was healthy and chubby, just like a baby should be. I remember thinking that with her coppery hair and hazel eyes she was more like my child than any other I had seen. But this time I was adamant. This was not my baby, and the marriage was over, and my name was not going on this child's birth cert. But like every other thing I tried to make a stand on, I caved in on that too.

After a couple of months when Elizabeth was in better shape, she came back to the London house and brought Amber with her. Stevie was mad about her, and played peek a boo all day long with her. Elizabeth was listless and weak and pottered around in a dirty dressing gown listening to records and leaving the baby to Breda.

And it began again.

The late nights, the telephone calls where she would bang the phone down if I came in the room. I knew she was having an affair with someone but I didn't care. She went out more and more and this time I didn't even try getting her help. Maybe I should have. By the time the baby was a year old she was as bad as ever.

I tried to protect the kids, but it was hard. Stevie was in school and I would bring him on the way to work in the offices in London, and after I left the house she would go out, in the little red mini her father had given her, and do God only knew what. I tried really hard to be normal, with baths and bedtime routines and homework done to rote. Trying to cover the fact that she was either out or strung out all the time.

And then one day she vanished. She took the baby, and the car and she went. Breda went to her sister on a Wednesday normally, but when we went to the sister's house in Clapham, they said that they were gone from there since before Christmas. Breda went into thin air too. No one knew where. She had been seen in the airport and hadn't been seen since. There was no record of Breda Storey leaving Britain.

They pulled the car out of the Thames on a Friday morning in November 1973. The back seat was covered in the little toys that Amber loved to play with, and there was a plastic bag with nappies and her soother in it. The little pink duffel coat was on the floor covered in dirt. Elizabeth was in the front seat, all the windows were open. They called them the *"Angels of the Thames"*.

Suicide I thought.

Murder, they said.

They found that the brakes were faulty in the car and they said it was me who did it. I had been seen looking under the bonnet the day before she went away.

I had been fixing something for her, she said that the battery wasn't right and I thought I would have a look and see, and I had found a loose cable and fixed it up.

They said I cut the cables and the brakes failed.

They took the child to his grandfather and I was locked up. I swore I didn't do anything to hurt her, but her father told them that I had asked him to help me divorce her. They charged me with murder and I was sent down for life.

My four year old son was taken up to Scotland and sent to a boarding school and the London house was sold and some of the money put into trust for him till he was twenty one. I spent the time in prison thinking and wondering what could I do to get out and get away from the mess my life had become.

Come to think of it; it *was* all over the papers at the time so maybe that's where Carries mother knew me from, I didn't want to relive all that again. Five years was long enough the first time around. And Carrie doesn't need to know.

In 1978, there was a major crackdown on the drugs trade in Britain and every week there was a new admission to the prison.

Some big shot from the drugs scene, or the common or garden junkie caught in possession.

I was in the kitchens one day working when a guy came up to me, and he asked me if I was married to Liz Bard-

"I was, did you know her?"

"Yeah, and I know what happened to her an' all"

Apparently, this guy was hired by someone, a dealer, long dead, to kill my wife and he had doctored the brakes on the car, knowing that she would take chances and drive too fast.

"I din't know she was goin' to top herself though, did I?" he said.

"Did you tell them that?" I asked.

"Wot d'ya take me for? Nah, but you do me a little favour and I'll help you out"

I promised him money, and he agreed to confess to my wife's death being in some way down to him, even though it *was* suicide, according to him.

"I'm doing life anyhow, nothin'to me if there's another ten years on it" he grinned.

I was to pay a certain amount into a bank account when I was let out, and he would do what needed to be done now.

"I got kids an' all" he said.

It was my word of honor that got me out of there, plus the fact that my being free meant the proceeds of my house in London were mine and I could get at them again.   I got on a train and went north to the school where my son was and I took him with me. We came home to Ireland the next day.

And we live here now, since 1978, and there hasn't been any trouble from the Bard Family. Old Man Bard is old now. He must be hitting ninety years of age. But not once has he ever tried to contact his grandson, even to see were we dead or alive. I am proud of the fact that I coped alone. It's good that. I used what money I had to set myself up in business and in time, earned enough to buy a home and give Steven the stability he was denied for so long.

And tonight made me so proud, him and Carrie going off to the debs together, and mad about each other, it made it all worth it. I swore on the ferry coming home to Dublin, that night long ago, that no one would hurt my son as long as I lived, and I have lived to see him happy. That's all I ever wanted.

I never hurt Elizabeth, but I *would* kill anyone who hurts that boy again.

But sometimes when I look at him I wonder-

Why was he not enough for Elizabeth? Why could she not have loved him enough to live for him, if she couldn't for me? What made her destroy herself the way she did?

And when those thoughts come, I sit in them for so long that they threaten to smother me, because to the normal person there is no rhyme or reason to it all, there's no reason to kill yourself the way she did.

Unless the thought of living was worse?

I will probably be asking the Gods this question for the next millennium. And I still haven't found the answer I need. Jesus, I don't know what answer would make me feel better!

And my heart, such as it was, was drowned that morning too and now, all that's left is the body, this soul less shell, I live in, for however long it's going to take before I can let it all go.

4

Carrie

The taxi dropped me at the door and I stood there. I suppose I didn't know what to do, I mean the only reason I lived there in the first place was because I was with Steven and now that it seemed my relationship was coming to an end, then maybe my tenancy would too. I saw the light on in the living room and I sneaked past the window and round to the back gate of the house and into the garden. There was a little chill in the breeze now and I was glad to get inside the mobile. I looked at all the make up and the damp towels on the floor from earlier, when I had been getting ready and I sighed. I picked them up and made the tea and was sitting in the half dark drinking it when there was a tap at the door-

"I take it you ran away then?" David asked.

It was too much, the tears came falling down my face and I sobbed. David knelt and held me tight and made shushing noises now and then, till I calmed down.

"I'm sorry David" I sniffed.

He handed me a hanky and he made another cup of tea-

"What happened honey?" he asked.

I told him everything, from the row that morning with Becky to the events of the night in the hotel.

"I thought that it might be a bad one all right, but I didn't think he'd hurt you that way" he sighed.

"I'll never speak to Becky Whelan again"

"Yes you will Carrie, you will, she doesn't mean what she did, she doesn't mean to hurt you, its just the pills are turning her head, making her vicious, you'll patch things up when she's more herself" He smiled.

"But... doing that with my best friend, what the hell was he thinking? And her, such a dirty fucking trick to pull" I was sick, I couldn't get the image out of my head and I couldn't think of forgiving them.

"Becky's an addict and Steven... he's a mess at the moment, I should have warned you, I just thought that things were okay with you"

I had too. Three months or more of heaven, and then this. I was gutted, totally and utterly devastated.

I waited for a minute, and then I asked-

"Why David?"

"You don't want to know sweetheart" he smiled

"I do, because if I know it, then maybe it won't hurt so much, I mean, if its something I can't do anything about then fair enough, but if I can help him through it, then maybe I will feel better, because I feel terrible now, really terrible" I sniffed again.

He sat there and sighed, resignedly and I waited. Then he told me the story, about Stevens mum being a druggie and how he would try to cheer her up and make her happy even as a tiny little kid, and how it never worked. And how it was this time of year that it hit home what she had done and how she had died-

"Suicide, she drove her car into the Thames" he said.

"Oh God that's *terrible*" I cried.

"It was, really terrible, oh if you'd known her, and little Amber, two of the most beautiful people you ever saw, both dead, although they said that Elizabeth was unrecognizable, and Steven looks so like her, its uncanny, and, of course, they never found Ambers body, they reckoned that it went out to sea, she was small enough to float out the car windows I guess" He looked desolate. I felt so sorry for him.

And now this. His son going off his head and probably seeing in Becky the mother he had lost and trying to make her happy and stop her going off the rails and in the meantime, hurting me, the one he really loved, or so I hoped.

"Look Carrie, I know your upset, and you have every right to slap the head off that idiot son of mine, and tell him to sling his hook, and I wouldn't blame you if you did, but please, try to understand, its not the real him doing this to you, he adores you, and I know it, try to understand that it's the eight year old, abandoned by everyone he knows, that's playing the fool tonight, and listen, no matter what, you have a home here as long as you want it, don't let that eejit son of mine make you go when you don't want to, okay?" He left me then, to think, and I fell asleep a little later.

I don't know what time it was when he came home.

He was a mess, I'll grant you that. He looked like he had been sick a couple of times, and he had lost the jacket off the suit. He was red eyed and funnily enough, sober as a judge. Though he stank to high heaven of Jesus knows what.

I'd been lying on the couch and leaned up on my elbow when he came in-

"Well, look what the cat dragged in"

He leaned against the door.

"You look like shit" I said. I wasn't going to make this easy for him.

He laughed softly-

"If I look anything like I feel inside me, then I must look terrible, oh Carrie, what have I done to you?"

"If you don't know I ain't going to tell you, you fucking arsehole, what the hell did you think you were doing?"

"Oh God, I know, I know, I can't believe I did that, what have I done to us, to you?" He rubbed his face, his eyes bleary.

"Well, apart from getting off with my best friend in front of the entire class, making a fool out of me in front of people who don't expect any better of me, and literally smashing my fucking heart into smithereens, not much, but hey, who's counting?" I got off the couch and went into the kitchen for my cigarettes and flicked on the kettle. What a fucking *arsehole!* What has he done? There weren't enough hours in the night to tell him what he did to me tonight!

He leaned against the kitchen door-

"I'm sorry, I really am so sorry Carrie" he stretched his hand out and touched me on the arm. I could feel the fizz of electricity in my arm under the robe; he always got me that way. But sorry wasn't enough, not for the humiliation and the hurt.

"Don't put your hands on me Steven" I pulled away.

"Carrie?"

"I mean it, don't touch me, I don't want you fucking near me tonight" I turned my head away so I wouldn't see the hurt in his eyes, the rejection. I'm hurting too! I wanted to scream at him. I felt, perversely, that I needed to make him suffer, even though my heart was aching with love for him and I was suffused with the terror that I might lose him.

You see, when I was in school I was never one of the hip crowd. I was into rock music and hung out with hippies and rockers and I just knew that they hadn't been expecting me to turn up tonight with a guy, especially not one as gorgeous as Steven, and then for him to go and do something like that, in front of them, well it kind of confirmed their suspicions that I was a loser.

And even though me and Becky had been thick as thieves all this time, they had never quite grasped the concept of the Doctors daughter and the "scruff" from the estate hanging out and having anything at all in common.

I could just imagine them in the bathroom at the debs gossiping and saying "I told you so" all night.

And it stung.

I felt the way I used to feel when I was picked last for basketball teams or when I was left out of the invite list for someone's party. Sad and ashamed and hurt.

I tried to take heart from the idea that I wouldn't have to see them again, for as long as I lived, but boy, was I pissed off at my triumphal march being ruined.

It wasn't just raining on my parade, this was a fucking monsoon!

Right now I wanted to sleep and I really didn't care where Steven went or what he did and told him as much-

"I don't want to talk about this tonight Steve, just go to bed and we will talk in the morning, I need to get my head straight and figure out what I want, go to bed"

"Here?"

"You can have the sofa, or go into your Dad's place, or better yet, go find Becky and finish what you fucking started, either way, leave me alone, and I'll talk to you in the morning"

He tried to grab my hand and I pulled away-

"Carrie, please...listen"

"Good night Steven" I snapped, coldly. He sighed and nodded-

"Okay, okay, goodnight Carrie, see you later"

"Maybe you will"

I took my mug into the bedroom and lay there in the dark. A while later I heard the shower running and I drifted off again to sleep.

I was in that place where you're half asleep and half awake. It was morning time, because the sun was shining, and I half opened my eyes to see it. I drifted away again, I was being held, tight, and he was kissing me, and I realized that I couldn't let him go. No matter what he did, or what had happened, I couldn't leave him. Over and over he told me he loved me and he would never hurt me again, and I clung onto him like I was drowning until it was over and we lay still. I remember that was the last time in my life that I felt at peace with myself. Just lying there and knowing he was with me, looking at the blue-black shine the sun made in his hair. I remember thinking that love had never been so painful and so beautiful. That maybe we weren't meant to have the easy life, but that anything could be made right once we were together like this. No one came into this part of us, only us. And if were together, we could conquer the world.

We never did have that talk.

Becky went back to London a couple of days after the debs, and it was Serena, her big sister, who filled me in, telling me that she had just packed her gear and went without a word to anyone. She had been very upset the following day and Serena got it out of her what she had done-

"I slaughtered her" she said "that was fucking unforgivable"

"I know it was, but she must have been angry with me"

"Jesus, you're her best friend in the world, why do something so mean to you?"

"Its okay Serena, she probably feels terrible about it, we'll sort it out another time"

"Too fucking nice you are! I'd have slaughtered her, and him, but I tell you what, she told me that he ran away from her, nothing happened, bar a kiss, she said, but still and all, was he pissed or what?" she was sitting in a café with me, down near the four courts, dressed in her suit and with a pile of files on the table that she was supposed to be reading in her lunch break.

"I didn't make it easy for him anyhow, that's for sure" I sighed.

The days after the debs, I felt like I was walking on broken glass, afraid to think too much. David had pulled Steven aside and had a quiet word and there was something very strange going on now, in that Steven, while not being openly hostile, was being cool to the point of curtness with his father.

I presumed they would sort it out. Best left to them, I supposed. One thing you learnt in my house and learnt fast, was that you never, ever got involved in a row that wasn't yours.

Because you usually came off the worst of it. And then some!

Serena was still talking-

"I'm worried about Becky a bit. To tell the honest to God truth, you know she moved out of the flat Dad got her and into a loft with some photographer? Some head from Jamaica, called Jacques, or Jacko, or something, well anyhow, my Ma went spare when she heard Becky was living with a black guy, and then, Da hit the roof when the landlord asked him why the rent wasn't being paid and had a massive row with her the day she ran off back to England, he wants me to go over and suss her out, and see can I find out about the guy she's living with, and I'd love to go, but I mean, I'm up to me tits in work, I can't think of taking a half day off for a haircut, never mind a bloody week to swan round London with Becky, hey?" She dropped the spoon she was fiddling with-

"Maybe you and Steve might find your way over to her, I think it's a great idea, you could bury the hatchet and she might open up a bit about this Jacko guy, cos he sounds a bit too good to be true to me, I mean if he's so shit hot as a photographer and agent, why is he still working on penny h'apenny magazines?, Yeah, you guys go over, I think that's a brilliant plan Carrie, hey what do you think?... Carrie?"

I was in the middle of a world class yawn that almost split my face in two-

"Fuck Carrie, am I boring you or something?"

"No, sorry about that, I'm just a bit wrecked, is all" I smiled

"Not a bit surprised, all that riding with lover boy is enough to tire anyone out...tell him you need a sleep or you'll be like a fucking zombie!" she laughed.

"Serena! I will not!" I blushed.

"Get away, I'd hate to see the state of him trying to stand pulling pints half the night and him in bits...shameless, that's what you are! You'd know the pair of you hadn't had a decent nights sleep in months!"

I was too tired to think straight. I couldn't seem to get myself together lately. I was in town trying to do some Christmas shopping and I couldn't rise myself to buy anything. I'd wandered aimlessly for hours that morning and hadn't bought a thing, and still managed to be five minutes late meeting Serena.

Serena had the type of gaze that was sure to put the fear of God into whoever she ended up facing across the bench in court and she fixed me with a stare now.

"Carrie, are you okay?" she asked.

The funny thing about her was that she was like my big sister too. She had been the one I went to when things got me down and when I needed answers to questions that I couldn't ask Ma. I smiled, remembering the time she told me about periods and how to take care of my self, knowing that Ma was going through her drinking phase and hadn't the sense to realize that I was growing up fast. I shook myself-

"I'm grand, I just feel a bit fluey or something, must be a viral thing, I haven't the energy to wag" I sighed.

"Do you mind if I say something? I think that, lately, I'm kind of getting second sight with Becky, I know she is in the shit, and she is going to be in need of serious help soon, and I hope I'm there to give it, and then there's you, Carrie, I know you love him and he loves you, but I get this feeling over me sometimes that the shit is about to hit the fan in some way, so I think, I wondered, like, could you be pregnant or something?"

I felt myself go ice cold.

"Why do you ask?"

"Its just you look so tired, and greener round the gills than I ever saw you looking, it's just a thought I guess, have you been careful?"

"Yes, I think so, except." I remembered the morning after the debs; I didn't think we had been as careful as usual that time, and, oh Jesus, Connemara! Was it possible that I had got caught?

"Well, it only takes once, you know that, look; go up to Dame street, there's a place there will do a test for you free, and you can decide then what you want to do, I have to go back to work, otherwise I'd go with you"

I told her I would go up and see them and when she left the café I sat there for a while, trying to do the Math.

My periods had always been irregular, I never knew when or if they were going to arrive, but I had them in early September, I was sure of that. The debs was on the fourteenth of October. So if Serena was right, and I was pregnant, then I was about two months gone.

Three hours later I walked out of the office in Dame Street in shock.

I was Pregnant. And further on than I thought. Three months or so, it was the night under the boat, just as I suspected it was.

I had a handful of leaflets telling me what to eat and what to do and where I could find support if needed. I got on the bus home in a daze and went into the mobile and sat at the kitchen table, praying that Steven wouldn't be late home.

I didn't know how he would take this at all. But tell him I must.

I sat there for a long time, thinking and planning what I would do if he didn't want to know, and eventually had built myself up for the fall.

Then he came home and I told him and his face lit up.

"Really?" he asked.

"Yes, I am, I found out today"

"Oh wow, that's amazing Carrie" He grabbed me and hugged me really tight. Then, let me go and held me a little less tightly-

"The baby, don't want to squash it" he laughed.

"Your, your okay about it?" I stammered.

"Its great news, I'm delighted, are you?" he looked straight at me-

"You do want to have it Carrie? I mean, I'm here for you no matter what happens, but I want you to tell me what you want"

"*Of course* I want it, oh I was terrified you'd say you didn't and I'd have to leave you" I was weak with relief. I couldn't have stayed with him if he'd wanted me to get rid of the baby. I knew that it would never be the same after something like that.

He was thrilled, I could see it. And he was pacing the room unable to sit still, and then he stopped and looked really serious-

"Let's get married"

"*What?*" I nearly choked with the fright.

"I said, let's get married"

"Jesus I heard you the first time, but *why?*" my legs went weak and I sat down with a thump on the sofa. I couldn't believe my ears. It wasn't as if a baby born out of wedlock would carry any stigma nowadays. The day of the shotgun wedding was well and truly past.

"For the baby, so we can be a proper family, what do you think, come on, say yes, it'll be great, you'll be Mrs. Me, and I'll be Mr. You say yes, go on, please?"

I couldn't speak and he took the silence as a hesitation-

"Carrie, I'll look after you, I won't ever let you down again, I love you, I swear to God I won't hurt you ever again, please... please say you'll marry me" He was kneeling in front of me now, holding my face in his hands, staring into my eyes-

"Oh God Steve, I..."

"Carrie, please..."

And I thought about all the reasons against this, the fact that I wasn't nineteen yet and he was only twenty two, and we had no where to live bar with his dad, and most of the young marriages I knew had been grand for a couple of years and had broken up then, and we had no money because I wasn't earning great money in the shop and he was only part time with his dad.

But then I looked at him and realized that he was the one I wanted to be with for the rest of my life and whether I married him now or in ten years time, that wasn't going to change, and so maybe I should throw caution to the wind and say it-

"Yes, I will" I smiled.

He grabbed me and kissed me and then, pulled me to my feet and into the bedroom-

"No point in locking the stable door when the horse is gone. Lets make double sure of this baby, Mrs. Williams" he grinned.

I actually surprised my self in the weeks that followed, getting things organized for the wedding. I discovered that I didn't want a hole in the corner affair, but that I wanted a nice little church service and then a few drinks in the hotel. White didn't suit me so I got a purple frock that didn't make it too obvious that I was pregnant, and we went to see Father Green about the service, which we wanted in late January, or at latest mid February. Father Ray was there the Saturday in December, when I went up to arrange things and he told me that I would need a couple of things, baptismal cert for both of us and our birth certs-

"For the civil part of the thing, the register signing, have to be sure you are who you say you are" he laughed.

"So it all worked out nicely like we thought Carol-Anne?"

"Looks that way Father"

"How long are you together? Its not that long is it?"

"Since August Ray" I smiled. Ray always put me into good form.

"Not that long, are you quite sure about this?"

"As sure as I am about anything Ray, we want to be together and then there's the baby to consider"

"Ah, that's a horse of a different colour altogether, and Steven is happy about the wedding too?" he looked at the form I had filled out.

"Delighted Ray, about everything"

"And your mother?"

"*That's* going to be a problem, she doesn't know yet, but I am going to go up and tell her, I need my certs. anyhow, and she has them, so I'll let you know how I get on" it was the one part of the proceedings that I was not looking forward to.

"Best of luck Carrie, your going to need it, I take it things are bad there at the minute" He waved me off from the porch and I walked down and through the park and over to the estate.

The place hadn't changed in the few months I was away and I laughed to myself. I had lived there for seventeen years, and nothing had changed in that time either, except the snotty little kids I grew up with were now rearing their own little ones. The houses were blank and uniform. Dreary. Even if every window had a Christmas tree twinkling behind the curtains.

My Ma was in the kitchen when I came in the back door. She was on her knees doing a pile of laundry, sorting it into whites and coloureds.

"Well?" she asked.

"Hiya Ma, how are you?"

"Busy, what can I do for you?" she seemed very narky or something.

"I need my birth cert and my baptismal one too"

"Oh? Why?"

"I'm getting married"

She stopped sorting the dirty washing and leaned back on her heels-

"To who?"

Who did she think?

"Steven"

"You're not serious?" she said.

"I am, look at my ring" I held out my left hand with the small chip diamond ring on it. She barely looked at it.

"I don't believe you! I really don't believe you! What does his father say?"

"He's delighted, it's what we want" I couldn't understand this, she was up in arms about us living in sin and now we were getting married she was in the horrors again.

"Are you pregnant?" she snapped.

"We are very happy about that too and..."

She stood up, with difficulty, and reached into the press behind her for a brown envelope.

"You can't marry him, you can't marry that man, I mean it Carol Anne, you have to stop this now!"

"Jesus Ma there's no pleasing you! You should be delighted for me, not like this, trying to ruin everything, what the hell is wrong with you?"

"If your Da was here he would stop you, I knew this would happen, I told him back then that nothing good would come of lies and now look at the mess your in!" she was literally tearing at her hair and I couldn't believe it!

"What has he to do with this? Ma tell me?" I jumped off the chair and grabbed her by the arms-

"Tell me what's wrong, please?" I shook her.

112

"We lied and I knew that it would go wrong, I told him not to do it, and he did, oh Jesus in heaven help me!" she wailed.

"Ma, for fucks sake…tell me"

"Your ruined Carol Anne, ruined"

I looked at the envelope and picked it up.

"I'm opening this now Ma, and I want you to explain to me whatever it is that's in it, no more bullshit do you hear me? Ma, please, this is my life, help me" I tore at the ancient paper with shaking hands.

"He's your brother Carol Anne! Your pregnant for your own brother!" she said it, and I felt my stomach turn.

"What?" I gasped.

Suddenly the ground shifted under me and for the very first time in my life I passed out cold on the floor.

5

Doris

When I was a child, my mother always told me not to do a bad turn if I could do a good one-

"We reap what we sow Dorrie, you remember that!" she used to say.

We lived in a lovely place, in the midlands, a few miles out of Mullingar. Daddy worked on the railway and Mammy kept house for us all. Though we were a small family by all standards of the time. Breege, my sister, and Michael my little brother. I was in the middle. Times were hard and the money was scarce, and there was no money for university or anything like that. So when Breege or Breda was seventeen, she took training in a hospital in London, and went off nursing.

I followed her over two years later and worked in a sewing factory in Islington. We shared a little flat and we used to go to dances and hops in the city with her friend Mary.

My little brother wasn't as bright as the rest of us and he was at home on the farm with Mammy and daddy.

Daddy retired from the railway and got sick with Parkinson Disease and died when I was nineteen. So there was no one to give me away at my wedding.

But I wasn't too upset about that.

I met Peter Conway in a dancehall one night. It was during lent, when all the big show-band stars would come over to England and play for us when the halls were closed back home.

He was gorgeous, he really was. And he was doing well for himself. He was working on the building in London and was a foreman now. He was twenty five and built like an ox.

I thought it was Breege he fancied but I was wrong. He made a bee line for me and stayed by my side for the night.

He was respectful and loving, and we never did anything before we were married properly. Mammy taught me that much. A man never buys the loaf if he can have a slice for free.

We got married in 1969 and moved into a lovely little flat in Clapham and settled into married life, waiting for the babies to start coming.

Breege would come over on her day off from the hospital and would be full of gossip and tales and she told me about Mary's fiancé doing a runner with some posh one up in Scotland and breaking the engagement off in a note the day he eloped with the other one. Mary was never right after that and she went home to Belfast afterwards. I heard, oh, much later, that she had married a man much older than herself who she had been nursing.

But it was Mary that put Breege on to the job with the couple. Mary had thought about doing it herself, but she had really loved David Williams and couldn't bear the thought of looking at him day in day out with his new family. So Breege applied for the job of nanny/private nurse and went to live in their big posh house.

I went to the doctor to see was there a reason for us not having babies when we were married two years and nothing was stirring. The doctor told me that these things take time and to be calm and serene and not be worrying about it. Peter said I was a worrier and that it would happen in its own good time and not to fret too much.

I decided to go back to work in the factory until it did happen and my life was fairly occupied and busy then.

Breege was finding her life more than she could handle at the moment. She was the nanny for the little boy, Stevie, and she adored him. The things that went on in that house! My God, the things she saw!

Drugs and drunkards and terrible things going on while that man was at work and the child locked into the nursery with Breege for his own safety.

I thought that David was certainly repenting at leisure his hasty marriage! Breege told me that Liz was pregnant again but that the state she was in, she wasn't going to have the baby at all.

It was around this time that her father asked Breege to be her companion and nurse when she was locked into the secure unit in the hospital in Glasgow, until she had the baby. She wasn't to be trusted see, she was running away all the time and getting off her head on drugs, and she with the belly out in front of her.

"Its so unfair Breege, that someone like her, that doesn't give a damn about the baby that *she* can get caught and I can't"

It was out before I knew it and before I knew where I was I had told Breege the whole story of how we were now three and a half years trying for a baby and nothing was stirring. Nothing.

Breege soothed me and told me that God was good and things would work out for the best, wait and see.

I was getting tired of waiting and waiting to see what God had in mind. He might be good, but he wasn't very punctual, was he?

Breege was paid very well for her work with Liz Williams.

When the baby was born healthy, she was given a load of money as a bonus payment from the grandfather of the child.

I noticed that she didn't speak too much about her life there anymore. She told me that coming to my place was a rest, and escape, and she couldn't bear to think about the place when she had so little time away from it.

The bits she let slip told a whole story of their own.

It seemed that the mother had a serious problem, she didn't want anything to do with the boy, but the little girl went everywhere she went. In a little red mini car. It was as if she was trying to protect the child from something but couldn't tell us what it was. And she took so many drugs and drank heavily and somehow got involved with a rough gang that were up in the city and who had girls out working and all that.

She didn't need that kind of work, she had money! Her father paid her an allowance. Breege reckoned that one of the pimps had some class of hold on her and that's why she did it.

One day she told Breege that she thought she was in serious danger and she was thinking of taking the baby and going out to America or somewhere.

"Far away, somewhere they won't find me" she said.

Breege thought about it and then asked her to let her mind the baby for her, till she got settled in the states, and then she would bring her over.

"I won't tell David anything" Breege said.

Breege remembered what he did to her friend and she didn't have any loyalty to him at all.

That was why, when it all happened, she never helped him. She could have saved him from jail and she didn't.

But I'm ahead of myself.

Breege told us that there was a baby, and that we needed to get everything ready, that she would be coming soon, and we had to be ready to run with her, back to Ireland. Peter got all that was needed and one day, we were in Holyhead, waiting for Breege to get off the boat train with the child.

I fell in love with baby Amber the minute she was held out to me. I wrapped her in the blanket we had bought and we went onto the boat. I stuffed the brown envelope into the bag of nappies and baby clothes and rocked her to sleep.

We got to Dublin and got a flat and everything went well. We went out for walks with the baby, up to the Phoenix Park and into the Botanic Gardens. One evening we were coming back to the flat and Peter went into a shop to buy cigarettes and came out white faced.

"Doris, she's dead! That Liz Bard is dead" he whispered.

I grabbed the paper and read that the red mini was pulled out of the Thames that morning and that David Williams was being charged with murder.

I found a phone box and rang Breege.

But she was gone. She had vanished off the face of the earth. No one knew where to, or how she had done it.

We had the baby and we brought her home. I sat in the chair, holding her and crying. Peter paced the floor and smoked.

"We have to tell the police, we can't have this child now" I wept.

We had her for a week all ready, and we kept telling ourselves that we were fostering her till her Mammy got sorted out. But she was beautiful and we both wished she was ours.

"Why do we have to do anything of the sort? Isn't it better she is with us?" he said.

"But Peter, suppose they find out?"

"How can that happen? They think she's dead, they'll look for the body, but in time they'll issue a death cert and won't be any the wiser, think about it Doris, our own little girl, and no one will know" He was totally charmed by the child and I knew he ached to keep her with us.

All that night we talked and talked and eventually we came up with a plan.

The baby was to be called Carol Anne, after his mother and mine. If anyone asked us, she was our baby. The only person who knew the truth now was Breege and until she came forward, no one would be any the wiser. Maybe she was dead too?

We were keeping this child. She was ours now.

I knew even then that no good would come of lying like that and I made him promise that when Carol Anne was old enough that she could be told she was adopted. Maybe I had a sixth sense about something happening like now. I clipped the newspaper and stuffed it into the envelope with her birth cert and hoped that I would be able to keep the secret.

I don't know how I kept going all this time. I remember once, the letter coming with the money in it from Breege, No address on it, no clue where it came from, but I knew it was Breege. It had to be. Everyone else thought that Baby Amber died in the Thames, didn't they?

When Peter and I split up, he took himself back to London and I took up with Noel. The money came in handy then. But in my heart I knew that this would all fall down like a house of cards.

And now it has.

Now there is another baby coming into the world, destroyed before it ever draws breath. A tissue of lies the only thing they have behind them. That's no life. No life at all. I wish I could turn the clock back.

I took that little baby and promised that I would take care of her and I let her down, I neglected her and didn't love her as much as I ought to. Peter idolized her and I ruined that for him too. I let him leave when I should have worked at my marriage for the little ones sake.

She was so hurt when he stopped coming home to see her. I close my eyes some times and I can hear them in the living room, Carol Anne sitting on the arm of his chair in her little pajamas singing songs with him and taking sips from his glass of beer. I know she missed her Daddy, so much, and Noel was no replacement, I see that now.

I cannot understand why he is so horrible to her. Because he wasn't that mean when I met him, it's like over time, it's built up like steam pressure and now it's at the point of exploding and I don't want to see the carnage it causes when it does.

Because the only one that's going to be hurt is my little one, the little one I held in my arms all night on the ferry from England, the one I swore to love and protect and care for in the absence of her Mammy, for ever and ever if need be.

The little one I sold, the little one I neglected.

The little girl who was so empty and craved love and affection so much that she fell in love too soon when she saw someone she recognized as part of her self.

The little one who ran away because I couldn't be there when she needed me.

It's all my fault, I should have told her. But I never dreamed that this could happen. Not in a million years did I dream that she and Steven would meet, and its no surprise that she had her head turned, because honestly, he is the most beautiful man I have ever laid eyes on, and from what I see, he's a good soul too.

But now both of them will be irreparably damaged by the sins of their mothers, Liz Bard and me.

Liz, at least, has had the mercy of God, she died before any of this came to fruition. And maybe where ever she is she understands and sees the bigger picture.

It is me that has to face the music now. And pick this child up off the floor and finally do right by her after so much wrong.

6

Carrie

When you have never fainted before in your life, it's a weird sensation, especially the coming around part. There I was lying on the floor in my mother's kitchen, the smelly laundry in piles around me, and her kneeling beside me holding a wet face cloth to my forehead.

I sat straight up and nearly fainted again-

"Take it slowly Carol-Anne; you've had a shock, stay easy for a minute"

I felt dreadful, I knew she was trying to be nice to me but all I could think about was poor Steven in work, thinking of coming home to me, thinking I'd have news about what day we could get married. Now it could never happen and I hadn't a clue how I was going to tell him.

"I'm grand, let me up Mam" I clambered up to the little two-seater sofa she had there for when she wanted to watch soaps in the kitchen.

"Tea!" she said and bustled around boiling the kettle and getting cups-

"I don't want it" I said, but you'd think I was talking to the wall. She approached with the mug of weak tea and I knew by the smell it was as sweet as treacle.

"You can't leave here till you do, you have to think of the baby too you know?"

The baby, oh fucking hell.

I took a sip of tea to wet my mouth, it was vile, but my mouth felt dry and gritty and salty. I felt like I had bitten my tongue, it was sore.

"What *are* you going to do about the baby?" she asked.

"For fucks sake Ma, will you let me think? I need to get over the one shock before I fucking think about the next one!" I snapped.

I surprised myself by drinking the tea down and then she gave me more-

"That's better, there's more colour in your face now" she sighed.

"You will have to think about what your going to do, the baby will be, well it won't be right with him being your brother, and in a couple of weeks, it will be too late to think of anything"

I had visions of a mutant, deformed baby, not even able to cry or take a bottle, and I shuddered. I didn't know what I wanted to do, yet, something was telling me to follow this through, that somehow it would be all right. I believed in the right to choose, but I never saw myself having an abortion, it just wasn't me. But in this case...

"I don't know what I want to do yet, I need to talk to Steven" I said.

"Ha! Him? Your days with him better be numbered miss!" she snapped. The dose of niceness never lasted long with Ma. Her old snappiness was back in minutes.

I didn't answer her; I just pulled the envelope towards me and took out the papers that were in it-

Some yellowed newspaper cuttings were first, grainy photos of David being led into a police van and one of a child I was sure was Steven being held by the hand by an old Man. *My granddad?* Then the wad of papers inside-

A birth certificate, my name was Amber Bard Williams. My date of birth was as I knew it, that hadn't changed. Just the name. Place of birth; St Andrews Hospital; Glasgow. Mothers Name; Elizabeth Mary Bard Williams. Fathers name; David Francis Williams.

There it was, black and white, and frayed round the edges. My life, destroyed.

I put all of the papers back into the envelope and looked up at Ma-

"I don't know what I feel, what I'm supposed to feel, but I need to go away and think about this, and, is it okay to take this stuff with me?"

She nodded.

"Why didn't you say anything to me, when you knew what, who I was, and who David was? Why did you stay quiet?"

I couldn't understand it. Surely the best thing would have been to tell me, warn me of what I was walking into.

"I couldn't, there were reasons, old reasons, I would have been in terrible trouble Carol-Anne, you have no idea"

I sighed.

"Not half as much trouble as I am in now Ma, I'll see you soon, thanks for the tea"

I walked down to the village in the dark, and headed for the library. I looked up books on pregnancy and birth and none of them said anything about what happened to babies conceived between brother and sister. The ultimate taboo, the love that dare not speak its name… that used to be homosexuality, didn't it? But I reckoned that incest was up there now.

I sat in the reading room and rubbed my belly. The baby felt healthy, I had begun to feel the little flutters of life and was so thrilled by it. I couldn't believe that this child was going to be born a monster. It couldn't happen. Maybe we would be lucky?

But what had luck got to do with my life. So far, it seemed the only lucky thing that had ever happened to me was that I didn't end up in the river with my mother. And now, even that was debatable.

I tried to think clearly about me and Steven too.

But it's one thing knowing that what you're doing is wrong and illegal and terrible, and another thing entirely not doing it anymore. I loved Steven, absolutely loved him. But it appeared that the chemistry and *knowing* of each other was not a result of finding a soul mate at all.

Instead, it was because we came from the same gene pool.

Tell that to my heart! Try and reason with my emotions, when all I wanted was us to run far away and never come back to this fucked up reality again.

That was it! We could run! Out of Ireland and go where nobody knew us. The other choice wasn't a choice at all. I couldn't live without him. Let them say what they wanted; they should have warned us before it got to this. Fuck them all I say!

I ran out of the library and home, hoping I still had time. I packed my bags and sat there, nerves jumping and yet feeling incredible. I was in control again.

"What's going on Carrie?" he had sneaked in silently when I was in the kitchen and had seen the bags.

I grabbed him and kissed him-

"Come on, we have to get out of here" I pulled him toward the bedroom, where his clothes were in bags already.

"What? Are we eloping? How rose-mantic you are for a weeknight" he laughed.

"Please Steven, please, I will explain everything, but you have to come with me now" I was frantic, pacing the small floor and looking at the door, expecting something to come in and get us, but not knowing what "something" could be. Police maybe or the Priest?

"What is it? What's going on Carrie?" he sat on the edge of the bed, and just stared at me.

"Jesus Carrie you have to calm down, the baby..."

I was gasping for breath, panicking. I could feel the walls closing in on me.

He grabbed my hand and I pulled away and went into the sitting room to where my rucksack lay with everything stuffed into it.

I rummaged in the side of the bag and took the envelope out of it. I handed it to him and he took the papers from it, his face blanching at the sight of the newspaper clippings-

"Look, just read that, then you'll see" I hugged myself round the waist and felt the baby flutter inside me.

He scanned the pages and, when he came to my cert looked up at me-

"Who gave this to you?" he whispered, face white, his eyes actually looked frozen with fear.

"My Ma" I whispered. I felt like a deflated balloon, all the fight gone from me.

"This can't be fucking right" he cried.

He read and re read my birth cert and even as he did, I knew he was hoping that the words would be different the next time he looked. I had done that too. But the ink didn't dissolve and the plain truth stayed the same.

"It can't be right Carrie, Amber drowned, she was the Angel, she... You *can't* be her, you and me; it can't be true, for fucks sake what's going on?"

I started to cry.

"I know, I can't believe it either, oh Steven what will we do?"

He stood up.

"I know what I'm going to fucking do, I'm going to kill that bastard in there" He went storming off to the house and I heard the back door nearly coming off the hinges, followed by shouting and banging.

"Did you *know*? Tell me!" I could hear him shouting.

"Know what? Stevie, Jesus what is it?"

I arrived in the sitting room as David took the cert from Steven's hand. Steven had him pinned to the wall and it was hard for him to hold the cert so he could read it.

"Steven for fucks sake let him go!" I screamed.

"Read that, go on, tell me you didn't know anything, how could you not know? And yet you let me... you let us, oh Jesus, the baby; we can't have the baby now, can we? This is *crazy*, and you fucking *knew about it?*" Steven was in tears now, shaking. He let David go and punched the wall.

"You *must* have known, you were the adult back then, you remember Amber better than I can, you must have seen" he growled

David was stock still-

"I knew nothing about this, I swear to you, I knew nothing at all, I *wouldn't* have...I couldn't have let you, I swear I didn't know, Stevie you have to believe me son, I... I wouldn't have done this to you, to either of you, Carrie, do you believe me?"

"Was that why you hid me? Is that why I wasn't allowed do anything for fucking years?" I'd never seen him so angry, it terrified me. I knew bits of his life by now, the fact that he had few mates and no best friend and had been a real loner as a child and teenager, missing out on all the usual things young fellas did back then, going to football matches and drinking cans up the canal and getting off with young ones. He'd been as lonely as I was in my little box room, playing my albums and staring at the walls.

"I was trying to protect you, you don't understand what would have happened if they knew where you were"

"They? They? That's all I ever hear about is them! I was a fucking hermit for years and now, the first time I find something I want, the first time I'm happy, you manage to fuck it up again, I've never been free, never, let them send me to prison, I don't care, I've lived in it for years anyway"

"Steven I love you, I wouldn't hurt you, or Carrie, you have to believe that, I did it all so… I thought I was doing what was right, do you understand?" David was in bits, white faced, and I was worried he would keel over any second.

I understood, and I believed him when he said he didn't know.

"I do David"

"I don't know what to say, this whole situation is crazy, there has to be a mistake, there has to be"

He sat down, I felt so sorry for him too. I went to the side board and poured a very stiff brandy and held it out to him.

He grabbed my hand-

"I should have told you about the whole court case and everything, but I thought it was dragging up the past and Steven and you were so happy, but I swear I didn't know you were Amber, Carrie you must believe me pet"

"I believe you David, I do, but now we need to think about what we can do next, I think we need to get away from here, as soon as possible"

He nodded-

"Yes, yes you do, you need to go, quickly, you need to leave" He whispered, his face chalk white.

"This is fucked up, *it's sick*, she's my *sister*, for fucks sake, how *can* it be fixed? Where the fuck will we go that this won't matter? Everywhere we fucking run, no matter where we run, the fact remains, she's my fucking sister and I… we didn't know and now… the baby" Steven was able to verbalize his feelings and I was stuck inside my head on the merry go round, not able to find any solution..

I felt physically wrecked and mentally drained. I just wanted to sleep. But we stayed there till the small hours and we tried to think, I guess we were all trying to make things right, so that I wouldn't have to leave Steven and that the baby would be all right too. But nothing worked.

There is no solution when you're teetering on the abyss and the forest fire is three inches from your heels… its jump or burn, no choice really, is it? Either way, you're doomed.

I walked down to the mobile at some time after three a.m. and collapsed into bed. I heard Steven come in a little later and he sat on the end of the bed-

"Carrie?"

"Yeah?"

"I love you"

"I know you do love, and I love you too, so much it hurts, oh babe, I wish it was different"

He lay down beside me and put out his arms to me-

"C'mere, I won't touch you, I just want to lay here with you, is that okay?" he whispered.

"Course it is Steve, just get into bed cos it's cold" I shivered.

I snuggled into his familiar body and we just lay there, breathing the same air for the longest time.

"Tell me its going to be all right?" he whispered.

"I don't know how, but it's got to be a mistake, we don't even look alike"

"I still want to marry you Carrie, I love you, and I don't want anyone else, do you believe me?"

"Of course I do, I love you too, and I want to be with you, but we have to face the truth, if this is the truth, we won't be marrying, and we won't be able to be together at all"

To the best of my knowledge there was no place on the face of the earth that could or would condone incest. I felt sick when I thought of it. But the fact was there, that's what our love was, if the certs were genuine and we shared a bloodline.

"No, no I won't think of that, look, this isn't a fantasy, there isn't anyone else for me, not now and not ever, I couldn't be with anyone the way I am with you" He was getting agitated again.

"I know pet, but we couldn't, not if, I don't think we could anyway, its illegal isn't it"

"I suppose so, we could run, go to Germany or Holland, or somewhere, and just live, where no one knows us, Oh Carrie, I'm going to do everything in my power to stay with you and face this, I can't bear the thoughts of never touching you again or making love to you again and I won't be able not to, you know it as well as I do, what we have is special, no one else can come close to you, you know that don't you?"

"I do believe you, and I love you too, more than anything" I smiled.

And then we were kissing.

And because I couldn't stop myself, couldn't help myself, I sat up and slipped the nightdress I was wearing off and threw it onto the floor, and then, helped him take his clothes off.

This time it felt different, because it felt like, against our better judgment, against everything we wanted for us, it felt like reality had bitten and this was the end.

We lay there entwined as always, afterwards and I was upset, crying silently, as he stroked my little bump and I tried to sleep.

"I can't lose you Steven, I can't, not now, not after everything" I wept.

He leaned up on his elbow and kissed me hard on the mouth-

"Listen to me Carrie"

I stared at him and nodded.

"Wherever you are, there I'll be, whether I am there for real, or it's only my thoughts that follow you, you're my woman, for ever and ever, and no one will change that" he whispered.

"I know, I know but, I want you so much, I can't think about life with no you in it" I said as I stroked his back. I could feel my tears running down my cheeks and plopping onto my shoulders.

"I'll always want you, always, this doesn't happen every day, this is us Carrie, this is how we are, I'll never as long as I live want anyone else"

"Then take me away Steven, don't let this happen to us"

"I will my love, whatever happens, I promise, *I promise* I will never leave you, ever"

And so we made plans and we thought that we might get away that weekend to another country, he had a passport, I didn't, so we'd have to sort that out, but then, we'd be free.

"England for a start, tomorrow, dad can sort your passport, then maybe to the states, after Christmas, then when we get there, I'll change my name or something, or you can, and we'll live real quiet somewhere that no one knows us, when the baby comes, we'll see what happens, it might all be okay"

As we built our new life and prepared to say goodbye to the old one, I felt my eyelids drooping and sleep came. He kept talking, building me a castle in the air, so beautiful and real that I began to trust in it and believe that it could happen.

"Goodnight Carrie" He whispered.

I muttered something in reply. Maybe if I had known what was around the corner, I would have told him not to stay. To go back into the house, and sleep there. To stay safe. I had already made up my mind to tell them that someone anonymous was the father of the baby and therefore cut out the investigations. If the child was born deformed then I'd know the truth was told and he was my brother. But it was hard to think that the way I felt was wrong as I snuggled into him and nodded off in the darkness. How I wished afterwards that I had listened to my gut feeling.

Because the next thing I heard was the door being booted and about four coppers landed into the mobile. He was unceremoniously pulled out of the bed, I screamed for David who came running from the house-

"What the..." he was still half asleep.

"Get back sir, we have a warrant for your sons arrest" the guard at the door said.

"Arrest? For what?" He cried.

They were handcuffing Steven now and I was kneeling in the bed in shock.

"Jesus Christ! What are you doing to him?"

"Stay back please sir" the ban Garda was in my room now.

"You'll have to get dressed and come to the station too miss" she said, and they dragged Steven out into the squad car and then drove away.

I got dressed in the bathroom and shivering, went out into the front garden. Despite all the noise, there was no one out in the street staring and I was glad of that. We drove in the squad car to the station and I went inside with the ban Garda.

"Why? Who made the complaint? Why did you come tonight?"

"You know a lady called Doris Conway?" she snapped.

"Yes...yes I do, she's my adoptive mother" I said.

"well, she took a bad turn today, a kind of stroke, she's in the hospital, her partner found her on the kitchen floor this evening and when he got her to hospital, he asked her what had happened and she told him you'd been up there today, and why" she brought me into a room and I was told to sit down and wait for someone to come and talk to me.

"Where is Steven? Can I see him?" I asked.

"That's the least of your problems Carol Anne, sit there now till the sergeant comes to see you" she closed the door and I put my head in my hands.

The sergeant came in about fifteen minutes later I thought. I had no idea what time it was because the room was completely bare, except for the two chairs and the table which was bolted to the floor. I looked at him and tried to smile-

"Hello" he said. He had a piece of paper in his hand.

"Hello"

"Do you know why you're here?" he asked.

"I have an idea" I replied.

"You and your brother are in quite a lot of trouble, it appears that you are carrying his child, is that correct?"

"I am carrying a baby for my partner, yes, but..."

"Your partner being Steven Patrick Williams?"

"Yes... But" he cut me short with his hand.

"You are aware that you and Steven share a birth mother and, it would appear, the same father? Do you know what Incest is Carol Anne?" he leaned across the table.

"It's when people who are related have sexual relations with each other" I said, realizing that I was hanging myself and Steven with every word.

"Indeed, and it appears that you have been sleeping with your brother, and if is not a crime to live with, or sleep in the same bed as your brother, it certainly is a crime to have sex with him, and you apparently have done so, if it is his child your carrying" He put the piece of paper on the table and smoothed it out.

"You will have to go to court, you will be charged, and you will most likely do time in prison for this, do you realize that?"

"Prison? I... What about Steven?" I gasped.

"He is being told the exact same thing as you. Now, what I have here is an undertaking, signed by him and to be signed by you, and what this says is that you and he are admitting to the unlawful carnal knowledge of each other, and that you are carrying his child and that you will stay away from each other entirely until the court case, that you will have no contact, no phone calls or letters, until the courts decide if you are guilty of the charge" he slid the paper towards me.

"Read it and sign it please" he snapped.

We were being treated like criminals. How could love turn into this?

"Your forgetting that I live in the same house, almost, how will I not see him if I live there?" I asked.

"You won't be living there, he is entitled to live there as it is his fathers house, but you will have to go back to your adoptive home or else make other arrangements, either way you will both have to sign on in the local Garda station daily" he tapped the paper and I sighed.

"Look, we only found out about this today, its so much to take in, please, can I just see him for a minute?" I guess I was trying to appeal to the policeman and his better nature if he had one.

"Sign that"

"Can I see him, please?"

"Sign that first and we'll see" he smiled crookedly.

I signed the document condemning us both and felt like I was betraying Steven. And the upshot of it was that I wasn't allowed to see him. The paper I signed was what was called an exclusion order which meant that he or I couldn't be within any distance of each other, ever. I couldn't go to his house or his street, and he couldn't come to mine. Where ever that would be now, because I was darned sure I wasn't going back to live with Noel!

"Can I phone someone, please?" I asked.

"Who?" Papers signed and being shoved into a manila folder, the Garda seemed to have lost interest in me and how I felt.

"My workmate, Nancy Jones, she has a flat in town, she might let me stay with her"

"Very well, you may phone her" he brought me out to the reception and I used the phone. My bags had been brought to the station from the mobile and soon as I had the phone down, I was in a car and heading for Dorset Street.

"...I can't see him, or ring him or anything Nance, what am I going to do? We could have got away but... oh Nancy we could end up in jail for this!" I had told her the whole sordid story and she was totally gob smacked.

"You're not fucking serious!" she had blurted when I rang her from the station.

"Come here, don't fuckin' go back to that madhouse in Corduff" she said.

"Thanks Nancy, thank you" I whispered, trying not to let the coppers hear me getting upset.

"Don't you cry in front of them cunt's, you don't let them see you cry, do you hear me Carrie?" She hissed.

"Be strong kid, be strong, everything is going to be okay, you wait and see, but don't let the coppers see you cry, that's right up their alley"

Nancy hated the police, for good reason, she said, but never elaborated.

"Come here now, I have the kettle on the hob, come on hen, its all right" she sounded like she was trying not to cry too.

I sat numb in the squad car and when we got to the flat the Ban Garda went into Nancy's flat first, I guess to take her details and make sure I was with whoever I said I'd be with. Then I was given the letter for Fitzgibbon Street and told to sign at 12 noon the following day and to ask for a Sergeant Curtis. Then they were gone-

"That cow has the right personality for the job anyway" Nancy was in her dressing gown and was smoking a fag at the door.

"Nance, I..." I was lost for words.

"Come on, come in here to me, pet, and tell me the whole story" she held out her arms and hugged me.

"Oh Nancy they wouldn't even let me see him to say goodbye, I mean what did they think we were going to do, go at it on the table or something, fucking hell, this is nuts, I don't think I can take this" I was shaking like a leaf.

She brought me in and made tea and listened.

"Come on chicken, spill the beans, from the beginning" She lit another cigarette and leaned back in the chair.

The whole story, from start to finish as I knew it took hours and we were blessed that it was Sunday morning.

"So basically, all you have is that bit of paper that *says* you're Amber Williams? That's the only bit of evidence you have to say you're his sister?" Nancy asked.

"Yeah, isn't it enough?" I sniffed.

"C'mere till I tell yeh hen, if *that* was all you needed to say a child was someone's child or relation, d'ya not think Bono would have three million love children, nah there has to be serious proof of relationship and even I know that this bit of paper isn't enough" she lit another cigarette.

"You need blood tests or something, *and then* you'll know"

"Surely the police know that too?"

"Ah you wouldn't want to mind those fuckers, they don't know what day it is half the fucking time! No, you need to get a blood test, something to show them that this is all a load of bollocks" She blew out a load of smoke.

"You mark my words chicken, this will all be a storm in a teacup, you'll be back home with him by Christmas, you wait and see, now come on and get your head down for a kip, otherwise you'll be in bits later" she brought me into the bedroom and I got into my pajamas.

"I hope to God your right Nancy" I said when we were lying in the bed.

"Course I am, now asleep with yeh, and no throwing your leg over me thinking its Steven your in with!" she giggled.

I was too tired to answer, but I went to sleep feeling a whole lot better.

I signed on the next day and asked the sergeant about the blood tests and he told me that the courts would order them as and when they saw fit. I was reminded that I couldn't contact Steven at all or I would be breaking my bond and would be in prison quick as a flash.

"Can I not get the tests myself?" I asked.

"No, because that would be breaking your bond, you'd have to get Steven to do it too and you're not allowed contact him, wait till the courts order them, that's the best thing" he said.

So it looked like I was to live in limbo a while longer.

Until the court decided otherwise.

What is that old saying? Something about the mills of God grinding exceedingly slowly, but that they grind exceedingly fine? Well that was the way my life felt now, like it had slowed down and was at a standstill. Christmas came and went, and new year, and there I was, still waiting for the police to get around to ordering blood tests so we could get back to normal.

Nancy had been fantastic.

I had stayed in her flat in Dorset Street for a month or so, and then, a bed-sit came free on the top floor landing and I grabbed it. I was going into work as normal and was more than beginning to "show" and actually looked six months pregnant.

Spring can be lovely in Dublin. The trees are beginning to bud out a bit and people are not rushing around, paralyzed with the cold any more. It was good that year and I was trying to enjoy it.

Mrs. Chandra in work had been nice enough about my pregnancy and she never asked me anything I couldn't answer, and I needed the job so I just went in and did what I was meant to do and went home. I signed on in the Garda station every evening when I got off the bus and then strolled home to my flat.

I couldn't allow myself to think of Steven. I couldn't think about "after" or what would happen when I had the baby. But Jesus was I lonely. I went to bed in my little flat and lay looking at the damp stains on the ceiling and thought of all the lovely times we spent together in our place, all the times we had lain in bed waiting for morning, looking at the candles flickering on the walls and the whispered conversations we had.

I missed him so much, it was worse than if he'd died, knowing he was climbing the walls in Blanchardstown as much as I did, eight miles away on my own.

I never thought he would be with anyone else, I knew I wouldn't be, because none of it would be the same. I figured that it would only be a matter of time before this was all sorted out and we would be back together. It's like Nancy said the whole situation was so farcical; Monty Python couldn't make it up.

But sometimes I thought about it seriously, and realized that the world and its wife would brand us perverts, would call us dreadful names and we would be shunned by everyone we knew probably. But even if he *was* my brother, how would I stop myself wanting him? It's like they say, when you have crossed that line once, how can you stop yourself doing it again.

"It's the last deadly sin left really, used to be being gay or being an adulterer was the worst thing you could do, but I think you guys have the pervert award now" Nancy said one evening in April, when the sun was still shining through the windows and we were feeling a little more positive than before.

"Yeah, but how do you stop it from happening?"

"Look, no one can tell you how to live, if you guys are happy, and you can face yourselves in the mirror every morning, then who can tell yeh how to be? I mean, there must be other couples in the same boat, since divorce and all that came in years ago"

"Even here? In Ireland?" I asked

"Course there is, there must be, people didn't just start having sex in the nineties, sure how many people ended up in the laundries when they were pregnant outside of marriage years ago, its not beyond possibility that the kids they had back then are out there married to people that could be related to them" Nancy shook her head-

"There's a way round this babe, I read up on it in the Ilac library, you know when the baby comes, and, if it's not okay, and it... you know?" She stopped.

"I know Nancy, I know what might happen" I sighed.

I knew that there were dangers when the parents of a child had a close blood relationship. But I hadn't the nerve to look into it properly yet.

"Well, in some countries, couples who, well... who are like you guys, they can live together legally, if one of them gets sterilized, so that there's no more kids born, you know?" she looked terribly sad.

I wondered if our love could survive this, and survive long enough to allow one of us to give up the chance of ever holding our own child. Would having him be enough to pay that terrible price? We hadn't talked about children; not really, the whole issue was in the abstract, something that would come when we were tired of having fun and wanted them to come. This baby was unplanned, though it wasn't unwanted.

I thought we were a forever love, but at what cost? And could it make up for me never having a baby again.

I read *flowers in the attic* and knew the turmoil Cathy went through. Only hers came from being thrown with her brother at a formative age and mine came from never knowing he existed till it was too late to stop what we had done.

I definitely thought we would have to do a runner and change our names when all this was over. I could live anywhere if it was with Steven. I prayed for the chance to see him and run. Soon. I was sick of being alone, it had been almost five months since I'd even spoken to him and it was killing me.

I went to the Rotunda hospital for my visits every month and they did a scan and asked me did I want a social worker assigned to me. Nancy told me to be cute and to tell them nothing of the situation and just tell them that me and my partner had split up and that I would be going it alone. Apparently they ask everyone do they want a social worker. I didn't so they left me be.

And here's the odd thing.

The scans were fine.

I was expecting sharp intakes of breath when the ultrasound showed up whatever deformed little creature I thought I would be carrying.

But there was nothing.

I took the scan home and carried it in my handbag like a talisman against whatever was to come.

"The baby is perfect Nancy" I said one night, sitting in her living room, feet up on the sofa while she painted my toenails.

"See? I told you it was all a load of crap" she looked up over my bump and smiled.

"It shouldn't be though should it? If he is my brother then there should be all sorts of things wrong"

"Like what?"

"Well, I went to the library in the Ilac too, and there were case studies and stuff on file there and God, the things that can go wrong"

"You think too much, that's your problem hen"

"No really, there's a thing called sialic acid storage that happens when you have babies with close relations, its to do with two people with the same defective genes and it gets doubled in the baby, it causes all sorts of things, underdevelopment of the lungs and the brain, everything"

She looked at me real closely-

"My, we are reading up aren't we?"

"I wish I could see him, even for a minute to tell him that the baby is okay, Nancy, what will I do when it's born, he won't be able to come into the hospital or nothing?" I felt my eyes beginning to prickle and I sniffed back the tears.

"He's okay Carrie, I promise you he is doing fine"

"What do you mean?" I sniffed.

"I mean, your not allowed to contact him... but I can, and I did, and he knows that your okay and he has seen you from a distance so he knows all about how you look and..." she faltered.

"Are you mad at me?" she asked.

How could I be mad? I mean I was feeling wretched because I thought he was still in custody and was going crazy because he didn't know where I was and how I was, and good old Nancy had saved the day again.

"He's going nuts up there, hassling the police every day for blood tests and all that, and our Serena is fighting a losing battle with them too, its like out of sight out of mind, you know, and now she has to try and get over to the queer one in London, because she's going off her rail too, isn't it all fun an' fucking games, this life?" She asked the wall.

"And, I promise, your not going to be going through this alone Carrie, I'll go in with you when you have her, cos it's a girl you know, I can feel it in my waters, and she'll have two Mammies that will love her till all of this is sorted" she squeezed my hand.

"So what happened to him, when he, when they arrested him?"

"Well, they held him for twenty four hours and they kept asking did he know you were his sister, apparently he was four or so when she died and they reckoned that he must have remembered you from then, I mean, I ask yeh, I can't remember what I did last weekend and they want him to remember twenty fucking years ago! And then they tried to make out that he raped you but you put the kibosh on that when you said he was your partner, and then they let him home and he was told to stay away from you and the first night he was home some spa came and threw red paint on his dad's car and threw a brick through the front window, so they had to move till the culprit was caught, because the police thought that the next thing would be a firebomb and they'd be killed"

"Jesus, poor David, that's awful, who would do a thing like that?" I knew the answer before I asked the question.

"Do yeh have to ask? Noel, that's who!" She snorted "he got four months in prison for it and I'm fucking delighted"

My mind was a bit easier knowing that he was safe and sound and that his dad was okay too. I couldn't think of David as *my* father, just a father figure.

The buzzer shrilled as we were drinking a coffee and Nancy got up to answer it-

"Whoever this is, better have a good reason for buzzing me at this hour of the night" she laughed.

"What? Like I did?"

"Exactly, always there to bail out a buddy, that's me" she pressed the door button and went out on the landing-

"Well fuck me, look what the cat dragged in!"

I looked over the back of the sofa and nearly died from the shock.

Becky stood in the hall, bag and baggage, pale as a whitewashed gable and skinnier than a broom handle.

"How's it going? Any tea in that pot?" she smiled.

Nancy exploded-

"You have a neck Becky Whelan, coming in here like this, bold as brass, like nothing happened, the fucking cheek of you!"

she stood in the doorway and for a minute I thought she was going to throw Becky out on the street again

"Don't start Nancy; I've had a bad day"

"Fuck you and your bad day, do you know what Carrie has been through, since you and your little stunt at the debs, oh yeah, *you had a bad day!* Selfish cow!"

"Nancy its okay, stop shouting" I was staring at Becky, there was something strange going on in her eyes, she looked dead or something.

"You have everyone going bananas here over you, your Serena couldn't even take a fucking holiday because she wanted to save days for a trip to see you, an' you swan back in here and expect it all to be grand" She slammed the kettle on to the hob.

"What did you do? Break a nail? You have no fucking idea what's been happening here..." Nancy was making the tea and ranting at the same time. I threw my eyes up to heaven and saw the ghost of a smile on Becky's lips.

"Well try and tell me then and stop giving out to me!" Becky snapped.

She came around the sofa and stopped dead in her tracks-

"A baby? Oh Carrie, are you pregnant?" she whispered, wide eyed with delight.

"No, its fucking constipation, you dozy sod, heres your tea, sit down and drink it before I fuck it over you" Nancy held out the mug.

"How far along are you?" she asked.

"Seven and a half months" I replied.

"Steven?"

"Yes"

"Wow, that's amazing, I'm glad for you, and you got a new place, I take it, is he working?"

"You see, *that's* what we have to tell you about, there's been a few developments since you went to London, how long are you staying by the way?" Nancy glanced at me; I think she was looking for the nod from me, to tell her was it okay to spill the beans.

But Becky didn't seem to notice. She had, when Nancy asked her the question, put her head down on her knees and burst into tears.

When she stopped crying, a long time later, the whole story came out-

Seemingly the photographer she had taken up with, Jacko, was known as a bit of a boy around town, who used drugs habitually and liked to party. Becky must have seemed like manna from heaven for him. A young, beautiful Irish girl, all alone in the big city and feeling a bit lost there. Within days of her getting over there, he had her firmly in his clutches and wouldn't let go. He was choosing work for her and doing all her publicity shots and basically was at her side all the time.

"I thought I was in love with him, you know?" she sobbed.

She was only a couple of weeks with him when he started giving her his energy pills, to keep her going when the going got tough. We knew about that, oh how I knew!

"Is that what you were taking at the debs?" I asked.

"Yeah, speed, uppers, you know?" She sniffed.

I didn't know, not having taken anything stronger than an aspirin in my life!

"You fucking eejit Becky!" Nancy snapped.

"I thought it was the way everyone went on, you know?" She sighed again and went on.

After two or three weeks of no sleep, and constant work and partying when she went back from the Debs, was taking its toll on her skin and hair and there were questions asked and so she went on to smoking hash to bring her down.

"After a while that didn't work so he gave me something stronger to take me down, and I smoked it"

143

A couple of months of that and she woke up one morning in bits.

"I thought I had flu or something so I stayed in bed, but I was in terrible pain and so I called out the doctor and he couldn't find anything wrong with me, and told me it was a weird viral thing and to stay in bed, so I did, I stayed in bed till Jacko came home later that night and told him I was in bits, and he just laughed"

"Baby, you're just strung out" he said.

"What do you mean?" I asked him, cos I really didn't have a clue.

"You're an addict" he sat on the end of my bed smiling at me. I remember feeling like I was going to vomit and I ran into the bathroom. I was leaning over the toilet puking and he was outside the door and when I went out he handed me a syringe and told me that the best way to get rid of the illness was to inject it into myself.

"So I did, and it worked and I was able to get up next day and go to work and I had my stuff with me in my bag and once I could get into a toilet and do it a couple of times a day...I was sorted" she shivered.

"Heroin, that's what it was, wasn't it? Jesus Becky, you stupid, stupid bitch" Nancy started to cry. Of all of us she was the one who walked on the wild side, hanging out with the musicians and being queen of the Dublin groupie scene, but she drew the line at anything stronger than tequila and the odd joint.

"Strung out, for fucks sake, is this what happens when I take me eyes off yez for a week or two? I tell ya, I'm never going to let you'z out of me sight again" she wept.

Becky handed her the box of tissues she'd been nursing-

"Ah Nancy, it was bound to happen at some stage, its all part of the scene over there"

"It's fucking part of it here too, and you didn't get sucked into it, cos we all stuck together so we did" She dabbed at the stream of eyeliner that ran down her face.

Becky smiled- her first real smile since she arrived home.

"Well I'll knit you a hair shirt later on, just shut up for a second till I finish"

Jacko worked with her nearly every day for the next month or two, and it was easy for him to cover her little trips to the toilet. But things were about to get a whole lot worse-

"He told me that I was using a lot and that I would have to pay him for anything I wanted from here on in, and I asked how much and he said three hundred a day, so I laughed and said he had to be joking, but he wasn't.

I hadn't got that sort of money, so he said we could find a way to get it, but I had to do as I was told and just be a good girl, he would give me my medicine at the end of the day"

There never seemed to be enough in the little paper bag to get her through the day and so by afternoon she would be climbing the walls.

And that's when he started bringing men home to the flat.

He would sit in the living room watching television while the pile of cash on the coffee table grew and grew, and his girlfriend had sex with however many men he brought back. Always, at the end of the night there would be a pile of money and the little paper bag for Becky.

"And then five weeks ago, I found out I was pregnant, and he didn't want to know, so I figured that I would work as long as I could till I got the fare up to come home and get sorted out" she took a cigarette out of her bag and lit it-

"So I went to do a shoot for a Sunday Magazine, summer fashions, you know, and he was there and I wasn't feeling too good, and he took out a bit of gear and gave it to me telling me to go up to the top floor toilets and shoot up and get myself together. I was in the loo, just putting the needle into my arm when the fucking door nearly blew off the hinges and I was hauled out. It was the editor and the security man, they caught me, and from then on my name was mud. He'd tipped them off, there's a new girl on the scene now, and she's polish, beautiful, Tiana Mae, I knew there was something going on, cos he pointed at me and said to her-

"See what happens when you do drugs?" and laughed at me.

I went home and packed my stuff and took every bit of money I could find in the flat and ran. I went to a clinic in Brighton and had... I had an abortion, and then, came home to Ireland, but my family doesn't want me, and Serena is in France and... and I didn't... I didn't..." she broke down again and sobbed.

"I went up to the house and David, he told me you were in with Nancy, and so I hopped into a taxi and came here, he said I would find you here, and, he asked me was I all right and I said I was grand, but he said that he knew I was sick and so I told him I was going to get sorted soon, and he said he hoped so" she sighed.

"I have to go into a clinic somewhere, I only have enough with me for the next couple of days, I need..." she began

"Hold on a fuckin' minute!" Nancy hissed.

"What?"

"Do you mean to tell me that you have heroin in your possession right this *minute*?" she was whispering, almost as if she expected the drug squad to burst through the wall at any second.

"Well, yeah"

"Ah Jesus, this gets worse by the minute! You're in London less than eight months and you turn into Marianne Faithful, and now you're a bloody smuggler, fucking brilliant that is!" Nancy slapped her hand over her eyes.

"Do you *realize* that this place is *crawling* with fucking coppers?" she hissed.

"Why?" Becky asked. Bewildered.

"How did you get it home?" I asked. I suppose I'd watched Midnight Express too often. I imagined her shoving condoms full of white powder up her arse in the train toilets or something. This was the first time in weeks my mind was off my own problems and I really was genuinely interested.

"Do they not have sniffer dogs or something?"

Nancy groaned-

"Jee-sus Carrie, you watch too many bad movies! Not on the boat for fucks sake!"

"I only asked? Go on, tell us, is it all up your fanny or something?" I giggled.

"Fucking hell, that's it, I'm going to be in the nuthouse by morning!" Nancy laughed.

Becky was looking from one to the other of us and shaking her head-

"It's not funny, I could have been caught, and that's why I didn't fly home"

We were helpless with giggles then, I was thinking of her perched on a toilet seat trying to hide enormous amounts of drugs in her orifice and the sniffer dogs outside howling. Nothing like gallows humour at times.

"I put my works in my handbag, I took a hit before I left the guesthouse and then wrapped the gear up in a bathrobe in my case, I came on the boat you see, no hassle there from customs, told them I was heading home for the holiday, and I have my Irish passport, so hey presto, here I am" she looked smug.

"Someone should tell Howard Marks, save him all that time in the Bangkok Hilton" Nancy laughed.

"Ah come on, I'm not stupid, I know how to move the stuff round, and not get caught" Becky stopped-

"How come the place is crawling with coppers?" she asked.

"Do you wanna tell her or will I?" Nancy drawled.

"Tell me what?"

"Jesus I don't know where to begin after that, my little story is going to be very tame after your escapades!" I smiled.

"What? Will you tell me?"

"It's a very long story, brace yourself Bridgie" Nancy nodded at me-

"Go on, spit it out"

And then I told her.

".... So the bottom line is that they think you are having your brother's baby? That's mental, and a little bit sick too, in a weird sort of way..." Becky grimaced.

"T'is a bit isn't it?" Nancy was making yet more tea.

"Sort of like the Blue Lagoon, 'cept Brooke Shields has a better arse" I laughed.

"Yeah, but your eyebrows are so much better Carrie" laughed Nancy.

"Yah think?"

"Yeah... less bushy..."

"Thanks, I think so too..." I grinned.

"And what about you? Do you think he's your brother?" Becky interrupted..

I thought about that. I wondered if the chemistry we felt was the same as the love between siblings and I had to concede that it wasn't the same at all. I felt like there was lightening in my veins when I looked at him. I couldn't see me feeling like that about a brother at all. But like I said, even if he turned out to be my brother, I didn't think our relationship could, or would change.

"I dunno Becky; we were pretty close, pretty quickly"

"Yeah, but look at the guy, he's a ride for fucks sake, who wouldn't?" she blushed scarlet. Then silence fell. It was like a gorilla had suddenly appeared in the corner of the room and none of us wanted to admit to its being there.

"Eh... Carrie, about that night, the night of the debs, I want to say how sorry I am, nothing happened, he pushed me away

the second he saw you, but you were gone, he didn't want me, but I was high and I... I'm sorry, really and truly I am..." she stopped.

"Why did you do it then?" Nancy was dangerously quiet.

"I suppose I was jealous, I was finding the London thing more difficult than I thought and there was Carrie all loved up, I just felt angry with myself, and I swear..." she knelt down in front of me-

"I'll do anything for you, to make it up to you for what I done, I mean it, anything" she started to cry again and I hugged her.

"C'mere yeh gobshite" I laughed and hugged her.

"D'ya know what? We should be on fucking Oprah!" Nancy sniffed.

So that night ended on a high note.

Wouldn't it be great to say that life went on, on that high note, and that all was fine and dandy from there on in?

This wasn't an episode of Oprah or the Walton's unfortunately, this was my life and it was gradually getting more bizarre.

Serena came home from France and there was another night in, talking and putting the world to rights. She said that she would get Becky into a good drying out clinic and she did so, within a couple of days.

"Don't ask me what I had to do, I nearly had to sell me body for a place in there" she said, and then looked at Becky and blushed-

"Sorry Beck's, I didn't mean it that way" she grinned.

Becky went off to the clinic and a couple of days later, Serena came down to the flat.

"When are you going on maternity leave?" she asked

"End of next week" I said "it can't come soon enough for me, my legs are killing me"

"Have you any idea what your going to do?" she asked.

"When?"

"Have you any idea of when this is going into court for a start?"

"No, I sign on daily and that's it, they tell me fuck all" I sighed.

The police were trying every tactic they had to make me admit that the sex was non consensual, they even sent out a social worker to the desk one day and she spent the whole time I was there patronizing me with stuff like-

"Such a nice young girl like you, surely now you can put all this nonsense behind you when the baby is born, no body blames you for what happened, you can give the baby away and you could go to a nice new place, have a fresh start, maybe in England or somewhere" She patted my hand.

"I mean, he's older than you, he took advantage of the situation, you were the innocent in all this Carol Anne, we know that, we spoke to your stepfather and he told us"

I could only imagine the bullshit Noel must have spouted to them, justifying his actions and making Steven out to be a monster! I had to grit my teeth and listen to this patronizing codswallop even when my head was telling me to let rip and tell the truth.

I wasn't going to give my child away; I had made up my mind. I knew the baby was a hundred per cent healthy and there wasn't a chance of me putting it up for adoption.

"I'm not going anywhere; I want to stay here with my baby and my partner"

"Your *brother*" the voice syrupy and sickly, the smile false.

"My *partner*, I don't give a flying damn what you say or think, there is no way on this earth that he is my brother and I'm going to be proved right one way or another" I slapped the pen back across the table and went out of the station into the sunshine.

Serena listened and made notes.

She shook her head.

"I dunno, I wonder is there anything else I can do for you. I mean, I'd have access to stuff that you couldn't get access to, things like old court reports and stuff, maybe I could find out what the craic is, get things moving on the blood test front" She clicked her pen impatiently.

"I have tried to get things moving but its like everyone is on a go slow with this one, it's the whole nature of the case, brother and sister more yah, and they think that the longer they keep you apart the less likely you will be to offend again, but honey, Steven is going crazy and I don't think your that far behind him, are you?"

"Nope, I think sometimes I am just about *this side* of sanity, God I miss him like crazy Serena, I just want this sorted and over and done with" I sighed.

"You see, if they find you and Steven guilty of incest...you have a couple of choices, either stay away from each other, which is hard enough in a village like Dublin, or one or the other of you could volunteer to be sterilized so that the baby thing wouldn't happen again" she smiled sadly-

"*They* don't care what you two do in private as long as you don't show it, and unfortunately that's what you did"

"I know that Serena, I just wish I didn't feel like it was all a big mistake" I sighed.

"How d'ya mean?"

"We don't look anything like each other for starters; surely there should be some resemblance? The baby is perfect, nothing amiss at all, and from what I have read, that's a billion to one chance when you share a gene pool, I should think that I would have recognized him somehow, physically, even when we went to bed, it was perfect, lovely, and I have to say, I think it would have felt wrong somehow, if we were related"

"So what are you saying" she asked.

"I think there's something really amiss, something not right, there has to be someone knows what happened here, someone can clear this mess up, I just don't know how to find them" I was frustrated by the lack of action by the courts too, there had been four months of nothing and now I was into my seventh month and I hadn't seen Steven since the third month. It was getting to me big time.

"Show me what you have, the cert. and stuff, let me see them and I'll have a think" she said.

I handed them over and she read them-

"o-kay, the birth cert looks okay, except the fathers name is in different ink to the rest of it, so that was added afterwards; that's a bit odd" she looked up, frowning.

"I'm just so tired lately I can't think straight, I can't be bothered bell ragging policemen when they won't listen to me"

She waved the papers at me-

"Your in real trouble here Carrie, serious trouble, if you get convicted, both you and Steven are looking at three to five years, more even, they could give him a life sentence for this, do you realize that?" she snapped.

"You're not serious?" I felt weak at the thought.

"I am, deadly serious, so you better fucking well get your shit together and do something about this before its too late!" she took the papers and put them in her folder-

"I'm going to ring around a few people, see can we even get it so that Steven can be there when the baby is born, see what we can do for you, keep your chin up Carrie, I'll be in to see you with news soon, okay?" she hugged me hard.

"You're going to be all right" she whispered.

7

Serena

I couldn't believe what had happened when I was in France with Michel.

There I was, off on the first bloody holiday I had in three years since I started working in Moraine and Clancy and my little sister picks it to start on heroin! I came home to my mother wailing and my father going round the house banging doors and cursing under his breath and none of them doing a damned thing about it in case the younger five got to know about it-

"Conor is doing the leaving, it's a sensitive year for him" Mam said. She was only worried that Becky might get pregnant for that Jamaican and we'd have to explain a half caste grandchild to the neighbors.

And heaven forbid that the foundations of "The Pines" might be shaken by that revelation! Having said that, she knew about the Carrie situation too and seemed to take comfort in the fact that bad and all as Becky's life was, there was no chance whatsoever of a blood relation to Jacko... not unless Ma's extracurricular activities in Trinity included a shag with Harry Belafonte or someone like him. But she and the Da had met in their first month in college, eyes met over the dissection table and that was that!

"I always knew that girl would come to no good, living in that estate and all" Ma sighed. I thought she was being a smug cow and said so. Carrie was my friend too! And I knew she had a good, basically decent, soul, and she wouldn't do a bad turn on anyone. Not even Becky, who, between us, bloody well deserved it!

Of course there was a row, and I came off the worst of it.

My parents were all for leaving Becky to sort out her own mess. And I knew the poor cow wasn't up to it. Dope sick and rail thin, she wasn't capable of making a phone call, never mind sorting out a detox for herself.

So muggins had to do it. Go down and see the poor kid in the flat with Carrie and try getting her into a centre. I did it and she went, the poor cow, I guess she hadn't a clue what was in front of her. Though, I'm told she's doing grand, she is not allowed visitors till next week or so, and I can drop down to her then. I might bring Carrie if I can fit her into the car. God help her, she's enormous!

Michel thought I was gone stone mad when I rang him-

"I can't see you for a couple of days, I have family stuff to sort, my sister and her friend, its all gone pear shaped!" I was rifling through the London phone book as I spoke, on my lunch hour, trying to eat at the same time.

"You haven't gone cold on me *Cherie*, have you?" he asked.

"No, No darling, its just… complicated" I found the number I was looking for and scribbled it down.

"I will be waiting for you to call me, are you wearing the ring?" he was smiling; I could hear it in his voice.

"Of course" I looked at the little amethyst and diamond ring he picked for me in a little market in Dieppe. I was engaged and no one had noticed!

I had gone to see that David guy, the evening after I had been to Carries flat. I asked him for his version of events and he told me a pretty gruesome tale about that wife of his. I found it all a bit peculiar that there had never been any contact from the Bard family even to see was the little fellow still alive and well.

"I tried to ring them, but they said that Mr. Bard, James, was sleeping and that I couldn't disturb him" he said.

"Okay, did you ring back?"

"Repeatedly, the day and night Steven was in the cells, but they stonewalled me"

"Bollocks to that then, we need an injunction" I said, sounding a bit more confident than I felt.

"What?"

"If that oul bastard won't talk, then we have to make him talk" I said.

"What can he tell us that we already don't know?" he asked.

"I dunno, I just want to hear his version of events"

I left there with something bubbling in the back of my mind and it wouldn't go away. I went into the office and got onto the computer. We have this brilliant system linking our offices in the UK and here and Europe. Any old files and cases are stored on it and we can check something up when we need to.

The name Bard was ringing a bell with me and I wanted to see why.

I typed in the name and the files came up on the screen-

Bard, Sarah Hospital memorial wing Glasgow

That's one, I thought. I printed it off and looked again. Some of it was stuff in the financial paper, not much use to me, I thought.

Bard Williams the inquest into her death.

The Angel of the Thames 1974 Photos of Carrie as a baby, you could see even then it was her. How in Gods name had David not seen?

I was there for ages waiting on it all to print out and then I brought it home.

I was sitting in the living room and was wondering how to get the medical information I needed when Dad came in.

"Dad?" I asked

"Yes?"

"Could I ask you something on a medical issue?"

"Hmm" he had his nose stuck in the paper already so I had to be very quick.

"D'ya know when someone uses heroin, or hard drugs?"

"ye-es" he looked over the paper at me.

"And say if they got pregnant" I began

"Jesus Mary and Holy saint Joseph! Becky isn't pregnant as well is she?" He was bright red; I could nearly see his blood pressure flying off the scale!

"NO Daddy!!!" I cried "it's a case I'm doing, for my exams, an old one, I was wondering what the effect of hard drugs were on a fetus?" I had to laugh, this was the narrow minded oul get who had thrown his daughter away from the front door when she came home sick and needed them to help her. He could be a right, narrow minded prick when he wanted, could my Dad. But I needed information. So I swallowed the retort and waited for answers;

"Well, in the vast majority of cases, the child is born craving the narcotic, most will be underweight, some will be underdeveloped because some will be premature, not all though" He leaned forward and thought for a minute-

"They *are* generally sickly and have a very unusual cry, high pitched and squeaky almost, then there's jaundice, of course, that can be tricky" he sniffed.

"Is it possible to go full term with a pregnancy when you're a using addict?" I asked.

"Not impossible, but rare" he answered.

156

"Hypothetically speaking, could a heavy user of heroin, who had overdosed twice during the pregnancy, give birth to a healthy, seven or eight pound baby at more or less, full term?" I asked.

He laughed-

"Anything is possible I suppose, but I have never seen that, if the mother was overdosing on drugs, it is unlikely that the child would be full term, of good size, totally healthy etc, its possible, but highly unlikely" he looked into the newspaper again and I went off upstairs. The little niggles in the back of my mind were beginning to grow into something a little less vague.

If everything my father said was true, then it was damn near impossible that Carrie was the same baby that Elizabeth Bard Williams had carried. It couldn't be the same child. Hadn't David said that she was perfect, chubby and healthy, two weeks after birth? It couldn't be the same child. But if she wasn't Amber Bard, and she wasn't Carol-Anne Conway, then who the fuck was she?

I started the long trek through the files I had printed off on my office computer and I thought that they wouldn't have much in the line of information I could use, until I opened a copy of the newspaper, the Glasgow Herald, and saw him standing, cutting the ribbon on a new hospital wing-

James Bard, of Baird and West publishers, today opened the new maternity wing of Glasgow's St Andrew's Hospital. He said it was in gratitude for all the care and attention his daughter and grand-daughter received when they were patients there in 1972.

It was dated November 1974.

Even to my mind, this seemed like a bloody extravagant way to thank a hospital for delivering a baby. I mean, there was no big reward when Steven was born, was there?

The photograph was very grainy and faded looking and I squinted trying to see the faces clearly. You could see that Bard was a looker. He must have been in his fifties when that was taken, and he still looked good. Steven must get his looks there. Though David wasn't a bad looking man either. Our Becky didn't seem to think so anyhow.

Some one, somewhere, had to know what had happened and how that little baby ended up being reared in Blanchardstown. And the only person who could tell me was Doris Conway.

I grabbed my bag and keys and got into the car and drove out to Corduff.

I had to speak to Doris, now!

I pulled up at the house and locked the car. I often wondered how someone as lively and funny as Carrie used to be had grown up here in this mess of a family.

The last time I was here, Noel was sneaking around the place. He was the type of person that you never heard coming, you know, you'd be up to your ears in mischief like any other teenage girl, and then he'd be there, slithering in the door grinning at you. I never liked the man, he was a bit too pervy for me. I used to feel like he could see through my clothes when I'd be there.

I'd heard he had done a bit of time inside, for criminal damage to the Williams house. I prayed he wouldn't be there tonight. But luck wasn't on my side; he opened the door and held on to it tight-

"Yeah?" he asked.

"Hi, is Doris home?" I smiled. You catch more flies with sugar than you do with shite any day. I wanted to sweeten him up a bit.

"Who wants her?" he grinned. His teeth were yellow. I swallowed hard.

"My name is Serena Whelan, I'm an old friend of the family, I heard she was sick so I came up to see how she was" I tried to push my way in. He must be a better actor than I thought, pretending not to recognize me. It had been a while mind you. Maybe I had changed.

"She was sick all right, but she's okay, we're having a bit of dinner to celebrate"

"Oh, is it a birthday?" I feigned surprise.

"No, I was away for a bit, on business"

Business my arse. I thought. *Peeling spuds in prison for the last four months.*

"Well, I just want to see her for a couple of minutes, please?" I flashed the smile again and he opened the door.

"Come into the parlor, I'll see what she says"

I sat there for a couple of minutes while a whispered conversation took place outside the door. Eventually she came in, and even I was shocked at the state of her.

Doris had never been what I would call a looker, and she had always been thin, but she was cadaverous now. She was wearing a drab looking jumper and a skirt that could be a lot cleaner.

"Serena, love, long time since I saw you pet, how are you?" she was forcing herself to be jolly and nice to me.

"Grand Doris, your looking... better" I finished lamely.

She stared at me and sighed.

"Serena, I look terrible and I know it. I deserve it, because of all the things I did in my life that should have been different, I should have been better as a mother to Carol Anne... I'm only reaping what I sowed" she lit another cigarette off the first one and threw the butt into the fireplace. The grate was full of paper and old butts. The room was cold.

"Ah no, Doris, you mustn't think like that" I patted her hand. It felt cold and papery to the touch.

"I know you mean well love, but there are things that I did that I could have done different, things that would have made my life, and Carol Anne's better" she sighed.

I knew that this was my chance-

"Well, have you anyone you can confide in? You have a sister, haven't you, could you talk to her maybe?"

"She went away a long time ago, after...." She stopped.

"Doris, please, I'm trying to help, please tell me" I whispered, looking at the door. I could nearly see Noel skulking round outside the door, listening.

"I can't, it's the money you see, the papers" she whispered.

"What papers?" I felt my blood run cold.

She nodded at the door-

"*He* sold his story to the papers, being imprisoned for protecting his daughter from an incestuous relationship" she whispered softly.

"Oh God, oh Jesus no..." I moaned.

The story was going into the Sunday paper this weekend and Doris was petrified at the thought. I thought wildly of getting them to stop the story being printed. The shit would really hit the fan when this whole mess was public knowledge and any hope I had of getting Steven access to his child would be slim to nil. Public opinion made a heck of a difference, particularly when it was fuelled by sensationalist stories in the Sunday paper.

"What paper?"

She whispered the name of the most gruesome of the Sundays and I winced-

"Jesus they'll both have horns and a tail by the time that rag finish with them"

The paper in question delighted in the sleazy side of Ireland, with stories of incest and child abuse regularly making the front pages. I didn't mind so much when it was justified, and real perverts were being named and shamed, but this was going to be so hard on Carrie, and she and Steven didn't deserve the lambasting they were going to get when this story came out.

"Doris we have to stop it going public, I need you to help me, please?" I hissed.

"How can I help you, I don't know what to do!" she looked wild.

"Tell me where your sister is?" I pleaded.

"I don't know, I swear to you I don't know" she moaned.

"look Doris, its Thursday night now, I have one working day to stop that paper going to print, but I have to have a good reason for it, you have to give me something to work on, something more than a vague maybe, please Doris, tell me what happened"

She began to talk, one eye on the door, telling me a rapid and condensed version of the illegal adoption of baby Amber and how she and Peter ran away to Ireland and kept quiet about everything.

She'd carried the worry of this for years and it was no wonder she was cracking up inside.

"Doris, listen to me..." I had been about to tell her that I would help her and she wouldn't go to prison for kidnap or whatever she was terrified of, but the living room door burst open-

"The Rotunda is on the phone, Carrie's gone into labour" Noel grinned nastily-

"Let the games begin" he hissed.

I drove out of the estate and onto the Navan Road, heading into Dublin City. I was just at Castleknock when I got a feeling over me, like I couldn't describe. I remembered lying in that lovely bed in Paris, with Michel, the morning after our engagement, and I remember thinking I was so lucky, that this was a man that could go the distance, and not desert me when times got hard. And by God was he about to be tested mightily!

I thought about what would happen if I got pregnant and for whatever reason, my Michel couldn't be with me. How would I feel? How lost would I be? And how would he feel not being there to see his child born? I thought that unless Michel was actually dead, he would be there with me, and that it was only right and proper.

Carrie would be petrified, probably, and without her man beside her she would be a million times worse. And poor Steven wouldn't see his child for months, unless he was there today. But how?

I thought for a split second and made the decision.

"Fuck it" I said-

I didn't even bother to indicate and swung into the right hand lane and spun round the roundabout to Auburn Avenue to a cacophony of beeps and roaring from other drivers.

"Yeh stupid bitch, what the fuck are yeh doing?" one guy roared, burying the horn into the dash he pushed it so hard. I'd missed him by a millimeter, but he was in a big Jeep and wouldn't have sustained too much damage had my little banger hit him.

I flipped him the finger and shouted-

"Fuck off and save that horn for your wife, you asshole" I got into the right lane and floored the accelerator all the way to Castleknock village. I didn't even bother my arse watching out for the police. If I was stopped I'd explain myself and take the ticket.

I knew it was probably going to cause a mountain of shit, but I didn't care. Carrie needed her Steven to be there, and that little baby needed him too, so I was going to get him.

Steven needed to see his baby being born. Because the way things were going, it could be the last time for a long time.

8

Carrie

The pains started in the middle of a May Thursday. I had been sitting on the sofa with a pile of baby grows I had bought in Penney's on Mary Street, trying to see which ones I wanted to pack into my bag, when I got the first twinge.

I counted and waited and the next one came about seven minutes later-

"Well, my little baby, you must be ready to come out and see us" I muttered.

I was almost eight and a half months pregnant. I sat there and calmed my breathing thinking that this might be a false alarm, and I would wait and see.

By the time I heard Nancy running up the stairs that evening I was puffing with the exertion of not screaming aloud.

"Mother of Jaysus!!" she roared when I opened the door. The bag of shopping she was carrying went all over the floor. A box of eggs cracked and made a nice big mess on the carpet... Not that I was in any state to care.

"Nancy, I have pain" I gasped "But its too early, I'm not due for a couple more weeks, but I think its coming now"

"Your fucking tellin' me?" she laughed. She went over to the bookcase and grabbed the ancient copy of "Everywoman" we read when we needed to know anything.

"How far apart are the contractions? I think that means pain?" she asked.

"They started at seven minutes and went on to five, now three...no. *two...owwwwww*" I moaned.

"Fuuuuuuck! I better get an ambulance! Oh Jesus oh God!" she ran around the kitchen and I stared at her.

She was in more of a panic than I was. And *she* was going to be my birthing partner in the hospital.

"Nancy, the ambulance for fucks sake!" I gasped.

She clattered down the stairs and into the hallway. I could hear the coins dropping all over the floor as she tried to find twenty pence pieces.

I leaned over the banister and shouted-

"Ring 999 Nancy for heavens sake" I panted, white knuckled, gripping on the banister rail. I had the overwhelming urge to pee. I lumbered into the bathroom and was sitting on the loo when my waters broke, the door to the bathroom wide open.

I could hear her talking, repeating the address and thanking someone for helping her. She ran back up the stairs and grabbed my bag.

"Carrie where the fuck are you?" She yelled.

"The jacks, I think me waters are gone"

"Oh shite, that means its happening all right" She helped me out of the toilet and into the living room.

"Come on, down to the door, we wait there" she looked flushed; maybe she wasn't the hard chaw she liked to think she was.

Before I knew where I was I was in the pre natal ward in the hospital, and then a few minutes later, I was wheeled into the labour ward.

"This is it Nancy, Oh God, I want Steven, Oh fuck it hurts" I tried not to scream.

Nancy grabbed my hand and I squeezed for dear life.

"Nancy he won't even kno-ow" I wailed.

"I'll tell him, I swear to Jesus I will, I promise you I'll phone him, just breathe for fucks sake" She rubbed my hands.

The nurses were like cheerleaders, urging me on, telling me to breathe. I gulped the gas and air, I was too late for an epidural and I felt like I was being torn apart.

"Go on Carrie, your doing great" Nancy cried. She rubbed my back and I felt myself gearing up for another pain.

"Here it goes again" I yelled.

"You're nearly ready to push, wait for it Carrie and when I tell you to, then bear down" a nurse smiled.

"What the fuck does that mean?" I asked.

Nancy didn't know either-

"I think it's... lookit...Pretend your from Thailand and your firing a big ping pong ball out of your gee" She muttered.

The midwife exploded into giggles-

"Nancy this is not the time for jokes" I held my breath again.

"I'm only trying to help, fucking hell, I don't know what it means either" Nancy laughed.

"Come on love, you're almost ready to go" The midwife had another look below-

"It won't be long till you have your baby" she was so excited herself, you'd swear it was her own child, come to think of it; I wished it was her on the bed and not me! Fucking hell, I wished it was *anyone* on that bed apart from me!

I had never felt anything like it, I felt like I was being torn apart on a rack. But I tried to listen to the nurse and the midwife and I pushed when they told me to.

"I'm gonna sue the makers of Casualty when I get out of here" I puffed on the gas and air again.

"Why?" Asked the nurse.

"Cos it's not like this on the bloody telly" I groaned as another pain hit me square in the back.

"Fucking BBC, bunch of liars!" I gasped. Sweat rolling down my face and back, legs cramping as I tried to bear down. I was holding on to Nancy so tight I thought I'd break her hand.

Then, I heard Nancy gasp and she let go of my hand, I opened my eyes and looked up.

"Steven!" I burst into tears.

"You're here, oh God, you got here, oh Steven" I grabbed his hand and held on for dear life.

"Come on little darlin' your doing brilliant, I'm here" he kissed me and put his other arm around me. I felt the pain again and this time, I pushed as hard as I could, I thought my eyeballs were going to pop, I was straining that much, and then I heard the midwife saying that head was crowning.

"Do you want to see the baby's head?" she asked Steven.

"Yeah" He nodded.

He looked, and a smile lit up his face-

"It has your hair Carrie" he laughed.

"God love the poor kid, red hair, it'll hate me!" I gasped.

"No it won't baby, it'll love you. Like I do" he rubbed my back again and I felt my muscles contracting and pushed again-

"A lifetime of being called Duracell and ginger pubes, that's all I got" I felt my skin rip down below and winced with pain. Though it was a drop in the ocean against the labour pain itself.

"One more Carrie, come on" The midwife said-

And that was that.

A couple of minutes later our daughter was born.

She was six and a half pounds in weight and perfect. The midwife wrapped her in a towel and put her straight into my arms.

"Here's your daughter Carrie, isn't she gorgeous?" she laughed.

"Is she okay?" Steven asked.

"She's perfect Steve, look at her, look at her" I whispered, tears falling down my face.

She had perfect little rosebud lips, and her eyebrows could have been drawn on in feathery copper pencil lines. Her cheeks were chubby and the skin so soft it was like touching feathers.

"Beautiful, gorgeous little baby girl, I am so happy to see you" I whispered.

Her chubby little arm was sticking out of the towel and her fingers were grasping the air, Steven touched her with one finger and she gripped him.

"Carrie...look" he whispered, voice choking.

"That's your daddy little woman, say hello to your lovely handsome daddy" I kissed her head.

He was in shock, I could see it. I suppose my not being around him when I was pregnant made him separate from me in some way, and this was like being brought down to earth in a rush.

"She's gorgeous, thank you Carrie, she's so lovely, I couldn't imagine anything better" he was nearly in tears, and I held her out to him.

"Come on Daddy, hold her" I smiled.

"Can I?"

I nodded, and settled her into his arms.

"She's so tiny isn't she? Look at her little hands" He kept saying.

"We made a little person Steven; we made her, isn't she lovely?" I stroked her cheek and her mouth made a sucking motion, and he laughed.

"Like her Daddy, always hungry"

I could have looked at them all day. He looked beautiful; the look on his face was beautiful. I felt like all my birthdays and Christmases had come at once. Thank God he was here to share this with me.

"What will we call her?" I asked.

He stared at me for a second and then he smiled-

"I was thinking about it for the last couple of months, and I thought we could call a little girl Saoirse" We had picked Daragh for a boy; both of us liked the Celtic names. Saoirse suited this little one, it really did. Our little red haired Celt.

"Freedom?" I whispered.

"Because one day soon, that's what, we will be, and I wanted her to have it, as a symbol, you know?" he rocked her gently in his arms.

"Saoirse Elizabeth?" I said.

He smiled-

"Nah Carrie, Saoirse Amber"

He sat on the edge of the bed and we held the baby and kissed and talked and all around us the midwife and nurse tidied and cleaned as unobtrusively as possible. It was a precious moment in our lives and they wanted it to be as peaceful and happy as they could manage it.

I heard voices outside, and he turned white.

A couple of seconds later, Serena came into the room and stood at the end of the bed.

"Carrie, she's gorgeous, I'm so sorry to intrude, but Noel phoned the Gardai and told them that you were in here, and they came to see was Steven here, their downstairs now, he has to go, now Steven, please, I'm so sorry Carrie" she cried.

I panicked.

"He'll end up in prison, Serena, do something, please" I tried to get out of bed.

"Carrie, I am trying to do something, I swear, I am trying to help you, you'll see later when I tell you what I found out, but he has to go now, right away" she grabbed my hand, and he stood up.

"Okay, I'll go" he bent and kissed me again.

"Carrie, you take care of my baby, and of you, I won't be long, and..." he smiled

"Oh Steven, run, get away from them" I was distraught. I couldn't bear this.

"It'll be grand pet, you'll see" he whispered.

He hugged me really hard-

"It was worth it, do you hear me? Even if I spend the next ten years in prison, it was so worth it"

Then he was gone.

Steven

I knew the police were waiting for me so I ran. I got out of the hospital and into some kind of garden that seemed to back on to the Gate Theatre and I ran across the grass and climbed the fence. Out in Parnell Street I got as far as the lights and looked back. No blue lights or sirens yet so I thought they must still be in the hospital. I jumped into the first cab I saw outside Checkers and told him to take me to the boat.

"North wall?"

"No the other one, look I need to get out of here fast so please, help me"

"You in trouble?" He looked a bit worried about his fare and I pulled out my wallet and showed him I had it.

"My motto is never question anything" he muttered.

"Good motto" I slunk down in the back of the cab and we sped away.

In Booterstown I got out and used a phone box and dialed Nancy's number. I told her what had happened and asked could she come and meet me-

"Jesus Steven I only came home for a few clothes for Carrie, have you anything at all with you for yourself? Where are you going?"

"I have about a hundred quid and nothing else, I need a change of clothes and some cash, and I'll pay you back when all this is sorted out"

She said she'd meet me in Dunlaoighre so I got back into the cab and we drove on.

I hung around for about an hour and waited for her to come.

She arrived with a rucksack and a wad of cash that I stuck in my wallet.

"Tell me what to say to Carrie, where are you going?"

"To see that Grandfather of mine, I want to sort this out once and for all"

"I know, I know, but, listen man, be careful won't you? You don't want to end up in prison"

Then she left and I went on and got onto the boat.

I took the late sailing and ended up on the train to Euston at midnight. I remember sitting there waiting for the train to start moving and feeling the tiredness overtaking me. I had to stay awake, stay alert. The whole train seemed full of people with Irish accents and they were drinking beer and chatting about home already, like they had been away for a hundred years.

It was only a matter of time before someone started singing the "Fields of Athenry" and they all joined in.

There was one guy who wasn't singing and who sat hunched into the seat facing me across the aisle. Maybe he had nothing to sing about. He was wearing scruffy trousers and one of those padded plaid shirts you see a lot on bricklayers and builders under their high visibility clothes. He looked like he hadn't slept in a while too.

Every time I closed my eyes I could see my daughter and her little face all soft and her tiny little fist waving. The train began to move and I promised her, that I'd be back soon and that this whole mess would be sorted out and we would all be together the way we were supposed to.

God I was tired, so tired. What a long day it had been.....

Somewhere in Wales I dropped off and when I woke, I realized that my bag was gone.

"Who took my bag?" I cried. I looked around the carriage and realized that the guy opposite was no where to be seen.

"Where did that guy go, in the plaid shirt? Where did he go?"

Everyone looked away, no one said anything, and I decided to go to the bathroom and clear my head for a moment and then maybe get the guard to help me.

I found my empty bag in a corner of the toilet and picked it up. The clothes Nancy had got for me were gone and so was the money I had stuffed into my wallet and into the bag, foolishly thinking it would save me from pickpockets. I had nothing left. I had the clothes I stood up in and nothing more than that. My empty wallet was in the bottom of the bag, and I realized with a pang that the git had even taken the little silver ring Carrie bought me. I stuck my wallet into my jacket pocket, even though it was empty bar a photograph of us, and went out again.

By the time I got to Euston I was already thinking up ways to get to Scotland with no money and the only way was to get onto the northern motorway and hitch.

The small change I had bought me a coffee and I asked a station guard where to go for northern routes.

I walked for about an hour and just when I was beginning to give up I found myself on the motorway and basically just walked a bit and hitched a bit.

The weather was getting cold, raining hard, and I was dog tired. I had gotten as far as Manchester when the artic came and stopped.

"Glasgow?" I said through chattering teeth.

"Gerrin" He grinned.

There was another guy in the back who basically shrank into the corner of the bunk and said nothing to me bar a nod. He had on a fleecy thing and had the hood pulled up so you couldn't see his face too well.

Bit by bit we started a conversation. His name was Gary; he was going home to Glasgow and was hoping to sort out the problems with his wife and the kids. He'd been a

bit heavy handed with her and heavily into the booze and basically hadn't sent any money home to her or anything. He had been in Ireland for a while and hadn't managed to make good and then came back to London and was now on the way home.

All the time he spoke, he kept his eyes glued to the window on his side of the cab and barely moved. It was really disconcerting to be having a conversation with the back of a head!

I wished him luck. I was shaking with the cold and after flicking his eyes and looking at me for a second Gary took his jacket off and handed it to me-

"There, put that on you, your cold, I'm okay"

I slipped my own jacket off and put his on. It was a fleece type thing and it was warmer than the sodden thing I was wearing before.

I felt tired, more tired than I ever knew I could be. My eyes were closing and I felt my head nodding. I wished I could be at home with Carrie and the baby, that's all I wanted. I knew that the only way to get that was to find my family, my grandfather and have this out with him. Find out the truth, and then go back and take them far away from it all, make a new life for them somewhere else.

I leaned my head against the window and nodded off again-

"Hoi, climb into the bunk at the back there, your all in mate" the driver said, and gestured to the curtained bit of the cab.

The bunk wasn't long enough but I could at least get the head down. I smiled, remembering the little tent in Connemara and how my legs stuck out of the ends no matter what way I lay.

"You're like a fucking giraffe Steven" Carrie had grumbled when the sleeping bag wasn't long enough to cover her arms and my legs properly God I was so tired, I could sleep for Ireland right this minute. I yawned.

"How long will it take to get to Glasgow?" I mumbled.

"Long enough for at least forty winks, go asleep lad" he laughed.

I lay there drowsing, my eyes half open and listening to the wind and the rain over the sound of the engine.

I curled into a ball, somehow I couldn't get comfortable, there was something digging into my hip bone and I sat up again and felt it-

It was a small lump, and I asked-

"Gary, have you something in this pocket, it's digging into my side?"

And then I knew who he was.

The plaid shirted guy from the train, which meant that this jacket was probably one of the things in the bag he had robbed.

"You bastard" I snapped His eyes were filled with fear, but I didn't care...

"What's to do lad?" the driver asked.

"He fucking robbed me, took all my stuff on the train" I fumbled in the pocket and took the silver ring out of the pocket-

"You fucking bastard, this is my ring"

Gary knew he was cornered and he held his hands up.

"Right, okay I did it, but here, you can have it back, no harm done, yeah?"

I stuffed everything back in the bag.

It was all there, the money, the clothes, everything. I felt like I'd had a lucky break at last. I stuck the bag under my head and went asleep. I held the ring in my hand like a lucky charm, and my last thought was of Carrie and my baby girl.

"I'll be home soon" I thought, nodding off to sleep.

I woke up in the teeming rain, lying in wet grass, half of my body draped over a fence of some kind. I could feel the wet on my face and boy was I in pain. My legs and my ribs hurt beyond belief. There was the smell of burning but I couldn't see it, I could hear the screaming and eventually someone found me and I was put into an ambulance.

I remember feeling heavy, I couldn't even speak, and I felt myself slipping away, and the funny thing was, I didn't want to come back. They were shouting and roaring at me and I didn't care. I slipped into the dark as easy as pie. Someone died that night, and when I woke, I couldn't remember anything more than the things they told me. And by the time they let me think, I couldn't remember anything at all.

They had my coat and my identity card, really a sign on card from the labour exchange in Dublin. My name is Gary, they said. But somehow I know that's not right, and that a different name and a different person is what I am and who I am...But they say that it will all come back in time, how long they cannot say and that it will take something simple to pull the two bits of my person back together and then I will be whole again.

Carrie

They took him away then and there to the prison, I presumed. Serena stayed for a while and then went off promising that she had something up her sleeve that would solve our problems and would have us all back together in no time at all. I remember feeling very tired and they took Saoirse away and put her in an incubator for a while as a precaution because she was a little early.

"You can go and see her any time you like Carrie" the nurse said as I drifted off to sleep. I felt like my body was made of lead.

Two days, that was all I had with her. Late on the Saturday night I sat in the nursery holding her and talking to her, having fed and dressed her and told her all the things we would do together when we left the hospital.

The nurses were fantastic. They showed me how to hold her and funnily enough, none of them mentioned the scene in the labour ward on the day Saoirse was born. They treated me like a normal everyday Mammy and I was delighted that the baby was so lovely and perfect and surely that *meant something.*

I kissed her goodbye on Saturday night and went to bed. I told the nurse to wake me when she wanted feeding and that I would come down.

I fell asleep, full of the thoughts of my lovely daughter and that one day we would get this mess sorted out and be a real family.

I woke with a splitting headache and a sore feeling in my leg. When I looked at it I saw a little pinprick like a needle mark. The sun was streaming into the ward, and I had been moved to a private room in the night. I sat up and looked for my house coat and slippers. They were dumped in a heap on a chair and I slipped them on and staggered out onto the hall.

"Where are you going?" a nurse came running towards me.

"To feed the baby, it's late" I gasped.

"Baby has been fed already, you go back to bed now" she tried to turn me around and I fought back-

"I want to go and see her" I yelled.

I pushed her away and ran down the hall to the stairs, I got to the nursery just before the nurses and security men did, and was standing staring into the empty cot.

"What happened?"

"She's been taken into care, I'm sorry, but it's this you see" one of the nurses held out the paper and I could see a picture of Noel looking solemn and holding a photo of Steven and me at David's house before the debs.

I remembered I gave Ma a copy so that she could at least see my dress, as she hadn't been there on the night.

"Where is she?" I screamed "I want my baby"

"She's quite safe Carol Anne, she's safe where she is" They grabbed hold of me and pulled me out of the nursery.

"Why is this happening? Its crazy, someone has to stop it" I wept.

"Carrie, you never told us the circumstances of the pregnancy and we have to do what social services say, Steven broke the barring order by being here, we had no choice but to let the baby go with them" I know the nurse was trying to be sensible and kind but it didn't wash. Now I had nothing.

Our story was in lurid detail, splashed all over the Sunday paper that I knew 99% of the people in the estate read. It was full of stories about gangsters and their wily ways and accounts of the extravagant weddings among the travelers and also stories about young women being sold to old men for the price of a car. Now what we shared was reduced to that level.

I now knew why they had moved me to another ward, because it seemed like I was under siege. Someone had told them that I was in the hospital and they were coming in droves, reporters from other papers, asking me questions and trying to scoop my side of the story. Even an English paper came over, trying to photograph the "miracle of the Thames" the angel that lived when everyone thought she was dead. Security beat them back and I lay listening to them in the hallway and couldn't go to the window to look out, because they were out there too and the once I did look out they caught me on telephoto lenses.

I couldn't even go to the toilet or to the smoking room; the other women in the place turned away, disgust written all over their faces.

I went in and lit up a cigarette when the room was empty and sat staring at the walls.

Two other women came in and sat as far away from me as they could-

"Is that her?" One of them whispered, and the other nodded.

"Yeah"

The spit landed at my foot-

"Fucking pervert, bringing a baby into that situation, you should be locked up"

She was hard looking, her hands covered in heavy gold rings and home inked tattoos on her knuckles. Before all this had come out she told me she was in on her fourth baby, and that her husband only had to get out on temporary release for a night and she was pregnant again.

"He'd rob the eye out of your fucking head, my Paulie would, and the only thing is the stupid fucker keeps getting caught!" She'd laughed.

"Its not like you think it is" I started to say, and she hopped off the chair and stood over me-

"You had a baby for your brother, your own brother, that's fucking perverted so it is, you're a scumbag and so is he and I'm telling you, they better lock him into solitary in the prison when they get him, cos my Paulie is going to kill him, dirty fucking pervert like him" He shoved me hard against the wall and I felt my shoulder hit the radiator.

"And you better watch out leaving here tomorrow, cos it's not only the papers that are waiting to get you, you dirty slut" She hissed.

"Mrs. Cronin?" A voice from the doorway.

I looked past her and saw the Matron, a tall dark woman, beautifully made up, who had helped me feed Saoirse the night she was born.

"Your baby is crying you should go to him" She said.

The other women walked out of the smoking room and I sat there shaking.

"You all right Carrie?" The midwife sat beside me on the seat.

"I think so, I... I don't even want to think about tomorrow and going out there to face anyone, I don't think I'll be able for it" I sighed, too tired to cry.

"Look, can I call someone; get you brought out later today, maybe in the night when the place is quiet?"

I thought for a minute and then asked her to call Serena, the only person I knew with a car and who I knew I could trust.

"Don't worry love, everything will be all right, that child is perfect and there's no way she would be if you were siblings, its all going to be all right" She patted my arm and went off to make the call.

Serena came that night and brought me out through the warren of corridors in the basement to her car. I lay on the back seat with a blanket over me and we sped out into the night. We drove to David's house and I slipped in through the back gate like before. David was waiting in the kitchen.

"Carrie darling, you poor child" he wrapped his arms round me and I sobbed.

"David, what will we do?" I gasped. I wiped my eyes on a wad of kitchen towel and blew my nose.

Serena was making coffee and she leaned against the worktop.

"Carrie, there's a couple of things you need to know, first of all, Steven isn't in prison, he's gone, He got out of the hospital while they were arguing the point at the reception desk, and he did a flit, my guess is that he's in the UK, looking for answers, he spoke

to Nancy and told her he was heading to see his grandfather"
She lit a cigarette and blew a long stream of smoke into the air.

"But we have no way of knowing where he is and what he is doing and the Gardai, bless them, have contacted the police in Britain but until he surfaces we won't have a notion what he's doing, secondly, The baby is with Doris, she's okay and you will be allowed contact soon…" she put the mugs down on the table and I wrapped my hands round mine.

"Thank God, Thank God he isn't in prison, Oh Serena, I've been so worried about him in there"

She nodded-

"Listen Hon, there's more to tell, I've unearthed a bank account in the name of Amber Williams, with regular amounts being paid in for the past number of years and nothing touched, opened in 1972 and steady deposits into it all this time, and I wonder what that's all about, why keep a bank account open when they person is dead, sounds weird to me anyway? Unless, of course…"

"Someone knows that Amber isn't dead" David looked tired, but his eyes lit up.

"Exactly, and that someone might be Mr. James Bard, who is not talking right now and who won't talk unless we go and make him, which is why you and I are heading to Glasgow on Tuesday morning Carrie" Serena sipped her drink and grimaced.

"No chance of a bit of brandy in this is there?"

David grinned and fetched a bottle from the living room.

"My kind of woman" he smiled.

Something flashed as she poured the spirit into the mugs and I cried-

"Serena! You're engaged!"

She looked at the ring and smiled-

"Wondered when you lot would notice, I guess that it's hard to think about this type of thing when your whole life is going at 300 miles an hour" She held out the hand and I admired the ring.

"You want a wish?" she asked softly.

I shook my head and smiled.

"I have only one wish and I don't think any ring will make it happen, even a ring as lovely as that one, thanks anyhow" She patted my hand.

"We'll sort this out pet, mark my words we will, someday soon it will all be put right"

So there we were, sitting in the living room, drinking brandy laced coffee and working out flights and money and all that we would need for the trip. Serena was fantastic. She seemed to be so organized and matter of fact, knowing what could be done and what we would need an injunction for.

"We have to get to Bard, that's the only thing we can do, and failing him, we get to Doris' sister, but that's going to be really hard because she went off to the states a long time ago and Doris says she hasn't been in proper contact since"

"She sent the cheques!" I gasped.

"What cheques?" Serena asked.

"They used to come in an envelope with American stamps on, airmail, with no letter or anything sometimes, maybe a short note but that was all, and no forwarding address ever so Ma couldn't write to Breege ever!"

I began to have a feeling that this could be sorted and that there was hope now.

"Breege?" David asked.

"Yeah, Breege, her real name is Breda I think, Breege is a pet name"

"Her name was Breda Storey, she was your nanny I think David" Serena smiled.

"Fucking hell, that's a blast from the past, can we find her?" He breathed.

"I'm gonna try my best, she knows what is going on here and she might be able to help us, she'll have to help us, fill in the gaps and all that" Serena looked delighted that her investigative skills were bearing fruit!

It was late, very late, when we heard the door bell. I was sitting in the big leather chair in the living room, and Serena and David were chatting about France and he was asking about Becky and how she was doing.

"It's probably some journalist figured out where you were, I'll get rid" David went out to the door.

"He's a nice man you know..."Serena grinned.

"Yeah, he is, he really is, nice and kind and sweet and caring"

"If I wasn't with Michel I tell yeh, but I think he has a soft spot for my little sister, how old would you say he is anyhow?" she whispered. We were able to hear muttering from the hallway, whispers, and then someone, David, saying "no" repeatedly. Then he was shushed and the door opened and he came in, followed by Nancy.

I felt the room go quiet, so still I could have sworn the clock stopped ticking. I could feel the blood thudding in my ears, my mouth went dry and I felt like I was freezing.

"David?" I croaked.

"Carrie, listen to me honey, there's a bit of news, the police came to the flat, Carrie, look at me, please?" Nancy was talking to me but all I could do was stare at David, transfixed.

"David?"

David wasn't an old man; he was young enough to still be regarded as handsome by my age group. He took care of himself and was tanned and fit. But just then, right there in that moment, he was old, his face was bleached white and there were tears falling down his cheeks. I just stared.

"David, tell me" I whispered, trying to quell the rising dread inside me.

"Carrie, he's dead, he's dead, my son, my baby..." He shook all over.

"Nah, Nah, your fucking messing, it can't be right, stop this messing now, Nancy?" I grabbed her arm.

And then I realized that it must be true, because she was sobbing and Nancy rarely cried, and from then on, I could see the room beginning to spin around me-

"Nancy, please, How..." I stopped, and sank into the armchair, Serena was behind me in a second, pushing my head down so that I wouldn't faint.

"Breathe Carrie, for fucks sake!" she was saying and I felt my stomach turning.

Bit by bit, it came out, a crash on a motorway in England, up near the midlands. He must have been hitching to Glasgow, but why that was I didn't know, Nancy said she gave him enough money for the train fare at least, and somewhere to stay, so what was he doing? A crash, a lorry it was, jackknifed and he was killed there and then.

"They think the driver fell asleep, he's in intensive care in Leeds, Another guy that was in the cab, sleeping in the back was badly injured, they reckon when he wakes up he might be able to tell them what happened, but he's in a coma since Friday, he was a hitcher too, he only got out because the back blew open and he was thrown clear, Steven and the driver were trapped in the cab" Nancy was shivering.

"Why did they ring you Nancy?" I asked

"I was the last person to see him here. He rang me when he was in Dun Laoire and asked me for money, I went out in a taxi to him Thursday night and gave him a change of clothes I nicked from the lads downstairs, and two hundred quid that I had saved for the holidays, the police found the bit of paper with my address on it, it was all that was left of his address book after it happened"

After it happened. My Steven died in agony, he burned, oh Jesus. I thought.

"A bag was in the lorry too and though it was well burnt it had the clothes and the few bob I gave him in it, and the ring you gave him, they found that too, its him all right, God Carrie, its him" she sobbed.

Serena was on the phone to the police and was asking to speak to someone who knew about this accident. She was getting transferred to different extensions and was having no joy.

"Someone must know what's going on here!" she was shouting.

She banged her hand hard on the wall beside the phone-

"What hospital? Have they tried to identify him? Why not?" she listened again.

"Oh no, oh Jesus" she whispered rubbing her hand across her forehead.

"David, I need you here for a minute" She held out her hand and he came out to her in the hall. They were whispering about dental records and he was shaking his head.

"Nothing?" she whispered. David nodded.

"Nothing, no tattoos or birthmarks, no fillings, broken teeth" she said to whoever was on the line.

Serena put the phone down and came into the living room again.

"They'll release the body soon, I'm so sorry Carrie, it looks like it is him, we, they say that we should have him home in a week or so"

All I could do was sit there and nod and wait for the tears to come. They lay like stone inside my chest and I shook all over. But I couldn't let them out. I felt like I was standing outside myself looking at the room full of people in shock, and wasn't part of it. I felt like I was dead, and honestly, that night, I thought it was only a matter of time before I was dead for real.

There wasn't much point in going on with the search for Breege and the trip to Glasgow wasn't going to happen now. We waited in suspended life for the word to come that Stevens's body was being released and was being brought home.

Every time I closed my eyes I could see the crash, I could see the panic and the last moments of his life when he realized that he wasn't getting out. That all the hope and the thought that he and I could make a life out of the nightmare our lives had become, if he could get to his grandfather and sort out the riddle, that it all came down to that last minute of life, before the smoke and the flames took him from me.

I hadn't thought much about what comes after. I sort of believed that there was a God and a spirit world and thought that maybe we live on somewhere, and I knew that if this was true then Steven would have found some way to tell me so.

But there was nothing. The silence was deafening and I couldn't bear it.

I spoke to Becky in the clinic and listened to her weeping and felt like I was made of stone. Ma arrived with Father Ray and we sat in the living room while the sun streamed in through the windows and she asked me to come home to the baby.

"She needs you, you're her Mammy" Ma gripped my hand tightly.

"You weren't saying that when you took her away from me, were you?" I snapped.

"Carol Anne, things were different then, the Law..." Ray began.

"The Law" I cried "The law is what started all this crap, anyone with an eye in their heads could see me and Steve weren't related, and the law said otherwise, and now he's gone and I can't..." I choked.

"Carrie, please" Ray knelt in front of me and held me by the arms.

"No Ray, there's things I have to say, I loved him, I loved him with all my heart and you lot and the law took him away from me and I will never forgive you or God as long as I live, NEVER!"

"I know you loved him, he was a great fella altogether, and ye were happy" Ray tried to soothe me.

"There can't be a heaven Ray, he... There mustn't be a God, why would he do this to us? Why would he take him when I loved him so much?"

"I don't know, Carrie, I ask myself that question all the time, but there is a purpose for everything, even if you cannot see it right now, one day you will understand"

I calmed down a bit, and they left, and I was sitting there drinking vodka a while later when David came in. But it didn't matter how much I drank, it still didn't take away the emptiness and the cold feeling of longing inside me.

"He's been released, he is being flown home tomorrow, the funerals on Saturday"

"Okay"

He went out and up to his bedroom and closed the door. I sat there, drinking and smoking and waiting till it got dark. Still I felt nothing. I remembered what Ray said, that God was love.

And somewhere in the mist of time, at the back of my mind, I remembered reading something about love, that said the destiny of most people was to remember love, to have it and lose it somehow was what most of us got.

I had read that out loud to him one morning before I found out I was pregnant and we had been lying in the bed out in the mobile.

"Then we will have to cheat destiny, because I want to be with you for ever, I want to be with you when I remember this, not far away thinking of you" he'd said.

"I dunno Steven, people die and fall out of love, it happens" I'd been upset at the notion that something like death could come between us, because falling out of love could never happen to us. I was sure certain of that.

He'd reached over and taken the book out of my hands and kissed me.

"Listen here missus, when I die, its going to be when I am a very old man, living in a house with a stair lift, drinking Guinness through a straw, and your going to be with me, when your a cranky old woman with Norah batty tights and slippers, and incidentally, you'll still be my little darlin' then too, I won't die now, not when we're young and alive and mad about each other, so put that book away and lets do something less depressing" he grinned and tossed it into the corner, and that was the end of that.

And that was what played in my mind all night, I closed my eyes and saw that scene over and over again, and I could feel him beside me, all through the night, when I thought I was awake, but must have been dreaming. I lay in that half sleep, my arm thrown across him, sure that I could smell him and hear him breathing. Afraid to open my eyes, because I knew he was a mirage, and all I would find was a rumpled duvet and a pillow in my arms.

They brought the coffin into the house on the Friday night. It was sealed. So all I got to say goodbye to was a box. They had sent some things over with him, all charred and tarnished the clothes in the bag bloodstained and torn up. And in a little cellophane bag, the ring I had slipped on his finger a couple of months before. They had found it on the road, about ten feet from the wreckage.

I sat holding that in my hands all night, waiting for them to come and take him away. I found a silver chain and strung it onto it and wore it next to my heart.

Ray had said he would do the funeral and I had let him. David was agreeable and he asked me to pick a song for the ceremony.

I handed a tape we made of our favorite songs and told him to pick one. It hardly mattered. Steven was dead, he wouldn't hear it. And I wouldn't be bothered listening to it either.

It was a beautiful day, sun streaming through the windows of the church, cherry blossom blowing in the breeze. The box at the top of the church meant nothing to me, I couldn't relate to it at all. I looked at the photo on top, one I had taken in Connemara that time, and it seemed like another lifetime altogether. He was leaning on a rock, looking sideways at the camera, that smile, the grin he reserved for me, on his face, eyes half closed in the sunshine. I couldn't believe that I would never see that smile again.

Not surprisingly the church was packed. People wanted to see the freak show ending, and that was what my life had become.

I know there were readings and what not, but I couldn't tell you who did them, or what they said. I remember the undertakers coming in to carry the coffin out, David at the front and three more men we didn't know helping him. I got up to walk out of the church, behind the coffin, Nancy on one side of me and Serena holding my arm on the other side. Ray had chosen "Parisian Walkways" by Gary Moore, and the opening bars made me feel ill, I shivered and drew my coat round me tightly.

"You okay?" Nancy whispered.

I nodded. *It's not fair, this shouldn't be happening. We should be walking out of this church together, not like this.*

We got to the door and stood on the shallow little steps of the church porch, and for a second, the cherry blossom swirled round us like confetti. People were staring at me, waiting, I suppose for me to go hysterical, for something to happen. I could see them standing there but the faces were a blank to me. I saw a woman coming forward, a bundle in her arms, which she handed to me.

"Take her home" she said.

"Doris, this isn't the time or the place..." Serena began, but she stopped her-

"Serena, I made a big mistake doing what I did eighteen years ago, and I cannot do it again, This child belongs with its mother and its family and I won't stand in front of that again, I was talked into doing wrong back then and I cannot do it now" She touched my arm.

"Please Carol Anne, bring her home and mind her, she's all you have now"

I was transfixed by the child. She was awake, and looking up at me with what were unmistakably Steven's eyes.

"Poor little baby, that's your daddy they have there, he only got to see you once" I muttered.

"I wonder can he see you now." I bent my head and inhaled her baby scent and felt the trapped tears leaking from my eyes at last.

People were moving away, probably pissed off at the lack of histrionics by the church door, and were heading to the pub across the car park. I sat into the second car and rocked Saoirse. David sat in with me and stared out the window. We didn't speak, both

lost inside ourselves. I doubted then that I would ever come back.

I looked over at David for a second; this was the second time he had to do this, go through the loss of someone he loved-

"David?"

He looked at me, his eyes dead inside him-

"What love?"

"Does it ever go away?"

"Does what go away?" He asked, as the car started to move slowly from the church and into the car park.

"The pain"

I knew he would know what it was like, the gnawing emptiness inside, like a longing, like a hunger, like your body is crying and wanting something and there's nothing that can assuage it, nothing to give except what is gone forever.

He'd lost Liz, and he would know.

"No honey, it gets so you can survive it, but it never really goes, I'm sorry" He reached over and took my hand and I held his tightly.

I stared ahead, looking out at the car in front that was taking my love to the graveyard, to be buried and gone from me forever.

"How will I live without him Dave?"

"You'll live, it's going to be hard though" He sounded like I felt, hollow inside.

"I don't know how, I just don't know how I'm going to do this, its killing me now, I want him back so bad Dave, I can't see my life without him"

As the car in front pulled in and stopped for the last time at David's house and waited the couple of minutes before pulling away again I felt the baby stir in my arms and looked down at her.

"There aren't any words, Carrie, there's nothing I can say to make it better when he's gone, but you have the baby to live for, so you have to try" He whispered as the car moved down the Main Street, past the Greyhound and the shops.

"Try" I sighed.

That's all I could do, that's all I was going to be able to do from here on in.

Part Two

Chasing shadows

Standing in the street
I hear you calling
Turn around and you're gone
Chasing the shadows
The dragons are falling
And I'm not the only one
Outstretched arms run out of steam
Dance with misfortune
And follow the dream
Not knowing what to say or to do
Don't flatter yourself
I wasn't thinking of you

9

Christmas 1991

"Good morning Gary, how are you feeling today?"

Some times, the relentless cheerfulness of nurses gets to me. I ask you, how you would be feeling if you were lying in a bed for close on six months not knowing if you were able to move or do anything for the rest of your life.

For the first while, they kept me asleep, sedated they called it, mainly because I was thrashing round the place and they thought it would cause more damage and they needed to see what was wrong internally. Right into June I was kept sleeping, and into the first week of July. A medically induced coma they said.

But they reckon I am a miracle. Imagine that? Me, a miracle.

I shouldn't have survived at all, and the other poor bastards in the lorry didn't. The driver was in a coma for three weeks and he died, and then the other bloke, he burnt to death they said. I wasn't meant to hear that, they were whispering when they thought I was asleep. The police came and asked me questions, but I remember very little. There are patches, like the driver, he had three kids, and the other bloke had two. He was heading home to Glasgow for a week with them; he was separated from his missus. Hoping to give it another go he said. And now she had to bury him, poor thing.

But they say that this is wrong, that it doesn't tally with what they have, and that the knock on the head must have messed with my memory. You see, they know I traveled round a lot, they said so, and that I must be remembering other trips in other lorries with other people. I don't know, honest to God I don't. I keep my mouth shut then, because somewhere in the back of my mind I know there are problems, prison looming, and trouble. I don't trust the police.

"Am I going to prison?" I ask them once, and they say that I'm to shush and that it wasn't my fault, the driver lost concentration for a moment and that was it.

But still I get the feeling that there's something they aren't telling me, and I feel like I should be running away, not lying still.

I was thrown from the lorry. The back opened like a can of tuna, they said. The cuts on my face and head were caused by the metal ripping into me. Twenty feet away I went, over the median of the motorway, lying in the bushes I was. I fractured my skull, broke my collar bone, three ribs, punctured my lung, and broke both legs… I was like a jigsaw. But they say its cos I was asleep, I didn't see it coming. I wasn't tensed for the impact like the other two.

And they put me back together and I'm alive.

Though what I'm living for is debatable. They told me I was married with kids but when they contacted the wife, well, she was in another relationship and there's no way I'm coming back into her life to torment the hell out of her. But the funny thing is, I have been laid here in this bed for weeks, months, and there's not a jot of memory about her, or two kids or anything. Either way, she didn't come to the hospital and when they tried to contact her again, she'd moved on to another area and no contact details were left for them, not even for the mailman. Have to say though, if I was as big a bastard to her as she maintains I was, I couldn't blame her running away, could you?

Somewhere in the weeks after the crash, I could see a baby, one that was mine, that I was holding, and a woman, but with all the drugs and the sleeping and everything I can't be certain that it's not a dream. There's no point in telling the doctor, he just nods and then fucks off to his office and forgets what I told him.

The nurses come in and tell me it's a matter of days now before I can get up and go in the wheelchair they have beside the bed. I watch them coming and going, they seem to like me for some reason; they sit by the bed and talk to me when I can't sleep and they call me handsome. They won't let me see myself though. They shave me and all that. I must be a mess.

"Well Gary, its Christmas Eve, will Santa be coming to you?" one of the nurses is nice, Colleen her name is. She's from the Wirral, in Liverpool.

"Most likely, depends on if you told him I was a good boy" I smile at her.

She rattles on about her family, her Mam and her Dad, and her brother Robbie. She's a nice girl. She has lovely auburn hair, she ties it up in a bun when she's working but I know it is curly. She's almost eighteen and she's a first year trainee. Robbie is seventeen and he's going to college to be a vet. Her mam and dad worked really hard to make this happen; they run a pub in Birkenhead.

"They must be proud of you, training in nursing and your brother doing college too, they should be delighted" I say, meaning it.

"They are, they didn't have it too easy themselves you know, things were tough starting off, Dad was, well he tried being in a band first and then gave it up to do his training and Mam was working in a shop, but then they got married and Dad qualified, he's a chef, and they got the pub then and that was that" She was fixing the sheets on the bed as she spoke.

"Are you going home for Christmas?"

"I am, I'd have to go home, Mam would be heartbroken without us, especially when we have the mass and all that to go to"

"Mass? You're Catholic then?"

"I am, it's funny though, Mam only goes once a year, to this mass she has said for my sister, Rachel, though me Mam, she calls her Layla, you know, after the song? Well, she only lived a couple of days, she was born before they were married and she wasn't allowed to bury her or anything, so she does this Mass once a year, on New Years day like, when we're all together, its nice, though she gets upset"

"That's sad, your poor Mam" I say. What else can I say? She bustles around the room a couple of minutes longer and then she is gone.

There is a nice atmosphere in the hospital over the Christmas. The patients that have no families to take them home, or who can't go home for some reason or another, are all put into one big ward and we watch the telly and have a nice meal. You really count your blessings when you see the state some of them are in. One poor git is paraplegic after a bike accident, and seven of his mates arrive up in leathers on Christmas day to see him. Once my legs are okay, I'll be up walking again, they were well mashed up on me, but they operated and they will be okay soon.

New Years Eve is a bit weird. There's a party in the nurses home and the staff are all going to it. Apparently they get the chance to get off with some of the young interns and Colleen is mad into one of them.

"So while you're off dancing, who's goin' to be minding us poor sods?" big Geordie in the bed opposite mine asks. Geordie is funny. He was a brickie, working on a high rise development and fell, he won't walk again but he reckons that he prefers being in a chair for life rather than getting up on the "fookin' scaffolds agin" and that the claim he is making against the bosses will pay off his mortgage and give him a few bob to do what he really likes to do, racing his pigeons and drinking in the local.

"Aw, don't you be worrying Geordie, we have someone coming in to baby-sit you while I'm off dancing, she'll take none of your oul chat" Colleen laughs.

"Aye? Who is she then?"

"Oh, she's very high up an' all, from an agency, hard as nails she is, you won't get away with your bottles of ale under the bed with her"

Geordie's wife Vera brings him up six bottles of beer a week and he stashed them in the locker for New Year. We were all offered a drink to bring in the New Year and had been looking forward to it.

"Go on, I'll charm her into having a drink wi' us meself, you wait and see" he grinned, showing the gums where his false teeth should be.

"Geordie, if your goin' to charm any woman you need to put yer teeth in lad, an' your Vera will kill yeh if she hears you chattin' up anyone" Phillip the biker snorted in his bed.

"Get away, its animal magnetism, teeth don't make a blind bit o' difference" Geordie was a tonic. He cheered us all up no end. By nine o clock the nurses were gone and we were all drinking our ales and talking about other new years. Rather, they were, I was listening.

There were too many holes you see. I could remember bits and pieces and then I thought that I was mixing things up, I would be thinking and something, so sharp an image that it made my heart pound would come to me, and I would try really hard to hold onto it. But it was no use. It would slip away.

One of the nurses was wearing a perfume I recognized one day and I had suddenly seen a room in my mind, a small sunny bedroom, with some kind of hanging on the wall, with like an Indian design on it, and the scent of that perfume in the air.

"What's the name of that perfume?" I asked her.

"This?" she laughed.

"Yeah, what is it?"

"Oh its very expensive, three quid a bottle from the Indian Market, Patchouli oil, do you like it?" she grinned.

"Eh, I thought I smelt it before" I replied. *I did, I know I did, but where?*

"Its kind of heavy or something, I'll bring you in some next time I'm down there, okay?" she went off, and before long a doctor was round to see me.

"So Gary, you're starting to remember things are you?" he asked.

"I, it was just a smell, that's all, it seemed familiar"

He droned on for a while about smell being a powerful memory aid and that this was all very exciting and we would work on this in the New Year when he came back to work. I tried to think and remember more but it was no use.

Something bumped the end of my bed and I sat up.

"Not asleep already lad? You lot are supposed to be better drinkers than that!" Geordie held out another bottle of ale.

"Are you drunk in charge of that vehicle Boyo?" Phillip laughed.

"I am, nicely pickled, and more to the point, I'm going to be even more pickled by midnight, because Madam Hitler hasn't shown up, its boys night down here for sure" He held out the bottle and I took it.

He scooted across to Phillip in his wheelchair and I couldn't help laughing. Madam Hitler, as he called her, was slowly creeping up behind him-

"... and when she does make an appearance, I'll tell her that you cannot infringe on the right to get pissed to see in the New Year, and no woman will tell me...." He was in full flow when she tapped him on the shoulder-

"Mr. Patterson, are you drunk?" she asked, the twinkle in her eye belying the stern tone.

"No, indeed I'm not" he belched softly.

"On the contrary Mr. Patterson, I believe you are very drunk, but far be it from me to tell you that you shouldn't be in that condition, after all, I'm only a woman myself"

He grinned.

"And a fine looking one too I might add, will you have one with us, for the new year like?" he proffered a bottle.

His gummy grin completely disarmed her and she roared laughing-

"Thanks but no, I have work to do, you boys carry on, I'm going to do blood pressure and all that in a minute and then I'll leave you to it, just try keep the noise down and don't get too sloshed"

She went off down to the nurses station and Geordie looked at her behind-

"Not bad, and not as frosty as I thought"

He nodded at me-

"What you think? Bit old for you mind, but there's no harm in looking"

"Nah Geordie, too skinny for me" I gulped some of the beer.

"Aye, there's nothing like a nice round woman to warm the bed" he sighed.

"Better not say that to your Vera" Phillip laughed.

Vera was skinny and small, the total opposite to her big husband.

True to her word, Biddy, the nurse, only came back to take our blood pressure and make sure that we weren't all in danger of being ill from alcohol poisoning. She went back to the nurse's station and left us alone for the rest of the night. We watched the ringing in of the New Year and were all asleep by one a.m. Geordies snores echoing round the ward.

My last thought that night was a prayer to my people, whoever and where ever they were, that somehow I would find them again, and that they wouldn't forget me.

ℚ

Down in the glass fronted office, at the end of the ward, Breda Storey sat shaking. She slipped a small silver flask out of her bag and poured it into the tea she had made for herself after she had done the blood pressure checks.

Of all the things she thought she would be facing back in England, this was never going to be one of them. She had decided to come back from America in the fall, following the death of her charge, who she had been nursing for more than ten years. She had enjoyed looking after her, found private nursing an easy life, with the perks and holidays she enjoyed as a carer to the wealthy. She had arrived back in England and joined an agency and decided then to base herself in Leeds, and went up the week before Christmas. They sent her to this hospital, and for a week she had been working in the ICU, and then transferred to the orthopedics unit for the night.

She had always been vague about her previous work, her connections with the Bard family had ensured she would be received by the best families in the States, and indeed had been her trump card in securing the post looking after Senator Donavan's wife in Nevada.

Of course, once Mrs. Donavan passed away, her children didn't want her around. They had made no bones about the fact that her mothers care was no longer an issue, and she was surplus to requirements. Breda had thought that the senator himself would fight for her, maybe keep her on, in light of their deepening relationship, but he had been out of the state when Cathy, the hard nosed cow of a daughter, had presented her with her pay and her walking papers.

The house she had lived in for ten years was no longer hers, she had to pack up and go, leaving her memories and her life behind her.

She had always had the paper sent out to her, the Independent was her choice, and she had a stockpile of them in the garage, and she was using them for packing. While wrapping up her china, she tore a couple of pages out of a recent issue and a picture caught her eye.

There he was, in a smudged and grainy photograph, somewhat older than she remembered, but then, so were they all, she thought. David Williams, his hand up to ward off the photographers, his arm around a tall girl, in a dark coat, coming out of the four courts. September 1991.

Final hearing in tragic incest case, Baby Saoirse goes home for good.

She read on avidly, and felt her blood run cold when she realized that the girl in the photo was Doris' daughter, and the baby was hers.

"I had no idea things were that bad" she muttered.

She went back through the papers and found the previous issues and sat thumbing her way through them, cutting and tearing the articles out and shaking her head in disbelief. The photographs of Steven's funeral knocked her for six! She had truly idolized that boy; she had practically reared him till all the trouble started. And now he was dead, and she could have prevented it.

She read till the light failed and then sat in her kitchen, drinking whiskey and smoking.

She decided that she couldn't go back to Ireland, not now, she couldn't face seeing the tragedy she had visited on this family for real.

She lifted the phone and dialed.

"Do you know what's been happening to the children?" She asked.

"I do know, and believe me, its not easy standing back and watching, but I have to for now" the voice answered. Breda knew that there were tears in that voice, even if it stayed calm and cool.

"But Steven, he's dead" She cried.

"I know Breda, I know, I can't begin to think about this now, now we're finally getting somewhere"

"What will I do now?"

"Go back, Even if we can't change what's happened to Steven, we have to try and keep going, for Amber's sake"

It was an easy matter, to tweak her name, call herself Biddy Donavan, apply for work and get a job. Her reference was passable, no one could dispute that this woman was a great nurse and had cared for her patients well. And she had enjoyed being part of a team again, enjoyed her little apartment in Leeds, and being able to shop and do what she wanted without being on call twenty four hours a day.

She had even relished the thought of being on the ward tonight; Big Geordie was a legend among the hospital staff. He had flirted with her while she slipped the cuff over his arm and she had gone along with his chat.

But when she got to Gary Stanley's bed, she had felt the world tilting and her knees went weak.

He was badly scarred, his head shaved with black stubble poking through, and he was skinny from lying there so long. But his eyes hadn't changed, and when he looked at her and grinned sleepily, she knew who he was, because they were the same eyes that had looked up at her when she was giving him a bottle, or cleaning a cut on his knee when he fell off his bike in the garden.

She gulped her whiskey laced tea and sighed. Obviously there was something wrong here, and she wasn't going to be able to do this all alone. She had the cuttings from the paper in her bag in her bedroom, but she didn't know what effect it would have on the child if she just blurted out what she knew.

There was no time to call America, and she couldn't do that here anyhow, it would draw too much suspicion to her. No, America could wait; the other would have to be first.

She fished in her handbag and took out a notebook.

She found the number she wanted and dialed-

It was answered immediately.

"I want to speak to James Bard, it's urgent" she said.

"Mr. Bard is sleeping at present, can I take a message?"

'You wake him, you tell him its Breda Storey, and I want to speak to him now"

ॐ

"Well, you're a dark horse and no mistake!" Colleen smiled at the end of the bed a week or so later.

"How do you mean?" I asked.

"Gary, your leaving us, going up north, to Scotland, your family have been found"

She looked delighted.

"Aren't you pleased?"

"I didn't know I had family there" I was baffled. I really didn't know what they were talking about.

"Duh! That nurse, Biddy, she knew your grandfather, used to nurse him apparently, she recognized you from a photo he kept in his office and rang him, he's very old, but he wants you back" she played with the edge of the bedclothes.

"But you are very naughty, you never got in touch with them for ages, and they are really rich too, you never said you were loaded!" She smiled.

I shook my head-

"Me? Loaded, come on, why was I hitching instead of traveling by private jet then?"

She held out a card-

"This is for you, when you're better, maybe you could come and see me sometime, in Liverpool, and my number is on there... I, I'll miss you a lot" she smiled sadly.

I took the card and held her hand.

"I will, I promise you"

"Grand"

I felt something familiar in her that I wanted to hang onto. Life was becoming too uncertain lately, with me not knowing what and who I was. I needed something familiar to keep me grounded and safe.

"That will do Colleen, off you go" a voice cut into my thoughts and I let go of her hand. Nurse Biddy was standing at the end of the bed, a plastic bag in her hand and a folder in her arms.

"Well Gary, your moving on today, we're going to put your things into this bag and get going, it's a long drive" she was emptying the locker as she spoke.

I swung myself into my wheelchair and pulled on the hooded top I was wearing as daytime clothes in the ward.

"Have you no coat?" she asked.

All my clothes were cut to shreds in the lorry.

"Where am I going? Who...?" I began.

"You're a lucky man, your family have found you, they want you home, your grandfather is waiting to see you" she tied the top of the bag and shoved it into the net at the back of my chair.

"Come on now, we can't dally" she pushed me out of the ward and into the lift.

It was freezing cold outside and I shivered. I'd forgotten about winter and snow and sleet, in the twilight world of the hospital. It seemed like life had begun to move again, they had gotten me into a chair and moving around, I had been doing physiotherapy on my legs and was able to stand for a little while, holding onto the bars in the therapy room.

They hadn't been able to keep me from mirrors then, and I had wheeled myself into the bathroom one morning and looked at my face. I had a scar down one side, along my cheek, and a ripped mark along my collarbone. They said that it could be sorted out in time; maybe plastic surgery could be an option. But I couldn't look at myself. I knew I was too different to what I thought I had been.

It was the strangest thing; I had gotten really upset about my hair.

I had looked at it, growing in different directions and chunks of it shorter than the rest and had closed my eyes tight, thinking that I had long hair once, but I was damned if I could figure out when.

"They had to cut it" Biddy said.

"Oh? Right"

"You had a bad bang on the head Gary, they thought they'd have to operate, you were lucky"

She calls this lucky. No idea who or what I am anymore, where I am from and even this grandfather who has appeared out of the blue means nothing to me. How the hell am I going to rebuild a life I don't even begin to remember?

There wasn't anything else to say was there? I just wheeled myself out into the day ward again and got on with it.

Hours later we came to the house.

We had been driven in what I would call a limo, which had been waiting outside the hospital for me. I initially thought we were going to another hospital, but Biddy said no, that she was going to be minding me from here on in, at my grandfather's house. I was warm enough, and looked out at the scenery we passed, hoping that something would jog my memory and make me remember anything about my so called family. But nothing worked.

In through two gates, and about another twenty minutes of a drive, and we were there. It was getting dark by then, and I couldn't see the house well. I was wheeled in and up to a room-

"When can I meet my Grandfather?" I asked.

"Tomorrow, you're to rest now, sleep, its time enough for all that tomorrow" Biddy was flushed with excitement.

I lay in a huge bed, hours later, staring at a ceiling, listening to the rush of trees in the wind, mind racing. None of this meant a thing to me. I remembered nothing of this house and these people. I looked around; there wasn't as much as a photograph. Nothing to jog the memory. I got out of bed and into my chair again. I wheeled myself round the room, looking in wardrobes and into the bathroom. Nice place, but it wasn't mine. I didn't fit.

I pulled open the heavy door to the hallway, and slid out on the thick carpet.

Silence. Heavy oak paneling all along the walls, with pictures that might have been ancestors or maybe were just hung there to pretend that the family were rich longer than they were, and a deep red carpet down the middle of the floor. I was sweating because it was a darned sight harder to pull a wheelchair along on heavy carpeting than on linoleum in the hospital. I could hear voices and I heaved my chair along the carpet till I was at the base of the staircase. They were in a room to my right, the door slightly open-

"Will you tell him everything?" Biddy was asking.

"Well, his mother is dead, and his father, well, he's otherwise engaged, so of course, he must stay here, we are his family, he never should have left in the first place" a deep voice replied.

Grandfather?

I moved closer.

"But what about…"

"Breda, may I remind you of your role in this affair, and the serious consequences you will face if it should come to light, what is the sentence for fraud and kidnap these days? Hmm? Ten years? Twenty?"

Fucking hell!

"But that was by your orders! You were the one who…" Biddy gasped.

I heard a chuckle and it chilled me to the bone.

"Breda, I'm a very old man, a very sick one, they tried to collar me last year and they couldn't, my lips are sealed, and the lawyers I pay ensure that it stays that way, you on the other hand, are dependant on my protection and discretion, and it would be advisable for you to remember that and *do as I say!*"

"But surely, the business, your not still…"

"Breda, its none of your affair, what I do or what I say, and you know better than to ask me questions or get too inquisitive don't you? I mean, you recall what happens to those who do?"

"Yes Mr. Bard… I certainly do know" She said.

I actually pitied the poor cow. Imagine being under that buggers thumb. I turned to go, and got jammed in the end of the stair rail. I could hear Biddy coming towards the door and gave up. I was caught, and knew it.

"What on earth!" she gasped, when she saw me, sweating and flushed and tangled in the balustrade.

"Hello, I wasn't able to sleep so I came out looking for you" I smiled.

"Is that my Grandson?" the booming voice from the room called.

"Yes Mr. Bard, it is" she pulled at the chair till I was free.

"Bring him in here"

"Oh, its late sir and..."

"Biddy" there was a warning in his voice.

Hadn't he called her Breda?

"Right away then sir" she pushed the chair into the room where he was sitting in a huge armchair, in front of a dying fire, drinking a glass of something that might have been whiskey.

He didn't look like a granddad type to me. He looked willful, and tough. He must have been a good looking man; he still had strong features, even in old age. But he was thin, obviously there was some sickness. His hands were large, nails manicured, his suit was expensive, and even I could see that.

"You may go *Biddy*" he smiled. He was just the right side of respectful, I realized that there was indeed a family resemblance, his eyes and mine were the same anyway. But he was cold, I could sense it.

She shut the door behind her slowly, and I got the feeling she didn't want to leave me there. I felt like I was being thrown to the lions.

The clock ticked loudly-

"Do you drink?" he asked.

"I don't know"

"What do you mean you don't know?"

"I mean, I don't remember, I did have a couple of beers over New Year but..."

He sighed.

"Then you drink, here..." he handed me a glass and I sipped it cautiously.

"Whiskey and soda, its very weak, drink it slowly"

He sat again and stared into the embers of the fire.

I knew I shouldn't speak, that he was the type of man liked to take the lead.

He stared at me-

"You're like your mother" he began.

"Am I?"

"Yes, the colouring is the same, she was magnificent, dark as Diana the Huntress, and fearless, she could have been a rare beauty"

"Is she, is she dead?" I asked.

He nodded.

"And my father?"

"He is also gone, we don't know where he is, we think he's dead, I'm sorry.

"Is there only me? I mean, have I brothers or sisters?"

"Only you"

"I see"

"You will, in time" he sipped his drink.

"What was I doing, when the accident happened? How did I end up in that lorry?"

And that's when it began. He told me, his version of the story of my life so far-

"...you were working for me, you had gone to London to file some documents in my bank and see some of our agents in the area, you were in your car, it was stolen and you had no way of getting home and I suppose you were worried about telling me that you had slipped up so you hitched a lift and that's what happened...Quite simply, wrong place at the wrong time, but its no matter now"

"I work for you?" I asked "Doing what?"

"I am a publisher, the largest company in the north, you're my heir, my agent, as it were, and you will be back out there in no time at all, I have no doubt" he yawned.

That rang bells with me. Publishing, yes, I knew that it must be right. At last some of the mental jigsaw was beginning to slip back into place.

And then it struck me-

"If you knew I was on the way home, why didn't you look for me sooner? I was seven months in hospital, and you never came to me then"

He sighed.

"You were going through some personal difficulties, you had stopped coming here for a while and you and I weren't on the best of terms, you see"

"Right" the clouds were forming again.

"Your car was found at a place in the south, called the Black Leap, a well known spot for suicide, we thought that you had jumped into the sea, we looked for a body but..."

"Well I guess that explains it"

"You have to get well, strengthen yourself, get back on your feet, we have work to do, huge work, you have to be ready to take over when I go" he stood up and opened the door to the hallway.

I rolled past him into the hallway and stopped.

"Can I ask you something?"

"Go on"

"Was I married or something, I just, I see things all the time, like flashes, and there's one, of a girl, I remember being with someone, but its gone, I don't know anything about it, other than she was red haired and tall, and we lived together"

He sighed heavily-

"Yes there was a girl we believe that was the reason for your personal difficulties, you and she were engaged, a young love thing, but she threw you over for someone else, and you couldn't take it"

"Oh, so that's why I was so upset about everything and you thought I'd killed myself"

"Yes, now go to bed, sleep" He turned and called me again as I was leaving-

"Gary, don't listen to any one else when it comes to your life story, ask me anything you want to know, just don't listen to idle gossip"

I nodded and went on my way. But when I was back in my room I remembered the conversation I overheard. *Fraud and Kidnap and ten years in prison.* Was that what I was running from? It couldn't just be a broken relationship could it?

I wondered would I ever know. Maybe if I waited and asked Biddy she might tell me. That's if she wasn't afraid of the tyrant in the library.

10

July 1992

"Oh Gary, you look lovely so you do!" Biddy clapped her hands together in glee.

I was standing in front of my bedroom mirror, fixing my tie and feeling like a fish out of water.

"Do I? You're not just saying that to make me feel better" I smiled.

"Oh No!" she cried.

Six months had passed since I came to Baird Hall and I was, almost, as fit as a fiddle again. I had been training with some of the best physiotherapists my family money could buy and I had my own apartment in the house and a small gym and spent my time working out and getting fit again. The weather had been unusually good and I was out and about so much, I had gotten tanned and looked really healthy. Most of the scars had faded, on my legs and the ones on my face were hardly visible. The only one that you'd really see was on my shoulder.

I was working a little with my grandfather and was traveling round the country for the past month seeing the way the business worked and meeting the men and women who would be part of my life from then on in.

One of the first trips I made was down to Liverpool to see Colleen. I took her out to dinner and we talked like old friends. She was thrilled at the change in me and brought me to meet her family. I felt right at home, especially with her mother. She was a sweet, quiet woman, who, when she heard I was related to the Bard Family was delighted to tell me that she too had a link with them. Seemingly she had been a patient in the same hospital as my mother, when she had had her baby Rachel, and she had seen her walking up and down the corridor-

"...we all did that, when we were in labour, do you have a brother or a sister Gary?" she asked.

I shook my head-

"Neither, I'm an only child" I smiled.

"But, she was having a baby, I know she was" she insisted. She called her husband-

"Jimmy, do you remember that woman in the hospital when I was having Rachel, that Bard one? Didn't she have a girl?" she asked.

Jimmy came in wiping his hands-

"Jesus love, I don't remember details like that, all I remember is us losing our little one, I don't know, honestly"

"Mam, can you leave it please? Gary doesn't need to know all this, its ancient history" Colleen was scarlet with embarrassment.

"All right love, I'll stop, but true as God, I do remember her being pregnant" she closed her eyes.

"Maybe she lost her little angel too" she whispered.

I felt sorry for her, standing in the kitchen a tea towel in her arms where her little baby should have been. She shook herself and turned back to me and smiled, and my heart leapt. I turned scarlet.

"You okay love?" Colleen touched my arm.

"Grand, just someone walking over my grave, I think"

I knew that smile. It spoke to me. Somewhere in my past I had seen it before, and my heart leapt. I felt like someone had hit me with a hammer. Why would I feel such joy? Only to come back to earth with a bump when I looked around and saw nothing else there.

"Could we go for a walk? I'm supposed to walk an hour a day and I'm getting lazy here" I asked.

Within minutes we were out and about, and from then on, when I visited Colleen, we didn't mention the family or the train of thought her mother had been on when I was there the first time.

And we met quite a lot, and we got closer, and then I realized that Colleen felt something more than friendship towards me, and that I was very fond of her. Perhaps not in the way I should be, I wasn't head over heels or anything, but I figured she was a fine person with a good solid background and she would be a great partner in life. For some strange reason I seemed to think that I had lost a chance in love and would never find anything like it again. But I liked being with Colleen and her family and of course, my own business was beginning to take off too, Granddad was really helping me and I figured it was time to pop the question and settle down.

From that day on the dream started.

Have you ever woken up in a cold sweat because you have been chased in your dreams by some malevolent entity that you couldn't escape?

Or had one where you were falling and just before you hit the ground, you waken, heart pounding with terror?

Mine was the same dream every single night.

A garden at night and knowing that someone was with me, opening a door into a place I knew was mine. Laughter and feeling at one with myself, and then reaching out to *her*, and touching her, pushing her hair back behind her ear and kissing the skin on the side of her neck, breathing in her scent, warm and woody and gorgeous.

Knowing she was mine, knowing she loved me.

And in darkness that was soft and warm, feeling her body with me, feeling myself inside her and all over her, her arms round me and touching my skin with fingers like air, wanting to call her name and it wouldn't come, knowing she knew mine and I couldn't hear her. Maybe this time she would say it and I would know.

"Who am I?" I whispered and she smiled, tilting her face to me in the dark to kiss.

"My love, my love" she sighed.

"Tell me who I am" I asked, knowing what was going to happen soon.

"You're mine, my love, mine" She breathes and I hold her tighter. Her skin is like water, or silk in my fingers, her hair covers her face and I reach to brush it away again. I just want to see her, just once.

And then the panic, they came and took me away, tore me from her and left her crying in the bed, took me away, until all I could hear were her cries

And the next time I see her she is head bowed, sitting on a bed in a lonely place, crying into her hands, and I can't touch her or help her any more.

And sometimes, I would reach out in the dark, trying to find her and I would touch something, someone, and hold them close to me, pushing inside, looking for her.

"Mine, my love" I whispered, finding her lips, touching the skin I can't see.

215

And this time no one came to take me away, this time I would go on, lips would find mine and her breath on my cheek, her hands, solid now, stroking my back and her legs wrapping around me. I shut my eyes tighter, waiting. This time it will happen. This time I will know.

"Who am I? Tell me?" I say, over and over.

This time the smell of her perfume is different, the room begins to feel different, I close my eyes tight as I can and keep moving, deeper into her, hoping that it will change everything. I can hear her breathing and she holds me tight, I feel myself changing, being engulfed by her and I know that this is it, that soon I will know.

"Gary, Gary.. Oh, Gary" She says and I fall apart.

I fall away from her and back into the darkness.

Her hands are still on me and I cannot move.

I open my eyes and see Colleen, and I know that it's all a lie.

The dream is over.

∞

"Biddy, do you like the ring?" I held out the box to show her, the small diamond with the white gold band.

"Oh it's lovely Gary, gorgeous; she's such a lovely lass, your going to be so happy"

Colleen had arrived today, her mum and dad and her younger brother in tow. He immediately went off to the stables and spent hours there talking to the groom.

This was a small intimate party, Bard style, with about a hundred people invited, to celebrate my return and now, my engagement to Colleen. I hated being under scrutiny, and wanted to see Colleen before the crowds got in on us. I left Biddy tidying up and went downstairs to find her.

She was out in the yard, clapping as her brother rode one of the hunters at break neck speed round the paddock, whooping like a Navaho and being chased by about twelve dogs.

"What the hell…" I asked, laughing.

She turned to me, eyes gleaming-

"He's always wanted to do that, they haven't got enough room for a real good gallop in the riding school, so he asked the groom here could he do it" she laughed out loud, her head back.

"You're lovely Colleen"

"Am I?"

"Yes, you are, I was wondering, if you'd think about getting married to me?" I held out the ring, and heard her gasp.

"Oh Gary, Oh, I will, Yes!" she threw her arms round me and kissed me on the lips.

I slid the ring on her finger and we kissed again.

"I'm going to make you happy Gary, I really will" she looked at me with such trust in her eyes that I felt weak inside. I hoped to God that I was doing the right thing. But why wouldn't it be? She was lovely and a good girl. What could go wrong?

And the answer to that was damned nearly everything.

She wasn't marrying the real me, because I didn't have a clue who the real me was.

Colleen, bless her, was buying a shell. Even I knew that and knew how wrong I was.

Pity no one else saw fit to pull me aside and ask me what the hell I was playing at.

The party that night was great. Okay so there were lots of people we didn't really know, and early on in the proceedings Colleen was borne away by a gang of women to show off the ring and talk about the romance, to a couple of women who wrote for the romantic fiction market. I laughed at the thought of us ending up in a Mills and Boon novel. It was a bit sweet, I had to admit. But I liked her; she was a silly little thing.

I was standing at the doors into the garden when someone tapped me on the arm-

"You are to be congratulated; your fiancée is a lovely girl, when will the wedding be?"

He was smaller than me in height, unmistakably French.

"Michel Moraine" he held out his hand.

"Gary Stanley, I mean, Bard" I shook his hand.

"I am pleased to meet you; your name takes a little getting used to hey?"

"A little, so, what do you do? Do you work for us, or with us, I mean?"

He explained that he worked for a legal firm that looked after our contracts in France, but that he traveled a lot to England and to Ireland-

"And soon, to Italy, you will be working there too I see" he grinned.

This was something that was in negotiation. We were trying to branch out a little into Europe, I had suggested Ireland as being a good place, being so close, but Granddad wouldn't hear tell of it and chose Italy instead. I was going to be living there for at least six months of the year and Colleen was too. Her nursing career had to go by the wayside for a time, but I had promised her that she could take it up again when the Rome branch was sorted and we could come back.

"Your young Colleen, you're not twenty yet, you can do it"

"I'll miss Mam"

"She can visit, it'll be lovely, you'll see"

"Well, all right then, I'll do it, for you" she kissed me, and I held her tight and promised her we'd do great things in Italy, all sorts of traveling. We were both learning to speak Italian and it looked like it was going to be fine.

I turned back to Michel-

"Are you married?"

"Non, I too am engaged, she lives in Ireland"

"Is she here?"

"Non, she is working on a very difficult case right now, someone stealing from their employer, who says the items were a gift, she too is in law" He smiled-

"She is a wonderful woman, she is the joy of my heart, but she is strong and strong willed, and doesn't want to settle down too soon, and there is her family and her friends, they have troubles, but soon, it will happen" he sighed.

The joy of my heart, a wonderful woman… I didn't feel that way about my fiancée and I knew that I ought to feel more than fondness, but it was granddad pushing and pushing for me to be wed and settled.

"I hope you will be happy Michel"

"I will be, once my Serene comes to me and marries me and is my wife, its too hard being away from her so long"

I looked at Colleen walking towards me. I also realized that what I felt for her didn't include yearning for her when she wasn't with me. It seemed that when I was with her I could concentrate on her, but once she left me, I yearned for something nameless, faceless, that she had no part in. I realized then that I was marrying the wrong woman, but that it was too late now to be backing out. I smiled as she came to me and took my arm-

"Lets dance, come on" she half pulled me to the dining room where the dancing was.

And I went, because it seemed like the right thing to do.

11

September 1991
Carrie

I heard the baby moving in her cot and I groaned. She was still in the habit of the four o clock feed. The nurse said it was because she was premature, that she would grow out of it soon. I was bushed; I hoped it would happen soon.

It was the hardest job in the world being a mother at the best of times but I had to admit, it was double hard for me. I had gone back to my flat the week after Steve's funeral. I couldn't look at David any more, the pain in his face when he looked at the baby and not being able to get three words out of him a day was taking its toll. Rumour had it, well, Nancy told me that he was back in work, that he was trying to put his life back together-

"But you'd know by him he's not with it at all" she sighed. She had spoken to him one afternoon when he was up in Grafton Street, supposedly looking at new offices for the business.

He told her he would be in touch with me. He had to be, there was an inquest hearing and then, the whole custodial hearing that would in effect decide if Saoirse should stay with me. It was all a formality, Serena said; anyone could see that the child was loved and thriving.

Thankfully the papers had died down, leaving us alone. However the law was still on my tail, and I had all sorts of social workers breathing down my neck about Saoirse and the situation. I leaned into the cot and lifted her out, her warm little body curled up in her pink baby-grow.

"Hungry again baby?" I whispered, and reached for the bottle that was warming beside the bed. Between Becky, Nancy, Serena and myself, we had managed to get every bit of baby paraphernalia under the sun and it pissed the social workers off no end. I supposed they thought a woman of "ill repute" like me should be lying prostrate with a syringe hanging out of her arm all day.

"Not me baby, not your Mammy" I crooned. She was growing more like her daddy every day, with my hair and his eyes, and she was perfect, she was developing normally and seemed to be very alert. Sometimes I wondered how I could go on, how could I continue without him. And then, when I looked at Saoirse, I knew I had no choice. But it was hard, very hard. Sometimes in the night, tears would catch me on the hop and I would lie for hours weeping, railing at God and at Steven for leaving me alone like this.

In pure desperation I had gone to see a medium. Not being into that kind of malarkey it had taken Nancy about a week to get me to her offices out in the back of beyond.

"Tell her nothing right? See what she says" Nancy, bless her was trying to help me and she had gotten this woman's name from a friend who swore by her.

I went into her house, the reading was to take place in her living room, and she was friendly, a chatty type of girl, in her thirties, not at all the Mystic Meg figure I envisioned.

"You at this long?" I asked as she set up the tape player.

"Ah, years, I come from a family of Clairvoyants, it's in the blood" she smiled.

"That must be strange" I smiled sadly.

"No, it's nice to be able to show people that life continues, even when they think someone is dead and gone, they live on somehow"

And I thought about the black void I was in, the only shining light was my daughter, and the nights of crying and the silence. I knew that if there was a spirit world, Steven would be champing at the bit waiting to talk to me.

And the reading began and I listened-

"You have gone through hell pet" she began and I started to cry.

"I'm sorry" I sniffed.

"That's okay, I'd be rich if I had a pound for everyone that cried, it's natural, but listen honey, there's a young man here, by the name of Gary, do you know him? He talks of a lorry crashing and him dying"

"But his name was Steven, not Gary"

"No, his name is definitely Gary, he says the crash happened in the middle of England going north... does that make sense?"

"Yes it does" I listened hard, maybe it was Steven trying to get through and she was messing it up.

"This man has two children in this life, a son and a daughter"

"No, we have one child, a daughter"

"He says to tell you he is sorry for what he did; he stole something special, a ring"

"I have it here, look this is making no sense" I was getting angry now.

"He was married to Angela, that's not you is it?"

"No, I'm Carrie, look this is all wrong, totally wrong, me and him were not married" I blustered on.

"Oh dear, there's something about incest, or an inquest and he says it was all wrong"

She seemed to get agitated-

"Look love, I have to tell you this, you have to listen to me, no matter what your going through now, it will be okay, you will be happy again and you family will be reunited soon, there will be weddings, your own included and you will be so very happy with the way your life turns out, can you believe that?"

I stood up and literally shouted-

"My Steven is dead, he's buried for the last few months and I'm going through hell without him, and you sit there talking about someone I don't know and tell me its all going to be all right and how can it be, he's gone, he's fucking gone and left me here on my own with the baby, you, you liar!"

I crashed out into the hall where Nancy was waiting and she jumped about three feet in the air-

"What is it, what happened?"

"I was mad to come here and listen to this garbage!"

"Calm down for fucks sake, what did she say to you?"

"Nothing, nothing at all, Nance I want to go home"

Nancy got me to the car and ran back, on the pretence of fetching her jacket which she said she left in the house. It wasn't, it was in the boot of the car, she'd put it there. She was gone for a good while and I sat, fuming and smoking in the car. We were half way home from Navan when she spoke-

"She knew all about the accident Carrie, and the ring, you have to admit to that"

But I shook my head-

"He wasn't there Nancy, there's nothing left, I don't want to think about it any more, just let me be, okay?"

She said no more and to give her her due, she was very good at listening to me and stopping me feeling too lonely.

I was lucky, what with Nancy downstairs and Becky too, now, and they acted as a buffer against the more inquisitive of the social workers that came.

"...The child is the product of an incestuous union, we are aware of that" one Social worker, christened "vinegar tits" by Nancy, had sat in my flat with her notepad open staring at the baby.

"Are you expecting her to sprout another fucking head?" I snapped.

"Not at all, but you must realize that a woman who knowingly sleeps with her brother..."

"I didn't know!" I was stung.

"Ah, I think you will find that on the morning of your arrest in December 1990, you were in fact sleeping in the same bed" she grinned maliciously.

"But we weren't doing anything"

"That's as may be dear, but you all ready had, hadn't you?" she nodded at Saoirse.

I felt weary suddenly-

"I suppose so"

"And who is to say that it won't happen again?" she snipped.

"*That* would be a fuckin' miracle, the chap's dead; can youse not leave her in peace?" Nancy arrived at the flat with Becky in tow. She stood leaning on the doorjamb, arms folded, and eyes glinting with temper.

"How many times have youse been here this month? Asking the same bleeding questions and getting the same answers, she's a great mother, no question, and the girls trying to cope with losin' her partner too, why don't you fuck off out of it and leave her alone?"

"Losing her *brother*" Vinegar tits must be enjoying saying that, she said it often enough.

"Whatever!" Nancy roared.

"Listen here you, take your shit and your innuendoes and fuck off out of here, *My* Sister is a barrister and she will be making a complaint against you, this is harassment" Becky grabbed the woman by the arm and frog-marched her past Nancy who growled at her. She clattered down the stairs dropping half her handbag in the process.

I sat on the sofa bemused-

"And since when did Serena get called to the bar?" I laughed.

"Fuck off you, I was trying to help, and trainee solicitor hasn't got the same ring to it"

"In anyhow, Serena should be a judge or something, she can be vicious when she gets her teeth into something, she ate the head off Dad yesterday when he started at me over the drugs thing and about going to college, She reckons I need a year to get myself together and not be thinking about the points system again" Becky had changed a lot since her brush with the wild side. She was still as sharp as a tack and could put you into your place in seconds, but she seemed warier and a little more forgiving.

"What do you want to do Becky?"

Becky shrugged-

"I dunno, I think I'd like to be a counselor, help people off drugs or something, but I really don't know right now"

"Will you go back into modeling?"

"Maybe, I don't know, I sent my photos round the agencies but I haven't heard anything yet"

I knew how she felt, floating along in a dream, not knowing where our lives were going. Both of us were on the verge of something. A leap into the unknown. She had gone back into work, with Nancy. There had been some lovely developments there for her. Chrissie, the manageress had decided, on her trip to India, to throw in the towel properly, and had gone off to join an ashram. Mrs. Chandra's immediate reaction was to offer Nancy the manager's job and she grabbed it. Her first task was to re-hire Becky and she told me my job was there when I wanted it.

"The terrible threesome back together in work again!" she laughed.

"God help Grafton Street" I smiled.

I couldn't go back to work yet. I had to get sorted with this court thing first, and then think.

I winded Saoirse and put her back into her cot.

"Nanny is coming to see you today, so go asleep chickadee" I stroked her cheek.

That was the best thing that had come out of all this mess. Ma had come round, and was really sweet to me. She came to the flat the odd time and even stayed over with me, helping me with the baby. I had to give her her due; she was trying very hard to be a mother to me as well.

I knew that she was hoping I got to keep the baby and she had, against Noel's wishes, made a statement to the police saying that I hadn't known about mine and Stevens blood relationship, and that therefore I hadn't gone into the relationship knowing it was incest. She and Noel were on the rocks now. But as far as I was concerned, they had been for a long time.

Later that day she arrived, and she was sitting holding the baby, when I asked her-

"Mam, why didn't you tell me? You knew long before I did about Steven, why did you keep it from me?"

She went into the bedroom and put the baby into the cot and came out again.

"It's a long story Carol Anne; I suppose I was afraid, I thought that I would end up in prison"

"You? Why on earth..."

She sighed-

"You see, I didn't adopt you in the conventional way, it was all very unorthodox, illegal, I suppose, I should, when I heard what happened to your mother, I should have sent you back to your family, but something inside me wanted to keep you, and Peter did too, and at that stage, the only person who knew where you were was Breege, or Breda, and she was gone"

"What do you mean, unorthodox? Did you kidnap me or something?"

"Not at all, no, it wasn't like that" she laughed.

"Well, how was it then?" I persisted in asking her, I had to know, not that it made a lot of difference now, but still.

"My sister Breege worked as a nanny, for David and Liz Williams. She had been a friend of David's ex fiancée, Mary Taylor, who was nursing with her in the London hospital. We shared a flat in the city when I went over first and I remember meeting Mary a couple of times. David broke her heart when he left and married Liz, she never got over it, but I heard that she married well, eventually. So, Breege took the nanny position for the little lad, Steven, with plenty of opinions as to the sort of man David was and with no real love lost for him. I married Peter and we moved into a place in Clapham, and we were trying for a baby. I had tests done but he didn't, and it turned out that it was his fault all along, I blamed myself till I had the boys" she lit a cigarette and I opened the kitchen window.

"Your mother was a serious addict, very heavily into the drugs from the time Steven was about one year old, Breege used to put him into the pram and run to my place when she could, and I could see she doted on him. Her opinion changed a little about David, she used to say that he was repenting the haste in which he had married, and I had to agree. She became very embroiled in the family, very involved. It got to the point that she hardly had a day off from them. She loved your mother. Absolutely adored her, and she was a stunner. I remember thinking that Steven took his looks from there, and I couldn't blame you falling for him. She minded her for the three weeks or so before you were born and went back to the family home in the highlands when she had you to look after her and you. And then the whole family came back to London"

I was standing making tea and she stopped-

"Go on, I'm listening"

"You might not like what's coming, are you sure you want to hear it?"

I nodded and put the mugs down on the table.

"You were the most beautiful, sunny little baby, with those curls and those hazel eyes. Breege was mad about you. She used to try and go where you went, but Liz had other ideas, bringing you out at all hours, like she was afraid to leave you behind. And obviously, Breege couldn't have gone into drug dens and that kind of place. It was nothing short of a miracle that you weren't hurt or something. Her father used to ask her to go up to the house, to bring you, but there was no way on earth she would do it, even when Breege would try and coax her into it, she'd refuse point blank.

Breege thought that there was something amiss between the two of them, because on one hand her father idolized her, and then she seemed afraid of him or something. It was in the autumn, you were about one year old then, she came over to my flat, and told me that Liz was seriously unhinged. She owed a lot of money, but she had been putting money into a bank account for you, not Steven. She carried your birth cert and a bag of essentials everywhere, and Breege figured she was frightened of something. There were a lot of late night phone calls, so David thought that she was having an affair, but the one time Breege pressed redial, she went through to Baird Hall, Liz's home.

Breege asked me, if there was a chance that she could get you for us, would I take you and mind you for a while. Liz was talking wildly about America and Breege didn't want to let you go into god knew what over there.

She's trying to escape something Doris, I know it. She'd say to me. I told her we would have you no bother till she would sort things out and find a place to say. Peter knew you were her child but he didn't know the ins and outs of the deal. He thought it was legal and above board till the day we had to pack up and run to Holyhead and meet Breege with you in her arms. She had a blue jacket on you that had belonged to Steven, not your little pink coat. I only realized why later on.

Get her out of here. Was all she said, and we went straight onto the boat, and into a flat in Glasnevin. And you were ours for about a week when we heard that your mother was dead. I was afraid of what might happen, and tried to contact Breege but she was gone. I haven't laid eyes on her since that day. I know she's alive though, for certain. And she was in America; she used to send those cheques, so she was making good money over there. There was never a forwarding address though.

"Your mother is dead, they found the body. But you were safely tucked up in your cot in Glasnevin, not floating out to sea like they thought. Your mother had put your little pink coat on the back seat of the car to make it look like you were there too, because she wanted them, whoever they are, to think you were dead too. Whatever she was running from, she wanted to save you"

I waited a second before I asked.

"But the bank account, why is that still there for the last seventeen years, who would do that, unless they knew I was alive?"

":Let me tell you something Carol Anne, I am not a brainy woman, but I have learnt a lot this past couple of years, and I know this much, Liz Bard was terrified of her father, terrified enough to keep you with her twenty four hours a day for a whole year, and then, knowingly send you out of the country before faking your death as she died herself... she didn't want you in his clutches, and God forgive me if I am wrong, there had to be a fair fucking reason for that, I think he was abusing her, and she didn't want him getting you!"

"You mean...?"

"Yes, your grandfather, the wonderful James Bard, I think he was a pervert, and that's why she hid you"

"But then... who's holding that account open all this time"

"The same person sent those cheques all those years, Breege, of course, she is the only one knows for sure where you are, and more to the point, *who* you are"

It was a lot to take in. Far from feeling the hate and resentment I had been feeling against my mother, I had to feel pity for her now. I wondered was she afraid, dying the way she did, or was it quick. They did say that drowning was the best way to go, not like fire...

Stop that! It gets you nowhere, come on, shake yourself.

I sat in the flat mulling it all over, and I wished that there was some way of finding it all out, clearing up the mystery, once and for all. One day I was going to go over there and see that grandfather of mine and see what sort of man he was to drive his daughter to drugs and suicide, and who had brought such misery to so many lives. That house of his was like a magnet, drawing us to it, Steven was on his way there when he died, and my Mother had died when she was running away from it.

"It must be some bloody place" I said aloud. Saoirse grinned up at me.

I had visions of an old man, sitting fishing, reeling people in and destroying them.

"Well he won't get me, and he certainly won't get you baby"

It was the last week in September when Steven's inquest was held, in the coroner's court, and then the following day we went to the four courts for the custody hearing. My head had pounded all night, after sitting through the details of how and when he had died. I tried to think of something else but the words kept coming back-

Broken leg, trapped on the passenger side of lorry, driver on top of him, probably unconscious when fire began, lorry was torn apart passenger two was flung out onto the road, driver was pulled out by bystanders, but the fire was too advanced to reach Mr. Williams in safety. The cab of the lorry was on its side, passenger side down. Mr. Williams was unrecognizable when removed from the vehicle, necessitating a sealed casket.

David sat stony faced through it all and accepted the condolences of the court. I wasn't even acknowledged. I was in the catch all term, "Family of the deceased" and Saoirse wasn't even mentioned.

Ma came down to the flat to baby-sit while I went to court the next day. I sat in the waiting room with Nancy and Becky and Serena. David was opposite me. When it all began, I listened to them, tearing my life apart, hearing the oohs and ahs from the people who sat in on cases like this, for entertainment, and the scratch of the pens belonging to the couple of hacks that sat taking notes.

They couldn't fault me for my mothering of the baby. Steven was dead now, there was no danger we would be corrupting the life of an innocent with our carry on, as the judge put it. I could have her back, for good. It was over.

I heard someone cry out and realized it was David. I went over and hugged him hard-

"Its over now, come on, lets get out of here" I said into his shoulder.

There were a couple of photographers outside and we pushed through them and into a taxi and up to my flat.

She was feeding her when we got in.

"I won Ma, I get to keep her" I smiled.

She nodded, looking past me at David.

"That's nice, and now here's her granddad come to see her" she beckoned him over.

He took her into his arms and smiled.

"Steven's eyes, she..."

"I know, she's gorgeous, isn't she?" Ma stroked her little cheek.

Looking at him, with Saoirse, I knew no matter what happened that we would survive. I could do this, I could make it work.

I was lucky in a lot of ways. I had three of the best friends a girl could ask for, Becky and Nancy, living downstairs, and Serena out in Blanchardstown, all of them there for me when needed and I did need them a lot.

Saoirse's first birthday, May 1992, approached and I really didn't want to think about the week after when it would be one year on, Stevens's first anniversary. I still had days when I just couldn't believe it, when it would hit me like a ton of bricks that he was never going to come back. There were so many things I wanted to say to him and couldn't. He would never hold me again. On days like today, when the spring sun was shining and the blossom was beginning to come out on the trees, it was especially hard. I would put Saoirse in the pram and walk for miles when the blues hit me hard. Ma was having a tough time too and as we had gotten closer, she shared a lot of her life with me. Noel was being vindictive and mean, and barely communicated with her past a grunt now and then.

"Its over, but he just won't bloody leave" she said.

"Get a barring order or something, he has to go, it's your house"

Eventually he moved out, and still came to see the boys, and stayed close enough so he could see where she went and what she did. But she was so relieved that he was out of her home that she didn't mind.

We had a little party for the baby on her first birthday. It was a bittersweet day, all of us thinking of how it could and should have been. Ma finally came to David's house and she talked to him for the best part of an hour in the kitchen, I suppose, explaining her reasoning for the way she was in the past, and making amends. Her youngest son ran round the garden and I sat on the back step with the girls, smoking.

"How are you getting on?" Serena asked.

"Up and down, I suppose I never saw this coming, never thought I'd lose him this way, its hard, to think of how he died, how scared he must have been" I gulped my coffee, trying to hold the tears back

Nancy put her arm round my shoulders, and hugged me to her.

"It'll get easier hen, some day" she smiled sadly.

"He was a good guy, and he did love you, and not everyone gets that in life" Becky rubbed my arm.

She hadn't. Although, she was coming on in leaps and bounds, studying to be a counselor and loving it. Nancy gave her flexi hours and she was getting out and about socially, and men naturally flocked to her, but she wasn't into them.

"I want someone that will look after me from now on" she said.

Serena grinned-

"A sugar daddy maybe, and one not too far from us hmm?"

Becky blushed.

"Stop that, he's just, he's helping me with my studies, that's all"

Nancy spluttered and coffee went all over her new top-

"Yeah right, *that's* what they call it now, is it?"

I couldn't help it; I had to say it-

"You *do* realize that if you get with David you will technically be Saoirse's granny... At what, twenty? That should be enough to get you an anti aging cream campaign anyhow!"

"Will you shut up? He's way too old" she was as red as a cherry.

"Think of it now Becky, you'll be the most glamorous granny since Tina Turner!" Nancy said.

"Not so old, I always thought he liked you, what is he? Mid forties? Look at Mick Jagger for heavens sake" Serena was really going for it, teasing her mercilessly.

"He's forty four so he is! Mick Jagger is way older and he looks awful, Dave..."

"Ooooooh, *Dave* now is it?"

Becky laughed and threw the cushion she had been sitting on at her-

"Feck off you, enough"

"Okay, okay, I quit, he's nice anyhow, not a bit too old for you" Serena grinned.

Nancy broke in-

"What's the story with you and the Frenchman? Any sign of us buying a hat any time this century?"

Serena's romance with the gorgeous Michel had been going on for more than two years, but the wedding plans could never seem to be finalized. She was working so hard and he had been spending a lot of time in Europe, so that they could never pin a definite date down for the wedding.

"Ah I don't know, we are thinking of Christmas time for the big do, that's if we can get the time off for a decent honeymoon, we're like ships in the night lately, he's hardly here at all"

She laughed-

"Sure he has a wedding to go to in July, I'm supposed to be going to it with him, some rich fella in the north of England, from the Italian office I heard, but I don't know if I can get the time off myself, we have this big case on at the minute, honest to God you wouldn't believe the things couples fight over, it'd put yeh right off marriage and men"

"Make the time Serena" I said "you never know what's round the corner, and I wish..." I didn't finish the sentence; they all knew what I wished.

"Well as for Nance, I can tell you that I am staying free and single" Nancy grinned over the cushion she held to her chest.

"Oh yeah? What about that guy? Eddie? You know, Spinal Tap?" Becky giggled.

"What about him?" Nancy replied warily.

"Hangs around a lot doesn't he? Like a bad smell, though that could be the oul afghan he wears" Becky mused.

"We are just friends, that's all, friends"

"I'm not in love, so don't forget it" Serena sang under her breath.

"Enough Serena, I mean it" Nancy muttered. And Serena shut up.

I knew why she wouldn't go with Eddie again. She had been with him the night we heard that Steven was dead and she couldn't bring herself to do it. Eddie was a real sweetheart and he loved Nancy to bits, but she was killing herself with guilt over being the last to see Steven alive and the more I told her that I didn't blame her the more she beat herself up.

"If I hadn't given him the money Carrie, he wouldn't be gone, he might be here, okay in Mountjoy maybe, but alive"

"Maybe, maybe not, when its time to go its time to go Nancy, and it's really not your fault, please don't give up the chance of happiness for the sake of what might have been"

But she wouldn't be moved and though Eddie tried, she wouldn't go back.

"She's special, I can wait Carrie" he said.

I just wondered how long it would take for her to see sense.

Doris took the baby home to her house that night so that I could spend a bit of time with my friends. I went back to the flat and got dressed in anything that wasn't too tight or covered in baby sick and we went into town to a gig.

The gig was in the Baggot Inn, Christy, the ex lead singer from the eighties band Aslan, had gone out on his own with a guy called Conor Goff and they were packed to the rafters to see him every week. Nancy was devoted to him and dragged me there, almost kicking and screaming-

"Nancy, I don't listen to music any more, not since, well you know"

"Well you should listen to this lad, he's the biccies, and you'll love him"

"Right so, you win, what will I wear then?"

"Good girl"

It wasn't a bad night, the gig was brilliant, and the craic with the girls was great, and I was laughing my head off when we were walking up to the flats. Serena was staying in with me, she was very drunk and had rung Michel from a phone box in O'Connell Street, to the amusement of three Gardai who were standing listening, and being told by Nancy that it was a serious proposal of marriage and they couldn't come between a woman and her true love. The upshot of the call was that Serena capitulated, and promised him she would marry him at Christmas come hell or high water.

"Your cornered now kiddo" Nancy laughed.

"Fuck, I am, aren't I?" she grinned.

"I don't care, he's so lovely I want to be with him forever and ever n'ever" she threw her arms out lost her balance and fell on her backside in the road. Her response was to sing at the top of her voice-

"I'm gettin' married in d'mornin'"

I nearly split my sides laughing at her, and we half carried her up Parnell Street and headed for Dorset Street.

"Tell you what bridey...you'd want to shift a few stone before this wedding of yours. You're a ton weight" Becky laughed and slapped her backside hard, making her screech.

"He'll never get you over the threshold if you get hammered like this on the wedding day"

"When I get my man on my weddin' night you can bet your ass that I won't be drunk, I'm gonna lock him in the bedroom for a week" She giggled.

I remembered feeling like that about Steven and wished that I could just feel it one more time. Life was looking very empty and cold without him and I wondered would I ever love anyone the way I loved him.

"Hoi" Nancy tapped my arm.

"What?"

"No time for the blues tonight, okay?" She hugged me one armed as she held Serena up with the other.

I forced a smile and kept walking. Nancy smiled.

"Good girl, come on, home for a cuppa tay, I'm parched"

Serena was sobering up by the time we got to the Waxworks at the top of Parnell Square and wasn't as in need of help and we were all delighted. It was no mean feat dragging her along!

We turned the corner and the blue flashing lights were everywhere it seemed, in front of the flats.

"Aw Jesus, not the drug squad again, when will them hippies learn?" Nancy groaned. I hated the squad raids too, whenever they happened we were sent out into the street at whatever time of the morning it was to wait till they went through the flats downstairs with sniffer dogs and a fine toothed comb. There were four lads in the flat downstairs and we knew they were dealing hash. And the police did too. But we took the brunt of it all.

"I'm bursting for a wee, I'll ask them can we go in" Nancy said.

We got Serena on her feet and Nancy ran up to the steps in front of the house, a guard got out of the car and asked her something, she shook her head and pointed at me-

"For fucks sake, what now?" I moaned.

He was coming towards me, his face stern.

"What? What the fuck do you want now? I finished with you guys a year ago..." I started. But he held out his hand to me and I stopped.

"What is it?"

"Can we go inside to the flat?"

"Why? Have I been robbed or what's happened?" I could feel my stomach freezing up.

"You're Carol Anne Conway, are you?" he asked.

"I am"

I saw Nancy talking to the Ban Garda who had stepped out of the car and was holding her by the arm, stopping her from running back down the road to me. Nancy was screaming at the top of her voice, her knees going from under her, I was staring at her, wondering what the hell had happened.

"Tell me here, what's going on?" I asked.

"I'm sorry, Miss Conway, there's been an accident, an incident, in your mothers house, some class of a fire, your mother, and three children were killed, they had no chance to get out" he was saying it but I couldn't take it in.

"My baby is up there in that house, did she get out?" I could hardly speak.

"Three children died, the oldest boy managed to jump from the upstairs window, he's alive, just" I closed my eyes and just let go. I didn't care if I died, I wanted to.

"The lad might have seen someone, the person responsible, we have an officer in the hospital, waiting till he comes round, they had no chance, none at all, it was over in seconds" He was still talking, Becky and a sobered Serena were sobbing, trying to get me to speak. But there was nothing I could say, nothing I wanted to say. I wanted this life to be over. Steven and now the baby. I had nothing left to lose.

I broke away from them and ran into the flats, up to the kitchen and pulled every pill I could find, stuffing them into my mouth, swallowing and gagging.

Please God, let me die too, I can't do this any more, it's too much to expect of anyone, let it be over, I want it to stop.

"Carrie, for fucks sake!" Serena grabbed me and stuck her fingers into my mouth-

"Let me go" I sobbed. She shoved her fingers further into my mouth and I gagged and the half swallowed pills came up.

"I can't, Jesus, Carrie, please don't do this to yourself, please" she was crying too, her make up all over her face.

"I want to I want to, please let me go, the baby Serena, why, the baby" I was kneeling on the floor, the packets and bottles smashed into the lino, Saoirse's high chair under the window, her teddy on the floor. That was enough for me. I put my head down and closed my eyes.

They brought me to hospital and watched me for the night. I didn't care. I couldn't wait to get out and have another attempt, one that would work this time.   Serena and David went and identified the bodies, Doris, Paul, Robert and my Saoirse.

"There's not a mark on her Carrie, she looks like she's asleep" Nancy's eyes were raw from crying.

Young Peter was in the ICU recovering from smoke inhalation and burns to his hands and feet. He still wasn't talking, and up to the time I was transferred to the psychiatric unit, he was still not responding.   They said that there was no reason for it, medically, it was shock. He was only sixteen; it must have been terrible for him. They told me that he had tried to get the baby out; he thought he had her in his arms when he jumped, but he'd dropped her into the cot again, and took the blanket. He'd nearly lost his reason when he realized what he had done.

Ray came up to see me in Unit Nine. He wanted me to talk about the funeral. I sat and said nothing. There was nothing I wanted to say anyway.

I'd gone to the funeral and sat staring at the altar, not even able to cry. They buried her on Stevens's anniversary. I vowed in my heart never to set foot in that church again as long as I lived.

They took me back to the hospital and gave me something to make me sleep and I swallowed it gratefully and closed my eyes again.

May 1992
Doris

I really love being a grandmother. It gives me the greatest pleasure of my life to be able to go out into the street wheeling the baby in the little pram and having people stop me to admire her lovely curls and her little smiling face.

God bless her, she has her daddy's eyes anyhow. Oh, she'll be a beauty when she grows up. And it's great that Carol Anne and I have managed to patch things up. I know in my heart and soul that she is a good girl and a good mother to Saoirse and that makes up for a lot.

David seems to be genuinely fond of her too. She has a good group of pals in the girls too, that's something I missed out on, having someone to confide in, someone to share my troubles and triumphs with in my life. Noel didn't like me being too friendly with anyone, but now that he's gone I might try and get something back together with the other women who go to the prayer meetings and all. They have socials sometimes and trips to Knock and places like that. That would be nice.

The estate is quiet for a summer evening. There are a few kids out playing and Saoirse is asleep in the pram as I walk towards the house. She'll want her bottle and her cot when I get in. The curtains look a bit grubby too, maybe I might wash them tonight, get them back up damp so they don't crease.

"Robert, come on, help me with the gate" I call him before he goes off with his pals.

A nice cup of tea and a smoke and I'll sort the baby out and do the curtains and then sit down and watch the telly for the night. I hope Carol Anne has a nice night out; she needs to have a little fun, maybe meet a nice lad to look after her and the baby. Maybe she might move back in here what with Noel being gone now, I must say that to her when I see her.

"Doris" I hear someone call me as I close the door.

Marie Mc Donald, three doors up, is waving a letter.

"That postman is a feckin' eejit, he dropped this into my house yesterday by mistake, I saw the Yankee stamps on it and knew it wasn't mine, here now" She handed me the letter and I stuck it into my bag.

"Come in and have a cuppa Marie" I asked, more out of politeness and she came in and sat down on the sofa in the kitchen.

"Where's your lads?" She asked me.

"Peter is going to the disco and the other two are out playing, I have the baby here for the night, it's her birthday today" I'm filling the kettle and chatting at the same time.

"Ah you wouldn't feel that year flying by, hows her Mammy?"

"Up and down Marie, up and down, but maybe things will get better for her soon"

I don't like to talk about Carol Anne and her troubles although they were common knowledge in the estate and that was probably why she would never come here to live again. Can't say I blamed her.

Marie left after an hour and the baby woke up for her supper and I bathed her and put her little pajamas on her and into her cot she went. She fell asleep immediately and I blessed her and sneaked out of the room.

I'm a bit too tired to do the curtains now; maybe I'll do the rest of the washing and do them tomorrow.

Paul and Robert came in and then went up to bed, and it was only then that I remembered the letter from America. It had been a while since I heard from Breege and I wished that she would give me a forwarding address so that I could write back to her. I missed her in the beginning, really missed her, but I knew why she stayed out of my life, to protect me and the child.

She didn't want us getting into trouble was all.

This letter was longer than normal; at least, it looked that way.

I pulled out the sheets of paper and started to read-

"Jesus Christ what is this?" I gasped.

There was the usual bit of a letter addressed to me, with a cheque stapled to the top. The one page on lined paper, with all the little snippets of her life in America.

It was her writing, like always.

But there was more.

Four sheets, folded in three, typed, addressed to Noel.

How in hell did she know that Noel was here?

Dear Noel,

The time is coming closer now, take a little look at the picture enclosed, we have him this time, he is going to be caught, he was careless, and we have him now.....

I read. Then looked through the sheets and found the picture.

I have to admit that it made me ill.

That evil, wicked man, with that child, and there as plain as day, the picture over the mantle of that, that horrible Bard man.

I trembled as I stared at the grainy photo and then retched into the sink.

I could hardly bear to read on, but I felt like I had to know.

….. Breda is with Steven, he is living in the home house, though I think that will change soon enough, I hear that he is to marry, another of Bard's Machinations, but nothing will be done that cannot be undone, you know that.

Noel there is no way of telling Amber what she needs to know, we need to let time and fate take its course. I am sure that things will work out and that they will find a way to be together.

You need to sit tight for another little while, give us a month, Maybe a little more, certainly by the years end, this will all be finished and Bard will be behind bars forever and you and I will have justice for the little girls he destroyed.

You have been so brave Noel, so good; I know what it cost you…..

"What it cost him?" I gasped.

What could this mean? Who was this person? I read to the end of the letter and found no clue to the identity of the writer.

But if this letter was to be believed, then Steven was alive. Carol Anne had to be told. And who would know that she was Amber?

There was only one person other than Breda who surely knew that.

Elizabeth Williams.

Dead in the river for the past twenty years or so.

I could feel my head pounding and got up to take some paracetamol and wished that there was alcohol in the house. I heard the key turning in the front door and looked out into the hall, expecting to see Peter home early from the dance.

But it was Noel.

"By Christ have you some explaining to do" I snapped.

He didn't fly off the handle as he would normally, just nodded and came into the kitchen.

"You better tell me what the hell is going on here" I grabbed the letter and waved it at him.

"I was here yesterday, I thought that I would catch that before you did" He nodded at the sheaf of paper in my hand.

"You were here?" I had thought that the house felt like it was haunted by something. Little had I known that he was coming in and out like a ghost when I was out?

"Yes, Doris, I had to get the mail, you see, we..."

"Spare me the details; tell me what the hell is going on here? Is Steven still alive?"

"Yes" he sighed.

"And how long have you known that?"

I couldn't believe him. How could he do this to Carol Anne? How could he see her in such a terrible state and not tell her what he knew.

"New Year, or thereabouts, your Breda found him in hospital, purely by chance, and brought him to Scotland" He looked old, tired. I couldn't feel any pity for him.

"Five fucking months! And you let that girl suffer? You let that innocent baby be without her daddy for all this time, and you *knew?*"

"I know, I know, but Doris, listen to me" He grabbed my hand and I pulled away-

"No, NO, I will not listen to any more lies, I am taking the baby and I am going to the Gardai and then I am going to find Carol Anne and tell her that her Steven is alive and he..." I was shrieking and I couldn't stop.

"Doris, listen to me, we are so close to getting him, so close to nailing that bastard now, you can't ruin it on us, you just can't, please, another month or two and its all over and we can get Steven back for Carrie, I swear to you, another couple of weeks is all we need"

But to me it was cut and dried.

244

There had been too many lies told in my lifetime. And look where it had led us all, into hell on earth. I had lied to Carol Anne and lived with the consequences of it when she lost her Steven. If I could make amends to her, if he could come back, then brother or not, I would let her be with him with no interference from me till the day I died.

I shook my head-

"Noel, this ends now, here and now, I'm going to the police and I am taking the baby with me, I can't lie any more" I got up and went up to my room for my coat.

Noel followed.

"Please Doris, please don't do this" he begged.

"I'm sorry" I slipped my coat on and went to walk past him as he stood at the door.

For the longest second he stared into my eyes. I saw him change, tears filled them, and I watched in wonder as one fell slowly down his cheek. For that couple of seconds, I saw him as he must have been in his younger days, before the drink and hard living took a hold on him and changed him.

"Noel, let me pass" I tried to push by him and he didn't move.

"Please Dorrie, please love, don't" he was crying now, properly.

"Noel?" I felt something gripping my insides, fear, and my stomach turned over.

"Let me out Noel, let me out" I was calmer than I thought I'd be.

"I can't let you Doris, I just can't let you" He wept.

I stood firm and waited-

"Noel, I'm sorry, I have to go now" I moved a little closer and waited.

"I'm sorry too" he whispered.

The blow from his fist knocked me to the floor and I felt him on top of me and his hands round my throat.

I never was able to fight, and less so now as I felt life leaving me.

The last thing I felt was his tears falling on my face.

Then it was over.

1992
Carrie

The days seemed to drag by slowly. David came to see me a lot. He couldn't think I suppose, what to say to a woman who had lost as much as me. I tried to talk to him of all people, the last link to the happiest time in my life. I asked what had happened and he told me he would tell me later. God help him he was grieving too and I was too far gone to care. I lay holding the little pink teddy bear that had been her favorite and just thought of nothing.

It was Nancy who told me the truth.

It was Noel again. He'd gotten into the house and done something to the fuse box, and in the night it had smoldered and gone on fire. He thought the fire would destroy any fingerprints that he'd left but only the inside of the house burnt away, his prints were all over the front door. He would spend the rest of his life in prison. He would never see daylight again. And I didn't care if I never saw daylight again myself.

I lay there for days looking out the window and not even able to cry. People came and went and I didn't talk to them much. I held it all in, afraid of letting it out I suppose.

But inside me was one long scream of agony. If I started to cry, to give voice to my feelings, I might never stop.

David still came up every single day and sat by the bed and waited and watched hoping I guess that I would snap and talk to him, something more consequential than the weather being nice or cold or whatever. Then one day he arrived with a big black case and plunked it on the table at the end of the bed-

"If you won't talk, write" he said.

"What?"

"Write it down Carrie, do something for fucks sake, you have to come back to us, come back to me, we need you Carrie"

"Why? Why the hell should I come back?"

"Because, Carrie, you're the only link I have to my boy, you're the only one who understands the way I feel and you're the mother of his child, I was thinking that there has to be a way to make good of all this and clear your names, the more I think about all that trouble back then, the more I think there are holes, gaps in the story and maybe its time to plug them up, find out the truth and finish it all once and for all"

"David, even if I clear my name, what good will it do me? Steven's gone, Saoirse is too, me Ma, everyone, it doesn't matter any more Dave, not to me"

"Well it should, we can do this Carrie, we can fix this somehow, but you need to get well" He left then and I took a deep breath. I opened the case and smiled at the ancient typewriter inside. The paper was in the zippered compartment and I took out some sheets and began.

It took me about three weeks to do it. I worked into the night and through the night sometimes and sometimes I couldn't see the keys or the paper for the tears. But I kept going, and hundreds of little black words, laced with the anger and pain and sorrow of my loss and my life came pouring out of me.

Till one day I typed the last word and finally knew a kind of peace.

I knew that I was only in the beginning of life without them. I knew it wasn't going to be plain sailing and all rosy in the garden, but I felt like there was something left now, something left of me that life couldn't destroy or take away.

So there I was, on my own again.

I got out of the hospital in September and went to stay with David. I wouldn't sleep in the mobile, but sometimes went out there and sat there looking around, the faint smell of my past life and little reminders of how it used to be all round me. I put the teddy on the bed and sometimes lay there and talked into the air to them both.

But never once did I hear anything other than the sighing of the wind and my own voice.

Before I knew where I was, winter arrived and Christmas was coming and people everywhere were planning parties and of course, Serena's wedding on the horizon and everything there for me to take up the reins and move on.

So bit by little painful bit, I tried.

I hadn't been around for most of the planning of the wedding. I had been lost for most of 1992, in a daze, a dream world of sorts and she had tried to keep her plans secret from me, I guess not wanting me to feel bad when she felt so happy.

Her fiancé had come to meet her family and by all accounts he was great.

Not one to do things by halves she had decided that the best place to get married was in France and we were all flying over.

"Makes sense really, Michel is all caught up in this European thing and he can't be far from the office, so we'll have a big party and honeymoon over there" She smiled.

"And tell me" laughed Becky "Does he realize that half of Ireland is coming on your honeymoon too?"

"And that half of us haven't a word of the lingo and he's going to be worn out interpreting things for us" interjected Nancy.

We were all staying in the wedding hotel, a chateau, if you wouldn't mind, for a couple of days.

"Of course, the more the merrier and his interpretive skills are fine" She grinned.

"Well, they say the language of lurve is universal!" Nancy sang. She was looking much happier now. Seems there was a new man on the scene, since Becky had moved out, Nancy had been spending a lot of time holed up in her flat. Poor Eddie was walking round like a drooping hound, wondering what this new man had that he hadn't.

I didn't tell him that the new man was someone fairly spectacular, someone that even I thought was the cat's pajamas. And the little bits that Nancy let out about him sounded pretty good, like that she had met his mother and he and she were practically living together already. I hadn't met him yet, but Jesus you'd want to be living under a stone not to know who Denny Palmer was in 1992. He was everywhere, back then.

It had been love at first sight with them, or lust as she dryly remarked. And seeing him on the television with his band was a revelation, because you could see he had star quality in spades.

Nancy being Nancy was quite pragmatic about it all and made out that she was only having a fling or something because she knew he was going to hit the big time and probably leave her behind him. All to stop her being hurt. I prayed that this wouldn't be the case for her. That he wasn't going to leave her when his star began to really rise.

David and I were going to the wedding in France. We didn't want to be in Ireland for Christmas, personally, I wanted to forget the whole thing, so with that in mind we were flying to Paris with Becky for Christmas Eve and then down to the south of France on the 28th, for the wedding. Nancy was meeting us on the 28th herself, having spent Christmas with Denny, before he flew out to Hamburg for a load of gigs.

It was snowing and bitterly cold when we landed, and the lights in the city were pure magic. I felt lonely, especially watching Becky and David and how happy they were, with the relationship blossoming between them. I spent a lot of time wandering around alone in the night time, looking st the lights and the amazing things in the shop windows that I couldn't begin to afford. Although that might be changing soon.

David had taken what I wrote in hospital and read it, and had asked me about publishing it-

"God Dave I don't know, do you think it's all right?"

I didn't think anyone would want to read it. There was too much misery and pain in it.

"Maybe a bit of work on it and it just might, its kind of raw at the minute"

So I took it and some days I just re read and wrote bits and pieces, fleshing out the story and making it more understandable for anyone who might read it and who hadn't lived in it.

And it was hard sometimes because in re writing this stuff I was reliving it. I could close my eyes and be back there in the mobile, listening to Leonard Cohen and watching the smoke from the incense winding into the air, and feel Steven's arms round me and his breath on my skin.

Some mornings I would wake up and hold my breath, because he would be there and I just didn't want him to leave me. If only I could hold on for one minute more, the spell, the curse on my life, would break, and there he would be, and all of this would be a bad dream. I would cling on, sure that I could feel him, sure that he was there and it would only take a minute more of blind faith, and I would get my reward.

I'd try to pray, begging God for one more minute with him. The prayers nothing more than me repeating "Please God, please" over and over.

But it was like the day I went to the medium, and got so disappointed, nothing ever came of it and I had to let him go. The alarm would go off or someone would knock on the door and I'd be forced to open my eyes and face reality.

Gary

Colleen and I were married in 1992.

I had been so busy with everything with work that I barely had time to think about what I was doing. I was working hard, going between Italy and London and France and basically doing all I could to get things moving and keep the London office afloat. The staffs in the London office were a bit strange at first, I guessed it was because I had left them in the lurch for so long and then stepped back into my old role. I suppose there was a certain amount of resentment, you know, the old "Bosses son" thing happening.

I mean for at least eight months they thought I was dead and buried or at least washed out to sea and I suppose that someone had been given my job and now here I was back there and into it all again.

Colleen and I took a flat in London and she transferred to a hospital in Westminster and worked shifts. She wasn't looking forward to the move to the continent and I knew she would miss her mum.

She's a nice girl Colleen. I mean, I knew that I was lucky to have her in my life, she was trying to build me back up, put me back together and hold me when I didn't know what I wanted.

Sometimes I felt so confused and lost. I could sit for hours trying to untangle my mind, trying to remember something but the truth was, I just couldn't. It was all there, I knew it but it was out of reach.

We hardly made love; we barely slept in the same bed. The only time I reached for her was when that dream came and then I went into a depression that lasted days on end. It hardly seemed worth it.

I was walking to work one morning and passed some road works and the smell of the tar they were using near drove me out of my mind. I couldn't think why. But for an instant I could smell the sea. As soon as I found something it would go, and I would be depressed again.

I tried everything I could think of to bring back my memory and it just didn't work. I spent ages going back and forward to the hospital and even there they told me the condensed version of my life so far and I was told just to go out and live and it would all be okay. But I knew in my heart that this just wasn't right! There was more, there had to be.

One Saturday morning I was lying in bed and Colleen got up to make coffee and something about the way she turned and looked at me gave me a jolt-

"Carrie" I said. And this feeling of elation came over me, like I had found a diamond or something in a muck pile. Like I had found something at last that fit into my memory.

"What?" Colleen looked white as a sheet.

"Do you know someone called Carrie?"

"No, I don't, do you think its someone you used to know?" she asked. I hated to see that worried look on her face; almost as if she expected me to take flight and go to the place I'd come from and leave her there.

"Colleen I really don't know where that came from, I just seemed to remember someone called Carrie for a second and then it was gone"

"Maybe you had a friend called Carrie or something" she said.

"Maybe" I didn't know. Somehow the seed was sown then and I figured it was a matter of time. If I had a friend in my old life called Carrie, then where was she now? I mean, I was here and alive, so where was she? Surely anyone I was friends with then would be here now? I realized that I didn't have any friends, not people I remembered anyhow. I thought that at some stage I was going to have to start seriously looking into my life and my past and see what the truth really was.

So did Colleen, evidently, because when I looked at her again she was sobbing-

"Colleen, what is it? What's wrong?"

"I'm afraid that one day you will find your old life and you will run away back to it and leave me and, and I love you so much, I couldn't bear that" she wept.

I climbed out of bed and held her. I tried to comfort her and she quietened after a few minutes, and we went back to bed, but, did you ever lie there thinking-

"This isn't it; this isn't the way it's meant to be"

It's almost like my body knew, even if my heart and mind didn't know, that there had been more, that there had been something, and that something, literally, was what I was missing!

I never felt with her that I was one with her. I always knew she was a separate person, a separate entity to me, that the act of making love didn't make us one, not even close. I knew she was afraid of losing me, and God, I was afraid of being kept!

For some reason I felt that we were wrong, but by that stage we were on the rollercoaster to the wedding and I just couldn't get off.

But I couldn't figure out why, every time I lay in bed with Colleen, I felt like I was betraying someone. And every time I slept, I felt like I was betraying Colleen.

The wedding was a quiet affair, the end of summer, just before the weather really turns in Scotland and winter draws in. Originally it was planned for July, but Granddad wasn't well, he was prone to getting chest infections and things were ropy for a while with him, so just in case, we put it back a couple of months.

We had it in the little church in the village and the reception in the house. Granddad like the old man of wisdom in his chair in the library, looking over all and nodding his head now and then.

We didn't honeymoon, we decided to wait till the following Christmas and go somewhere nice then. So it was cool when the invite to Michel Moraine's wedding came.

If truth be told, things were getting bad between me and Colleen by then. She felt claustrophobic not being able to work and she wanted to spend a lot of time in her mother's house and I needed her with me when I was working to bring a bit of normality to my life.

Somehow I don't think being married was what she thought it was going to be, it was like the idea had sounded good but the actual reality wasn't?

And let's face facts here; she hadn't gotten the bargain of the decade in me, had she?

So the thought of Christmas in Paris was a good diversion-

Except she wouldn't go for Christmas day, but down to the little terrace in Liverpool to her family and then, onto a plane for Paris on the 27th December.

I had to keep telling myself that she was a kid in a lot of ways and that I should give her a bit of leeway and not be too hard on her even though she cried all the way to Paris because it was the first time out of the UK for New Year and what would her Mam do without her calling her?

"Can't you ring her at midnight, I mean the wedding is the 28th, we will be free to do whatever we want by then" I tried to comfort, but ended up opening a can of worms.

She asked could we fly back to Liverpool that night and be there for New Year and I sighed and said that I had booked us into a hotel for a few days honeymoon and did she not want to do that?

But she didn't want to do anything. Right then and there I knew we wouldn't last. I felt stifled in this marriage and it was never going to make her happy.

So we got to Paris and we stayed in the fanciest of hotels and she spent the whole time watching BBC on the telly and ringing her mother. I walked around and around in Paris, going along cobbled little streets and down by the Seine where I had imagined bringing her but she was always too tired to go.

I woke up at four o clock one morning, the morning of the wedding, and realized that I hadn't even made it to bed. I was half lying on the couch and had a blinding headache. That happened sometimes. It was the bang on the head, the concussion, I got when the accident happened that did it. They said.

And somehow, in Paris, the dreaming was more real and lucid than ever.

It happened without any warning. I'd been there, trying to make love with Colleen, and then suddenly it was like I was out of myself and the place we were in, and it was someone else, not her, and I squeezed my eyes tight shut and tried desperately to hold on to it, to see could I finally find in Colleen what I was looking for, and then she said something or cried out, and I found myself snapped back into the real world again.

And she knew well. It had happened the previous morning, in bed in Paris, in the hotel, we'd pulled apart and I was lying with my eyes shut, catching my breath.

"Where do you go Gary?"

"What?" I was fighting the overwhelming feeling of loneliness, and wasn't up to thinking right then.

"Where are you when we have sex, because I know it's not with me?"

Panic struck me and I tried to make her feel better. Why, I don't know. Maybe I thought she would be hurt too much by the truth. I could handle another life and another being in my head and my heart. But it wasn't very fair on her when she was the one in my bed.

"Don't be daft, how could I be anywhere else?" I tried to pull her into my arms, but coldness was creeping between us like a wet blanket.

"No Gary listen to me" she pulled away and half sat up, the words tumbling out and her hands folded on her stomach-

"I'm listening"

"Sometimes you're with me and I know it, and then other times, you drift away, and you look at me and I know you're not seeing me, but that there's someone else, a shadow, that only you know is there, and that I will never live up to, and when I call out to you and you come back, the look of disappointment on your face is so awful, I can't bear it"

"Col, I didn't know, I didn't realize, I'm sorry" I thought that I had hidden it better than that. How could I have been so transparent?

"Gary, I love you, I know I do, but I'm not it, I can't be it, because you don't know what it is, and I'm afraid that when you figure it out you're going to leave me, so, I am going to have to do what I think is right now, to save myself, and that is to leave you"

I sat up and looked straight at her-

"What are you saying Colleen?"

"I want a divorce Gary, I, I just can't live like this, I can't be with you when its not meant to be me, I thought that I could make you forget her, but how can I when you haven't remembered her yet and your chasing her shadow"

"Colleen, for Gods sake, listen" I tried to grab her hand and she pulled away.

"All my life I've lived in Layla's shadow, and I am damned if I am spending the rest of my days living in this Carrie's shadow too, it's over Gary, I can't do it anymore"

"I don't know anyone called Carrie, Jesus Coll' what are you trying to do to me?"

"I'm trying to make you see sense, trying to make you understand that its over, what we had, it's gone Gary, and I can't do it any more"

So all that day we talked and into the night and she was adamant.

She wouldn't come to Michel's wedding but would fly home next day to Liverpool and her Mam. And I could do as I pleased. I sat up all night, and dozed off on the sofa, and woke early and went out for a walk.

The air was bitingly cold and I wandered around kicking the slush and thinking that my life was taking more turns than a bad film. Three months married and this happens! Grandfather would hit the roof! He had ways of showing his displeasure, subtle ways that made me wonder was I really all he wanted in a grandson, or was I a disappointment to him. He was quite a domineering character and the people who worked with me would clam up when his name was mentioned, giving me nothing in return for the questions I asked.

Colleen had been quiet and repeated herself a couple of times, talking about how her parents never got over the loss of her sister and how every time she did something good, or it was her birthday or whatever, Layla, as her mother and father called her, would be brought into it.

"I wonder would they have had me if she'd lived." She asked me once.

"Come on Colleen, you must know they love you, they were so proud of you going into nursing, you're being silly"

"Gary I don't expect you to understand, its like I am constantly trying to be what she might have been, because they look at me and what I am doing and they wonder wether she would be like me too, I can't live in someone else's shadow forever, and I thought when we married that finally I would be my own person, and now I see that I am not, that still there's a shadow over me, a faceless person that I can never live up to, just like its been all my life with Layla"

"But you are your own person, marrying me didn't change who you are"

257

"I thought that having a new name would be like being reborn, into a new life" She sighed.

"Colleen love, it takes more than a new name to make a person, you are what you are, and who you are, and changing a name makes no difference to that, its what is in your heart and soul and what you feel is what matters" I'd said, and with that hammered the final nail into the coffin.

"Well, now you know, you just said it, you're not what I thought you were and I am certainly not the woman you want, though you might think it so, Go away Gary, please, just let me go and be alone" She'd gone into the bedroom and left me on the couch in the suite, brooding until I finally slept.

Part of me was wondering was this the way I wanted to spend the rest of this life, at the beck and call of an old man who controlled every minute of my days at times. Even living in London gained me no freedom and I saw very little but work and home.

I knew that I wasn't easy to live with. There were times like I said, that flashes would come and I would try to make sense of the things I saw and felt and couldn't, and no one could tell me what was real and what wasn't.

Except for my grandfather who had plausible explanations for everything I did and felt and saw. Amnesia was a queer thing, he said, and it was obvious that something had disturbed the balance of my mind.

At times I thought he might get me locked up, thinking that I was a bit mad or something. The threat hung in the air many times. I had no doubt that he could do it if he wanted to.

Every single day of my life was a fight to keep my sanity. Because I knew that what I had, just wasn't what I was meant to have.

There had to be a key, a way to unlock this cloud that covered me. There had to be someone that could help me, tell me what I was doing wrong.

I couldn't even escape it when I slept, in fact that was when I felt I was in the right place and hated to wake up. I would see things; see images and people that weren't here and now, but that I must have known.

Sometimes I would feel angry, overwhelming anger, and all I could do then was go out and walk it off. Colleen would be working nights sometimes and I would walk and walk around London, trying to decipher what was going through my head, trying to figure out what was real and what was a dream.

I felt like I was living in a nightmare and couldn't get out of it, I got no rest and no help from anyone.

Somewhere out there was the truth.

And now, here I was, in Paris, the most romantic place on earth, on the verge of divorce after three months of marriage, and still walking the streets not knowing who or what I was.

Early morning is my favorite time to walk anywhere; I would roam around London at five am and not see anything mad in that. You get to see the other side of the city that way, when its all just kicking off, waking up to the new day. I kicked at the slush in the gutters and turned corners blindly. Not that that was a surprise to me in my present state of mind.

A clock somewhere chimed four am and I leant against a wall for a rest for a second, sometimes my legs got tired with walking and I would take a break and just people watch. Not that there were too many people round here at this hour of the morning.

There was a big hotel, not as fancy as my own, but nice all the same, over on the other side of the street. I thought that they might have somewhere I might sit for a moment. I was just about to walk over when I saw a woman, well, a girl really, come running out, her hair flying over the collar of a long black coat. She pulled it round her and walked up the hill, trying not to slip on the cobbles.

For some reason my heart leapt. I actually felt it move inside me. I put my hand to my chest for a second and watched her walk up the hill.

I decided to walk that way, for no other reason than curiosity. I mean, how many people, girls especially, go out walking at that hour of the morning?

I tell you, she could sprint along when she wanted to, and by the time I got to the top of the hilly street, she had already turned the corner and was talking to a couple of Gendarmes in the road, waving her arms like a windmill trying to make herself understood.

She had red hair, and it curled madly over her shoulders, and her face was pale skinned, and as I got closer, I thought I could see freckles. She was lovely, her eyes all sparkly with the cold. I got this feeling that I wanted to touch her, tuck her curls back behind her ears, and hold her... trace my fingers down to where her coat collar opened and I could see her skin.

I must be going mad! I should have turned and walked away, but I didn't.

I waited till she walked on and fell into step a little bit behind her.

She said something out loud so I figured she might know I was there and so I answered her. I must have frightened the life out of her though, because she stood dead still and asked me would I be there when she turned around.

I prayed she wasn't a nutter, a lunatic. But I was certain that it was a hotel she came from and not a hospital, so I told her I was real, and then she turned around.

And that was it, that was the click I was waiting for, that was the key that unlocked the memories, and once again I knew who I was.

"Oh Steven, I've missed you so much" she wept as I stood holding her while the snow fell again. That woody perfume surrounded me and I touched her face and knew, I just knew it was right.

Steven.

Is that me? Is that who I really am? Who I am meant to be? I was standing there holding her while her body shook with sobbing and was dying to ask her more and more questions, clear this mess up once and for all.

"Who are you?" I asked, as she pulled at her collar and took a ring out on a chain.

"Carrie, I'm your Carrie, I'm taking you home"

12

Carrie

We had flown out to France on the afternoon before Christmas. I had to admit that Paris was beautiful, there was real snow and twinkly little lights everywhere and the Eiffel Tower was all lit up with a laser show as well. Beautiful.

Silly though it sounds, I wondered if Steven could see it where he was. Could he see his father falling in love with Becky? What would he say? I guessed he'd be happy for him, and had to make do with that. No matter how hard I tried now, I couldn't conjure up his voice in my head any more, or his laughter. He was really and truly going from me and the thought of that killed me. I couldn't bear the silence. I tried to console myself with the thought that little Saoirse was with him, but it didn't work.

I had to try and deal with one thing at a time.

Walking and thinking for hours on end, I tried to come to terms with losing all I had and remembered that I had been blessed once, and maybe one day I would be again.

I just couldn't visualize being in love again, no matter how hard I tried or no matter what Nancy said.

"You know what kid, my motto is, best way to get over a man is to get under another" She said that one night in the pub, ages ago, long before all this happened.

I suppose it was a good method for getting over the general heartbreak inflicted by ninety per cent of the men we dated, but what did you do if it wasn't another woman or a bag of coke that took the man, how did you get over death?

I couldn't begin to think about seeing anyone else, starting over, the thought of making love to anyone was alien to me.

"I think I am destined to be alone forever Becky" I said, looking out at the lights from the hotel window our first night in Paris.

"I mean it, no more love, no more sex, no more babies or anything, I'll live like this, on my own forever, I just can't see any other way" My thinking was that if I had nothing then I had nothing left to lose.

"I know, it must be so hard for you Carrie, it's terrible, I just don't know what to say" She hugged me.

"I feel so selfish Becky, I lost my child, and it hurts, but it's losing Steven that still kills me inside, should it be that way?" She said nothing, and I continued talking-

"I'll never forget him, but its like, I'm losing even my memories of him, its like, God took him, but he, I can't even keep him in my head, I used to be able to hear his voice in my head, see his face in my mind, but he's going from me now, I'm forgetting him Becks, and I don't want to" I didn't want to be crying now, not tonight, but the tears would come despite my best efforts to keep them in.

"I know, I know, Oh its so unfair, I wonder sometimes is there a God up there at all" She was crying too, and we both reached for the tissues and laughed.

"God, it's always the same with us two, tears and snots when we're supposed to be happy" I blew my nose and tried to stop crying.

I truly believed that I would never ever be happy again though. I had lost too much of myself to ever truly laugh or feel joy inside me again.

I certainly didn't want to stop believing in God, but it was hard. I couldn't believe that this was all a part of a master plan, a bigger picture that would come clear one day.

All I had left were a couple of photos and a teddy bear and a caravan where the sounds and the visions of my life were fading like the wallpaper on the walls. I couldn't even bring myself to play some of the music or burn the incense any more. It was too painful, it brought back too many memories that I just couldn't handle.

And do you know what? I figure that if there is a God, some old geezer sitting in a long white nightie on a throne in the clouds, well he is going to have some serious explaining to do when and if I ever meet him.

How much loss is one person supposed to take before they die? How much pain is a human mind supposed to handle before it loses its grip on reality and closes down forever? I don't know why I was still alive, I figured there had to be a reason, but I tell you something, it was going to be one hell of a hard and empty life, because I couldn't see what would ever make me better, now that everything worth living for had gone for good.

We stayed in the hotel for Christmas day, and went sightseeing on St Stephen's day and I spent the next day, the last full one in Paris, wandering around on my own, down to the riverside and out to Marseilles and the palace. I thought about the revolution and the blood washing the streets that were covered now in slush, and I wondered if it was true, that life just carried on regardless, and that the past slowly dies away for the ones that have to go on living.

I mean, all those people that died were somebody to someone. They were mothers and fathers and they were flesh and blood and their blood would have stained the cobbles when the guillotine had done its job. And someone would weep and mourn their loss, wouldn't they? I remembered doing something about the Tudors in religion in school and about the way Henry the Eighth turned everything to suit him and beheaded Anne Boleyn to marry Jane Seymour and that his previous fight to separate from Katherine of Aragon was the foundation of the Protestant church.

And the nun had said that he had his wife Anne beheaded because she was a slut, a woman who took lovers, one of which was meant to be her own brother in the search for the heir for Henry's throne.

The thought that came to me back then was that some people, the day she was beheaded, called her whore, and yet some called her a sainted martyr. So some people loved her and some hated her. And feelings must have run high there and people must have cried.

But sooner or later the blood had faded and the people who loved her would have died too and the day came when no one remembered them and nobody cared. I mean the only reason I knew about her was because Henry was a king, and a mad bollocks if the truth be told, and the cause of the split in the church, which is what the nun was trying to hammer into our thick heads that day.

I remember the way she put it-

"Men will re write law and history for a woman, look at Parnell, sure even the law of God meant nothing, and the infallibility of the pope meant nothing to Henry the eighth, a bad woman can bring down a country, a government, anything"

I stood looking at the muddy green water of the Seine; watching it pass under the bridge and remembered the time when the nuns brought us to the graveyard in Glasnevin where all the old graves of the dignitaries of Ireland were. I remembered being bored to tears looking at the moss covered stone and thinking that I didn't care a damn.

And there were millions of graves, all over the world where there was no one left to remember and no one left to care.

Now a couple of years on and I was tending a couple of graves of my own and I understood better what it meant. And how fleeting this life was, because the day would come when the moss would creep across the stone that covered my daughter and my lover and my mother and my brothers, because there was no one left to care.

"Someday, no one will remember me, no one will care about all the things that happened to me, it will all be gone" I whispered, and turned away from the river and walked on alone. My memories are in my mind and that's all. And when I die they die too, and everything I learnt will die with me. I felt indescribably sad that there was no way of keeping it all real and alive. Such a waste, isn't it? Everything I know and anything I learnt, well, it would die when I did, because no one lives inside us only ourselves.

"Coffee, Conway, you're getting fucking maudlin" I shivered, and walked faster through the damp and cold. I found a little café and sat in the steamy gloom till they threw me out at closing time, and then slowly walked to the hotel.

On that, my last night in Paris, I sat up till all hours and re-wrote some stuff about our time together before the news broke about us and I fell into a strange sleep, in the chair, and woke with a blinding migraine headache. I tried to think what might have triggered it but couldn't, and tried to rest for a while. But the nausea and the thumping headache was getting worse. I looked in my bag and couldn't find any aspirin and cursed. I pulled on a coat and went down to the reception. I pressed my hand to my temple trying to relieve the banging inside my head and felt the room spinning around me.

I don't speak much more than pigeon French and couldn't make the guy on the reception desk understand me and so stormed out into the street, in temper and frustration, looking for a chemist.

"There has to be a bloody chemist here, look for a cross, that's what they normally have everywhere" I muttered, trying to think of a French word for headache, or aspirin...

I saw a couple of Gendarmes and tried to explain to them what I wanted.

"Pharmacy?" I said hopefully. I thought that I might have the right word but you never know. I could feel myself getting nauseous again and swallowed hard. That's all I needed, to throw up on a policeman and get locked in a cell!

He started into a spiel of words, rapid French and I waved my hand-

"Non, Non Parley Francais, merci" I thanked my lucky stars that I at least knew this phrase, even if my accent was so bog thick you could have cut it with a shovel! Good old Sister Rita in the convent, something from her interminable lessons in French grammar had stayed in my sieve of a brain.

He laughed and began again-

"Oui Mademoiselle, le Pharmacy, is there, you go to the left, and it is on that street, a big place, and opens all night, yes?"

Thank God for that, another hour of this headache and I'll be stone blind.

"Thank you so much, merci, au revoir" I waved and they went off. I laughed to myself as I went on-

"That's about as much French as I remember from my schooldays, thank heaven I remember something" I must have said it aloud, because someone answered me.

"I'm a bit like that too"

I felt my insides freeze and I stopped dead in my tracks. It couldn't be. It *couldn't.*

Oh My God, is this it? Am I going crazy? Is this the final act in my life? Is this the bit where I finally go fucking insane? Is it him? Could it really be him?

I took a shuddering breath-

"What?" I gasped

"I use up my whole repertoire of words when I am here and hope that they understand what the heck I'm saying, when I say it"

I had to be imagining it, the voice came from behind me and I shook with fear, or maybe it was longing. I had migraine before, but never had they made me hallucinate!

Please God, please, please. I begged in my mind.

The accent was slightly different, sort of English, a bit like a disc jockey, that non offensive, mid atlantic accent they all had. But the smile in his voice was the same.

Its him, I know it is, it's Steven, but how the hell can it be? I have to be dying, because I know his will be the first voice I hear when I die.

I was still standing with my back to him, afraid to breathe almost, afraid that I would move and wake up, in the armchair in my room and it would all be a dream, like so many other times.

"I'm going to turn round now; will you be there when I do?"

Please please be there, don't go away again, please stay there. Even if I am going to die, I want to go with you. I'll follow you into hell if I have to, please stay.

"Of course" He laughed, a little nervously, truth be told. He must have thought I was a nut case or something. Let's face it; I was acting like one, wasn't I?

Oh My God what is happening, is this a dream, oh God help me please. I don't care if the world forgets me in a second, if this is when I have to die then so be it, but, please God let him be there when I turn around.

I kept looking down and saw the snow in grey puddles in the gutters. I saw my breath in frosty clouds, I saw the shoes, the legs and then I lifted my head and saw him there-

Dressed in a heavy jacket made of suede and with jeans on, boots, his hair shorter than I remembered, but with those eyes still the same, the one part of him that stayed longest in my memory were those light blue eyes, the colour of the stars in winter, like iced water, heavy lidded and dark lashed. I would always remember them.

I closed my eyes and shivered, head spinning, I felt my legs buckle and the feeling of wanting to be sick came back with a vengeance.

"Oh..." I groaned, and he grabbed me to stop me falling into the slush.

"Hey, are you okay?" He shook me a little and I felt him, he was really there!

"You're... Oh you're really here" I gasped.

And I hate to say this, I hate to destroy all the romantic thoughts that would be racing through anyone's head when they have an experience like this, but I was shaking with fright and joy and a whole gamut of emotion, and the whole lot combined made me lose my grip on the ground, sink to my knees and literally puke for Ireland.

He held my hair away from my face and I suppose that he must have been dying to run away, but he didn't. I remember the sweat on my face freezing cold and the pain in my chest as I retched.

"God you're really ill" he whispered, pulling a wad of hankies out of his pocket and handing them to me.

I wiped my mouth and got back on my feet again. He made to let go of me and I grabbed his hand-

"Steven, oh God"

He frowned and stepped back a little-

"What did you say?" he asked. I remember thinking that he looked like a man in the dark, like someone had pulled a curtain down over his eyes, like he was dead inside, and that this was my opportunity to shine a light in and make him whole again.

"You're really real" I grabbed him tightly. I stopped shaking and held him. My headache was gone now.

"Darlin', oh God, Steven, come home with me, please don't leave me again"

He looked confused, as well he might, I suppose.

"Hey listen, I don't know what the heck is wrong with you but maybe I can bring you to..." He stopped and I saw it, something changing him, a look in his eye, and I held my breath, waiting.

"I know you, don't I? You know who I am?"

"Know you? For fucks sake! It's me, its Carrie, Steven it's me" I shook him.

"Carrie?"

"Steven you have to know me, I'm Carrie, remember me? Dublin and the baby and your Dad, he's here Steven, *please*, you have to know me" I was shivering with cold, the snow was falling again, the back of my collar was letting in flakes and I was getting wet, and yet I couldn't have cared less.

"I don't know who..." He was backing away and was leaning against the wall of the bank.

He was shaking all over and I could see him, closing his eyes tightly and pressing his hand against his forehead.

"God this is weird, you have that smell, that patchouli oil stuff, I remembered it before, I do know you, I have to remember something" he muttered.

"You have to remember me, Jesus we thought you were dead, we thought you died in the lorry, Steven please" I was sobbing now, so hard I could hardly talk or see, but I held the cuff of his coat like it was a lifeline. I couldn't let him go; he couldn't run away now, before he had a chance to know who he was.

"You *know* about the lorry?"

I laughed aloud. Not that it was funny, mind.

Know about it? Every time I tried to sleep I could see it, smell the smoke and feel the flames blistering my skin.

"Yes, I do, I know because we thought you had died there and we, we buried someone thinking it was you"

"Who are you?"

"I'm Carrie, I'm... Oh God Steven, it's been hell without you, pure hell" I threw my arms round him and he held onto me tightly. I must have smelt horrible and looked dreadful, Make up smeared and a big mucky patch on my coat from when I was kneeling to be sick, but he didn't seem to care and as for me, well, I was fucking elated!

He thrust me away and looked into my eyes-

"I have a father? Alive? My father is dead, he's gone... I only have a grandfather, he told me so" He pushed my hair back and stared at me hard. I looked up into his eyes and a wave of desire shot through me and nearly flattened me. I gasped. I didn't want to scare him away; I pulled away slightly and opened the top button of my coat.

"You've seen him? Your grandfather? What does he say?" I had to think of something to reach him, maybe he didn't believe in me, or believe what I was saying. I fumbled with fingers that had turned to jelly at the collar of my shirt.

I reached under my clothes and pulled out the long silver chain I wore round my neck-

"This is your ring Steven, your Grandfather is James Bard, he lives in Scotland, Your fathers name is David, and he's about three streets away in a hotel, we're going to a wedding later today"

"I don't believe you" he gasped. He reached out and took the ring, still hanging on the chain, still warm from being next to my skin, and turned it over to read the initials-

"Oh fuck, I remember this, you gave this to me, I wondered where it was" He half laughed-

"I wasn't going crazy, I was right all along"

"Come with me now and see for yourself" I half dragged him down the street and into the hotel.

Up in the lift we went and I ran down the corridor to the room where Becky and David were sleeping.

I hammered on the door and Becky came bleary eyed to the door-

"Carrie, its five in the morning...what the fuck?" She groaned.

"Look, look who I found!"

Becky screamed and grabbed the door to hold her up-

"David! Get out here now!"

I heard movement and David came to the door and went white-

"Jesus Christ, it can't be!" He gasped.

I held Stevens hand so tight I thought his bones would break-

"I found him David, I found him, and he's coming home again"

13

Carrie

When Nancy arrived over for the wedding later that day she literally screamed for a full five minutes. (In between thumping Steven every now and then and calling him a bollocks for dying in the first place).

Nancy never changes.

"Christ almighty Steven, if you only knew what we all went through, I could have killed myself with the guilt of giving you the means to leave the country in the first place, and then it was me that had to tell Carrie, you have no idea what it was like" She wept.

"I didn't know, I didn't know anything, I thought I was going mad because I could see things sometimes, I dreamt of all of you and thought I was going nuts" He kept saying.

I was in a daze, couldn't take my eyes off him. Where ever he went I had to be within arms reach of him and he seemed to know how I was feeling. There was no time to be alone, the story was told and retold and marveled over again and again.

It had been a tremendous morning. Its not every day someone comes back from the dead is it?

"Do you remember anything about what happened, anything at all?" David asked. Poor David's hands were still shaking and he was knocking back so much brandy that I thought we would never get him out of the hotel and into a plane to fly south.

"I remember the accident sort of, and then I woke up months later in hospital, and they were calling me Gary, so I thought that was who I was" He got up and went over to the window. And from what I could see, his lovely grandfather hadn't helped him at all, had just built the web of lies for him to live in and hoped that it wouldn't be discovered.

"But being here with you guys, I know it's where I belong, and I remember more now than I did before, because I know it's not just a dream, do you see?"

I suppose I understood. I guess when you're told that "this is real and what your thinking is not" you somehow stop trusting your mind and you fall into step.

But I couldn't imagine what it would have been like had he walked into Serena's wedding and we'd met there. I said as much.

Nancy laughed-

"Can you imagine the drama? Serena would kill us, and Michel, it's taken him this long to get her up the aisle he'd murder us all rather than delay the wedding"

But I thought that somehow this was all down to more than fate and karma and co incidence. I mean, as the song went-

"Had I turned a different corner, we never would have met"

I was beside myself with happiness. I thanked God and everyone in heaven for migraines and not knowing French and for this happy wonderful accident!

"The worst part of all this is that I knew there was another life that I just couldn't remember, and you see..." He was still explaining, and suddenly turned and stared at me and I could feel the shiver up my spine. Whatever this was I was not going to like it at all.

"Carrie, I know I, and you, we were something, I could feel it every time I, but the thing is that, I married someone else in September"

"Oh Jesus Christ I don't believe it" Nancy grabbed another drink and gulped it.

"Married?" I gasped "Who?"

"A girl called Colleen, she was one of the nurses in the hospital, she's actually a lot like you now I think of it, and..."

A lot like me.

But not me. Did this mean that he wanted to go away again?

"Do you love her" My heart felt like someone had poured ice water into it. My voice was flat and dead, and I felt tiny, insignificant.

"No, not the way I should, but you have to believe me I didn't *know*"

"Are you going to stay with her?"

"No, No way, she, she asked me for a divorce last night, she knows that you exist, even before I knew, so she told me she wanted out, she's in the hotel now, probably packing her things up to go back to Liverpool, I think I will have to go back and talk to her soon, tell her what happened"

"What will you say to her? I mean how will you explain this to her?"

"I don't know, but I tell you, now that I know who I am, I don't think I can go back to the way things were before, I need to find out everything"

"Oh, so you have figured out that there's more to this then?" David asked.

"Well there has to be, Why would Grandfather go along with some cockamamie lie about who I was when he obviously knows quite well, I mean, if I was quite happy in Ireland with Carrie and all of you, what the hell was I doing in a lorry on route to Glasgow in the first place?

"That's a bloody horrible, long story Steven, you'd better go back and sort things with Colleen first and then come back to us here, and we'll fill you in then" Nancy sighed.

Nancy usually got angry and stomped around when things like this happened. It was rare that she allowed her soft side free rein. But this time, when he had left us to go and talk to his wife, she buried her face in her hands and sighed heavily. A heavy silver ring on her finger tangled into her hair. I made a mental note to ask her about it later on, when all this madness ended.

"Carrie love, I don't envy you one bit of this"

"I know"

"How much are we going to tell him?" She sniffed and wiped the tears off her face. The green stone glittered on her finger. She saw me looking and shook her head slightly.

I nodded.

"Everything, I suppose, he has to know" I looked at David and Becky who were standing near the window.

"Don't you think so?" I nodded to them.

"Everything, and then we have to see what's next, because now, there's the small matter of him being alive, and the criminal prosecution that's bound to ensue when the Gardai get wind of it all, it might not be so easy for you still Carrie" David said.

"What? You mean they still might prosecute? That's crazy! I mean we all thought he was dead, we buried him for fucks sake!"

I just listened to the talk going round and round and said nothing. In all of my wildest dreams, I had never ever seen this happening. My Steven was back with me, where he belonged, and now it seemed that the can of worms was being reopened and re-examined.

"Well, if you want my opinion" Said Becky "you need to fight hard and keep him, and you need to do all the things we were going to do in 1990 to find out why this mess happened in the first place, because its fate, and you need to sort it before you can hope for any kind of life, I mean, how can you think that this is the end, that you guys will be able to go back to Blanch and live in the mobile again like nothing ever happened? They'll hunt you down and persecute you all over again, and this time it will be worse, because you'll lose him all over again"

And she was right. Time could not be erased and the past was still there, and for any hope of a future, we had to make that decision, either run for it, or face what needed to be faced and go home with our heads held high.

I knew that I couldn't live again without having him with me. I wasn't going to lose him to anyone.

But still I was on tenterhooks till he came back from talking to his wife.

He came back about three hours later. Colleen had gone and he had seen her to the airport. She had seemed stoic and calm about everything. All he told her was that he had met some of his family and was going to be with them for a while.

She thought he'd planned it. Though he told her he didn't, that it was all by chance.

"I'm going to travel with you guys to the wedding" he said. His bag in hand as he came through the door.

He came and stood in front of me, really close, till I thought he was finally going to kiss me. But he didn't.

"Is that okay with you?" he smiled. He still looked sad, along with the tiredness I saw etched into his face, maybe he loved Colleen more than he realized.

I nodded. I'd deal with that later. On our own.

"Course it is, come on" I took his hand.

"Right then, lets go, we can talk later" David went into his own room and stuffed his clothes into a bag.

We went off to the airport and started the last part of the journey to Serena and Michel's wedding.

And boy did we have a surprise for them!

The taxi pulled up at the terrace of houses in the Wirral and Colleen Bard stepped out. The twinkling Christmas tree was still standing in the front window and she rang her mother's doorbell and waited.

"Colleen love! We thought you were in France!" Jimmy opened the door wide.

"Val, it's our Colleen home, where's Gary?" he asked grabbing the bag in off the step.

"He's still over there Dad, oh Dad!" she crumpled into sobs and he grabbed her tightly.

"What's happened? Have you had a row?

"No, we, we split up Dad, he, he found his other family, he isn't who I thought he was at all, oh Dad, what will I do?"

"Come in off the step love, come on, get a nice cup of tea and we'll talk about this, god love you, you're frozen" He led her into the warm living room and she sat on the sofa.

She told them everything-

"I knew one day he'd remember himself and his life before me, and I couldn't live with him knowing there was someone else he loved more than me, so I left him" she wept.

"He said it wasn't fair to me, that now he had found them, now that he knew who he was and what he was, and now that he had found Carrie again, he realized that it was forever, the kind of love he always knew he had, and that I deserved better than that"

"Poor baby, poor Colleen that must be terrible" her mother patted her arm softly.

"His name isn't even Gary, its Steven, he's from Ireland, his father is still alive and do you know what? The wedding we were going to, they know him too, before he was Gary, I mean, so he's gone with them to it, and he said that I was too good for him, that he couldn't give me anything I needed, because he knew from the moment he laid eyes on Carrie again that it was her, it was always her, and he couldn't love anyone else"

"And what about old man Bard? Where does he fit into this?"

"I dunno, I don't think he knows" she sniffed.

"Well someone better tell him what's happened, I mean surely he will be pleased to hear that his grandson is on the mend?"

"Maybe I should ring him and tell him. I mean maybe Gary won't be back for a while and he will need to organize something about work or whatever?" She was already dialing Baird Hall as she spoke.

"Well I do think he should know" said her mother.

"He'll be glad you thought of telling him"

".... So the important thing is that we are the only ones who know about all this" Serena was standing in what was going to be her bridal suite that night, in dressing gown and curlers, drinking a glass of wine.

"Don't get me wrong Steven I am thrilled to see you here, but there's a whole big mess back home needs sorting before you think of coming back and taking up where you left off, and we are better off keeping schtum right now, go under the name Gary Bard for now, do what ever it takes, for now, except with us, of course, you can just be you here with us"

She smiled at me.

"Carrie love, I know its going to be hard, but you have come through worse, and it will get better in the end, I swear to you it will, trust me"

"What about Michel? Does he know anything?" Becky asked

"Not as much as he should, but I can fill him in tomorrow and we can get him working on this too" She laughed "After all I am going to marry him in two hours time so... where pray tell are my bridesmaids? The ones who are supposed to be dancing attendance on me all flipping day?"

"Right here bossy boots, lead on to the frocky horror show" Nancy giggled.

We got ready for the wedding. Serena bless her heart, had gotten me a lovely dress in a champagne coloured silk and asked me then and there to walk up the aisle as a bridesmaid.

"I didn't know if you'd like to, the way things were, you know?" She was a little embarrassed, holding the dress on its hangar, it was shining like molten gold and I reached out and took it.

"It's a lovely dress Serena, really beautiful" I whispered.

The other two were a darker coffee colour. And they weren't a bit frou frou or flouncy, but classy and understated.

"I'd love to be a bridesmaid, thank you for asking me" I hugged her.

"And then the next time you do it will be your own wedding" she hugged me hard.

"You think so?" I couldn't help my heart leaping at the thought.

"Yes I do, because, oh Carrie, I know you were meant to be together and love like that is too important and special to let go for anything"

"I hope you and Michel are really happy 'Rena, I honestly do"

For once Nancy didn't snort or make a smart comment, but was very quiet and I saw her ring glinting in the light as she turned it round on her finger.

And the wedding was beautiful.

Michel was nervous as hell, but Nancy asked-

"Jesus wouldn't you be petrified marrying bossy boots? That one could run the world, never mind the country, lets hope he doesn't mind taking orders" She giggled.

But Serena didn't look bossy at all; she was radiant and glowed with pure happiness as she walked up the aisle on her fathers arm.

I looked across the church at Steven when the vows were being exchanged and his eyes locked with mine as he smiled at me, and I felt the tears prickling the back of my eyes.

I want us to look back at this time, when we are old and grey, and smile, because it was all worth it in the end.

Serena was true to her roots. The music was a mixture of rock and Celtic traditional.

Within fifteen minutes of the reception starting we were all on our feet for a ceili and were having a ball.

David grabbed me and swung me off my feet and my shoe fell off.

"Oh Carrie what a day this is!" he laughed picking it out of the plant pot it landed in.

I knew what he meant. The joy was infectious. The night fell and there were fireworks out in the garden. I found myself beside Steven again, and he slid his arm round me.

"You're lovely, I can't believe I found you again, cos you are what's missing Carrie, I can feel it" he smiled and pulled me nearer.

"Did you know about me, somewhere in your heart, did you remember me?"

He sighed-

"Carrie, even the day I got engaged to Colleen, I knew, I knew it was wrong, I couldn't give her what she wanted, couldn't be a proper husband, and couldn't be anything at all because I felt nothing, nothing at all"

"Oh God Steven, I missed you, so bloody much it near killed me" I could stand there forever, just inhaling his smell and feeling safe with his arm round my shoulders. Watching multi coloured stars streaking the inky sky above.

"What happened? What were we? Back then, I want to know. Could you come and tell me, now?"

"Okay, come over here"

I pulled his arm and we went into a small summerhouse. It was chilly, but not as cold as Paris had been and we sat close together on the bench.

"Tell me the story of us" he whispered. He wrapped his jacket round me and I sighed, I could feel the warmth of his body through it.

"Us?"

"Yeah, all of it, I want to see it, the way it was, so that I know"

There was a sighing in the air, branches rustling and somewhere I was sure, was the sea, waves making a soft whishing sound on the sand.

"Jesus Steven I don't know if I can, do you really not remember any of it?"

"Nothing, start at the bit I know, the accident, why was I in London"

But I couldn't start there, it meant telling him about Saoirse and why he had run and also, inevitably the fact that she was gone, and how.

Truth be told I couldn't face that part myself yet.

"No, I'll tell you what, I'll tell you about the first night I met you"

I felt him smile in the darkness.

"You're avoiding me! Go on then" He leant back against the rough stone of the wall and I lay there against his chest talking-

"It was in the Summer, 1990, we, me and the girls, had gone to McGonagles for a night out, and I was getting fed up, so I was having my last drink out of the bottle down my boot when you called me, and you told me you had been there five weeks in a row and that you were waiting for the chance to speak to me, and so, that night I went back with you to your place, like a shameless hussy, and stayed... and then I moved in with you a few weeks later" Not quite the truth but the best I could do so far.

"I must have loved you from the start, its no wonder really, you're gorgeous" He whispered and I felt my heart leap inside me.

"You think so?" I smiled.

"Course I do, I saw you this morning and thought you looked beautiful, all that red hair and those eyes flashing at the policemen, I was going to ask you for a coffee, if we'd found somewhere open at that hour" He stroked the skin of my shoulder where the dress didn't cover and I felt my whole body tingle. I cuddled closer.

"Even though I puked on your shoes?" I teased.

"Yep, even though you puked on me, your still gorgeous" He smiled.

Just sitting there was magical, just feeling his fingers tracing the skin on my shoulder, knowing that this wasn't only a dream, that it was real. I didn't want to say or do anything to break the spell. I felt him take a breath-

"When I was with Colleen, I used to feel, I used to go away in my mind, far away from her, into another place, and it was you I was looking for, and she knew it before I did, she asked me yesterday, after we, after I..." he faltered.

Feeling sick inside at the thought, I knew what he was trying to tell me. That he had been sleeping with his wife. But in fairness, what did I expect? That he lived like a monk? That he forsook all others when he couldn't have me? Like I had? But then again, I had remembered him, he had no idea where or who I was. Up to now.

"Its okay Steven, I know" I whispered. I patted his hand and stood up, walking across the stone flagged floor to the archway window, that looked out onto the garden. The jacket slid off my shoulders and he caught it before it hit the floor and put it on the seat.

"Carrie?"

"I'm okay"

I didn't want to think about him being with someone else, doing the things we used to do and whispering the things he used to whisper to me. It was killing me, the thoughts of it. I rubbed my arms as a little breeze brought them out in goose bumps.

He was quiet behind me and I was afraid.

"I didn't love her, I just didn't know any better" He said into the darkness. His voice was flat, and so sad.

"Steven... "I began and then lost the train of thought as a door crashed open out in the garden and I looked away from him again.

There was the sound of raucous singing from the terrace and I giggled despite myself. Michel and Serena must be heading to bed; Nancy and Becky were serenading them with something that sounded like an old Irish song about bedtime high jinks.

I peeped out through the ivy and laughed. Nancy was on the little stone wall of the terrace, wine bottle in hand waving up to the happy couple who were in stitches laughing on the balcony-

"Oh I can and I musht get married, cos the humour is on me nooooooow" she howled.

Becky must have fallen into a bush because all I could see were two legs waving in time to Nancy's singing. One stiletto shoe still on her foot, the other standing on the wall.

Michel whispered something to Serena and she giggled, cuddling into him. They took a bow on the balcony and went to their room, and Nancy pulled Becky upright-

"Some fuckin model you musta been when you couldn't stay upright for a minute. C'mon now, h'up" A heave and she was on her feet. Nancy brushed the leaves off Becky's dress and steadied her on her feet.

"Me shoe" Becky took the shoe off the wall and made about five attempts to get it back on her foot. Nancy took it and stuck it back on for her.

"Yeh right? Big eejit yeh, a model for the coddle is all you are!" She laughed.

"Wheresh David gone?" Becky was obviously pie eyed.

"Inside you spanner, come on will yeh? That best man is up for a session and I want to gerrin there while the getting's good!"

"Awright, I'm all right now!" she hiccupped and I giggled again. They wove unsteadily to the patio doors into the reception hall.

"G'night Carrie and Steven" Nancy roared into the garden.

"Where they?"

"The summerhouse, they think I'm drunk and didn't kno-ow" Nancy sang as she wove her way back into the house.

Steven laughed.

"No secrets with that one eh?"

"No, none at all" I grinned.

"Carrie, did we have a baby?" Out of the blue, just like that. My heart stopped for a second, and I felt my ears thud.

"What?" I was trying to buy time, to think.

"Its so hard to explain this but, when the accident happened I kept thinking that I had to hold on, because of a baby, and that for some reason I thought that the police were going to get me and I was afraid, I tried to get out of the bed so much they had to sedate me for months, just so my insides would heal, and I can't think why the police would be after me, please Carrie, try and tell me the real story"

I can't tell you, it hurts me too much to even think of it, and we are going to be back to square one soon enough, running scared the minute I do.

I turned away from him to the window again, looking out at the lights and listening to the sounds of the party winding down. I leant on the window sill and sighed.

"I missed you so; can't we go in now and talk in the morning, please?"

"You really don't want to do this do you?"

I turned to him; he was still sitting on the little seat, looking up at me.

"Steven, darling, for the past two years nearly, I thought you were dead, and now you're here and I want you so much and you haven't even kissed me yet, I can't think of anything else bar touching you, and being with you again, please give me that much, I promise I will tell you everything in the morning, but just for now, please?"

"You want me?" he asked.

"Yes, more than anything, fucking hell, I'm crazy about you, always have been, so even if we just lie there and do nothing, just stay with me tonight"

"Oh" he breathed. Then-

"Haven't I kissed you yet? Why not?"

All afternoon I had been asking myself that question, thinking that maybe he didn't feel it anymore. When we'd danced I had to try and stop myself grabbing him there and then and it had made me nearly ill with anticipation at the thought of having time alone with him.

"Why not? God I don't know, it's taken me all my time to wait till you did" I said, trying not to cry. Stupid bloody pride again.

He had that little smile, the one I remembered from long ago, the half grin. I felt the tears come again and I swallowed them.

"No, you haven't kissed me yet, you know you haven't" my voice sounded so small in that little room. My insides were fluttering like a net full of butterflies, I waited, heart pounding. Wasn't this what I had dreamed of in the lonely nights when he was gone? I could see the open collar of his shirt in the glow of the moonlight, and the way his skin was darker now, he never used to be tanned.

"Do you want me to, after all that's happened?" he asked.

I laughed-

"Don't, for fucks sake, of course I want you to"

He smiled; it lit up his face like sunlight.

"You still want me after everything I did? Even though I didn't realize I did it, it must have hurt you so much, even to hear me talking about it all, you know?"

"Oh God yes, I do know, but Steven I want you so much I think I'll die if I don't get you" I was shivering and laughing and felt my cheeks wet with tears.

"Oh" Silence then for a second, and then he moved.

"Come here" he stood up and stepped towards me so that he was less than arms reach away-

His hand reached out and his fingers linked into mine and I felt myself going towards him. He slid his other arm around me like we were going to dance. When we danced earlier, strange, silent times in the middle of all the celebrating, I'd been almost holding my breath, afraid to speak, afraid that all the emotion inside of me would come spilling out in a stream of words and frighten him. But all the time he held me in the middle of that floor, I looked into his eyes and he into mine, saying with my heart those words I couldn't bring myself to say. God knows why, maybe I was afraid that he wouldn't feel what I felt. It had been a while and much had changed.

Early in the day I had watched him, watched him looking at the wedding ceremony and caught him looking at me now and then and I had smiled. I could barely contain myself, the joy inside me that he was here. And the desire, oh God, it was like fire in my blood, the longing to be with him, and the waiting was killing me.

His hand unlinked itself from mine and he twined his fingers into my hair, all falling down now out of my lovely up style for the wedding. His fingers brushed the back of my neck and I shivered.

Before today, I thought I was going crazy, in the nights when I lay alone, halfway between sleep and waking, and I could see him there, or feel him beside me in the dark. I wondered why my mind couldn't let me rest? When he was dead, why couldn't I let go?

I knew the reason why today, because somewhere inside me I had always known, that one day he would come back to me and that we would be together again.

Another breath and closer still, my cheek against his shoulder and I felt the open button of his shirt scratch my skin. I smiled and looked up at him. Was he feeling one tenth of what I was feeling now?

He was so close; I could smell his familiar smell and feel his heart thudding in his chest. I closed my eyes and felt his lips brush my face, on the forehead and the eyelids, his face raspy and rough against my cheek-

I slid both my arms around him and my hands up, under the back of his shirt. He was warm, and I could feel his muscles tensing up until I started to stroke his back, up and down his spine.

"Oh Carrie" he sighed. His voice caught in his throat and I knew he wanted me too. I felt my insides melting and pulled him closer. I wanted to be him, to be part of him forever, never to separate again.

Then finally our lips met, and I swear to God, I nearly died. If I never kissed anyone ever again for the rest of my life, I wouldn't care, because I had kissed him now.

"Now I know" he whispered hoarsely, still holding me tight and his breath warm on my face.

"What?" I smiled, and stroked his cheek.

"I know what it is to love someone, properly"

"Sssh, I know, will you come inside with me?" I took his hand again.

"I want you, I want you so much, don't make me wait any longer Steven" I whispered.

This time when we kissed, it was like someone had set us on fire. My hands went to the back of his neck and I felt the static prickle my fingers as I tangled them into his hair. We pulled apart-

"Where?" He asked, and I smiled.

"Come on" We ran across the garden like a couple of kids, and onto the veranda. He pushed me against the wall and pressed his lips hard against mine, and then down my neck to my shoulder, half biting, he grabbed my buttocks and pulled me into him, I wrapped one leg round him and leant against the wall, he pulled at the bottom of the dress and it rucked up to my knees, I thought I would go insane with longing, then and there. But I didn't want it to be here, I wanted him in my bed, in my room, for the whole night.

Someone inside laughed and I felt him stiffen and then he broke apart from me.

"Carrie, we better go inside" He whispered. He was like me, gasping for breath, shaking with desire.

"This way, come on" I pulled the light curtain back and we crept through the hallway and past the bar where the party was still in full swing, up the oak stairs and along the hall to my room.

Fingers shaking I fumbled with the keys, thinking of that first night when I stood on the step of his place, afraid to go in, and terrified not to. The door finally opened and we went into the dim bedroom. It had little furniture, a small wardrobe and a mirror, and a door to a tiny en suite. But the bed was big, a real four poster, with a soft white quilt and lots of pillows.

There was one light still burning, and I turned it off, lighting a candle I brought with me from home. I turned to unzip my dress and he stopped me-

"Wait, I can do that, stop a minute"

"All right then" I whispered. I slipped out of my shoes and stood barefoot. I had never felt so vulnerable in my life, just waiting.

"I just want to look at you" He leaned against the bed and my stomach flipped as he looked straight at me, almost without blinking. His hand rested on the wooden foot rail of the bed and I longed for it to be on me. I ached for him and yet I couldn't take the three little steps to him, to make it happen. Suddenly I was shy of him.

And I knew in my heart that he was shy too. It was hard. This seemed so enormous, so huge, bigger than both of us could imagine. Wasn't it easy outside in the dark to be what we wanted to be? I felt more naked, more, *vulnerable* there in that moment than I ever did before.

I could never have imagined it. Not in all the nights dreaming of him and thinking of how it used to be, did I ever imagine anything like that moment. Not ever.

It's like I was inside him and he in me. Like we were part of the one person, breathing and living. My skin prickled and my heart was pounding-

"Oh God" I moaned to myself, not able to hold on any more, I couldn't take any more waiting. I bit my lip and tried to hang on.

He took a deep breath.

"What?"

"For heavens sake, please, come here" I grabbed the bed rail and closed my eyes, biting my lip harder still.

He smiled-

"Wait" he whispered.

An echo of the past and my eyes opened wide.

"You know?" I breathed, and he nodded.

"I know" that smile like a flash of lightening and then he moved and was across the floor in half a heartbeat, his hands on my shoulders, finding my zip and slipping it down my back. My skin tingled as his other hand slipped into the back of the dress and his fingers traced my spine.

"You're beautiful, you're so beautiful" he whispered.

So slow it took forever, he slid the dress off my shoulders and onto the floor. The silk making a molten puddle round my feet. I unbuttoned his shirt and slipped it off, and couldn't stop myself from kissing the line of hair on his chest. I could feel how he wanted me, even before I unbuckled the belt he wore and opened the button of his trousers and slipped them off. He was working out, it was obvious, his muscles were harder than they had been, and his skin was taut. I scratched his back lightly with my nails and shivered as he moaned softly against my cheek.

The clasp that held my hair was next to go, and my curls fell round my shoulders as he twined both his hands in my hair and kissed the top of my head, then down to my lips again.

The scar on his shoulder stretched down his collar bone and across his heart, a jagged line, silver white in the candlelight-

"Yours was broken too" I said. My tongue traced the line and he shivered. I could taste the salt on his skin.

"What was broken?"

"Your heart"

"Not now its not" he slipped my bra off my shoulders so that finally I was naked.

I slid my arms round his neck and pulled his head down so I could kiss him again and again, loving the feeling of his mouth on mine, and feeling the wooden bed post digging into my back. His hands went round my hips and down pulling me tight to him so I could feel him hard against me. I grabbed the post and pulled myself up to sit on the bed rail, still kissing him hard and wrapped my legs round him tightly.

"Now Steven, now" I gasped.

He knew what I wanted and gripping my thighs he pushed into me and I gasped, biting his shoulder in an effort not to scream out loud. I wrapped my legs tighter still, and he pushed into me harder, and deeper than ever. I felt him moving faster and my muscles contracted with him till I came, and held onto him while waves of heat and unbelievable pleasure broke over me again and again till I couldn't stand it any more.

I cried out, calling his name over and over again, wanting him to stay hard inside me forever but at the same time, wanting him to feel what I was feeling, wanting him to come too.

I hit the top of another wave and couldn't speak any more, I dug my fingers into his back, nails bared and bit him hard, harder than I meant to, and left a mark on his shoulder.

He groaned and pulled my head back and kissed me, his breath quicker and moving harder and faster than he had before, so I knew he was near.

He came, kissing me so hard I tasted blood on my mouth and his fingers dug into my skin till I thought they drew blood too.

He held me, talking into my hair, still shivering, sweat in beads on his skin, trickling in droplets on his back.

"Your mine, your mine again, Oh God Carrie, I love you so much" He whispered, his lips traveling across my mouth and down again.

"I love you too, you came back to me, I'll never let you go again" I wanted to laugh aloud, so happy did I feel, and so alive. But I didn't, I pulled him into the bed and lay there, wrapped round him, a cover like swan down over us, listening to the strange sounds of the unfamiliar night.

We lay for hours, or so it felt, touching and kissing and finding each other again, finally feeling alive for the first time in so bloody long. In the nights alone I had remembered being with him in Connemara and remembered how he had trembled under me when my lips and hands traveled all over him and I would waken crying, thinking it would never be again.

But it was happening now, as I traced my lips down his body, from his shoulder to his hip bones, and lower still, discovering him all over again. I found the scars on his legs and kissed them, and moved up again, taking him in my mouth and making him hard again with my tongue.

When I looked up at him, he was watching me, and my insides clenched with desire.

"Carrie, come here to me" he muttered, and I crept back to him and into his arms. He laid me back on the bed and moved so he was on top of me and into me again.

He kept talking to me, kept whispering, and I lay there listening to his voice, afraid to speak, afraid to break the spell. Hardly able to breathe.

"When I slept it was you I followed, in my dreams I chased your shadow and couldn't find it, couldn't reach what was just before me, couldn't touch what I knew was there, you were always there Carrie, always, every time I closed my eyes I saw you, I saw your smile and heard you laugh, and I wanted you, I knew one day I would see you again, that all I had to do was turn the right corner and there you would be, waiting for me...I love you so much, I'll never ever leave you again, I swear to God I won't leave you again"

I couldn't speak, it was like he was casting a spell on me and I didn't want it to end-

"Your everything, I've found what I was searching for, and I want to be here like this for ever, we're never going to be apart again, I love you.." His lips moved against my skin his breath making me shiver.

I actually wept when I felt him moving in me, so slowly and gently, like he wanted time to stand still. Silly I know, but that's the way it was. And all the time he was there, inside me, he looked at me, into my eyes, like he was looking into my soul; he never took his gaze away once. Never stopped holding me tighter and tighter, and when he came it was like we were dying. But this time, when I opened my eyes he was there, his body heavy on me, my hands still touching the back of his neck, the answer to every single prayer I'd ever said.

He moved, shifting his weight off me a little and I held him tighter-

"Don't go, not yet" I wanted to stay as close to him as was humanly possible for as long as I could.

"Your not a dream anymore Steven, your real, and I want this to be for ever"

"We are forever Carrie"

We lay there facing one another, the way we used to. Still entwined and lazy, watching the candle light dance on the walls.

"All the time I was away from you I knew there was something missing from me and my life Carrie, you were like a shadow I was chasing, something just out of reach and it broke my heart not to be able to find you. There might be a bit of you everywhere I looked but the whole you was never there, I smelt your perfume one day and it nearly drove me crazy trying to remember you, I could see something, a place with incense in the air and music playing, that was our place wasn't it?" He stopped.

"Yes, it was our place"

"And then I thought that if I had someone that loved me and had a place called home, then why didn't they come and get me? Why didn't you?"

"Because they told me you were dead Steven, they sent a body home and we buried it, your ring was with the stuff salvaged from the crash, your address book and your wallet, but the body was too badly burnt, we couldn't see you, it, I mean"

"I know I had to hitch because I had no money, my bag was nicked with all my stuff, and the money, and the ring, why did I take off the ring?" he whispered.

I took a deep breath-

"Okay, heres what I know, listen to me my love, you might not like this at all"

"I'm listening"

"Me and you were together about four months when I discovered that I was pregnant, we decided to get married and went up, well, I did, to Father Ray up in the church to arrange the wedding. You might not remember this but I am adopted, and this is where the trouble started, because when I went to my mother's house, Dorrie, my adoptive mother, she gave me an envelope filled with papers and it seems, unlikely though it looks, that you and I have the same mother"

I felt him stiffen and he pulled away from me slightly-

"No darling, listen to me" I leaned close again.

"The police found out about us having a relationship and they came one day, the morning after I found out and took you to the station and I was made to sign a confession that you and I were together. We were separated and we were waiting for this to go to court so that we could get blood tests and prove it was all a lie, and it is a lie, I never felt anything so strongly in all my life, you have to believe me!" I kissed him again and he responded, a sound like a growl or a sob coming from his throat.

"Serena has folders filled with stuff that she is going to tell you about tomorrow, and I did my own research before the baby was born, and it's damned near impossible that two people with the same mother can have a healthy baby, and we didn't have the same father, for sure"

"So what is the baby like?" he asked

"Oh Steve, she was beautiful, she had your eyes and my hair, and she was so bonny, and clever... you would have loved her"

"Where is she now? How old is she? She must be walking and all now, does she know I'm her daddy?" he stared at me hard.

"She saw you once on the day she was born Steve, you held her and you kissed her and you told her you'd come back and get her soon, when everything was sorted out, but the police were waiting and they tried to get you but you ran and went out to the boat and met Nancy who came and gave you clothes and money and all and that's how you ended up in the UK, I guess that's how you were robbed too, we had come to the conclusion that your Grandfather knew something more about the situation than he was telling us and so you decided to confront him and see what the story was, so that's why you were on your way to Glasgow, the hard part is trying to figure out how he knew it was you in the hospital, for I'm sure he didn't know you were coming to him"

"But, the baby?"

"Oh God Steven, she's dead, she died a year to the week after we buried you, or thought we did, a house fire started by Noel Holliman because he was mad at Ma for throwing him out, he killed four people that night, two of his own kids and her and our baby girl"

"Dead? Oh Carrie, that's, how did you cope on your own?"

"I didn't, that's the thing, I was in hospital myself for the best part of this year, and I only got my sanity back because your dad fought tooth and nail for it"

All the while I am talking about the past, I'm also thinking, will there ever be a time when joy is not tainted with pain and worry and sadness.

"Well you aren't on your own now Carrie, whatever the outcome of this, I know in my heart that I am not going to live without you, not now and not any more, so we will face this, and be together no matter what"

And then the warm buzz of love started all over again. Hours later, we tried to sleep. I lay for ages just listening to him breathing and looking into the dark.

My last thought that night was that there has to be a God, because someone up there has a fucked up sense of humour.

14

We didn't surface till lunchtime the following day. Nancy was in the bar, a large bloody Mary in front of her looking green as grass round the gills and Becky was apparently up in bed in a darkened room with David dancing attendance on her.

"Will you look at the pair of youse" she grimaced

I blushed scarlet. Like I thought, I was glowing, and there was more than one bite mark visible on my skin, and his. No point in trying to hide them anyhow, and Nancy and her gimlet eye would know regardless.

"No need to ask yez what the hell you've been doing all night anyhow"

Steven put his arm round her-

"Aw Nancy, what about you and the best man then?"

" Best man my arse! That bugger was more interested in the mini bar than my frilly French knickers...and my motto is, don't beat them, join them" She groaned as the smell of food wafted out of the restaurant.

"Oh Jesus the champagne, never again!" she bolted to the bathroom and I laughed.

It was all so normal.

For the remainder of the night, in between making love, over and over, we had talked and talked, I told him everything he needed to know including the fact that we were still in real trouble and could end up being locked up for this, until we proved that the relationship was all right. He needed to sort some stuff out too with Colleen. I was mad at him marrying someone else, but I guess in the circumstances it was bound to happen.

"What will we do now? I mean, if they figure out that you're here and alive and I am with you there may be a lot of trouble"

But Steven thought that the thing to do was get back to his grandfather and find out why this had happened in the first place, and more to the point, I deserved answers too.

"You look nothing like me, and yet I feel like I know you forever"

"Isn't that the confusing bit?" I smiled.

"Well, we face him, and we face this, and that way we can go out there and live"

So simple when you put it like that.

Everyone found their way to our room that afternoon. Serena, bride or not, was sitting with a pad and pencil, scribbling furiously. Her Father sat nursing a drink and staring at me and Steven now and then and shaking his head.

"O-kay, heres the story" Serena began "Back when you were in the accident, I had already made a bit of headway into the case, and there's a few bits that seem very relevant to you and that will be important to us all, firstly, you mother was a badly addicted addict, she was, by David's account, using heavily and injecting and was taken three times from the jaws of an overdose and near death, so basically, medically, its damned near impossible that Carrie is the same baby she was carrying, secondly, we need to find that nurse, Breda Storey, because my hunch is that she was paid to protect Liz Bard and would have done whatever it took, incidentally Carrie, she was responsible for giving you to Peter and Dorrie, and she dressed you as a boy for some reason, leaving your coat on the back seat of the car your mother died in, so that proved to me that your mother wanted you hidden and out of something, so finding Breda is the next step" She paused and Steven raised his hand-

"Are you sure she's still called Breda?"

"No, why?"

"Well, this could be nothing, but in the hospital in Leeds, a nurse came in temporarily and her name was Biddy, and it was then I was shifted to Granddads house in Scotland, and I remember on the first night I was there, they had words in the library I wasn't meant to hear, something about ten years in prison and kidnapping, and I am ninety nine per cent sure he called her Breda"

"And also" I gasped "The cheques, they used to come from her to Dorrie for my keep, she didn't ever write letters with them, just sent the money, and once when I looked at them they were for a bank in the UK but the stamp was American, I think that wherever she was for the past few years, your Granddad knew very well, and used her to keep tabs on me all this time"

It looked like James Bard knew everything, that he had kept his eye on us all this time and knew that his so called, beloved grandson was in trouble and yet never lifted a finger to help him and then, when he had fallen into his lap, so to speak, he had concocted a whole new life story for Steven, telling him he had tried to kill himself, confusing him and then putting him where he wanted him, under his control.

And he had known about me too! That was hard to believe. And it must have seemed to him like manna from heaven when I met Steven and all this trouble kicked off.

"He must be a bitter old man" I looked at David.

"I don't know, we're going to have to get to him and talk to him, see can this be sorted once and for all, Steven can you contact Breda?" He replied.

"Sure, I'll ring her and see can she meet us"

"Try not to let Granddad know, for fucks sake" Nancy snapped, still in a bad humour.

"I'll try, it's just, everything is linked in that house, every phone call is answered by his secretary and vetted, its going to be hard collaring Breda"

But strangely enough, when he rang he was put straight through to Breda and called her by that name, so it seemed we were right, it was her, back on the scene after all this time.

"What happened Gary? You and Colleen..."She began

"Me and Colleen are getting a divorce, I want to see you, I need to talk to you, can you meet me in London? I'll fly back tonight and meet you"

He pulled me closer to him as he spoke, and I could hear her on the other end of the phone-

"Look, Breda, this is very important, we know who you are, and you knew all along who I was, and, now you're my only hope, if I was ever important to you you'll do this for me, you helped me when I was a baby, help me now, please" He pleaded.

"But, Mister Bard, won't like this, I know it, son, I'm afraid"

"I promise you will be safe, just pack a few bits and meet me tomorrow morning"

She agreed to do it and we packed our stuff and were on a flight that night, arriving in London and going to his flat. The city was twinkling with lights and there was a lovely atmosphere but we stayed indoors, shutting out the world and whatever it would bring us the following morning.

Breda was nothing like I expected.

We walked into a restaurant in Camden the following morning, the place still not fully open, and she was already there, sitting with the cup of tea in front of her, her handbag on her lap, her hands nervously clutching it.

"Breda, thank you for being here, do you know who this is?" He was holding my hand tightly-

"Yes, its Amber, My God child, you look nothing like I thought you would, you're lovely, the only picture I saw of you was in the paper, you looked terrible" She held out her hand and I took it.

She was like Doris, just like Mam, and I felt a pang that I would never see her again, but Breda's accent was a queer mixture of American and Irish and I smiled as I sat down opposite her and we ordered coffee.

"It was a very tough time for me Breda, or is it Biddy now?" I asked.

"Call me Breda, or Breege, like Dorrie did, I cannot go on with this lying any more, Oh child" She grabbed Stevens hand "I knew who you were the minute I saw you in that bed, in Leeds and I rang your Grandfather, because I thought you were a down and out and needed his help, but he wouldn't let me go looking for your father, refused to let me even try, and so that's why the whole lot of us were in on the lie, everyone, absolutely everyone, in the business and the house, we all know the truth and who you are, and we were told to refer to you as Gary, because the cloudier we could make your memory the better for us all, but you shouldn't have been kept there, living a lie, you should have been home with Amber and your dad"

"I know that now, can you tell me why this is happening to us? Carrie, I mean, Amber isn't my sister, sure she isn't?"

"No child, she isn't, she is no blood relation to you whatsoever"

I burst into tears-

"I knew it, I knew it all along!" I wept.

"Then how..."

"I swapped her, the night she was born, I put the child your mother had into a cot belonging to a couple that weren't married, and took their daughter home with us, your father, David, smelt a rat, and of course the young couple must have thought it strange that their healthy baby should deteriorate overnight and die but that was taken care of, Your grandfather paid the hospital handsomely for their silence on the matter and then, the young couple, just happened to get a lovely house in Liverpool, left to them, and a legacy that came through some time later set them up in business, they own a pub now I believe"

She had Doris's eyes, the same gimlet way of looking at you. They sure as hell don't make women like them any more.

"Hang on, does this mean that Granddad kept tabs on them all along?"

"Oh yes, you realize, you have to realize, that Colleen is actually Ambers sister?"

"You're joking?" I gasped.

"I wish I was child, it's a mess" She sighed.

Jesus, this was getting worse. Basically, Steven thought that I was his sister, ran away to sort out the trouble and ended up marrying MY sister. This was fast turning into a rollercoaster I couldn't get off, and I hated to think that this was my life.

"God, Barbara Cartland couldn't make this up!" I had to laugh. I was ecstatic, this was better than I had hoped. I knew we weren't related for sure now, and all we had to do was tell the right people and prove it, and we were home and dry! Right?

"Did you know, all along Breda?" he asked.

"More or less, I knew when Colleen told me her name that it was all part of your Granddads master plan, that he had been plotting all along to get you back though I think it was pure luck that she ended up nursing you, he couldn't have foreseen the accident and all, look, Steven love, there's so much even I don't know, all I know in my heart was that your mother was afraid of your granddad and she would have done anything to stay away from him and keep her daughter safe, but when she got into the drug scene, he kept clawing her back, you know, when she was off the drugs the couple of times, it was him who paid for dealers to leave stuff lying around where she would get it, and in my opinion, he wanted her out of the picture, dead, maybe"

"And he got what he wanted, except he didn't get Carrie"

"Not in a manner of speaking, but he knew all along where she was and he waited, like a big old spider in a web, till she came to him, and now you will, you will have to bring her to him, face him, kill this once and for all"

"I'll kill him! What the hell is it with him?" He buried his head in his hands.

"Oh Steven, he has power, he knows it too…he thinks he is safe and secure in his own private universe, cushioned for ever by the money he has in his bank account, but there are terrible things going on there, things your mother knew about, things he wants hidden forever, and now its all on the verge of being discovered, none of us are safe"

She stared at me again and I shivered-

"Noel Holliman" she said.

My stomach turned.

"What about him?"

"Of course, you know him, he was very rough by the time you met him, but once upon a time he was incredibly handsome, I suppose drink and rough living took its toll, but one time, way back, he was a fine handsome man, and he was the best groom your Grandfather ever employed"

"Noel was working there too?"

"Oh yes, he was, but he, well he fell from grace, because, well, your granddad said, that he is the man who fathered you, Steven, of course, he was fired and couldn't get work any more, until the day, oh, years later your grandfather offered a lifeline, and he was paid once more out of the Bard purse to stay near you Amber, keep tabs on you by whatever means required, even though that meant breaking up my sisters marriage and living in a council estate, he didn't care, he had more than enough money to drink what he liked and I'm sure that he didn't go short of female company at times, so well, everyone is a winner" she called for more tea and waited till the waiter had gone.

"Noel Holliman could be my Father?" Steven shook his head.

"Jesus your mother must have had great genes then!" He looked nothing like Noel really, but then I was biased, I had hated Noel for a long time.

"David reared you, even though he knew, Bard told him, and it's to his credit that he took you away, tried to give you a better chance, you have to think that even money cannot buy love, even if it can buy privileges beyond most people's dreams"

"My mother was gorgeous all right, but boy was she sick, I remember hiding in the bedroom with you Breda, waiting till the loud music stopped and dad came home from work, why would my grandfather want my mother to be in that state?"

"Buying her silence, like he bought everyone else...I remember there was a time in the world where when bad things happened to people, in childhood say, we wouldn't talk about them, we would bury them and hope they went away, well, your mother was a troubled girl, she was known as the wild child, up in London, modeling and hanging out with musicians and artists, she was a muse for a couple of the designers, but that was the way things *were* in the sixties, your grandfather had doted on her almost to the point of obsession and she had very little to do with her mother, nor her mother with her, because she spent a lot of time under the care of a doctor, taking injections for a vitamin deficiency and sleeping, or so we were told afterward. But your mother, once she reached her teens, seemed to become closer to her mother, and then her mother killed herself, hung herself actually, and Liz saw it happening, this was when she was fifteen, on Christmas eve, can you imagine the effect that had on her? And then, she spent the next couple of years running up to London, becoming known more for her beauty and her friendships with famous people, I think she made a couple of films then, bit parts, you know, but always loved the party scene, and then, she announced that she was to be engaged to a young lad, the son of a baronet or something, Lord Thomas was the name I think, and her father was delighted, rubbing his hands in glee, I think myself that it was something to do with him aspiring to a title himself, she came home to Baird, and whatever happened then, shortly afterwards, she went off the rails, getting pregnant and marrying David, and I think your grandfather thought that David would, or could keep the lid on the can of worms, it was as though she hated her father, but wasn't allowed to be far from him, because he would always make things right for her when she was in bother, but a lot of the time before she died was spent trying to run away from him"

She sighed-

"There is a place no one is allowed go to in Bard hall, its part of the west wing, where your Grandmother used to sleep, there's a corridor and a locked door, to which only your grandfather and one or two other trusted employees have the keys, and though I have tried to get in there, I never did, and funny, your grandfather hadn't been going there much until all this blew up, the night Colleen rang him he went in there for a long time, and came out tired, almost an older man than he is, if that's possible" she stood up-

"If you want to get to the bottom of this mess, that's where you need to go, to that wing, and see what's in that room, I have my suspicions and think its something terrible, something evil, and your poor mother was part of it, but that's the place you will find answers" she shook my hand-

"Amber I hope that you find happiness, anyone with an eye in their heads can see that you love him, and its only right that you have a chance to be together, but James Bard is a bad man, he will stop at nothing to stop you, its Steven he wants, and you have to figure out why, because I know he has no intention of letting him go back to Ireland with you"

She left us then.

We were left sitting in the café, silently staring at each other, wondering where the hell this was going to bring us now.

But the answer was clear-

We were going to beard the lion in his own den.

"We have no choice in the matter Steven, I won't be without you again, we have to go and tell him straight that its all over and your coming home, that whatever he had planned for you will not be happening and that you and me want the truth, but either way, I'm not going home without you again" I said as we went out into the freezing afternoon.

"You know I'm going home with you Carrie, there's nothing in the world will keep me from you again" he said, wrapping his arms round me in the street.   And despite everything I knew it would be all right.

We spent the night in the flat watching the telly and saying little.

The following day, we went to Glasgow.

The Dolls House
New Years Day 1992
James

The dream begins as it always does, of the long stone landing and the sound of children's voices in the air, the sticky paint on the front door of the flat as I close it and go out and begin to walk down the stairs that smell of urine and disinfectant

The older ones play spin the bottle in the courtyard where the bins are and the young ones play skipping in among the washing lines and I'm watching them when she comes and takes my hand, leading me to the back of the close and in to a darkened corner...

"Come play with me Jimmy" she says, her lips clumsily painted with her older sister's lipstick and her blouse tight over her burgeoning breasts.

"What are we playing?" I ask her, already beginning to sweat, my stammer coming back in my nervousness.

"A special game of hide and seek" She slips her hand inside my trousers and finds my penis and starts to touch me, and then screams when the semen leaks out onto her hand...

"Dirty thing, your dirty, dirty..." the rest come for me then and attack and I cannot get away fast enough. Black faced devils in hobnail boots kick and hit till I am on the ground and dying. Humiliated on the spittle covered ground, dying dying...

And then there is no one but little Sarah, in the white nightgown, the angel that brought me to this place in my mind, the place where I have lived all my life Who came and gave me power and who helped me understand what I am and why..

"Sarah, Sarah, save me" I call... but she looks at me and in her eyes I see what I am and what I have done, and I know that I cannot be saved...

"You killed me James, you hurt me, I cannot save you, you cannot be saved, your going to die" She says, her voice like a whisper in the howling wind, whistling through the close.

"I'm sorry, I couldn't help myself Sarah, I'm sorry forgive me before I die," I cry, and when I wake, my face is mottled with tears.

Its fifty years or more since I met little Sarah, thirty since I saw Ellie, and yet the memory of their faces turned to me in awe and admiration still lives in my soul. I still feel pride inside me when I think of how I ruled.

But that only happens in the daytime, when the night comes and I lie in my bed and the dream that haunts me relentlessly comes, I realize that the look on their little faces wasn't awe, nor admiration, and that they hated and feared me and I can never begin to undo the damage I have done.

Oh what power I had. What glory was mine? I think I weep more for what I lost, than what I did.

"Oh Sarah what did I do?" I weep, but it's a momentary thing. Remorse is not for me, and I cannot and will not repent of what is not, and never has been a sin to me. It was a need, a need, a longing. And if I lived my life in its thrall and skulked in shadow, then so be it.

But still at night I pray that I won't dream, that there will be a night of unbroken sleep.

And still it comes to torture me, and haunt me in my slumber.

No pill can take away the faces that haunt my bedroom, Ellie, Sarah, Katie... No pill can take the realization that I have sinned and the fear that when I die I will go to hell.

Nothing can replace what I lost, nothing can bring me back to what I was before all this began, secure and loved and wanted.

I am destined for hell, I will never see the face of God, the God I tried to be, the God I tried to emulate and in mockery of which I controlled the lives, and the deaths of those around me.

I am banished, I am damned, and in the darkness of the night, I cry, because no one can save me now.

15

Somehow I knew that I would have my chance all over again.

Not to put right what I had done wrong, because in my world, there is no room for sentiment. No, there is no wrong, not in my life. I have lived as I saw fit, and if it hurt and destroyed those who said they loved me, well then, that is their undoing, not mine.

The Boy is my heir.

Flesh of my flesh and blood of my blood. More so than even he can know. The Girl, an asset once, but now, expendable. And it will be done. Without a doubt it shall happen. She will only impede him, stop him being what he has to be. Like all of the rest tried to do to me. There is no room for sentiment in my life and there shall be none in his.

This day is the final chapter in a story that started seventy or more years ago. When I was a boy, growing up in the mean streets of Dublin, I often sat and looked out over the chimneys and sooty wet roofs and thought about what I would do when I was rich.

For I knew that one day I would be rich, and anything I wanted would be for the taking.

My father was a merchant seaman. He worked out of Dublin Port, and was away a lot, leaving my mother in the flat with us children, for many a week at a time. My mother was a hypochondriac, constantly moaning, never happy.

Dublin in the 1930's was different to the place it is now.

For a start we were expected to obey.

When I was a child, this meant, that during my mothers frequent bouts of self pity, or illness, I was sent to live with my grandmother in North Wall flats. She wouldn't let me out to play once I came home from school and I would have to sit in her flat, reading tracts from the bible and learning them by heart.

Mass every single morning at seven o clock then, and back and out to school.

I hated every second of it and used to beg to go home. I couldn't understand why my sisters were allowed to stay when Mammy was ill and I wasn't. But I was the boy. That was why.

The children in the flats used to taunt me when I would walk through the terrace with my bible and the long black overcoat that once belonged to my dead grandfather-

"Heres the cleric" they'd yell, pausing in their games to throw a stone or cat call.

My name was James Bardon. I was the eldest of five children.

My father, on one of his rare trips home called me aside one day and asked me how I was getting on. He was a jovial type, my father, good natured and good humored.

By this time I was turning fifteen. Time to be leaving school and going looking for work. It was 1930, and times were hard.

"What d'ya think about coming on the ships wi' me son?" he asked.

I thought that sounded mighty good. See the world and go places like he did and most of all, get away from the young women in the flats.

Most evenings, especially in the summertime, the young people would congregate in the courtyard under the balconies and tell ghost stories and play silly little games, like Kiss and Chase, or spin the bottle.

But I never joined in.

By this time I was taller than any of the young lads in the flats, and thin. I liked to wear black sweaters and trousers and was fastidiously clean and neat. Most of the lads my age were working on the docks or the building and had calluses on their hands, but not me. Mine were as pale and slim as a girl's.

I had been besieged with desperate, nameless urges. With no father around for much of the time, I couldn't know what I was feeling. How would I know it was sexual feeling and that my sexuality was making itself felt?

I hated the girls I saw, with their frocks and little cardigans covering their bosoms, and the pious way they went to the Legion of Mary and sodality meetings, and then came home and kiss chased with the boys all evening.

The day I signed on to my Fathers boat, I joined the group in the courtyard for the first time ever.

They were playing spin the bottle and it landed on me.

I spun it again, to pick the girl and it landed on Mary Blanchard.

Mary was, what you might call, advanced for her years. Coming from a huge family she knew more about the "facts of life" than most and it was said, she could be held responsible for the awakenings of most of the lads in the flats.

She was small and blonde. Not too clean either, but to me, that night, she was heaven sent.

When the time came we paired off and went into the alley between the flats. She walked quietly, head down and stopped when we got to the place where the big bins were kept. They had been emptied earlier so there was no fear of rats. The smell of jeyes fluid was everywhere.

"Have yeh ever kissed anyone?" She asked.

"No"

"D'ya know how to French kiss?" she smiled, her teeth flashing in the twilight.

I shook my head.

"Its what they do in the films, C'mere" she took me by the shoulders and pulled me to her.

She kissed me with her mouth open and I felt it all wet and slimy. I recoiled a little, and then, relaxed.

She opened the cardigan she was wearing and I slipped my hand inside and felt her breast. She sighed and then did something that shocked me to the core.

She opened the button of my trousers and slipped her hand inside and began to move it up and down. I couldn't control myself and came. She screamed-

"You dirty thing yeh!" She held her hand out, semen dripping.

"I'm sorry" I gasped. My knees were shaking, heart pounding.

"What's wrong Mary?" someone called.

"He's after doin' somethin' on me hand"

"Wha?"

"Eh, I dunno, but it's disgustin'"

She ran out of the alley and I could hear the cries of revulsion among her friends and I ran home, up to the top floor and into my bed.

Next morning I sailed out of Dublin.

I stayed out of Dublin for nine years all told.

Sailing all through the different shipping canals, to Africa, India, even to America once.

My father died when I was twenty, in 1935.

He died on ship and we had no choice but to bury him in India. It would take too long to get him home. I telegraphed my mother and I am sure that she had masses said for his soul.

I went out and got drunk.

My father had known how awkward and gauche I was, and he had tried to help. Knowing how a young man can be bullied and terrorized in the navy, he taught me to box, and the second person who picked on me got the shock of their lives when I pulverized them.

I had little fear now, and no pity.

Some of the men on ship, found relief in the companionship of their mates. My father had been popular, but had never resorted to the type of relief some of his shipmates did.

And I couldn't imagine it either.

I liked girls. And that night in India I went looking for some.

Where there are ships there are sailors and where there's a sailor, there's usually a whorehouse. No matter what country you visit, the brothels are around the docks and India was no exception.

But in India, it was different.

Whores in Ireland and England were normally knowing, older women, blowsy and weather beaten. Whores in India were young, delicate little things, who looked up to me, with my pale skin and blue eyes, as a god.

I discovered that the only time I could obtain sexual release was in the company of the very young.

And for a while, after my father died, I could do that. I could seek out the youngest whores in the area and find what I was looking for. The others on the boat used to tease me about it. Asking was I going to rob a pram one of these days.

I just smiled.

War was looming and our boat was on route back to Ireland and stopped in Liverpool for the night.

It was the 31st August 1939, and every dance hall and bar was packed with people.

I went with two others and we had drinks in a wharf tavern, and then they asked me did I fancy picking up a bit of skirt.

"Why not?" I smiled.

I went with them to a place in a side street and we knocked on a door.

Opened by a bottle blonde in a tight wrapper, she grinned-

"Well hell-lo lads, come on in" she brought us into the living room and we sat there.

"Right, its five bob, who's going first?"

Bobby, the stoker, got up and hitched his belt, and laughed-

"Come on darlin'" and swung her into the back kitchen.

I looked at the room we were in and at the little knick knacks in the cupboard.

"I need to piss" I said to Mickey, who was half lying on the sofa.

"Out back, or wait" he called "Where's the bog?"

"Out in' back, go through the hall" she called, shrieking with laughter.

I slipped out into the hall and walked down into the dark yard.

The toilet was in an outhouse, with a door hanging by one hinge. I slipped inside and unbuttoned my trousers, and was in mid flow when someone came cannoning into my back.

"Sorry mister" a little voice said.

I smiled.

"That's okay, what's your name"

"Sarah"

"And how old are you?" I grinned.

She was blonde, her hair curled and her feet bare under her nightdress.

"Ten, mister" she whispered.

I closed my eyes and took a deep breath and sighed. The images of the little Indian maids came flooding through my head. They were the same age as this little one. And the things they could do. There was no harm in it there, why would there be here?

"Come here to me, Sarah" I whispered, and I took her into my arms.

Of course there was no police involvement. No one did anything about what I had done. The child was hurt, but what would the police have done? The mother a whore, bringing men to the house? What credibility would she have in a courtroom? It was laughable. The child lay sobbing in her bloodstained nightdress and the mother rocked her in her arms, and we left the house.

The men I was with were silent on the way back to the ship.

I felt curiously sated and relaxed.

We got to the ship and they stopped-

"You better go away, don't come back on this ship"

"Come on lads, what's the problem? She was a whore" I laughed.

Mickey was silent, Bobby snapped-

"She was only a babbie, she was ten year old, and you're a fucking animal!"

"That's your opinion Bobby, now I'm going to bed, get out of me way" I pushed past him and up the gangplank.

But the next morning, I woke to find the Second Mate standing over me with my pay and my kit bag packed.

"You're getting off here, get up and dressed"

"Why?"

"You know why, and there's not one man on this boat will sail with you on it" he snapped.

I got off in Liverpool and took a train north to Glasgow.

By the time I arrived, war was declared.

My money came from many enterprises. Having been kept out of the army by my Irish citizenship, I was happier to go into the black market and make my money selling drink and later on, the strange commodity that people became, when the war brought women out to earn a living when before, they had husbands to give them a wage.

It was a strange thing, back then; all sorts of women took to the streets and made a shilling. I had many of them working in flats and houses all over Glasgow.

I found that I made an excellent pimp. Wooing the women into my clutches with a little bit of flattery and promises of a better life.

I wouldn't sleep with any of my girls, leaving them to the punters. Instead I wandered around the streets and looked at the places I might buy and use as houses for them. Before all the munitions factories opened, there was very real poverty on the streets, and need and I liked to think I filled that gap in their lives.

It's a true thing that a man will have money for women and wine, even when his children starve and go naked.

Until one day I met Katie Hollis, and the whole scenario changed.

Walking through the Gorbals district one evening in the late autumn, 1942 it was, I saw a figure under a dimmed lamppost, plying for trade, and I stopped. This was my district, and I wondered what other pimp would have the gall to put a girl on my turf.

"Want a trick?" she lisped.

When I got closer to her, I saw that the rouge and the garish lipstick was a mask, trying to cover her obvious youth, she was no more than thirteen years old.

"Who told you to work here?" I asked, backing her into the alleyway.

"No one, it's the street isn't it?" she replied.

"Well it's my street" I grabbed her arm.

She cowered in fear, and not for the first I felt overwhelmed with the sense of my own power. She stared up at me with eyes wide open, as if I were God.

"I'm sorry, I'll go home now" she whispered.

"Where's home?" She named a district not too far away which had taken a fair amount of bombing of late.

"And your parents?"

"Gone"

"Dead?"

"Da is, Mammy left a while ago" she said.

"I see"

I did see. I took her home to my house. And yes, I took her. And as I did, a plan came to me.

"Did you have many men? Clients, people who paid?" I asked when she was sitting on the end of the bed.

"Some, not many, they wouldn't, not with me being young, not in the street, and I couldn't find a pimp to take me on" she replied.

Well, their loss was my gain.

I became known for it, in certain circles, men who had served abroad and who found that their tastes, while amply catered to in the likes of Thailand and in war battered Europe, were sparsely represented when they came home, and unless they could be satisfied with the blowsy tarts round Soho, there was no one to turn to, except me.

By the time the war ended in 1945, I had fourteen houses round Glasgow, but only one of them was my favorite, and that was the Dolls house. I had girls as young as nine in there, and it was always busy, night and day.

And don't get all moral on me, these were girls that would be out on the street doing it, selling themselves for the price of a few cigarettes, if it weren't for me to help them, and who put them in safety and comfort and fed them and dressed them. They were like my own children.

On Christmas Eve 1946, my son, through Katie was born. She was seventeen at this stage, a little old for what the clients liked, but I kept her on, looking after her like she was my own daughter. We named him Noel.

He took a lot of his mother's looks, very little of me came out in him, but I indulged them both.

Once the war had ended, the morals police started snooping in the red light districts and the vice industry went into panic. Not I, for over the years, I had more than enough money saved.

I was always searching for something better, something drove me to look further and further out there. I wanted to never smell the poverty and the decay that had been my life as a young man. I never wanted to live in a place with stairs that stank of urine and umpteen other families. So I worked hard, I strove to be the best.

Admirable, I thought it.

I drove the best cars and ate in the best restaurants. My needs catered to by Katie and any other of the dolls in my house. My family, my mother, a far distant memory. I never found my way back to Ireland.

I slowly sold off my interests in the other houses in Glasgow, when it began to get sticky and dangerous to hold on to. I began another little enterprise, two really, one my real love and the other, well, you could call it a beard, I suppose.

I started a publishers. I took on the works of the more obscure, gritty novelists. People were beginning to get tired of the soapy wartime romances and they wanted real life. Real life! I had more than my fair share of that in my day. By 1948, the north of England had a voice and I was the one who published it and brought it to the masses.

I was in a hotel one evening in Glasgow, sitting reading a paper and having a drink when my eye was caught by a young woman, serving in the bar. I called her to me and she told me her name was Maria.

She had an Irish accent, softer than the Dublin one and yet not the bog thick patois of the real culchie.

I thought about her that night.

It was being remarked upon that here I was, well set and prosperous and not married. Some of the women told me that rumour had it that I was queer.

The first man who said it in jest ended up in hospital.

I decided that the innocent Maria was the one.

I wooed her the way she expected to be wooed, with trifles and sentiment, until in 1949, she agreed to marry me, and we moved to my new home, christened Baird Hall.

A crumbling faded mansion set in parkland. With a wing, well, some rooms, going down into the basement, but well divided from the house, kept locked and staffed by completely different staff to the main house. One would think that any intelligent woman would have noticed something amiss, but not Maria. Too starry eyed with "love" and the thoughts of being lady of the manor, she swallowed the tale of it all being work related and nothing she would have to worry about.

I mean, this was a girl who had grown up in a three room cottage. Now she had a thirteen bedroom mansion in 76 acres of parkland all for her own. She was caught up in buying the latest style and décor for the house, and wasn't too bothered about the rooms that I told her were too crumbling and decrepit to be bothered about.

"We'll do it later dearest" I smiled.

Our wedding was small but fashionable. None of her family attended, nor mine. But we did have our pictures in the paper, on the society pages no less! I paid for that, and it finally put paid to the queer rumour.

By this time, in keeping with my literary ambition, I had acquired a new name, James Bard. It was to be Baird, but a clerical error made that impossible, so Bard I was. Lord of the manor and king of all I surveyed.

And what of Katie, and her feelings?

Katie didn't feel anything at all about my marriage, because Katie was disposed of, neatly and conveniently. A fall on the stairs leading to the wine cellar. Drinking again, they said. I buried her locally, and with her the past.

Married life wasn't much different to single life.

Oh yes, Maria shared my bed, but she lacked, something. I know now that it was the youth essence, and that she was more interested in being a dutiful wife than being a partner in any sense of the world, and she didn't look up to me. Women then were less liberated than they are nowadays, but still, she didn't have the awesome gaze when she looked at me, that the little girls in the dolls house had. I wasn't God to her; I was a man with faults and failings aplenty.

I could go in there, my kingdom, and be a hero, with the children vying for my attention.

And then Maria fell pregnant, and that was the end of her being a wife.

Sickly in pregnancy and overwhelmed by motherhood, she told me she wanted no more children.

One was enough, for she was beautiful.

Dark as a Spaniard and fearless, she was born in 1950. Elizabeth.

My very own living doll.

I had to be careful; I never let Elizabeth near the other children. Maria stayed in the nursery with her and the nurse a lot of the time and the occasional times I went away on business I gave strict orders about noise and locked even the shutters on the wing.

In 1955, Maria came to me looking troubled.

"James, I want to speak to you"

"Yes?" I was busy, some buyers in America were requesting some 8mm film of particular acts, some "playtime" in the dolls house and I was wondering who would be best to film and act the role. It couldn't be me, much as I would have liked it, no, it had to be an anonymous figure, dark and menacing, because that was the way the Yankees liked it. They read too much of the Bible over there and yet would marry off thirteen year olds to widowers in the name of Jesus.

"Well, what is it?" I snapped, shoving the letter into the drawer, and locking it tight.

"James, I would, I was wondering, could we move house?"

"Move house? Why?"

"I, I don't like it here" she whispered.

"Like it? You spent a fortune redecorating and restoring it, and now you don't like it, don't be so foolish woman, here we stay!" I snapped.

"Please James, please, I can't stay here, its, I think it's haunted"

I stared at her-

"Go on" I prompted.

"Sometimes, oh James, I hear the crying, like a lot of little children, weeping, and I can't stand it, it's terrible, and then the silence, please, please can we move?" She wept.

I knew I was on dangerous ground now. What happened next would determine my life from here on in. I considered the options-

Moving. To a bigger house, on a grander scale, with possibly more room for the dolls, well, that could be good, with maybe a proper film set for the movies that were so in demand in America, but then, how to get everyone out of here first, and how to guarantee the silence and discretion of the staff. They might not be so inclined to be silent if they were not my employees and under my eye all the time.

There might be whispers, questions, who knew where that would lead to?

I sat and looked at Maria and I realized that she meant very little to me. She hadn't given me the heir I needed, though my daughter was becoming the most outstandingly beautiful child. I decided to play the sympathy card-

"Dearest Maria, you are tired, the child takes it out of you, you must rest more, perhaps Doctor Banks can help, maybe I will get him to give you something to stop the nightmares, and you will be fine in a little while, this is our home, where our daughter will grow up and marry, surely you cannot want to leave, not really?" I slipped my arm around her.

"No, well, I have been tired, and you know, I do want to make you happy, you work so hard James" she sighed.

"Good girl, now, you run along to bed, and I will call Doctor Banks right away"

And there it was the solution to my problems.

Robert Banks, physician, respected pediatrician, working in the largest hospital in Glasgow, and regular patron of the dolls house. I called him and told him I had a little problem and he came and sat lugubrious in my study-

"Is it a child? Your child perhaps?" he grinned.

"My daughter will never be in the dolls house, you know that Robert, no, it's something a little more delicate, or dangerous, depending on how you see it" I smiled.

We came up with the perfect solution.

Vitamin injections. Daytime and night time. To keep her awake during the times when I needed her, for functions and receptions, and then, morphine at night to make her go into a sleep like death. And then the dolls could play and function as they pleased.

As I pleased.

Elizabeth was sent to boarding school. Kept well away and out of the picture.

I had the perfect life, and believe it or not I was pitied by the neighbors.

They saw a fine, upstanding publisher, making great inroads in literary history and bringing fine work to the masses at a price they could afford. And they saw his meek little wife, drinking too much and showing him up at functions and never being mistress in her own home.

As the years went on, Maria relied more on the injections and Banks remarked once that she seemed not to be able to survive at all without them.

He upped her dosage so many times that she barely ate or did anything but sleep, and life in Baird hall went on and on without her.

Every package of books that left my publishing house in the city, traveled to Baird hall on route to its destination, and was opened and repacked, filled with the pictures and film reels among the books, and then shipped on. I had my own drivers and shipping agents and paid enough customs men for their safe transport through customs and excise.

1965, the middle of the swinging and permissive sixties.

Elizabeth was fifteen years old and growing into a beautiful young girl. She adored me, plain and simple. Her relationship with her mother was brittle; Maria couldn't talk to her like she should. Elizabeth was what I imagined I should be, had I had her life. Free spirited and fearless. She was a tremendously gifted horsewoman. I bought her a beautiful black stallion for her fifteenth birthday, and she called it Shadow. She spent hours riding over the fields and parkland around the house.

She loved music and would often dance in the living room to the Beatles or some other band she said were part of the Mersey beat phenomena. She wore ridiculous shoes and tried to put her hair up into a beehive, and I let her. I drew the line at the chalky lipstick all though she did draw black circles round her eyes and mimed to the female singers when she thought no one was looking.

I was charmed and intrigued by her and in her I saw the same ruthlessness, like when she was goading Shadow over a fence, which I saw in myself. I thought that by the time she came out into society, she would possibly be a consort for royalty, or maybe a baronet. I planned finishing school and time away traveling.

But two things happened that year to change us forever-

Elizabeth, home from boarding school for Christmas, spent some time in the bedroom with her mother. Maria, who to my eyes was failing, had specifically requested that she be there, and she had gone and changed into jeans and a sweater and gone obediently to her mother.

I thought it was a girl thing, which maybe her mother was speaking about, well the things that mothers and daughters should talk about, long before the girl is almost sixteen.

Banks had been that morning and had left Maria's supply of morphine. But even so, she still looked unusually bright eyed when I bade her good morning and yet again in the afternoon, just before Elizabeth joined her.

"Are you all right dear?" I asked.

"Just fine James, are you going to work?"

"For a while, a new shipment needs attention, you enjoy your chat with Elizabeth" I stopped at the door and touched the frame-

"Did you take your medicine today?"

"Yes dear, this morning, and the needle is ready for next time, I just thought I would like to be awake for Lizzie's visit" she smiled sweetly, skin and bone in her lacy bed jacket. Another present from her devoted husband.

"Well, see you tonight then" I smiled and went off down the corridor.

There had indeed been a new shipment.

A young girl from Belgium, aged twelve, found wandering in the docklands by one of my drivers. Brought here and groomed and looked after for a spell, till she trusted me among all others. I dressed her in Elizabeth's cast offs and she twirled and preened like they were ermine and silk. With her limited English she still managed to speak little words of thanks and praise to me. Her name was Elise. I called her Ellie.

The nursemaid and the cleaning maid were old hands at the job now, and had the place gleaming, with the Christmas tree in the small living room, and the little parcels underneath it shimmering in the glow of the firelight.

Christmas Eve, the most magical night of the year.

And aptly, the night I chose to take Ellie as my own.

There was never any more than one child in the house nowadays. I could not risk the sound of their voices carrying anywhere outside. Not now that Elizabeth was home so often and the house was so often full of people.

This one was special. So pretty and petite. I had great plans for her.

I told her that she would be in a film, a movie and she was going to be a star. She nodded owlishly and smiled. I laughed, Hollywood had gone to the four corners of the world it seemed, and everyone knew about the films-

"Like Maryleen Monroo" she sighed.

"Just like that" I had patted her hand.

And tonight was the night I was going to prepare her for the role. But to my grievous cost, I was not so careful as usual.

I had been in the room with Ellie, for maybe an hour and was slowly bringing her round to the idea of a special game, my clothes removed and folded, for the walk back to the main house, and she, frightened, as well she might be, in the cast off underclothing of my own daughter.

"You won't be afraid, you're going to be a movie star tomorrow" I crooned.

"Movie star" she whispered, cowering in fright.

"Yes, a movie star, Ellie, shush now" I pinned her to the sofa and she tried to get out of my grasp.

"Stop, it hurt" she screamed.

"Now now, you be a good girl Ellie, or I'll slap you" I finally managed to get my hand over her mouth and the screaming was muffled.

But she wasn't going to co-operate, and I ended up slapping her hard, knocking her unconscious. And then, I could take her.

And as I was nearing my end, the door to the living room creaked, and in the frame, stood my daughter, Elizabeth.

I couldn't stop, and in my own mind, I knew that it would come to this. She was part of me, she knew me, and she was my blood. Her eyes locked with mine, hers wide open in shock, and I laughed as finally I came.

She put her hand to her mouth and ran, and I collapsed, breath heaving, on the half awake body of little Ellie.

I dressed carefully and called the nurse to come and look after the child.

You see, they were taken care of, I am not a brute.

I went out through the door, clicking it shut properly, this time, and into the corridor to the main house. It was late in the evening by now. The house was scented with a million different scents, Christmas food and cinnamon candles. I strolled along plush carpets and into the bedroom wing.

Elizabeth's room was up in the attic floor of the house. She always said she liked it there, she could see over the park and the meadows below us for miles that way.

Painted in pink and white, with all the gadgets and frills a little girl could ever want or need. The bed was a canopied confection of frills and cushions and she would sit there reading books and listening to the little dansette record player for hours.

I could hear music, loud.

I entered without knocking and she screamed. She looked wild, like she had been sick.

I never had her down as a weakling.

"Stop that this instant" I snapped.

I strode to the record player and pulled the needle off the disc with a loud scratch.

She stood in the bay window shivering-

I waited for her to begin; her eyes were open wide, the kohl she wore round them in streaks on her cheekbones. She was shaking like a leaf and her breath came in heaving sobs.

"What is it?" I asked.

"What *is* it? You ask me, you ask *that* after what, what you just, Oh daddy!" she bit her fist hard.

"You were mistaken, what you saw wasn't the real story"

She shook her head from side to side-

"How could I be mistaken, Mummy told me where to go and I didn't believe her, she told me what I'd find and I didn't believe, and then, I saw it with my own eyes, and you... you monster, you animal, how *could you?*" I saw her looking for something to throw at me, and she grabbed the crystal vase, usually filled with pink flowers and now empty, and flung it hard at me. I ducked and it hit the wall and then, I stalked across the room and grabbed her shoulders-

"*Elizabeth!*" I snapped.

She stood trembling, as though she knew she had crossed the line.

"Don't you ever raise your hand to me, I am your father and you will..."

"You're a dirty, filthy, disgusting..." she ran out of invective and I smiled.

So much for private education.

"You will listen to me, whatever your mother said to you..." I began

"Mummy told me everything, *everything,* including how you have kept her drugged for years to stop her making waves, and how you've been running this, this *sick* fucking business for years, in our *house, where we live,* and I thought it was her being evil, I ran out of her room when she told me, I couldn't believe that you would be so bad"

"Have I not given you everything you wanted?"

I waved at the room-

"How many girls have rooms like this?"

She was sobbing, tears falling unchecked. She shrank away from me.

She kept saying- *I don't want it, I don't want it, oh, I don't care, I hate you...I won't ever forget what I saw you do tonight.*

All the time I waited for her to stop her tirade and listen to me.

"Daddy, they, their only *children, how could you?"*

I wasn't about to explain where it all began or why, not to my own daughter, who should be obedient enough and respectful enough to accept her father and his word as law and accept that some people need to get their hands dirty to make a living.

She sat down suddenly-

"Is this all from *that?* Does it pay for everything? My school fees, my clothes? *Everything*?" She whispered.

"All of it, every stick of furniture and every rag on your back"

She looked up at me-

"Then I want no more of it" she spoke clearly, and in her eyes I saw a glint of steely determination.

"What do you mean?"

"I mean, I am leaving here, leaving this house and I will not come back, ever" she got up and brushed herself down, still shrinking away from me like I was poisonous.

I laughed.

"Your fifteen years old, you can't *leave home,* think of it, every time you go, I can find you, I have friends everywhere, and they will help me, the police, the judges, everyone, they will send you back again and again till I choose to set you free, don't you think it will be just as easy to keep you as it is that shambolic old bitch in the bed downstairs? Don't be a fool, girl, I can make your life just as hellish as hers, if I choose" I laughed aloud at the thought.

"You have no money only what I give you, you have no clothes, no friends, except the spoilt brats in your fancy school, and they won't want you now, not when you tell them why you're leaving home, what will you do? You can't make a living, what will you do Lizzie?"

She sighed.

"But... if you stay, and you stay quiet, then life will be as easy and as pleasurable as it was before tonight, you can keep Shadow and you can go to school and when you are of age, you can go, but I warn you, one word, one sound, one whisper of what you think you saw tonight, and I...." The sound of screaming from downstairs stopped me and I turned to the door.

"Mister Bard, hurry, please hurry"

Elizabeth ran to the door and out, down the stairs and into her mother's bedroom.

Maria was hanging, from the top of the bed canopy, the cord of her dressing gown wrapped twice round the post, and the empty syringe on the blood spattered bedcover.

Elizabeth stared with wide eyes. But this time there was no screaming.

I played the grieving husband for the servants' sake, pulling the cord from the post and cradling her in my arms as they watched-

Elizabeth was passive, standing against the foot of the bed.

"Get a doctor, ring Banks, NOW!" I roared and they scuttled away.

I stared at Elizabeth-

"Now you see what I mean, doesn't it make sense to be a good girl?" I smiled.

"I hate you" she hissed.

"You can hate me all you want, but never forget, this is my house, and you are my daughter, and I can make life hell for you if I choose, I never cared about love or hate, and I certainly don't care what you think of me, but you will be dutiful, and you will do as I say, as long as I choose to say it" I grinned-

"Because you are *mine* Elizabeth, you are my blood, and you are like me, and you will do well to remember that"

"You don't own me" She hissed.

"Oh I do, and I will, until I decide to let you go"

"You're a sick, evil bastard; I'll never let you beat me"

The poor child. She just didn't get it.

"Elizabeth, I already have, I've won"

Elizabeth decided she wasn't going back to her school and as she had just passed the legal age for school leaving, she decided that she wanted to stay at home. We buried her mother in a fine vault in the grounds of the house, and Elizabeth was the dutiful daughter, accepting condolences from the neighbors in her short black coat and mantilla veil she insisted on wearing.

For a time she took refuge in religion, attending church services in the local town with increasing regularity, and at one time, made enquiries into entering a convent! Imagine it? A daughter of mine? The heir to my fortune, in a nun's veil.

When she was sixteen she actually went to Skipton, down south, to see about entering enclosed orders, but the reverend mother, sensibly, sent her home, telling me, later in a letter, that she could not accept her until she faced up to what she was running from.

I replied that I couldn't imagine what it was, and sent a nice donation to the convent coffers for their troubles.

She hardly played music any more and she stayed in her room, sometimes only coming down to eat in the evenings, dressing in dowdy clothes and reading inspirational texts.

Until the day Noel came home.

In 1968, late in the year he arrived at the door of the house and was let into the study to speak with me. I had sent him to school too, and he was grown up well. Twenty two years old, broad shouldered and not as tall as I, but nonetheless a reasonably good looking lad.

"I've been working with the horses, down south, and I hear that you have bought more, and might need a groom" he said.

"You want to work here?" I smiled. "Why?"

He looked around the room-

"It was home when I was a kid, and you looked after my mother when she, when she was sick, sir, I just thought that maybe, well, you know" he wasn't as bright as I thought he was.

Maybe had he known that I was his father his attitude would have been much less servile.

I took him on. I put him out in the stables and he worked well. I silently congratulated myself on looking after my children so well.

Elizabeth was away, doing courses now, training in secretarial skills, because it was the vogue for young women at that moment. She took deportment classes too, and one of her tutors asked would she be a photographic model. I paid for her flat and she lived with two girls in Islington, in London. I kept close tabs on her and knew what moves she made. She was part of the swinging London set, the party girls who kept the gossip mill turning and whetted. Hardly a day went by that I didn't see her on the arm of someone in the papers. In the latest fashions and looking tipsy. Maybe she was more her mother's daughter than I'd thought.

I never let myself appear drunk. I never lost that control, that steely edge to my character. Others in my house for hunting and shooting parties would lose their grip and become tipsy, and I would watch silently, waiting for their first sign of loose tongue or indiscretion, and then they would be disposed of and never asked again.

Elizabeth didn't come home again till the summertime, 1968.

She immediately went out to the stables to her beloved Shadow, now getting on a bit, and not able to jump as well as he might. But still she insisted on riding him around the parklands, for hours on end.

Noel was her side kick.

It was becoming obvious that they were friends. And I indulged the friendship. I made it known that Lizzie, as she was called in the gossip columns, was almost engaged to the son of a Lord, and that she had come home to spend time thinking about her forthcoming marriage. Maybe I should have been more careful. I was trying to expand the publishing side of the business, trying to make my income, which was growing bigger by the month, more legitimate, to cope with new taxation laws the government was insisting on passing by the week.

They seemed to want to crucify the self made and the millionaires.

Rock musicians left in their thousands for Ireland, altogether a more liberal country, tax wise. But not an option for me. Not with my other enterprise.

I bought out two companies in Birmingham and Swindon. Browne and Stokes was the main publisher of school texts and academic works and I thought that they might be a good place to begin legitimizing my business. After all, quite a few of the contracts seemed to be government backed and they could hardly accuse me of wrongdoing or not paying tax on income they had paid me, could they?

Their top salesman, a young Irishman, called Williams, was pushing hard to earn decent money and by the time he came to my attention in 1968 he was well on course.

I met him at the initial meeting to buy out the business, and liked him. He had honesty, in the sense that he seemed to love what he did and had tried to make up for a lack of education by reading and seemed to have a keen eye for what might sell and what would end up in the bargain bin at Woolworth within the month.

I liked him, in as much as I liked anyone.

He seemed malleable and eager to learn and to please.

I returned home in August and as I usually did, went looking for Elizabeth.

My mind was elsewhere and I walked into the barn and didn't quite register what I was seeing.

They saw me before I saw them.

She managed to get herself decently covered before I was actually standing over them. I picked up the nearest object I could find, a harness, and beat Noel to within an inch of his life.

"What are you doing?" He roared, trying to cover himself and save his head and face from the beating.

"Get out of here, you filthy bastard" I screamed, incandescent with rage.

Elizabeth was cowering in a corner, her clothes barely on her.

Noel escaped and ran, and when he was found later, I ordered that he be cleaned up and paid off. He went to Ireland, with a letter of recommendation, for a trainer in the Curragh. That was the last I hoped to see of him. But later, he came in useful, as time will tell. The name might have changed, but still, what's bred into bone comes out in the spirit.

That was the start of it with Elizabeth.

She was openly defiant now, drinking heavily and sometimes, the sweet smell of marijuana would come down from the room up in the attic. She showed no inclination to go back to her career, such as it was, for the time being, and as summer turned to autumn, I realized, that there was a reason.

She had her own bathroom, but I was right underneath her room, and in the early morning, I could hear the water running and the toilet flushing repeatedly.

I listened every day for a week and then sent for her-

"Is there anything you want to tell me?"

She stared back-

"Nothing Daddy"

"You're sure?" I tapped my pen on the table.

"Absolutely"

I looked at her eyes; no doubt that she was smoking something funny, her eyes were glazed and her gaze a little askew.

"I want to tell you something, we are having guests this weekend, a shooting party, and I would like you to be here, to be hostess, people are curious about this engagement, to Lord Thomas' son, is it to happen or not?" I asked.

"Nothing has changed, I am still thinking it over" she said.

"Well, you have one more week and then I want a decision"

"Yes Daddy"

She turned to go, and stopped-

"Daddy, do you, are the children, still..." she trailed off.

"None of your concern, go now please, and tidy yourself up"

September 1968.

The party started on a Friday afternoon with cars pulling up at the door from all the major families in the district and many of the patrons of the dolls house in situ. I looked around the drawing room and sighed.

Elizabeth, hell bent on thwarting me, had gone out riding and was no where to be seen. My eye fell on the young, Irish man, Williams, who seemed to be wedged into the sofa beside Mrs. Doctor Banks, who was asking about "society" in Ireland and where he might frequent.

The poor lad in the cheap suit was trying to fend off her comments and I laughed to myself.

He had a similar upbringing to my own, piss poor family, in a tenement flat in Dublin. I'd say the nearest he got to the Shelburne hotel was walking past it, just as I did back then. But Millie Banks seemed satisfied by his answers, and was practically purring at him when Elizabeth made an appearance.

Even I thought she looked magnificent.

Still in her riding clothes, a long habit skirt and white blouse with stock, which I had expressly forbidden outside of the riding stables, she swept into the room and looked around with disdain before plunking into the sofa opposite Williams and grabbing a sandwich off the salver in front of her.

She barely passed the time of day with Millie Banks before turning her full voltage charms onto Williams.

If you could call it charm, that is.

I came upon them just as she was accusing him of involvement in the IRA and he was squirming in the chair, the colour of a beetroot and stammering.

I sent her away to change and the room returned to normal.

Millie Banks called me aside before dinner-

"You know James, I never ask questions, and I never talk out of turn" she stank of sherry and was slightly bloodshot in the eye. I recoiled and she gripped my lapel-

"But you need to be watchful, yes, watchful of that Irish lad, he's smitten with Lizzie, and you know, he comes from nothing, *nothing at all*" she hissed confidentially.

I smiled and removed her hand from my jacket.

"As do I Mrs. Banks"

She blushed-

"Yes, but the *lower* classes, they have more faith in the law, in honesty than we do, and you know, they have less to lose, they *question*" she swayed slightly.

I smiled fixedly.

How much does this old bitch know? I wondered. I made up my mind to speak to Banks about her and her problem with the drink. I couldn't afford this house of cards to be endangered by a tattle tongued bitch like this.

I patted her arm and passed her to her husband who led her into dinner.

Williams was all adrift through the meal and I could see his disappointment when Elizabeth didn't show up for dinner, the faint sound of music coming from the attic room and afterwards, he was standing in the hall drinking a small brandy when she appeared. I knew by the look on his face that she was there, even before I turned and saw her on the steps in her diaphanous white gown.

To a lad like him she must have looked like an angel. But to me, she was a she devil through and through. Knowing full well that I couldn't stop her, she took his arm and in full view of the company, went out into the gardens and away from sight.

I knew what she was doing that night.

The poor girl he *had* been dating before his visit north didn't stand a chance when faced with opposition like this. A dumpy, ginger haired nurse in the infirmary in London, against *my* daughter? His head was royally turned and even as he was on the train back to Birmingham, still picking bits of straw out of his hair, I was making arrangements.

For I knew what was coming next.

Elizabeth went back to London, in early November 1968, and within four days, she turned up, with her new husband in tow. She seemed to delight in the fact that she had blown out a title, that she was now going to be plain, Mrs. Williams and nothing more than that.

"Why him Elizabeth?" I asked, having brought her to my study.

"He's honest, and he's faithful, and *he* won't get involved in your filthy trade, and he can't be bought by you, *that's why*" she hissed, leaning over my desk.

"You will never be a wife, a mother, your better than that" I sneered.

"Oh but I will, I am a wife, in *every way*" she smiled.

"And a mother too?"

"Perhaps" she flushed a little.

"Does he know its not..."

She slammed her hands on the desk-

"You listen to me, I want out of here, and you can't stop me now, I'm a married woman now, and wherever my husband goes, so go I, and if you breathe a *word* to him about this, I swear I will burn this house and all in it to the ground"

I smiled.

"Lizzie, darling, *everyone* has a price, including your poor fool of a husband, and honestly, don't you think he has the right to know what whore he has married? And as for burning the house, well, if it burns, so do you, for you're an accomplice to a crime now, poor Elizabeth, you should have gone to the police five years ago, not let it carry on under your nose"

She went white and I thought she might faint. I rang a bell and a maid appeared-

"Take, *Mrs. Williams* to bed, and tell her husband I will see him now" I smiled as Elizabeth was helped from the room.

My new son in law had the kind of open face you saw on people who had witnessed a crime and were telling about it in the dock.

"I love your daughter sir, more than anything and, and I want to look after her" he started on about flats in Birmingham and working there himself. I couldn't see my daughter living in a two roomed flat with nothing more than washing nappies and making bottles to entertain her.

He didn't want to take the job, thinking that his marriage had been the only reason I offered it. But I laughed that off-

"On your merits then, start at the bottom and work up if you wish"

He liked that better and began work in earnest.

Of course they could have stayed living with me in the big house, but I had been working on another option that seemed to suit better.

The gate lodge. A small three bed roomed mews that had lain unoccupied for many years. I got builders in and they plastered and fixed and built a kitchen and bathroom and made it nice. The couple themselves decorated and the bills came to me at the house. A wedding gift, you understand.

I stayed away from them, in some way hoping that when they fell apart, it would be themselves that were the problem. But they didn't fall apart, certainly not as quickly as I had hoped.

I drove past one day and David was out in the garden digging and Elizabeth was sitting on a wall, laughing, her stomach protruding through her crocheted smock, and music playing on a little transistor radio. As I watched, he pulled her down off the wall and they kissed, and then danced to the music, his muddy hands making marks on her dress.

She seemed to be blooming with happiness.

By the beginning of May 1969, I was waiting for the child to be born. Surely a child conceived in late August should come soon. But still the weeks dragged on, until on the last day in May, Stephen Patrick Williams was born.

My grandson.

Elizabeth was worn out with the demand of motherhood so I sent the odd maid down to the cottage and they helped out when needed, and even I had to admit that the boy was beautiful.

With more of Elizabeth in him than anyone.

And the same eyes as me.

But then, wasn't he more me than anyone?

Shouldn't he look more like us than we did ourselves?

I laughed at the thought and watched and waited for the defects that were sure to be there and when they didn't appear, I put them down to luck. The luck of the draw.

Once more, the Gods smiled on me and I escaped detection.

By now, the beginning of the 70's, I was almost completely out of the game. Pornography as a genre was in the cinemas, mainstream now, and nothing shocked those who went looking for it. If it were possible for it to go out of fashion, then in my opinion that is what it did.

Ellie, dear little child, never did become a movie star.

She ran away to London herself, and faded into the strip joints and club scene, until she was found in a squat with a second rate guitarist, strung out and emaciated. I paid for medical care and was sad when she died.

She's buried here, not in the vault, but under a tree with little pink blossoms.

Apt, I thought.

The music scene was becoming exciting, and for a while I toyed with some of the musicians, hosting parties that of course, my daughter and her erstwhile husband would attend. I knew Elizabeth missed the bright lights and it was beginning to show. I let the brightest lights in the business come to my home, and how people clamored for invitations.

The daughters and sons of the original dolls house patrons came dressed in their outlandish fashions and yes, once or twice, romance blossomed and they went off with glad thoughts in their hearts for me, the benevolent old uncle in the mansion.

And then there were the others.

You see, being what I am, and knowing what I know, I can smell it, a like minded soul, when I see it. So sometimes, just for entertainment, I would arrange a selection of tableaux, young girls and boys, in the private wing, of course, making sure that my daughter was away in London. Usually she would go to visit Banks' daughter Stephanie, and her husband Nick. I would make sure that they had a call from a friend of mine, who supplied the finest cannabis and cocaine for their use, and of course Elizabeth did it too.

She went down to London quite a bit and it didn't surprise me when David asked to be transferred down there. I knew he was having it rough, trying to hold down a job, mind the child and watch her too.

I let them go and smiled.

She would think that this was her way out. But I would not be beaten.

Nothing that ever happened in her life was by chance.

I knew that to let her out of my sight or my mind once, would be a grave mistake. So I hovered, and watched.

The nanny they hired was vetted by me.

Breda Storey wouldn't have gotten within fifty feet of that house in London, and my grandson if I didn't think she was as gullible and innocent as David.

Or as stupidly honest.

Oh signs were, she idolized the child and that was all fine by me. I didn't want anything happening to him. Not yet, that is.

My new enterprise took me out of the country at times, trafficking children from the Far East to Europe. Altogether very satisfying work for a man of my taste. I became known as "The Spider" among the musicians and artistes that looked to me for their little gratifications. Flattering, don't you think?

I weave a web of contacts and they are all interlinked and interwoven, and it all still comes back to me.

And all the time, Elizabeth was going her own sweet way, going down the track to the point of no return.

Of course I knew what was happening! I knew about the wild parties she went to and the drink and drug sessions in her house when that fool was at work. Breda used to run with the child to her sisters, when they could actually get out of the house, that is.

David came to me and asked for help.

He actually told me he was considering divorce and leaving the country with little Steven, and I laughed-

"I told you you'd rue the day you married her!"

"I still love her, and as for the child"

"You finally realize that he isn't yours?"

He looked pale.

"I always though that maybe, well, since he was born I thought, but he's mine in all the important ways" he smiled sadly.

"Ah, how sweet, and now, let me guess, she's fallen again?"

His head shot up and he stared-

"How do you know?"

"I know"

I knew because I knew what she was doing and with whom every time she ventured out. I knew her dealer, I *paid* her dealer. I knew the lovers she had. Her current, a guitar player in a band called "Starlight" was a prolific drunk and user of heavy narcotics. He got what he wanted in Lizzie, and she got what she needed from his dealer. Little did she know that she need not have prostituted herself for it.

Did I not give it to her mother for free?

"Well look, James, I can't do this anymore, I can't take on a kid that I know isn't mine, She, she needs help, please can you help us, get her into a clinic or something?" He was desperate and I took pity.

"So we dry her out and what then? Divorce?"

He swallowed hard-

"I don't know, I, my religion won't allow it, you see"

"You didn't think of that when you fucked my daughter"

"That's a terrible way to put it"

"It was a terrible thing you did" I snapped.

"I loved her, I truly loved her, from the minute I saw her" he whispered.

"Humph, that's as may be, but your paying the price for the night in the hay barn now, aren't you lad?" I played the father scorned to a tee.

I dialed the number of a reasonably fine clinic in Aberdeen.

Elizabeth was in there by the end of the day and out again within the week. Four, maybe five times she ran and we kept bringing her back. The terror in her eyes was disturbing. She would beg them to let her go, leave her out, not bring her back home.

"Liz its not home, darling its hospital, they want to help you" David would try to console her.

But she would stare with wide open eyes at me, over his shoulder and beg him to let her leave.

He would leave the child with Breda and go to the hospital to her, sitting beside her, playing her music and talking to her, trying to build a life for when they got her well again.

Wild ideas about travel, emigrating even.

And I knew it would come to naught.

The final time she ran away from the Aberdeen clinic, she got as far as London again. How she did it will always be a mystery to me. She had no clothes, bar the nightdress she was wearing and a pair of moccasin slippers.

It was early June 1972.

I decided that enough was enough. The clinic wouldn't take her back anyhow, and she was too near her time. I put her into the Glasgow Infirmary, and put Breda in as her companion and nurse. I paid the hospital well for a private room and the best of medical care.

David had given up. He was working at home and with the boy a lot of the time.

The day she went into confinement, I went to the hospital and spoke to the Master.

I asked him how Elizabeth was, in herself, and what chance a healthy child-

"Slim to none Mr. Bard, I'm afraid"

He steepled his hands on the desk-

"A great pity, indeed, she being from such a good family to find herself in this situation"

I turned the tables and began to speak. I made David out to be a monster, a pariah who fed his wife's addiction.

"And its such a pity that she will have to face the music when its really he who is to blame, after all, how can I get her back to herself when she will be brokenhearted at what she has done to this poor innocent babe"

He sighed. I could nearly see his heart bleeding.

"Well, you must do what you see is fit, I mean, there's a case in here at the minute, a young unmarried girl, her boyfriend unemployed, and they having a baby too, when I think of that poor child going back to whatever squat and squalor they came from, and your daughter able to give a child so much when she gets away from that monster, well..." he sighed again.

"A sad time indeed, I shall talk to you later" I got up to leave.

The picture I had painted, one of privilege and happiness, ponies and wealth, for my daughters child once she, Elizabeth, had removed the husband from the equation, well, it must have stayed with that eminent doctor.

Because it was all so easily accomplished.

While my daughter slept, following the birth of her scrawny little daughter, with the ginger hair and small eyes of her father, I crept to the nursery where Breda sat, trying to get the child to take a bottle.

"She won't, sir" she whispered.

I looked at the child, and saw that she was very sickly indeed.

I looked around the nursery and saw another child, a bigger, red haired baby, with strong chubby limbs and cheeks.

"It's a pity" I sighed.

"I worry about this, Breda, the effect it will have on Elizabeth, the publicity" I murmured.

I reached into the cot and lifted the baby.

My eyes met Breda's and she stared-

"You can't mean..."

"Why not?"

"But, the mother...?"

She shook her head.

"I can't do this, you can't, its, oh Sir" she started to cry and as she did, I saw the child in her arms start, and go still.

She looked down and kissed the child, making the sign of the cross over it.

"Breda?"

She stood up, and without a word, put the dead child into the other cot.

I held out the baby to her and we walked out and back to Elizabeth's room.

The rot that set in all those years ago, when Elizabeth had seen me in the dolls house with dear little Ellie, well it was maturing and coming to bear fruit now.

This child, called Amber, after some character in a book she had read, was nothing to me. I was beginning to think that she might be an asset yet. For her mother, well, sedated and medicated as she was, was not bound to notice her half as well as she might, and maybe when she was older, she might make a nice little distraction for my old age.

She was, after all, no blood kin to me, and therefore...

Nothing as sacred as my blood, nothing so untouchable.

And in Lizzie's case, nothing so ruined, so desecrated, and so destroyed.

I thought that she would be staying in Baird Hall, but reckoned without David.

He arrived at the house and nothing on earth would do him but to take them back to London with him. Breda too.

How many times in the next few months did I try to lure her back?

God only knows.

I paid her allowance and her dealers. I tried to make her realize that the only place for her was with me and in her own home, Baird Hall. How could she live without me? But her stubbornness and her willfulness drove her further and further away.

This in effect was what I wanted.

She was becoming tiresome, a pain.

More often in the papers for the state she was in than the glamorous clothing she once wore. I was sick of her bringing attention to my house and to me, through the blackening of my name.

In 1973 I offered her a final out-

America.

I would pay for her to go, take the daughter she thought so highly of and go. But the boy stayed here.

He was four and a half now, started in a kindergarten near his home.

I wanted him in a private school; I saw Eton or Harrow, perhaps. The military school if he wished. But always, always, he would take over when I was gone.

I didn't want him to mix with the dregs of society; he had to know how to mix with the best. And let's face it, a scrubber for a mother and a fool for a father, well, that didn't make for fine society.

But Williams insisted-

"Stevie stays home too, thank you for the kind offer, but I am in charge of his schooling" he would say.

Elizabeth was back in the house in London on and off.

Her affair was fizzling out and she was in trauma. Panic had set in. Her drug habit was becoming so large that even my allowance didn't cover it. So I played my trump card.

I stopped paying her dealer and halted the allowance.

She started to sell her clothes, her possessions and finally herself. She drove everywhere in the red mini she had since her marriage to Williams, and would take the child everywhere.

I laughed at her naivety.

In her misguided attempt to protect the baby, she put her into more danger than she ever realized. The dolls house was a cake walk compared to the places she went to now.

October 1973, was her final descent. I rang her on Halloween night and asked her once more to bring the children back to Baird, that she could live there and get clean and the children would be taken care of.

"Elizabeth, there could be a better school for Steven, and for the baby, nursemaids and horses, the kind of life you once had, think about it" I whispered to her, and heard her sobbing on the phone.

"No I won't, I won't bring my children to that house, you leave me alone, do you hear me?" she banged the phone down and I laughed.

I laughed when they phoned me a couple of days later and told me she had disappeared.

Another attempt to escape me and her past.

Futile.

I waited for the phone call to tell me she was back, back in trouble, locked up and using again. And it never came.

I tried to contact Breda and she was gone.

I contacted Williams and he was frantic.

"She went a week ago, she went out in the car with the baby and she hasn't come back, I don't know where she is" he babbled.

I checked everywhere, but there was no trace.

Then a contact of mine told me that a woman, answering the description of Breda Storey was working in a bar in Camden.

I walked in there the following evening and she nearly fainted-

"Where is she Breda?" I asked.

"I don't know sir, I swear to you I don't" she whispered.

"The baby?"

She blushed scarlet. Breda could never lie.

"Listen to me Breda, I want her back, I want her and the children home with me, you better tell me what you know" I hissed.

And it came, a long tale of my daughter, handing the child to her nurse, her nanny, to take care of and then in turn, she handed her to her childless sister, who took her out of the country.

"Where to?" I gripped her arm tightly, so she cried.

"Ireland, I think" she sobbed.

"You have the nerve to think that I will allow my daughters child to be reared like a scrubber in Ireland" I spat the words out.

Breda pulled herself up in the chair and fixed me with a stare-

"But she isn't your daughter's child; you and I both know that, don't we?"

I dropped the arm I was gripping and sat back in the chair. She had me there. Maybe I could let go of the obsession with the girl, and concentrate on my real heir.

"You win Breda, Amber can go, but Steven stays"

She sighed with relief.

"I will pay an allowance, and you are to leave the country too, where do you think my daughter is?"

"America, I think, she, she mentioned it"

I smiled.

"America it is then, you be ready to go, the tickets and money will be ready on Friday"

My daughter was found on the 16th November 1973, drowned.

Her little red car was pulled out of the Thames when a spell of dry weather exposed some of the riverbed. The car was full of debris and silt but could still be forensically examined. Elizabeth, badly decomposed and unrecognizable, was in the front seat.

A bracelet I had given her was on her arm, the clothes she wore were recognizable to me also. I didn't see her, I didn't want to. I believe there was little left in any case. The fish and the water had done their work well. Perhaps that was how she planned it. Not to give me the satisfaction of looking at her dead. Who knows?

Amber's toys and clothing was on the floor behind her. There was no other body in the car. The windows were all open and the windscreen had caved in. They said that the child had been brought out to sea.

I knew different, but I let them think that.

The verdict was suicide, I thought.

Until they found the brake cables cut in half and a neighbor in the London street where she lived, came forward to swear that she saw David with his head under the bonnet the day before his wife went missing.

How I laughed the day he was tried and found guilty with double murder.

I took my grandson, the one I wanted all along, by the hand and away to Baird Hall.

My heir.

I would have reared him to be a true heir to my empire, an heir worthy of the dolls house and all that went with it.

Most of Elizabeth's consorts and junkie friends were dead at this stage, and any that weren't, were in such horrendous shape that they couldn't string three words together.

Breda was gone to America, her sister afraid to come forward in case she lost the child, and David rotting in prison.

There was nothing to stop me molding and making little Steven into a mirror image of me.

Oh how I planned the day when I would bring him to the dolls house, bring him to see what his grandfathers *real* work was.

I sent him to a great school. And though he was young, he was academically brilliant. He was thriving there. And then it fell apart-

Williams got out of jail in 1978. And immediately took him out of school and ran back to Ireland.

He thought I didn't know anything, but my web spreads a lot wider than he thinks, and I knew all along that he was there. I knew where he was and what he was doing. Even the house he bought was part financed by me, who paid the price again, on top to make sure he got it. And he went to private school and made few friends and still I knew. And I even knew about Amber.

In 1985 I received a letter from Noel Holliman, as he called himself now, asking about Elizabeth.

I heard that she drowned, and I am sorry to hear that. I also heard that the child died, but heres the thing, I don't think she did, because you remember that Breda Storey? Well her sister is living with me, in Blanchardstown, and the young one she adopted is near enough the same age as little Amber would be now, and to be honest, her and her husband were so paranoid about something to do with the kid, that they didn't go the distance and she and I had an affair, and now we have our own kids and I was wondering if there was any chance of a retainer, and I could keep you informed...

Noel, greedy as always.

Money was going to the child via Breda. She wouldn't allow me to have the address of course, but I could send it to her at the house she was working in and she would pass it on. So the child was well cared for.

Not that I cared really, she was too old for me at this stage.

Thirteen years old, and in the photo I was sent by Noel, she was a tall child, with curly hair, and wearing jeans and a sweater with something printed on it.

I gave him a trifle, a small sum every month to keep me informed and he behaved well.

You can barely imagine my delight when he wrote to me and told me of the events of 1990 and 1991.

Even in my wildest fantasies, I couldn't have thought that Amber and Steven would find each other again.

How I laughed when I realized that Elizabeth had handed over all the certs and documents, including the birth certificate, and there was blue murder going on in Ireland.

She would have been better to let the child go alone, with nothing.

Instead she did precisely what she set out to avoid.

She tore her children's lives to bits, and sent Steven back to me, just as I always planned.

The telephone call from Breda was hilarious-

New Years Eve 1991, after midnight, a call from Leeds.

I was in bed, a mild cold on my chest. I'm not so well lately. A viral thing I picked up in the Far East in 1986 when sampling some not so young merchandise, well it leaves me terribly susceptible to flu and suchlike. But I am old enough now, seventy five years old, and not as involved in business as once I was. Of course, I dabble, here and there, but the way things went in the late 1980's with the trials of that singer, the glam rocker and the disc jockey, I thought it best to leave it alone.

I thought that I would be dead before they found him again.

The doctors cannot understand it.

"AIDS is a young person's disease Mr. Bard" my doctor, a new one, said. Banks died of a heart attack long ago. They cannot find out why and how I caught it. I found no reason to enlighten them.

"I traveled a lot in my time" I smile.

I still have money, because my business thrives still.

I have enough for all the drugs that are new to the market and I allow them to experiment, so that my life is prolonged. But still I get tired, and bedtime is usually early nowadays.

So I was asleep when the nurse came and asked me to take the call from Breda-

"Sir, I think I've found Steven" She blurted.

I smiled into the phone.

"Breda, how lovely to hear from you after all this time" I grinned. Because I already knew. Holliman had told me that the lad was on route to me and though I expected him to take a while, seven months had been a bit of an exaggeration.

"Sir, I think he's a down and out, or something, he was in a bad accident, six months ago, he lost all his memory, but its him, I know as sure as anything it is" she babbled.

I closed my eyes.

She prattles on, telling me that he is called Gary now, that there was nothing on him to identify him as my grandson. Nothing except the Bard eyes. He still has them. And she knew him.

I told her to bring him to me.

And she did, and the final chapter in my life began.

I thought about the past year, and how some young woman in Ireland had tried to get me into a court room to talk, tried to get an injunction to make me talk! The impertinence of it, the audacity!

If I had stayed quietly here, waiting and biding my time for the last twenty years, what on earth made her think that she, a fledgling solicitor, could force the issue? Oh she could ring all the people she liked, but still I have contacts, still I have friends, and there is little concerning me that I don't know about, and that I cannot stop or start as I please.

But still I play with fate and play with time.

I pull them all into the web, closer and closer and I wait for my time.

She, the little solicitor, married to a Frenchman now, whose wedding I regretfully didn't attend, but sent a beautiful piece of crystal, the figure of a little girl, in hand-blown glass. Apt, don't you think?

I let Steven believe the tissue of lies, concocted to confuse him. I never enlightened him as to his real past. I made him well, with all the best medical care and help in the world, and watched as he married a woman who I had known since her birth.

Yes I was "good" to her too. Her family thrived and survived because of me.

They even got over the loss of their first born.

Taken for the sake of my own.

I cannot leave this life without him knowing what I did for him. I cannot allow him to throw his life away on a changeling, a child of no consequence, and leave behind the empire I have made for him.

Blood of my blood, flesh of my flesh. He is more mine than any other.

And now, one year to the day of my finding him again, he comes to me again.

His little wife rang me yesterday, and she told me that he would.

Breda ran out of the house this morning and she has not been found.

I find it lonely here for the first time in my life, because the only sound now is the ticking of the clock in the hall.

James Bard, who never needed anyone or anything, listening to the silence and wishing there was more.

I cannot look back and think that perhaps I should have done things a little differently. I think of the little girl, Sarah, in that lavatory in Liverpool, and wonder if I had not drawn blood then, would I have hungered for it all this time?

Would I have wanted my own flesh and blood under my control?

Could I have been a different man, better than I am, with hordes of children and happy with a fine wine and perhaps go into my final days with the love of a family around me?

Would that have been enough?

I think not.

There is no room for sentiment, no point in introspection. I educated myself and I am a self made man, disappointed by my family and driven by the longing, the nameless, forbidden lusts, that started all those years ago.

And now, the blood that moves in my body is what will kill me in the end.

I look in the mirror and I see a cadaver, a shell. I see a man who had everything and now must fight to keep what remains to me. And fight I will.

There is no need for an army of servants, because I find now that the house decays like I decay, from the inside out. Steven is the only hope. He is the flicker of light that remains when all else is dead to me now. And the sound of silence closes in, as I wait for what must soon come.

Somehow I think that I can feel time passing away with every tick that sounds. The clock, once the keeper of the hours that I spent in the company of like minded people, souls who would be nothing without me and now serves as nothing more than an hourglass for the time that I waste waiting for him to return.

I need the chair now. Walking has become too hard, at times, to attempt.

But still I dress well, and wait in my dinner suit, and I watch the hall, waiting for them to come. Oh, but I am but a shadow of the God that governed the dolls.

My mind still works; my mind is still as lucid as ever.

The sound of a car, coming up the track to the house makes me smile. I hear the doors slam and imagine them walking towards the house. I hear voices and I know that he has brought the changeling. The fool. Does he think that she will be allowed to live? That I will watch him waste his bloodline on a child of no consequence?

I lift my glass to the past and sip it cautiously.

Lately, my mouth has become dry, my tongue cracked, and wine is not the pleasure it once was. But tonight, is like a rebirth, and the glory of the Bard name will be restored. So I drink what makes me wince, feeling like splintered glass on my tongue, and I wait for my chance to come.

And as I shrink into the shadows of the hallway, and watch them walk into my house, I smile.

Waiting for the moment when I can once more, move into the light.

The family crest hangs over the stairs, *operor quis vos mos*, do what you will.

Of late, this life has been taken over by other things and what I wanted hasn't happened as quickly as I would like. But fate has intervened again and I believe that I am beginning to live by the motto again.

I will repaint the crest, which has faded and once more the name of Bard will be a force to be reckoned with.

And my true heir, son of my son, son of my daughter, will be the one to carry it on.

16

We hired a car and drove, literally for hours.

Steven didn't talk much and I sat looking out at the scenery, until it grew too dark for me to see.

The radio changed station five times until finally, there was nothing except Scottish traditional music on it and we turned it off, not having a clue how to tune it and not wanting the bother of it anyhow. There was a lot of snow as we went further and further up into the highlands, it might have been nice, in other circumstances, to see the place, maybe stay there for a while. Three hours after Glasgow and we were still driving half lost in the dark, doubling back a couple of times and finding the road again.

I kept looking at him, his jaw set like granite, his eyes unblinking as he looked ahead.

"Steven, what are you going to say to him?"

He sighed-

"Dunno Carrie, he has to have a reason for being the way he is, and that thing, the thing Breda said, about the house having a secret place, I don't remember it at all, I don't know how I missed it in the year I was there, its not that big a place that you could miss a bloody wing for fucks sake!" he grimaced as snow began to fall heavily and it got visibly colder. There were illuminus red and yellow posts along the sides of the road so that we knew where it was. It wasn't nice driving in it, let me tell you.

"Did you get to go round the house much?" I asked.

"Well, when I got there first I was in a chair and I was on one floor, naturally, and then when I could get out and about, I would go riding and then I was away in London with Colleen, so... I just didn't realize it was there, but I have an idea how to find it and I will, if it really does exist" he turned into a small petrol station and filled up the car for the umpteenth time.

I had no doubt that it did.

Breda had looked too sickened by it all for it not to be real. I was afraid.

I was afraid because tonight was only the start of it all for me. Okay, I had my man back with me, and he and I were as happy and as close as two changed people could be. But yesterday, Breda's revelation had shocked me to the core.

I had a mother and father. Alive and well. I had a sister and a brother, alive and well. I had to try and make amends to the sister, but surely that would all pan out in time.

I don't know if I could bear to forgive anyone for taking him away from me on purpose, so maybe Colleen won't forgive me, ever.

I thought as I watched him walking back from the garage shop.

"Jesus that was close" he laughed.

"What?"

"I nearly signed my name as Steven Williams, and not Gary Bard, for the credit card" he grinned.

"Must take a bit of getting used to"

He shook his head.

"You have no idea, honestly"

But I did. I didn't know who I was anymore. Was I Carrie, Rachel, Layla or Amber? And when would I know?

When would the four people I was, or that they *said* I was, when would they all click into place? And when would I feel at home again?

We drove for another hour on a sort of main road and then off, onto a narrow minor road, for another hour or more.

"God Steve, where is this place?"

"I know, the back of beyond isn't it?"

"You're telling me, God, I would never find it" I squinted out into the dark.

We finally turned up a laneway and drove slowly, over ramps and potholes the size of moon craters.

"Why doesn't he fix this road if he's richer than God?" He grumbled.

To stop the ones he didn't want, or to ensure that only the most determined would get in. I didn't say it, but that's what came to mind.

The headlights swept ahead and lit up, for a moment or two, what looked like a graveyard.

"Jesus, who gets buried in there? The family?" I whispered.

"I think so, my grandmother is in the vault there, but there's a few graves in it all right, haven't seen any funerals lately though, maybe it's full, or disused"

It was incredibly spooky, looming out of the dark like that, and I shivered.

"Cold?" Steven turned the heating up full.

"A bit freaked to be honest" I tried to smile.

"We're nearly there, it's going to be over soon honey, and then we can go home again"

Home. What a lovely thought that was. Home to my own bed and my life to start over again.

The house was lit up. The snow thick, but the gravel around the house was clear enough. He must have an army of servants here. We pulled in quietly and got out of the car.

The cold was biting. I pulled my coat around me and we walked up the stairs to the door.

"Carrie, whatever happens in here tonight, I want you to know that I love you, forever" he took my face in his hands and kissed me.

I slipped my arms round him and we held each other for a moment.

The door opened at a touch and we went inside.

The house was grand. Not overly so, but nicely furnished, if a little ornate for my taste. There was a glass door inside the hall door and it opened easily onto a tiled floor. The main hall had a wide stairway and it divided into two halfway up, so that the landings were like a balcony overlooking us. There was a lot of red and burgundy coloring on the walls and the carpet on the stairs.

Halfway up, where the stairs divided, was a huge clock. It ticked loudly in the silence.

"His study is over here" Steven whispered.

He pulled me into a room where the walls were paneled in dark wood, with a huge desk in the middle of the floor didn't even begin to use up the space. A fire burned, but it hadn't been fed in a while and was dying out. I shivered.

"Okay?" he asked.

"Hmm, nervous" I smiled.

"Don't be, we'll be grand" he took my hand.

I looked up at the portrait on the wall-

"Is that him?"

"Yeah"

"Wow, you do have his eyes" I stared up at the picture and felt a funny sensation in my stomach.

"More than my eyes, he has my blood" a voice, stronger than I expected, from behind me. I span around and came face to

face with James Bard. Author of every misfortune I had suffered in the past year.

I had thought about this moment all the time we were driving. I mean, what else could I think of, because I had learnt the hard way, never plan for tomorrow, because you just never know where the hell you might be.

In my mind, I figured on a tall man, someone with a clipped accent, someone dignified and with an edge, as if he was made out of surgical steel. I thought he must be a monster, ugly, a pariah, unimaginably ugly and cruel.

What I got was a skinny old man in a wheelchair, dressed in a dinner jacket two sizes too big for him, like a baddie in a B movie. His hair brushed back off a high forehead and the eyes, dimmed with age and cold as steel.

There was a curious smell in the room, chemical. And when I looked at the desk, I saw the packets and bottles of pills, lined up with a decanter of water.

So, the old man is ill. Well now.

Could that be the reason for all our troubles? In my own head I put the whole thing down to petty jealousy and spite. He lost Elizabeth and wanted Steven and David hadn't let him take him.

He stared at me and then flicked his gaze away to Steven-

"I knew you were going to come, but why bring *that* with you? She's nothing to you" he spat.

Steven gripped my arm.

"Grandfather, you can't say that to her, she's, I love her, and she's one of us too, isn't she?" I looked at him in surprise; after all, we knew the truth now.

He laughed-

"That scrubber is nothing to me, you're what I want, you're my heir, my hope, you're the one I want here, not some changeling brat that will drag you into the gutter" He wheeled himself closer. My heart hammered in my chest.

Maybe I had watched too many horror films in my time, but I was expecting the window to fly open and this man to take flight with a huge "ha hah" like Christopher Lee or some other vampire.

But the windows stayed closed tight and he wheeled closer and closer.

"You have a choice Amber, you leave now, or you never leave, either way, he stays" he hissed.

"What the hell do you mean by that? I'm here because I am finally going to find out why you have done all this, why you found it necessary to wreck our lives when..." Steven grabbed his lapel, and I pulled him back-

"Steve, he's old, please don't" I cried.

He laughed aloud-

"Old, yes, sick, that too, but I still have power, I still know what I can do and believe me, you won't beat me this time, any more than you beat me before" He grinned and wheeled himself to the table where a lot of drink in bottles stood waiting.

"Drink? No? Maybe not, but I shall" he poured and we stood waiting.

His hand shook a little and I cursed myself for pitying him. After all, he was old and sick and dying probably, because I could see that this was the last stand of a desperate man. Did he want Steven that much? As much as I did?

That he could happily kill me and see me dead to get him? And did he really think that he would get him even then? He'd have to kill us both to keep him here without me, surely he realized that?

"What is this all about?" Steven asked, breaking the silence.

Some colour had returned to James Bards face and he looked up-

"I am trying to decide how to tell you what you need to know, but I find that I need to dispose of the unusable before I can, so she needs to leave"

"She stays, now talk"

"Oh if you insist, but afterwards, it's my call"

Steven nodded and I shrank inside. I knew it was only a ploy, but still.

"Your name is Stephen Bard, I don't care what they called you on the birth certificate, that is your name, and that is who you are. And you are the product of an incestuous union, between my son, Noel Hollis, who you would know as Holliman, and your mother, my daughter, Elizabeth, not that I planned it that way, but throw two young people together without the knowledge of their roots and see what happens, didn't history repeat itself with you two?" He laughed softly.

"Noel, *Noel* is your son?" Steven gripped me tightly.

"Yes indeed, I had an affair, an acquaintance with his mother, Katie, in the war years and afterwards, a nice little thing, fond of the drink, she died, sadly, quite young"

"Huh, seems that a lot of people die young round you" I snapped.

He glared at me-

"And it's not over yet"

He smiled and continued-

"So, she was expecting you, and I waited to see what you would be, what the effect of such a close union might be, but there was nothing, so you were spared, and then I thought, well, you're my rightful heir, my rightful successor, and I tried to keep you close to me, to guide you, to teach you, to help you, and your *father* wouldn't let me do it, and your mother, well, you know where she is now, so there's no point dwelling on that" he drank from the glass, with an unshaken hand.

"I don't understand, didn't I go into the business with you this past year, what more did you want? Why kill so many people? Why the child, Saoirse? Why didn't you come over and tell them we weren't blood related, I mean, why put me through that? I might have worked with you happily if you'd helped us, instead you let them nearly kill us, and I nearly died, and Carrie..." Steven stopped. James was staring at him bemused.

"No, not the business, not the *publishing*, stupid boy, no, my *real* work, which I am going to show you now" He swerved and turned easily and I thought to myself that a lot of this wheelchair malarkey was a blind, to make us think he was frailer than he is.

We followed him, down the carpeted hallway, across the foyer and through a thick red curtain.

Another corridor and then a doorway.

"This is my work, my life, and you are part of this" he smiled, turning a key in the lock.

Inside it was dimmer than the rest of the house and I realized why when I looked at the walls and saw gas lamps. The furniture was like something you might see in a wartime melodrama on television. The floor, carpeted in part but lino in the rooms. No television or anything other than a wireless.

"Jesus it's like a museum piece" I whispered.

All the windows had black frames up on them; I took them to be black out blinds-

"Why black out? Don't you open the windows" I asked. It had made an optical illusion of the outside of the house, and I understood now why the house was lit up like a Christmas tree, because the blacked out windows would be almost invisible to anyone driving up to the Hall. Your eye would obviously be drawn to the lights. I thought the corridor we were in must be to the left of the front door, slipping into the trees, the opposite side would have the stables and the yard. I nodded to myself, clever idea.

The air was stale and the rooms felt dead. I realized he was speaking to me-

"Why, who wants light in here? There's nothing to see, unless you want to see it" He grinned, and he looked like a skull. I shivered. I knew the reasons for the tablets now; he had cancer or maybe, a strange thought for a man so old, Aids. He looked just like that rock singer who died last year of it, like a skull with skin.

But that couldn't be right, could it? Such an old man?

Into another hallway and deeper into the house now, it felt like we were going under the floor, and our very footsteps muffled as we walked on. He turned on a switch and a light lit up a room.

An oval shape, with seating like a cinema, and then a platform.

Deep red curtains and a screen.

But on the floor, toys, dolls and teddies, spinning tops and rocking horses.

"What is this?" Steven found his voice.

"Sit down, I will show you" he waved to a seat and Steven let my hand go and sat. I sat down on the aisle seat about ten rows back. It smelt unused and dusty in here, like it hadn't been used in a long time. Another button and the light dimmed and somewhere, music began to play-

The kind of music you hear when you go on an old fashioned merry go round. Organ music, the kind that was last in fashion in the 1950's.

This fucker is crazy.

I shivered. I pulled my coat tighter around me and listened.

On and on the music played and I thought it was getting louder at first, and then almost imperceptibly, a flicker of light on the screen-

A little girl singing a song, a light coloured dress with a standing out skirt.

A blonde wig looking silly on her. Her mouth lipsticked, like a parody of Marylyn Monroe.

"Ellie, Ellie, sing the song I taught you" a voice. *His?*

The child smiled and went into a lisping version of "My heart belongs to daddy" twirling and pouting and dancing for the camera. It could be any child playing up to a video recorder. But somehow I felt a chill and I felt tears coming to my eyes, because I knew, I fucking knew what was next-

They came out from behind the curtains-

Three of them, they grabbed her and danced with her, and one by one removed their clothes, not ashamed at all to be naked with such a small child, and then... I turned my head away and must have cried out in horror, because Steven was beside me-

"Carrie its okay, I'm here, Carrie, come on, we're going" he pulled me to my feet while the film still played and the child on screen screamed like a lost soul.

"That was Ellie, my favorite, my favorite little dolly, didn't you like her Steven? Don't you think she's beautiful?" Bard was laughing, his head thrown back.

"He's mad Steven, he has to be, please get me out of here" I shook so much I could hardly talk.

"Little Ellie, dead and buried now, under the pink blossoms, ah little Ellie wanted to be immortalized, wanted to be a film star and there she is" Bard never stopped looking at the screen, while he spoke.

I knew that Steven was finding it hard to get words out, all the while trying to keep his eyes away from the screen that drew us to it, even while it repulsed us beyond all reason.

"Your crazy, you're *sick*, Jesus Christ, what makes you think? How could you think that I?" He backed away, still gripping my hand-

"Because your more me than any other person alive, you're the son of my son and my daughter too, what flows in my blood flows in yours too, my sickness is yours also, what I am is doubled in you, and sooner or later you will see its true" He made a swift movement and was on his feet.

I knew the wheelchair was a joke. Steven began to pull me out of the room, even while the film played on and on.

"Fuck that, I'm not like you, I'm leaving here I'm never coming back here again, you can keep your money and this, this evil shit and live in it" he pulled me towards the hall, but even as we went, I knew it, I knew the door was locked.

I couldn't see for the tears, as we ran and clattered down the hall. Steven beat on the door, but who could hear us? Who would ever know we were there, apart from David, and the rest, only flying home now from France.

I thought to myself that this was the end. It had to be.

I leaned against the door and thought about life and how the hell it would all come to this, these last few moments, leaning against a door in this hell hole. I looked up at Steven, who aimed one last kick at the door and swore-

"Steven" I whispered.

He was sweating, and the tears were falling as fast down his face as they were on mine-

"I know your not like him, and if this is the end, then I am glad it's with you, not without you" I buried myself in his arms again and he held me tight.

"We have to go back into the room again; can you be strong and go with me?" He whispered. I could hear that crazy music playing still though the movie seemed to have runs its course.

I nodded.

"Okay, just stay quiet and go with me, okay?"

I nodded again and sniffed.

We walked slowly down the hall.

I found myself flung into a seat and sat there panting for breath.

"Right Grandfather, lets talk, just supposing I am more like you than anyone else, what good will that do me?, I mean, look at this place, its in bits, It's not been used in years, it needs fixing up if it's to be worth anything" He stood facing Bard who was back in the chair.

A triumphant smile spread across his face as he watched me cowering in the chair and Steven stood, tall and aloof before him. I knew what it must be costing him, knew he must want to kill him now, but he restrained himself and waited.

Bard didn't say a word.

He was staring into Steven's eyes, trying to read him. I felt like he was trying to pull the life out of him, kill him too.

I saw Steven's hands trembling and he shoved them into his coat pockets.

Finally he spoke-

"Oh, the room, that's all incidental, we can fix it up, the point is that you will carry on my legacy, for ever" He smiled.

"Well, I suppose that's what you want from me, and sure, I'd be denying myself and my nature otherwise, I mean, a Bard is a Bard, eh Grandfather?"

His voice was wavering a little, and I prayed he wouldn't blow it now. He was trying to sound cold, and it wasn't washing with me, I knew him too well, knew the sound of that voice when it laughed, and most of all, the sound of his voice when he whispered to me through the night. He wouldn't hurt me, I knew it. But he had to play a part or we were both dead. So whatever he did, I had to trust and have faith in him.

"Are you a Bard Steven?"

He shrugged-

"Dunno, maybe I am, maybe I just didn't realize till now what it means"

"Do you know what it means now?"

Steven smiled-

"I have to be just like you Granddad"

Bard grinned again-

"That's it, you must be cold and ruthless, and, I don't know if you can be ruthless?

Steven laughed.

"Depends, I can try" he shrugged.

"Good" James smirked and from under his jacket he took a gun.

Oh holy fuck!

I shrank into the chair.

Slowly, slowly he put his finger on the trigger and he pointed it. At me!

"Do you know our family motto?" He asked Steven

"I didn't do Latin at school Granddad" Steven kept his eye on the gun.

"*Operor quis vos mos*" he hissed.

"Do what you will" I whispered.

The old Man was surprised when he heard me say it. I hadn't been a Jimmy Page fan for years for nothing, hadn't "do what thou wilt" been his motto too? I felt a coldness the likes of which I had never experienced enveloping me where I sat. Bard looked at me and smiled-

"The classics in the slums, how clever, unfortunately not clever enough" he sat straighter in the chair.

The gun was leveled and he clicked the hammer back on it-

Oh fucking hell, oh God, this is it.

I screamed so loudly I felt it come up from my toes to my mouth.

I saw Steven jump and the almost imperceptible movement of Bards finger on the trigger and shut my eyes with the bang.

I hit the floor with an almighty thump and my last thought was Steven.

Mountjoy Jail
31st December 1993

My birthday passed in here without much fuss. I suppose I should count myself lucky to be alive at all. Child killers are the scum of the scum in here. So much so that I have had twenty four hour protection from the inmates since I was arrested and charged with the murder of Dorrie and the boys, and the baby.

I'm forty seven years old now, and since I can remember I have hated James Bard.

When I was arrested, found with the smell of the white spirits on my hands, I asked for nothing from them, just one phone call, and some paper. Since I have been here, I have been writing it all down. Not because I want to be free, Jesus, I have never been truly free, but because it's all coming to an end soon and I want them to know my side.

Dorrie died, I killed her. She finally knew the whole sick story and she was going to the police. I had to do something to scare her, stop her. It wasn't the right time.

But her love, yes love, of Carrie and the baby overwhelmed her. When she realized that Steven was alive she sobbed her heart out in that kitchen, with the eternal washing in piles around her and she begged me to tell Carrie and let them be together.

"But Doris, you have to realize that we are too close now, the old man thinks he has won, we have to keep going a little longer"

"Oh Noel, the child needs him, Carrie needs him, and now I know the truth, how will I not tell her!"

"Bard is a dangerous man, insane, he would do anything to buy your silence, but Doris you can't tell anyone about this, please, it will be okay in the end" I begged her.

But she wouldn't listen.

She was leaving the house, that very night, going to the police, taking the baby to them; she was minding her for the night. Her first birthday.

So I had no choice.

I killed Doris Conway, up in her bedroom, and then went to the other rooms, strangling the two boys in their bunk beds, and then, into the bedroom where Saoirse lay. It was merciful, damn it, she would have died in the fire otherwise. I'd rather die in my bed than in flames, wouldn't you?

Peter, the eldest boy, well... he was out at a disco that night, his first one. I was glad he wasn't there then, he was bigger than the others, would have put up more of a fight.

I went down then and did some work on the fuse box, dipping the ends of the fuses in white spirit, and pouring some on the endless extension leads in the kitchen and living room. And then to make the spark, took the fuse from an adaptor and plugged the washing machine in and the heavy old iron with its frayed cord, and set it to heat.

By the time the machine went to spin and the iron was at full throttle, the spark would be there to ignite everything.

I slipped out and went over to the field and waited.

It took longer to start than I thought it would. Long enough for young Peter to come home, all cheerful, I knew by his walk, must have met a young one.

It eventually started at two in the morning, and was an inferno in seconds.

Peter jumped from the top window into the garden, holding a blanket. I closed my eyes when the firemen took it and he realized it was empty. I'll take that boy's screams to the grave with me you know?

As I knew they would, the police took me in.

They brought me to the station and I was put into a room and told to wait.

I admitted everything, all of it.

The trial was over in a day and I got life. Me, who never had one worth living in the first place, they couldn't understand why I was cold and unemotional.

I'll tell you, by the time I finish this, you'll know.

It begins in 1946, when I was born.

I have hazy little memories, playing in a walled garden, in what was a big house to me, but now I realize was only part of a house. My mother was lovely, young and reasonably pretty and she doted on me. There were other kids there, older than I, but that didn't matter. Only thing was, they were all little girls.

The man who owned the house was called "The Bard" by the children.

My mother called him Mister. She was the only one of the girls in the house with good English and she managed to teach some of them to read and write a little. Oh I think she was only about seventeen then. Maybe less, it's a hazy time in my life, you know?

I do remember her accent, Glaswegian, not as thick as it was once, but still. Bard would visit the house and would always spend time with my mother, telling her to try and fix up her clothes and modulate her tone.

"How will I make you lady of this house if you talk like a fish wife?"

He would ask her.

So she tried, fully believing that one day she would be free to have the house for herself and me, and Mister, of course.

I knew he was my father, she told me from the earliest age possible that he was, and one day it was all going to be mine.

Until the day she realized that Mister was courting some woman he met up town. She started to drink a lot, and in hindsight, her screaming tantrums were too much of a liability for Bard. I mean, she would frighten the life out of anyone, the roars of her in drink. So, then, there was an accident, a fall down the stone cellar steps. And that was that.

The day his new wife came into the Hall, my mother was buried in the grounds of the house. And I was shipped off to school.

And don't think for one minute it was Eton I went to.

Bard had Irish blood and Irish connections, he knew people everywhere, and before the clay had been thrown on my mother's coffin, I was on the boat train and heading for Ireland.

A trip by boat and another train to the middle of nowhere in Ireland, and I was in school.

And what a place!

A low, grey building it was. St Martin's Reformatory. With acres and acres of fields, with little boys, some as young as four, digging potatoes and hoeing the frozen ground in all weathers.

I was thrown into it, and left to sink or swim.

Bullied mercilessly by the older lads, for my accent, I quickly dropped the Scots burr and developed a midlands accent. And then there were the others, the priests, the ones who came into the dorms at night and played with us.

I thought it was like home; didn't Mister do that, I'd heard them whispering about the times when he came to the dolls house? Except it was to the girls only, and I was never allowed to see it, not like here, where the boys were fair game.

Well, all that was there was little boys.

I discovered a love of animals there. Horses in particular.

Brother Jonquil, the man who took care of the plough horses, and not a bad oul skin, certainly not as bad as the other bastards who lifted me out of my bed and into the toilets at night, anyway, he saw that the horses would do for me what they wouldn't do for anyone else, and he decided to train me.

And then, when I was sixteen, in 1962, he got me training with a man in the Curragh, Kevin Keely, who bred racehorses and hunters. I was there till I turned twenty two and he let me go. I fell for the wrong woman. Got a bit rough one day with his daughter and he didn't like it. So he set me out into the world and I hadn't a clue where to go.

Except home to the Dolls house.

I went off on the boat and the train and found myself in front of my father in the study. I told him I wanted to come back. He decided to let me, and so I stayed, looking after the horses for him. He didn't have too many and so I had a bit of free time. I would mooch around and try and find the walled gardens and the entrance to the house I remembered.

But the garden was gone and the house seemed to be locked up tight now.

Before, when I was a kid, there were always at least ten kids living in the house at a given time. It seemed to be scaled down now. The staff in the kitchens would whisper about the goings on, rarely in my hearing, but the bit I caught was enough.

All the muddled memories in my head became clearer and I knew what Bard was then. And I knew then that my mother was murdered, and that she had been little more than a child herself when he first had her.

I felt overwhelming hatred and anger. I wanted to kill him for the things he'd done. But he was always away traveling now, rarely home for more than a day or two. His wife had died, hung herself in the bedroom a couple of years ago, and the upshot of it was that every one of us was afraid of what he might do to us if we opened our mouths.

I kept my head down and I kept plotting. One day.

The Elizabeth came home.

I loved her on sight, my little sister. But also there was a certain frisson of jealousy. Here she was, the legitimate lady of the manor and I was the stable boy, more or less.

She had a gorgeous hunter, Shadow. I used to saddle him up and me and her would ride for hours on the fields and parklands around the house.

She introduced me to marijuana.

She told me that it was the big thing in London and everyone did it, especially the Beatles, and she knew that I loved them. By the time I'd gotten back to England though they had stopped touring and all I could do was buy the albums.

It was an escape for me, my music, and Liz was the very same.

We were up on the highlands one afternoon, having ridden Shadow and Star for a good couple of hours, until hunger and the heat had made us stop to eat, and take a rest.

Elizabeth rolled a joint and we stayed there for a while, smoking and looking up at the clouds.

"I know who you are, you know" She said.

"Oh? Who am I then?"

"You're my half brother, aren't you?" She passed the spliff to me and I took it.

"Yeah"

She sat up and hugged her knees-

"Noel, your mother, was she one of, was she a doll?"

I nodded, and she sighed heavily.

"Which one of them?"

"Katie, the first one, I think, she died, fell down the stairs"

"Oh"

She stayed silent for ages, and I kept smoking and passing the joint back to her.

"Noel"

"What?"

"I know all about the dolls house, and what happens there, but, I'm afraid of him, really afraid" She whispered, her eyes filling with tears.

"So am I, but, Jesus Liz, we have to do something"

Only the night before there had been children in the house, I'd heard the music muffled but still audible, even from my room over the stables. I had felt so sick I played Sergeant Pepper at top volume till it stopped. How many lives would that man ruin before he was stopped?

"I don't know how, Noel, he's untouchable"

"The police?"

She laughed-

"God bless your innocence Noel, don't you think I tried that? I went to them in London, a long time ago, but they wouldn't listen, oh no, My Father has the world and its wife in his pocket, and as long as he can keep paying he can keep going, and as long as he keeps going, well" She shivered.

So that was the day we hatched the plan.

Liz knew that she couldn't marry anyone even remotely connected to her father and the guy she was supposed to be seeing was the son of a baron, the brother of whom was also a patron of the dolls house.

"My father thinks I am a stupid little feather head, and that I have either forgotten or chosen to ignore what I saw, and I bet he hasn't a clue that I know who you are either, so heres what we do, you and I will be found in, a compromising situation, that way he will throw you out, and I can fake a pregnancy, so that when I find someone to marry he will have to let me"

I laughed-

"And how will that help matters? Look, I think if we both went to the police they would listen"

"Noel, the only way he is going to be caught is red handed, but that might take a long time, he's paying money to everyone, the drug squad, the inspectors in Scotland Yard are in his pocket for fucks sake, how will we get anyone to listen to us? They already think I'm a junkie, a wild card, and they'd have me killed in a second rather than have all this come out" She grabbed my hand.

"There's a big party next month, some of the people from that place he's buying in Birmingham, they are coming up to hunt, and it has to be before then"

"But, Liz, what will I do?"

"You go back to Ireland, work, and then, when things start moving this end, I'll call you back, please Noel, please trust me" She begged.

I didn't know how it would work. God only knew how long it would take to make it happen, I thought maybe three, four years tops.

So I did what she asked me to do and got the whipping of a lifetime when her father caught us. Like we arranged, I went back to Ireland and worked away, for a few years, though not with anyone of the caliber of Keely. I kept the head down and stayed grafting.

But always, always I kept in touch with Liz.

She was on the drugs, that's true. But she had to have the personality and the determination of a lioness, because she kept fighting.

She found a young policeman, new to the force. He made her tea one day when she was in for possession of heroin, and he listened to her. Somehow she managed to make him realize how important this all was and what it would take to bring Bard down.

Another woman, Breda Storey came on board with us.

She fell into it accidentally but was so disgusted by what she saw in a hospital one day that she started helping us. It was she who told me where to find the changeling, Carrie. I moved immediately to the area she was living in.

"Watch her Noel, don't let her fall into their hands" she said.

That part was easy. It was easy to see that Dorrie was unhappy in the relationship with her husband, a workaholic. The best way to watch her was to live with her. So I went all out to seduce Dorrie and got into the house when Carrie was a teenager. Too old for the dolls house, but still in danger, such danger.

Breda was in America by now and in constant contact with Liz.

From the word go, Liz had known that Carrie wasn't hers. She might have been strung out but she was no fool, and she knew that Bard would never touch his own blood, but because Carrie wasn't hers he would use her like one of the dolls and the only way to save her was to give her away. She knew Doris and Peter were nice people, because she trusted Breda implicitly. But always the plan was to give her back to her family. We always knew who they were too; we kept an eye on them as well.

Liz got clean. She bought land with her own money, and set up a refuge. She planned to take as many of the Dolls as she could there so that when the time was right we would have witnesses on hand. It took so long because some of them went off and died of drug overdoses, and some just disappeared.

But any of the ones she got were happy to tape statements and then live there with her.

I used to go to the phone box, down in the village, right outside the station and wait on her calls, as she told me what next to do.

Breda would write with money for the child. It was in one of the envelopes that I steamed open, that she told me that the time was right now to tell Bard about Carrie's whereabouts.

So I wrote the letter, telling him I wanted money, which incidentally, I never kept a penny of, sending it to Liz, every single time.

"Don't be nice to the child, she has to hate you" Liz said.

So I was, I was a bastard to the poor kid. She hated me. But I couldn't allow her to be too close to Doris, I could not allow her to trust me. She had to be forced into running away, and it was all going to plan, she was talking about America for ages, bloody ages, from the time she was sixteen. She was trying to save the few bob and everything. That would have been fine, because

Breda and Liz would have got her safe and sound, and then we could have put the last part of the plan into action.

Taking Bard down. Forever.

Bard had cronies all over the place, it would have been nothing to him if Carrie disappeared like the girls that were doing so all over Ireland at one stage. I can't be convinced that he hadn't something to do with that either.

Steven was safe. He was a bloke after all, his father and him, even though they were under the watchful eye of Bard most of the time, and though we all knew that Bard thought he was mine, and therefore in some sick way, his too, and that he was plotting to get him, we never thought, not in a million years that the story would take the twist it did.

But when they met, and fell in love, I panicked.

I wanted to sit her down and tell her, but I was told to stay quiet. I wanted to tell Dorrie the truth, but the word from America was no. The time wasn't right yet. There was one last shipment, one last time, and then we could get him.

A picture had been found and thankfully, or perhaps foolishly, the old man had taken his perversion out of the secret room and into his study. There for all to see in the photocopy of the picture was his portrait on the wall. Liz photocopied it and sent it to me. A huge mistake and now, another turn for the worse.

But by now, Carrie had the baby and Steven was allegedly dead.

Breda had come home and found him by chance. Liz had thought she had no more to lose when her boy died, but Breda told her he was alive. And I knew all along too.

Old Bard did what we thought he might, grabbed the opportunity with both hands and took the boy to him, hoping I guess to mould him and change him and make him into a mirror image of him.

But Liz knew better.

"David is a decent fellow, he wouldn't have reared that boy the way he did otherwise, and though he knew nothing, and thinks to this day that I am dead, I have faith in him and my son, I know he will be all right" She told me, the last time I spoke to her that he was always the love of her life, that he was a good bloke, and that she hated destroying him when she faked her death, but like I said she had no choice.

The time came for me to tell Doris about the plan.

I was trying to pick a day, a time when it would be right. But she had gotten a barring order on me and I was out of the house. So when the letter arrived with the American stamp she opened it, for it was addressed to her. She never used to be up early enough for the post, I always got there first when I lived there, and got my information out of the letter before I resealed it and left it for her.

But she saw the picture and the letter from Liz.

She had been out that day, at the baby's first birthday party, and came home to the mail. She didn't open it till Saoirse was in bed, sleeping. And I arrived as she was re-reading it, trying to make sense of it all.

"Noel, What the hell is going on, Liz Bard is, is she *alive?*"

I nodded.

"And *Steven?*"

"Yes"

She exploded into a rage. Attacking me with her fists as I tried to hold her off.

"Dorrie, listen to me, please…"

"Listen? You want me to *listen*, what have you *done* to that girl? All of you, plotting and scheming and planning and that poor child up in the cot growing up without her father, and Carrie, that child cries herself to sleep every night without him, Jesus Christ Noel, what did you do? Why Noel? Just tell me why?"

"Dorrie, it wasn't what I wanted to do, it wasn't meant to be that way, Bard was too careful, too hard to catch, but now he's made mistakes and we have enough to get him at last, Carrie was always safe, she's only one of thousands he hurt, please Dorrie, you have to let me explain"

"You can explain this to the police, I am not listening to this any more" She shrieked.

But I couldn't allow her to blow it now, go to the police and tell them all, because one of the main men in the dolls house operation was a high court judge. Seventeen years of hard work would vanish into a mountain of red tape if this was allowed to be leaked now. Bard would know and he would run scared. To Thailand maybe, where he wouldn't be found. He still had the money and the contacts.

So I did it. I killed her.

I killed two of my own children.

And then I killed Saoirse.

I cried like I have never cried before as they died and then I wiped the tears away and got on with the job in hand.

And the rest you already know.

I listen to the bells now, ringing in the New Year and I know, I know for sure that it's coming to an end. I got a letter a week ago telling me that Liz was on her way home to Baird Hall for the last time. Breda had already been there for the past six months or so with Steven. It broke her heart not to be able to tell him what she knew, but there couldn't be a whisper, not a sound of this until we had it in the bag.

But she said that there was a hope that he might be reunited with Carrie soon, and now I hope that happens. Something good has to happen for them two; they deserve it, and each other.

And that young policeman who made the tea for Liz, all those years ago is ready now.

He's a detective now, on the vice squad. He caught a few high profile people in the past couple of years and some of them are in prison now. But with everyone he caught, the dossier on Bard got bigger and he held on to it, waiting for the chance to come.

I close my eyes and can almost see them walking into the dolls house and feeling the terror and the pain of it all, for it's in the very air. Forty years of misery, and sadness...seeped into the walls and floors, waiting for the light to come and blow it away.

They have me on suicide watch, but even they can't watch me all the time.

I don't want to live any more, but I shall wait till Bard is dead.

I'm writing the statement and I will pass it to them when I hear from Liz and Breda that it's over and all is as it should be.

When my mother's life and all those in the dolls house are known and accounted for, then I can let go. I don't ask for anything, nothing, not even forgiveness for what I have done. But at the bottom of the statement I write to Carrie. And I tell her I am sorry for what I did.

Because I really and truly am.

But as it goes, it was one little innocent among many. It was merciful and it was quick. I made sure of that, she felt nothing at all; it was like she fell asleep again.

More than James Bard granted my mother.

Steven

I saw him taking the gun out of his coat and I saw him level it at Carrie.

I hadn't time to think, I just jumped and grabbed his arm and pulled it up, the gun went off at the top and the bullet went into the ceiling. I felt the plaster coming down on me and into my mouth.

Carrie fell, I think she passed out in shock. I pulled the gun out of his hands and pointed it at him, but he wasn't moving. He slumped to the side in the chair like one of the rag dolls on the stage-

"Its okay Stevie, he's dead" She said.

I span around to the stage, and saw her.

Standing there, plumper than I remember her, with her hair cut into a bob now, but still the inky black of my memories.

"Mum?" I whispered. I thought that I was seeing things.

She nodded.

"But, how?" I felt my knees giving way and I sat on the arm of a chair. The soft whirring of the projector still running in the room behind us.

"Its okay baby, I know this is a shock, but I'm here, I'm real" she smiled, and my heart turned over.

She came towards me and I put out my hand-

"Why did you leave me? Why did you let this go on?" I croaked out the words though my throat was full of dust and tears.

She stopped.

"I had to escape him Steven, I had no choice, and I knew that you would be all right with David, I knew he loved you and would look after you, so I ran" she touched me on the arm and came closer.

She stroked my face softly and I closed my eyes, remembering all the times when I was a child and I had wanted this so very much, you know, like when you're sick and all you want is your mum. And she was never there. Even when I was tiny she was never ever there. I shook her hand away-

*"I can't take this in, you left me when I was a child, you let dad go to jail and you knew all along that it was a lie, that you weren't dead, and they sent him to jail, why do that to us? I loved you, **we** loved you and we missed you so much, and you let us go like that, you ran away" I couldn't believe it, I figured that my mind was playing tricks, that somehow I would wake up any second in the*

flat in London, or back home in Dublin and would know that it was all a dream. I'd lost my memory, my daughter, and my life. I'd ruined another woman's life by marrying her when I shouldn't have, and now, the reason for all of this was there, larger than life, in front of me, trying to play mother.

She stroked my head again, and I felt tingles of electricity run through me.

"I took care of you as much as I could, but he wouldn't have let me keep you safe, I had to let things happen the way they did, he would have killed me to get you, you were part of his empire, his power trip, he wanted you, and as for Amber, he wanted her to be another little Ellie, because she was nothing to him, Oh Stevie, don't think for one moment that I enjoyed running away, but I was sick, sick enough to die, but not sick enough to let him destroy you both" She looked down at Carrie, still lying on the floor.

"We better take her out of here, come on" she bent down and stroked Carries face.

"Amber, Amber, wake up" she whispered.

I shook my head-

"Mum?"

"What?"

"Her name is Carrie"

∾

Okay, they woke me, and for a second I thought we were all dead.

There was Steven, filthy dirty and looking like a coal miner with the amount of muck and dust on his face, streaked with tears and sweat and Jesus only know what.

And standing beside him was a sight to behold. So much so that I nearly passed out again.

"Fucking hell" I said, and grabbed him "Is that who I think it is?"

She laughed. A sound like a bell.

"Liz Bard, technically your mother, but not quite, as I am sure you know" she grinned and it was Steven's smile.

I shook my head like I'd been in water. The things that were going through my mind! How the hell had this happened? What the hell was going on?

"I need a drink more than I ever did in my life" I could barely get the words out.

She smiled-

"Come on, lets get out of here" and she led us down the hallway without a backward glance, to the door that had been locked.

She clicked the switch on the wall, that looked like a light switch, and the door unlocked.

"No keys, quite advanced for its day, don't you think?"

I nodded. Steven looked like he was going to collapse.

"What about *him?*" he asked.

Liz sniffed-

"He isn't going anywhere anyhow, he won't mind us leaving him there for a bit" she laughed.

"Betcha didn't think I could shoot so well, quite the cow girl I was, once upon a time" She walked ahead again and into the study where the portrait of the old man stared malevolently down.

"Old bastard, I told you I'd beat you in the end" She smiled up at him. She waved at the two seats by the fire-

"Sit down, I'll fix you a drink, you poor things" She mixed up drinks and I noticed she didn't have any herself, just a tonic water. I glanced into my glass, afraid to drink it.

"Carrie?"

I looked up, into her eyes and she was smiling with such love and kindness that I knew she couldn't hurt me.

"I'm a recovering addict, I can't drink alcohol, but you go right ahead, it's okay"

I took a sip and though I wasn't used to whiskey, it tasted nice, sort of like wine. I might have known the old git wouldn't drink the cheap stuff Noel did. I felt warmed by it and began to relax. The fire had been built up and pleasant warmth came stealing round the two of us, Steven was silent, quieter than I had ever seen him before.

"It's a lot to take in, isn't it?" Liz smiled.

"Jesus I thought last week was mental, this beats all" I grinned. Already a little tipsy.

"Yes, I heard about that, Carrie, you must love him very much"

"You heard? From who?"

She half laughed-

"Breda, she's been my contact, my eyes and ears for years now" she smiled softly

"A real friend is Breda, and so brave"

She got up and walked across the room to the desk again and the way she stood, I could see the nervous energy bubbling inside her, just like Steven when he was on a mad one.

"Breda gave me an identity to leave the country with, back in 1973, she knew that I would die if I didn't get the hell out of here, and she used contacts within her profession, to find me a detox place in Arizona. It turned out that my father never realized, and he, in turn gave her the alter ego she needed to get out of here too, and then, when my car was pulled out of the river, well, that was my freedom assured" she stopped and looked at Steven, her heart in her eyes-

"Many times, so many times, back then, and recently, I have wanted to come and get you, come and save you from the evil he was doing, but the time was never right, I had to see him closing in for the kill before I came, to do it before, well, it would have ruined so many lives darling" Her face became set.

"And he would have escaped, Scott free"

But if you'd come earlier, Maybe Saoirse would be alive, and Mum, and the kids, so many people hurt and for what?

"Who was in the car Mum?" Steven asked.

"Another girl, she died in a squat and they wanted her out, so they put her into the car and we heaved it off the bank of the river. She looked a bit like me, enough so that when the river did its job, she might as well have been me, and by the time they found her, I was already getting clean" She smiled.

"Father never thought I would beat him and he certainly never thought I had friends, but I did, and in the most surprising places"

She sat down on the rug in front of us and tucked her legs under her skirt-

"The strangest thing is, Father always thought he was invincible, that he couldn't be touched, that he was in the pocket of so many of the legal profession, and in fact many of them came to the house in the beginning, and the medical people too, they were all his clients, but when they all started to retire and leave their jobs and die off, he was actually more vulnerable than ever before.

They have been trying to get him for years now. But you see, his business interest isn't what it used to be, and believe it or not, he hasn't a whole lot of money left, and it was bound to get worse, because there's new technology in the states now, that means information will be transferred all over the world in seconds, no need to wait for the reels of film to come through the post, he was about to lose his source of income big style"

She smiled sadly-

"Not quickly enough to save Ellie and so many others, did you realize how many children he once had here, imprisoned in that dungeon? It was so easy after the war; many of them were refugees, coming in without proper English never mind proper identity papers. I was sick to my stomach when I realized how involved he really was, and in the seventies it got worse for a while, children from the Far East, Oh" she covered her face with her hands and her shoulders shook.

"Mum, what happened when you were in America, why did you never come back to me?" Steven asked.

"I went into detox, I had to clean myself up, and then, when I was clean and sober, Breda, who was by this time working for Senator Donavan, came to me and, we had already hatched a plan to fix him once and for all, we knew that David was in prison and for the time being we couldn't do anything about that, we had to hope that he would be okay, because I couldn't contact anyone for a while, and then I remembered that there was one young police man who I trusted, who I had confided in once when I was out of it, and I wrote to him, he's a detective now, you know, and he got David out of jail"

"He was the one I confided in, and right now, they are working on getting the people my Father worked with, here and in the states, because they think that if they do, they might be able to get the children used by them and let them go home to their families, you couldn't know the amount of children hurt in this ring, that's what they call it now, a ring, they pass the children round and round till they either die or get too old and then they dump them out in the street, in places like Thailand and Vietnam, and then they die, either on drugs or of Aids, but I have helped them, some of them"

She sat up straight-

I couldn't help myself, wasn't it bad enough that she knew all about her father and what he was at, but to live in America and do nothing, because that was how it looked to me, like she'd sat back and watched him destroy us and the little girls he tortured and did fuck all in her ivory tower in America. It was a whole heap of crap!

"Do what you will, it's a fine motto for a family that seems to suit themselves" I muttered. Liz looked at me sharply. Steven was lost in his own thoughts.

I knew Steven would never turn on her, he was in shock, I could see it all over him, and his face was like bleached bone so white was he-

"So, what the hell took you so long, what the hell is this? You knew everything for years, don't fuckin' tell me that the investigation took this long, No, Liz, there's more to this than your telling us!" I got up and walked to the window, pulling the dusty drapes aside so I could look out into the dark. It was cold and bleak and silent. A bit like my heart, I thought.

"I had to come, because I knew what he was going to do, call it a mother's instinct..."

I laughed-

"About twenty fucking years too late!"

"...but I knew he was going to try and implicate you in the ring and therefore save himself, he hadn't long to go, he was diagnosed with HIV in the mid eighties, and as far as I know by looking at him tonight, he was full blown a while ago, so him being charged wasn't going to make a big difference to him, but you, Ah Steven, to get you in there, get your name out there as the man to contact, now wouldn't that have been something, and believe me, its all happening, I heard whispers in the States about you, though I knew that you weren't involved, not really, but the men on the ground there knew that when Old Man Bard died, you were next in line... and they, the police, they have nearly all of them, all of the people he worked with and schemed with for the past thirty years, all of them caught red handed!"

Steven was still as white as a sheet, and he shook his head slowly-

"I'm not like that Mum, you know?"

"I do love, of course I do, but you might have fallen into it, not really knowing what you were doing, he has so many henchmen and helpers, who knows what might have happened?"

"It still doesn't answer my fucking question" I snapped. I was so angry; she'd known what we were going through, fuck

this being nice and waiting. A mothers instinct my hole! What sort of mother sees her son destroyed and does fuck all? I would have walked into an inferno to save Saoirse and had I been there, that's what I would have done. I closed my eyes as the pain of her loss, washed over me again.

"Carrie, listen to me, its not like you think, I haven't been sitting back waiting for this, I've...." She stopped and looked at the big oak door to the study as it creaked open.

I looked at the door as it was opening and Breda Storey came into the room.

"Breda" Liz was obviously delighted-

"Come in and tell them what we've been doing for the last twenty years"

Breda sat on the chair behind the desk and buried her head in her hands-

"You want the whole story?"

She looked at me quizzically and smiled-

"Dorrie always said you were the enquiring mind type, Carrie lovie, it's not as bad as you think it is, please listen to me..."

I exploded-

"Not as *Bad*! For fucks sake! Do you realize what I have lived through this past two years? I lose my soul mate, I lose him in the *worst* possible way, I grieve for him, I cry every single night when he isn't there, and I think that's as bad as it gets, and then Noel burns the house down so that the child I had with Steven, dies too, in the same way as he did, or so I thought, And you stand there and tell me that its all going to be hunky dory and nothings gone that can't be fixed! Well let me tell yez that there's *plenty fucking gone that won't be replaced!*" I screamed the last, and shook all over.

Steven jumped up and grabbed me-

"I have nothing left, *nothing*, my daughter, my home, my mother, and my brothers, did you know that young Peter hasn't come out of hospital yet? Sixteen he is and he's fucking traumatized by the fire and losing the baby, he was trying to save my daughter and he dropped her! He lost his reason when he realized all he saved was her blanket! He might never be right again, and he's only a child! *What about him, hey?* I lost my daddy too, years ago when Noel Holliman came on the scene and took Ma out of the happy marriage and the only safety I ever had went on the boat with Peter, what the *fuck have I got left now? Tell me!"*

Steven caught my face in his hands-

"You have me Carrie, we can start all over again, when all this is sorted, I swear to you, we will, we can do it" He pulled me into his arms and I shivered. I shook with anger, and grief. All the feelings suppressed for the past year or more.

"I don't know anymore, what we can do, I don't know can we save anything, are we able to, its too big Steven, this whole thing it's too big, I love you, I *love you*, but we can't erase what's happened, we can't! You only saw your daughter once and you hardly remember that, how can we give that back to you now? And its all your mothers fault, she could have stopped it years ago, but instead, she goes on a fucking crusade and we have to sit there and wait, You have your mother back, and you still have your father, and you have me, and what have I got? You aren't even free to be mine yet, you're still married to bloody Colleen, I'm the one who loses again" I laughed bitterly.

"Story of my fucking life that is, my life so far"

Breda was sitting listening to all this and she had so far not said a word-

"Carrie, you know what? You're not in the greatest frame of mind..."

I snorted-

"Well there's an understatement!"

"But..." She continued "We have been doing more in America than you think and I have to tell you the whole story before, before you condemn us totally"

I shook my head-

"Okay, I'll listen, I'll hear you out, but I tell you, as far as I'm concerned, there's nothing you can tell me that will excuse you for letting us be destroyed like this, and as for you..." I glared at Liz-

"*This* would be easier to take had you fucking stayed in the Thames in the seventies, I don't think I can ever forgive you what you've done to me"

"Carrie, you don't mean that!" Steven was shocked, but I didn't care what he or anyone thought of me now.

"Oh yes I do, as far as I'm concerned, she's a waste of time and space and she should have stayed fucking dead, instead of coming in here and breaking my heart again"

"I saved you both, remember that" she said quietly.

I laughed-

"Tonight? Is that when you think you saved me?"

"Yes"

"You saved me? Well let me tell you something Liz, the way I feel right now is that I'd rather that lunatic in the basement shot me tonight, because then I'd be out of this nightmare forever, you did me no favours at all, none, because when you pack your shit up and go back to the States and your life and your friends and your family, and probably, you'll try to bring your son with you, who knows? I go back to nothing, because there's nothing left for me to go back to, I'd rather be dead, I wish I was"

"Your so strong Carrie, we've watched you for years..."

"I know, I know you did, but its not helping me at all to know that, I swear to you, I just want this to be over, so tell us Breda, Biddy, Breege, whoever the fuck you really are, tell us what we have to know and then let me get the fuck out of here" I flopped down on the couch and waited-

She coughed and sat more comfortably in the chair, like a parody of a jackanory show, I couldn't help but smile-

"As you already know, I come from a poor family. There was always enough food to eat because Jesus be good to my father; he worked so hard to keep us. There was me, my brother, who wasn't all there, and then there was Dorrie.

I came to England, because there wasn't any work. I was called to training as a nurse in the late 1950's and was delighted, because in fairness, there was little else for me at home.

I loved it all. The training was hard and we had some right oul swine's over us in them days, but I was a quick learner and got on with the job with little or no trouble and qualified fairly well. I went to a different hospital then to do obstetrics and then gynecology. By the early sixties I was in theatre nursing and getting on fine at it.

And then one night, the call came to the nurse's home, to return to theatre for an emergency.

She was no more than eleven years old. Found wandering in the East End, disoriented and bleeding heavily.

The surgeon had no choice then and there, it was either allow her to bleed to death, or perform a hysterectomy.

Eleven years old and she lost her womb and her ovaries, before she ever had a period.

I remember standing with the surgeon and looking at the state that child was in and asking him-

"How can this be?"

And he had tears in his eyes as he stitched and cut and stopped the blood that seemed to come from a dozen wounds and he shook his head.

"She's not the first and she won't be the last"

I remember sitting by that child's bed for the night, still in my uniform, praying for her, because she was dying. This little child had lost so much blood that it was coming out of her faster than we could get it into her! At four am, in the darkness before the dawn begins, she opened her eyes and looked at me drowsily.

I just stroked her hand and she sighed.

She struggled to say something and I had to lean close, trying not to touch her, trying not to make her pain any worse. I could barely hear the word, so softly was it spoken, but then I realized what I was hearing, she was trying to tell me who had done this to her, but either hadn't the English or the energy to do so.

"Go on pet, tell me" I whispered.

The eyes, oh Jesus, the eyes. Never till my dying day will I forget those eyes"

Breda shivered, and I felt something akin to sympathy.

Didn't I remember the eyes of that little girl in the film; wouldn't they stay with me for the rest of my life?

Breda continued to speak-

"The Spider, the Bard" she said, and then, the little one, she died.

There was silence in the room. Steven was looking at the fire, small flames flickering, and I was lost in thought too.

The Spider, the Bard. I shivered. He had looked like a spider, an evil old insect, waiting on his prey.

Liz touched Breda and nodded-

"Go on"

"It went around and around inside my head. I stood at the funeral for that little scrap of humanity and wondered what or who "The Bard" was. I read the papers and looked for him but to no avail.

As time went by, children would appear in the hospital with injuries like the first, but I never got to be too close to them. All little girls and all destroyed. People told me not to think, that thinking would do no good, do more harm in the end. But how could I stop thinking when that child's little face was engrained, burnt, into my soul?

The Spider the Bard. What the hell could it mean?

I left the nurses home, and the London hospital, moving to a post in a different one, geriatric nursing this time, and went into a flat with another nurse, Mary. Now Mary was full of the joys of spring, having met a fine looking fella from Ireland who was keen and who seemed to want the whole deal, the ring and the wedding bells and all that.

He was working in a publisher in Birmingham and would come down to see her a couple of times a week. It looked likely that I would be looking for another flat mate shortly. By this time my sister Dorrie was over, she shared my flat too for a while till she met and married Peter Conway and I was thinking that I ought to get my skates on and meet someone myself. But things turned around very quickly and I lost all sight of myself.

And then one day Mary collapsed in the hallway, reading a letter she had just opened and when I read it, I couldn't believe my eyes, her fella, and the guy she was engaged to, had met someone and was on his way to Gretna Green to marry her.

Mary was never right after that. I remember her shrieking in the hallway-

"I'll kill him, and as for that Bard one!"

Bard.

For the first time there was a name, a connection. So they *did* exist.

I waited and watched, and soon, the fella, David, contacted Mary to apologize. It's just that Liz was expecting and he had to do the honorable thing. He said. I began to read up on this Liz character and to be blunt, she seemed to have a fairly vacuous life, full of the swinging sixties and the party life that the people like me, who worked for a living, couldn't begin to imagine. I knew that David wasn't up to the job, that he wasn't exciting enough for a girl like Liz Bard, who I imagined, changed her men as often as her handbag!"

She grinned at Liz who shook her head sadly.

"I know it was true of me then, but not now, eh?"

"No Liz, not now" Breda reached for the whiskey and poured a big dollop into a glass.

"And so, then, I heard that she was going a bit crazy and they desperately needed a nanny for the little boy. So I volunteered when it became clear that Mary was going to other places and would be leaving the flat. I moved into the house with the family and life went on.

Yes there were drugs. I saw all of that and there's no sense in saying that I didn't. But for a time, Liz behaved a little more decently and I could talk to her.

It was just before she fell pregnant on the little girl, that we were in the garden watching Steven playing, oh, one of the days when there wasn't a cast of thousands in the house.

"If you don't mind me saying so, that child idolizes you Mrs. Williams, you should try to stay sober and mind him" I said, thinking that she might listen.

She looked at me and smiled-

"Breda, you're a clever woman, trust me when I tell you that whatever I do, I know that my son is okay, for two reasons, one, I had the good fortune to marry a decent man, who adores me, and Stevie and wouldn't let any harm come to him, and two, I have the sense and the good fortune to be as far away from my father as possible"

I knew that her father was domineering and bossy, but I had thought that she loved him.

"Breda I might never tell you this again so listen up, my father is a bad man, a very wicked and evil man, who will stop at nothing to destroy me and what is mine, and I can't let him do it"

The words came out of my mouth before I knew what I was saying-

"Is your father the spider?"

"Yes"

"Oh, Elizabeth, Oh my goodness, what a thing to have to live with, I saw what he did to a little girl, it was worse than if he killed her there and then"

She smiled at me and patted my hand-

"David doesn't know, no one knows what I am living with inside my head, I saw him rape a child in 1965 and it stayed with me, poisoning me for all this time, and there have been thousands of them, hundreds of them, and there is nothing I can fucking do about it, I can't go to the police because he has them told I am unstable, like my mother, and the only way I can beat him is to get clean, but he keeps the drugs coming, even when I am in detox, I get shot up when I am asleep somehow. No one believes me yet Breda, some day they will"

I resolved then and there to help her. But by God, I didn't think it would take this long and be this hard.

His power was so great then that he could swap a healthy baby for his dead grand daughter and pay the hospital with new wards and equipment. When customs and excise men opened his crates they found books and reels of film. They never once played them, taking his respectable word that he was sending instructions about display of his wares to the morons in other countries who would throw them into baskets and forget to sell them if they were not shown how.

For years this went on.

You know about the birth of her daughter and you know what happened. I knew he wanted the child for what he termed the dolls house and I was determined that would never happen to her. Elizabeth, in her more lucid moments knew the babe's fate if she should fall into his hands, and yes; she realized that the child couldn't be hers. But in her own way she trusted that she could somehow find the real parents and get her back to them.

Elizabeth and I hatched the plot to fake her death.

We paid a guy, to pretend to order a hit on her. He paid someone to cut the cables in her car and then we took the car, with the body of a young woman who had already died of an overdose in the squat, a few days previously, and shoved it into the river.

She left the country then to go to the States and by then, Amber was on her way to Ireland with Dorrie and Peter and her new life.

And yes I realized that he would find me. After all, didn't he think I was in cahoots with him? Didn't I stand and watch him steal a baby and do nothing? But he unwittingly gave me more freedom to do him harm by handing me a new identity and the wherewithal to work and survive.

For the last fifteen or more years Liz and I have been in contact all the time. And we were in contact with Noel Hollis, or as you know him, Holliman, too. He did great things in his own way, though I wish my sister hadn't died, or your baby.

Liz got clean and sober and managed to get work. She's a life coach now, helping others who have fallen down and need help. And there is the other dolls house, of course." She stopped and looked at me-

"Carrie you may think that all we did was sat back and watched, but we didn't, all this time, we have been saving little girls, the little girls who have been discarded and outlived their *usefulness* to Bard and his cronies, I still had my contacts in the hospitals in the UK and I would hear very swiftly when a young woman was found in a similar state to the first little girl, and we would arrange it, for her to come to us, Liz had her own money, and what we didn't have we raised in the States, and now, there's a place for those women, who once lived in hell, they come and we fix them up, and some of them work now, some of them *married* decent men, and some of them counsel and help others who have been abused, so its not all bad, its really not all bad" She smiled.

For the first time I realized that there was a bigger picture.

"And you know, a couple of years ago, when I heard that I was a grandma, I re-named the centre, I called it "Saoirse's house" for

the little girl I prayed I would know one day, I know it's a Gaelic name, but what does it mean?" Liz asked.

The silence was deafening and I looked at Steven. He was the one who named her; I remembered it all so vividly-

"Steve? Tell her"

"Saoirse, it's the Irish word for freedom" he spoke so softly I barely heard him.

"Freedom, that sounds about right" Liz smiled.

Breda nodded-

"Of course, Bard knew where I was, but I like to think that never did he realize that Liz was alive too. We watched the two children, Steven and Amber and we knew through Noel, the way things were. He knew his origins and he wanted Bard done as badly as anyone.

Noel had to be a bastard. Because how else could he keep in with Bard?

Noel killed Dorrie and the kids before the fire did.

You have to believe me that he is devastated. It was never what he wanted to do. It was never meant to be this way, but Dorrie was so honest she wanted to tell the police and we couldn't let her till we had more to tell them, more than what we thought was happening.

We can look back at the last couple of years and wonder if we did right because we didn't send in the police when it was all in its heyday and honestly, I can't say what was right or wrong. There was nothing there to stick to him personally, nothing that would mean that Bard himself would be killed. He would have continued on for ever with another lot of minions, having lost the rest.

Until now, because finally they had something on him.

Three years ago, you might remember, a disc jockey in London was arrested for molesting children, and when they took him in, he sang like a canary about others in the business that were so inclined"

I remembered all right, watching the telly one night in Ma's house, before I ever met Steven and being disgusted at the way this man thought he had done no wrong. He was an eighties video jock, I remembered being vaguely creeped out by him when he would be on telly, something about his voice and his mannerisms hadn't sat well with me when he was on. I used to watch Kenny Everett instead of him. I always preferred Kenny's brand of lunacy to perversion.

I also remembered him, the DJ, protesting and proclaiming his innocence all through the trial and saying to Ma that there had to be more of them, more perverts like him, because they never acted alone, always there had to be a group.

But at the time, Ma had changed the subject and had made us tea.

God bless oul Dorrie, every time there was a crisis she turned to the teapot.

I said a prayer for her in my mind, and then turned back to Breda's revelations.

"After that trial, people ran for cover, and some who didn't were caught in possession of film and photos of children. Now, *one* of those photos, out of millions the police have seized, has, as a backdrop, this room, and stupidly, or thankfully, depending on how you look at it, the picture shows clearly the portrait of James Bard in its rightful place.

That detective, that young policeman that Liz confided in all those years ago, recognized the picture and we were hoping that the police were about to arrive at the same time as the film was playing in the dolls house tonight. Because either way, he *was* going to prison. It's just a pity that he didn't get what he deserves. Maybe God will give him his just punishment"

"So now do you understand why it took so long and you had to suffer so much?"

I didn't really, but I nodded.

Then Steven spoke-

"What I can't understand is how you and Noel, **being** related, had me, healthy and all that? It certainly seems **to be** one of grandfathers' obsessions, that I was more his blood **than** anyone else's... but it's just not possible *is it*?"

I had been thinking that myself, knowing what I knew about genetics and incest and everything, I had to admit it was unlikely.

Liz laughed her bell like laugh and looked at Breda-

"No, its not possible, its impossible, I was just clever that's all, I had to make him think that I had slept with Noel, I knew all along who Noel was and he was on his own revenge mission, even back then, so we hatched the plot, I never realized I would meet David, but the honest to God truth is, you *were* conceived in the hay barn that night, you are David Williams' son, honest to God, even if I had to convince David otherwise to save you"

"We would have told you everything eventually" Breda said.

"Its just you said that Noel was my father"

"I had to let on that I believed that, because to say anything else might have blown Liz's cover as she was coming here, to England, I mean, that night" she smiled.

"You have both been very brave, really strong and brave, and we are proud of you and I know your dad will be too" Liz said.

And it hit me like a ton of bricks.

David and Becky. How the hell was he going to take his wife *and his son* coming back from the dead in one week?

And more to the point, where the fuck did that leave them?

I cleared my throat-

"There's something you need to know, about David"

Liz nodded.

"I already know love, I know about the young model he's seeing and I know that he must be happy, and that she is something special, because he didn't go with anyone for so long after I *died* that she must have blown him away" She shook her head-

"David and I were special once, but that's dead and gone now... I have worked hard all these years and though I thought about what my life might have been had I stayed with him, I know for sure that I cannot go back to him nor he to me, he loves Rebecca now, and I am happy for him and when this is all out in the open, I'll give him his freedom and they can marry if they wish" she giggled.

"I never did divorce him you know...Maybe I'll be asked to the wedding"

Freaky thought wasn't it?

17

Carrie

Later on, after the police came and the ambulance men had zipped James Bard into a double thickness body bag, and wheeled him on a trolley out of his house, we left too.

I couldn't get my head around it all. I couldn't allow myself to think that this was it. It was over. James Bard was dead and gone, and Liz was back, and I knew that Steven was torn to shreds.

Loyalty to David and all he had done for him must have competed, that night, with the love he would have felt as a child for his mother, who now miraculously appeared in his life like a dream.

"I can't believe she's here Carrie" He said, as we lay in the big bed in the local guesthouse. It was off season and they were only too happy to put us up. They had seen the flashing lights and the ambulance going through the village and though curiosity must have been killing them they didn't ask us anything. Maybe they knew by the state of us that we were not in the mood. The big house was always a source of gossip for the locals all though James was very careful not to hire anyone from within fifty miles of his home, and that way kept the gossip and speculation to a minimum.

A line in one of the last diaries he kept had leapt out at me-

"No one can talk about what they have not known or seen for themselves"

I wondered what would happen now, when the police investigation began in earnest and they started to dig and find gruesome evidence. I got the feeling that the people round here must have known something, but like the ones who lived in sight of Magdalene laundries and concentration camps, they might plead ignorance.

I'd cried more tears and felt more anger and grief in that few hours than I had in such a long time. My euphoria at finding Steven again and then the sickening realization of what his bloodline really was, with that grand father of his, had shaken me badly.

For the first night since Paris, since the night of the wedding, we just lay there in the bed and looked at the ceiling and held hands.

"It's kind of hard all right" I whispered.

"I dunno, I can't figure out what I'm supposed to feel"

"How d'ya mean?"

"Well, she's been dead, you know? For years, and I let her go, I *accepted* that, and I moved on with my life, and I found you and, now, she's here and I wonder what exactly am I to do now? Do I try to play mother and son games again? Do I spend time with her? What? I mean, I don't know her!" he sighed.

I knew what he meant exactly.

I had known I was adopted for years and years. I used to fantasize about my mother and father, my *real* mother and father. At times they would be romanticized into a daddy and mommy warbucks scenario where, they would hold out their arms to me and tell me that they had never wanted to let me

go. And they would take me away from the estate and Noel and bring me to live in their mansion in America.

And now I knew that they hadn't wanted to let me go, hadn't known they were letting me go.

The choice had been made for them, by that evil old bastard, who took me from them and paid them in kind over the years, had they only known it. From what Steven had said about them, I knew my parents were young still, and I thought that maybe they had been too young and afraid and innocent to ask the pertinent questions back in the hospital, back in the seventies when authority was king and some people, like police and doctors and the wealthy, never stooped to the level of the ordinary Joe Soap in the street.

Back in those days, hospitals took new-borns away from the mother after birth. My mother wouldn't have seen me at all, only a quick glimpse of me maybe, and then she would have been told I was in the nursery. I also realized that it would be seriously frowned upon, the fact that she wasn't married; the hospital wouldn't have been very kind to her at all. And a Catholic hospital too, the poor girl. The nuns would have said it was "Gods Will" when I died...

Was my father even there when I was born? Could he have solved the mystery? I remembered a conversation I had with Ma, when I was expecting the baby and I remembered saying something like-

"Oh I wish that this was all over and that Steven could at least see the baby being born"

And she had said that in her day, when she was having her first, Peter, well the hospital wouldn't allow the father in the labour ward with you.

"Only right it is, there's no place for a man at a woman's work" she had said, folding another piece of the eternal laundry.

I lay in the darkness and wondered what would happen now?

I didn't know these people. This couple in Liverpool. But they were mine.

Already, I was going in there at a disadvantage. I was the harlot that stole their daughter's husband, after all. What the heck would they say?

"Steven, what will we do about Colleen's family?" I whispered.

"How do you mean? *Oh Fuck*, I get you now, their your family too!" he sat up. He buried his head in his hands, his knees bent up, and I traced the line of his backbone, funny isn't it, no matter what crisis hit me, I couldn't keep myself from touching him, from wanting him. He was always so beautiful, and I loved him so much, time spent not touching him or being with him was time wasted in my opinion. And we had the best part of two years to make up for. I shook myself-

Stop, you have work to do!

"Well, what will I do? I mean, I have to meet them somehow, but, I can't see them taking me in and wanting me, when I stole you from Colleen, I mean, blood is thicker than water, and they don't even know I exist, yet"

He smiled and took me in his arms again-

"Listen to me Carrie, listen, the man Colleen married wasn't me, he was a figment of my Grandfathers twisted imagination, when this is all over, the funeral and all that, and the police thing, we will go to see them, and I will tell them everything, and I will tell them that it wasn't your fault, that you loved me from the day you and I met, in Dublin, in that scruffy little pub...." He grinned.

"Where was it again?"

"Mc Gonagles, But..."

"You didn't take me from her, you hear me?"

"Steven that's not how they will see it"

"I don't care how they see it, she married me when I didn't know what I was or who I was, and I saw your shadow everywhere

I looked, you didn't take me from Colleen, because I was *never ever* hers to begin with!"

He kissed me and held me tightly, talking into my hair so I could barely make out the words-

I'm yours, always and forever, till the day I die.

"Steven, what are you saying?"

He pulled away and stared into my eyes-

"I'm saying that I am yours, always and forever, there is no life if I can't be with you and whatever it takes, and however long it takes, I will be with you, and I mean that, nothing or no-one is going to part us again, you hear me now?"

"Yes, oh yes, I hear you, Oh God, Steven, I love you so..." I laughed when he smothered the words with kisses again and again, till I lost my breath and the train of thought.

"You and I are going to be married, as soon as possible, I don't want to wait any longer to have you, to be with you properly, I don't give a fuck what anyone says, I want a home with you, a place where we can be together and be happy and put the past to rest, you want the same thing, don't you? Will you marry me Carrie?"

I couldn't speak, for the tears and the laughter and the pure happiness.

"Well?" he stopped talking and waited.

I shook my head-

"You don't have to ask me again, the answer is yes, let's do it, as soon as we can"

Much later, we lay talking, and I finally asked him about my parents.

"What are they like? My mother and father? Are they nice?"

I was lying with my head on his chest, and I felt him sigh as he answered.

"You're the living image of your mother, her name is Valerie, really, I never saw anything like the resemblance you have with her, wait till you see it yourself, and you're going to be amazed..."

"Is she red haired?"

He laughed-

"No honey, you get that from Jimmy, your dad, he's a great guy, totally down to earth and a great cook, he works as a chef, you know?"

"Oh" I wasn't the world's greatest cook, maybe he might teach me something.

"You have a brother Robbie, training to be a vet, nice kid, he's seventeen or so, dark haired and a real horse lover, I can see him owning a farm or something in time to come, and Colleen, well you know about her"

I knew all I needed to know about Colleen and I knew that I was going to be the most hated sister in the history of the world when she got wind of me.

"So they know nothing about any of this, do they?"

"Not a thing, as far as they are concerned you're dead and buried in Glasgow, not alive and kicking here and now... I just hope it isn't too much of a shock to them when we land at the door, I tell you something..." he stopped and looked down at me.

"What?" He seemed a bit embarrassed about something. Kind of cringing.

"We-el, way back, before I married Coll, I went to meet her family and there was this one time, I was in the living room and her mother looked at me and I swear I was speechless, it was as if it was you there in front of me and I couldn't understand why I was so shocked, and why I felt this, like, desire, for someone that was my fiancées mother, I mean, it nailed me there, I couldn't speak, but it was you I was seeing, before I knew who you were, do you see?"

I saw.

"That must have been freaky as hell, God some of the things you must have seen and done, even when you didn't remember, must have freaked you out"

"Yeah, they did"

"What was the worst bit? Of it all, what bits do you remember?"

"When I think back on it now, I remembered a lot more than I thought I did, obviously there was stuff about you that was like a dream and something I couldn't put my finger on, but now, I am beginning to think that Colleen knew more about me than she let on, because there was stuff that happened when I was with her that I couldn't understand, and now it begins to click with me"

"Like what stuff?"

"Like one day, out of the blue, your name came to me and she got really freaked out and started to cry, she said something then about me remembering and going back to my old life and leaving her..."

"So she knew I was part of that?"

"Yeah, and then there was the music thing"

Colleen didn't like music, which I found to be a bit of a shock in someone so young. I mean from the time I was a kid I loved music, it was something bred into me by Peter and his love of rock and roll. But not my sister.

"There wasn't one album or tape in her bags when she moved in, she never sang along to the radio, in fact she never listened to the radio at all, and if she came home when I had it on, she would turn it off, we never watched MTV or anything, I mean, don't you think that's a bit strange? I mean she comes from Liverpool for fucks sake, the birthplace of the Beatles, surely it's bred into people there to like music?"

"Sounds weird all right" I answered. I mean when I thought of Liverpool, I thought of the Mersey Beat, The Beatles and the Kop. Didn't everyone?

"This one day, I was in the shower, and I had a little radio in the bathroom and was listening to it, and this song came on and I was singing along with it, and I heard the door rattle like she was trying to come in, but I had it locked, so I kept singing along and then when I came out she was really silent for the rest of the day"

"What was the song, do you remember?" I asked.

"I can't, it was something by Thin Lizzy though, I know that, and I remember being chuffed that I could remember the words and all, but she wasn't too happy at all"

"Maybe she thought it was going to jolt your memory and you might leave"

"Whatever it was, the radio disappeared the following day and it was back to the silence, that killed me, the silence we lived in, it was like a tomb" he turned to face me and stroked my arm...

"You know what I think now? I think that Colleen was told to be on her guard for things like music, I mean, if Noel was tipping the old man off about us, he would have told him where we met and anyone could tell him what kind of club it was so Maybe that's why he didn't want music played round me, or when we were in Liverpool, we couldn't go to the cavern or to anywhere they played rock music, because anything might have brought me back, and it was in his interest to keep me here"

"That's a pretty shitty thing to do, I didn't think Colleen was as vindictive" I sighed.

"She was afraid of losing me, she said that she married me because she thought that by doing it she might get out of Layla's, your, shadow and be her own person, so it must have been terrible when she realized I was chasing another shadow and she wasn't number one with me either"

"Still, to know what and who you are and not tell you, that's wicked, isn't it?"

"She's young Carrie, she was only seventeen when I met her, she doesn't know what the bigger picture is"

And I wondered would she ever know, or understand what the bigger picture was. I wondered would she ever come to accept the situation as being the machination of a mean and twisted old Man, who thought he could rule someone and create a whole new life for him by pretence.

"I would have come back eventually, I was coming to Ireland anyhow, I was thinking of it when I was in Paris, the morning I met you, I mean, imagine me on Grafton Street and meeting Nancy? That would have brought it all back to me pronto, so it would have happened sooner or later, wouldn't it, Carrie? I know this might sound a bit crazy, but we are meant to be, this is fate, and what's meant to be will happen, no matter what, and Colleen will just have to accept that and live with it"

I just hoped that she and her family, my family would see it that way too.

March 1993

The courtroom was jammed with people.

Just like I had expected.

The papers had gotten wind of the story and for three solid weeks in January, there was blanket coverage. Every cog, every link in the Spiders Web was being pulled apart and analyzed and every scumbag arrested was cause for celebration.

And boy, were there scumbags!

Politicians, Musicians, Film people and bloody Barristers! All walks of life and all sorts of people. I mean, who knew?

Liz was still here. And we, well, we were still living in London, though Dave and Becky had gone home. But we had to stay, because there had been talk of Liz being tried for murdering her father. Thank God though, that didn't happen.

She was quite the celebrity now.

People came out of the woodwork to meet the Liz they thought they had known before. She was classed as another Edie Sedgwick, a tragic figure, but one who had managed to turn her life around and escape. There was even talk of a film being made, and they approached me for the notes I had made for myself, after Saoirse died.

But me and Steve talked about it and realized that what we wanted most of all was to be able to go home to Ireland and be happy and have babies and rear them in peace.

Because that was another link in the chain now, I was pregnant again. And though we were keeping it quiet for a bit, very little passed Liz and she had asked when we thought we were going to make her a granny again.

I liked Liz a lot. And she was trying. But she was caught up in the whirlwind of this inquest and the trial that never happened, and I guess it was taking its toll.

She was gentle with me and Steven, and she got so much out of me about Saoirse and what my life was like in the estate with Noel and Ma, that I could see why she made such a great life coach now.

She had insisted on her father being cremated. In fairness though, that was the law, then, when the person had HIV. He was in a sealed coffin, though that was nothing to us, I didn't want to see the old bastard anyhow. There wasn't going to be any flowers, and as we filed into the crematorium, I realized that the only people there were people who couldn't wait to see the back of him.

David and Becky, and Nancy, of course, had arrived in Glasgow the morning after James died. Worried because they heard nothing from us, Nancy decided to find the number and make the call.

She rang Baird Hall and Liz answered the phone.

I can only imagine the conversation, but later that day, when Liz arrived with Breda to the hotel we were holed up in, she nearly split her sides laughing at the things Nancy had said-

"If that one can write like she talks she'll make millions, she bawled me out, I mean, some of the words she said, I don't have a clue what they are!" She roared with laughter and she was transformed. I could see her when she was in her heyday, and I could see what David saw in her then, but as far as I was concerned, he deserved Becky, she was good to him, and good for him.

She wiped her eyes-

"Well knowing Nancy, I can just imagine what she said to you, totally unprintable, if past conversations are anything to go by" Steven laughed.

I smiled. I'd get it out of Nancy later when I got her alone. Loosen her up with a few drinks.

"Oh but she loves you guys, she really does, she told me they are on the way, I told them to come here, not the hall, its full of police and forensics people now anyhow, we wouldn't be allowed in"

"Here?" I cried.

"Well, yes, why?" She was puzzled.

"Well, you're here, and David and Becky are coming and…"

She laughed again-

"Your friend Nancy, well she said something along those lines too, like *listen here you wagon, you fucked up two of my friends and your not fucking doing it to another two, I don't give a shite if you're his wife back from the dead, I'll fucking kill you myself if you act the maggot with Dave and Becks, d'ya hear me?* I think that was the jist of it" She smiled.

"Whatever happens, I'm not going to try and interfere with David and whatever decision he makes, its up to him at the end of the day Carrie, but I hold no hope for a reconciliation, none at all, because time has passed and we are different people now"

"Well, that's fair enough, and I suppose he'd *have* to know your alive, we don't want a bloody bigamy case on top of us as well" Steven held me tighter.

"Yes, its time to move on, for good" she said.

The whole tribe descended by that evening-

Serena and Michel, who went straight to Steven and hugged him.

"You look so much happier; you found your soul again hey?"

Steven smiled at me-

"My soul, yes, I have"

Serena was kissing and hugging me so tightly I thought I'd burst.

David had walked into the room and stopped, and Liz, who had been sitting in a big armchair, got up and walked towards him-

"David"

I don't think he trusted himself to do anything or say anything more than her name.

"It's been a long time David; you look well, you look, happy"

He nodded.

"David..." she began.

The sound of Nancy's voice outside in the hall was enough to stop her in her tracks. She came into the room like a whirlwind, throwing her coat and her bag on the couch and standing with her hands on her hips. She looked amazing, in tight jeans and her fitted tee shirt, with the words Rock Chick picked out in diamonds. Her dark hair was full and her make up perfect, and I realized looking at her, that she is what Liz might have looked like when she was Queen of the Groupie scene in the sixties-

"Here you, Liz, me an' you are goin' to talk" her accent broadened with temper and I closed my eyes. I knew what was coming.

Liz walked closer and sniffed-

"Go on"

"Nancy, there's no need for this..." David began. But Nancy put her hand up-

"I'm going to say what I want to say and then I'll fuck off and leave youse to sort this out"

"Its all right David, let her talk"

Liz stood with her arms folded, her whole body language that of an equal meeting an equal. She recognized herself in Nancy and knew that Nancy had a heart of gold underneath it all. She must have known that her bark was worse than her bite, like the rest of us, but that she couldn't rest till she had barked her fill.

"Go on, say what you gotta say"

"These people are my fucking friends, they all are, Carrie and Steve, Dave and Becks and Rena and Mick, all of them, and they have gone through hell, fucking hell in the last couple of years, and you did nothing to help them. Now, I'm sure you had reasons that are none of my business, but heres what is my business, MY friend Becky is out in the car park, afraid of her life to come in here and face you, because *she* thinks that all you are doing is snapping your fingers, and your *boys* will fucking go running to yeh" She threw her head back and her eyes snapped-

I was still reeling at her calling the little Frenchman *Mick,* where the fuck did *that* come from?

"Nancy, I'm not here to do anything of the sort" Liz said, hiding a smile.

"Your damned right your not, cos d'ya see you, yeh fucking Mata Hari wannabe, I'll fucking drown you meself if you try!"

"*Nancy!*" all of us shouted, aghast.

"I fucking mean it, don't think I don't know what you were, and what you are, and I can see that you're a good looking woman, and Jaysus knows, they romanticized you enough over the years to make you untouchable, but I mean it, Becky adores him, she loves him so much, you can't come in here and destroy that now, whatever you might have been to him then, you just can't, she's waited two years damn it, for you to fade out of his mind, and then you appear again, like the fucking bad penny, so what are you going to do now?"

"Nancy, listen to me, for fucks sake" David grabbed her arm.

David hardly ever cursed and Nancy looked at him in shock-

"Well, your learning! Either that or your spending too much time with me lately!"

He grinned-

"Listen, this morning, after you told me about Liz being here, do you know what I did, right that second?"

"No, what?"

"I asked Becky then and there to marry me, and do you know what she said?"

Nancy shrugged.

"She said...." He began.

"I said I wanted to marry him more than anything on this earth, that he made me happy, so very happy, and I wanted him to be with me for the rest of our lives, that's what I said" Becky was standing in the doorway, dressed in a beautiful olive green trouser suit, her hair gleaming, and her face glowing.

Liz smiled-

"I'm delighted to hear that"

Becky stopped her-

"But the thing is, I said that I couldn't do it, because I thought that he was asking me, only as an insurance policy, that I would

be the decision made all ready, before he met you, and I told him, I told him that he had to come, and see you first, and if he still wanted to marry me tonight, then he had to ask me again, and I would give him my answer then" her lip trembled.

"Because I know what you were to him Liz, and for ages, I thought I could never live up to you, the young, beautiful, dead wife, who he looked back at with rose tinted glasses, and who he never forgot, but then came Paris, and I realized that he might be forgetting, or at least, putting the past to rest, finally, and we, we were together, for the first time, properly, at Serena and Michel's wedding, and it was the best time of my life, and I was so happy, so bloody happy that night, and all day yesterday, even though I was worried sick about Carrie and Steven, I thought that once I had David I could live with anything" Her eyes filled with tears and David came straight to her and hugged her tightly.

"You still *do* have me Becky, Jesus I was mad about you the first time I laid eyes on you, out in the mobile with Carrie, you remember? I went nuts that night thinking of you at the debs with someone else"

He laughed-

"Imagine it, an oul fella like me at the debs! They'd have thought I was one of the teachers"

I had to smile, that was unlikely, unless he had a sex change and took the veil!

Becky sniffed and wiped her eyes-

"I'd have brung you if you'd gone, but I didn't think, and I wanted to be with you, but I thought you thought that I was too young for you" she rooted for something to wipe her eyes. Her make up was beginning to run and David handed her a hanky.

"I look a mess, after all my trying to come in here and face me rival, look at the state of me" She wiped the last of the make up away and was there, so forlorn, and young, and yet, David still held his arm around her shoulder.

"I'm not your rival Becky, I'm delighted that you and David are together, I mean it" Liz glanced at Nancy who was still glowering.

"That's the thing, I applied for a divorce yesterday evening, I rang my attorney, it should be finalized soon, I said I deserted you David, no contest, no arguing, just fair and right, I want you to be happy now, you deserve it" she looked round the room-

"You all deserve it, every one of you, I'm not here to upset the apple cart or to be Mata Hari, though I am quite flattered by the analogy Nancy, thank you, although she led men to their doom didn't she? I'd like to think that I'm setting mine free"

Well, after that, we calmed down a bit and went for a few drinks. Nancy and Liz actually got on well together. I think Liz recognized a free and kindred spirit when she saw one and kept her on the edge of her seat with tales of Ringo and Paul, Mick and Keith, Marc and David (Bowie) and the antics of the late sixties London set.

And through the hum of conversation I heard Nancy going on about her own rock and roll people, Liam and Adam, Larry and Guggi, Gavin and Bono and of course, her Denny, apparently going to be the next big thing... I smiled to myself, because the nearest she had been to most of them, bar Denny, of course, was in the RDS when they played gigs. But she didn't want to lose face with her new heroine.

Rolling into bed later that night she was all chat about her-

"She says she has some genuine sixties gear in the attic and me and her are going to go through it, Ossie Clarke and Mary Quant stuff, Jaysus Denny will be tearing the clothes off me when he sees it!!" she fell asleep easily.

Hung-over the next day she remarked that at least Liz was still English enough not to think that this situation was going

to turn into an episode of the Walton's where the happy family reunited was going to go off into the sunset together.

"Though I think she has her own sunset to go to, if you get me drift?"

Becky and David were like two love birds, because she had accepted his (albeit drunken) proposal in the bar the night before, and he had slipped a ring on her finger before she could change her mind.

Liz was still on the mineral water and I nudged her-

"You okay? This must be so weird for you, looking at us all"

Michel, drunk as a lord and ecstatically happy was singing some weird French song of love, on one knee to Serena who was telling him to get up and stop making a show of her. Steven was arm in arm with Nancy who was talking intensely to him while he smiled and kept looking at me and shaking his head.

"It is strange, I'll grant you that, but I think it's the right thing, and listen, I don't want you to worry, I won't come over all grand motherly with you guys, I know you have your lives to live and your journey isn't over yet"

I sat in the cold crematorium a week later and remembered what she said.

David and Becky, Nancy, Steven, Liz, Breda and Me were the only people there.

It was like we wanted to see the story ending. We didn't have any service as such. There was no eulogy. What could you say about a man that was widely known to be evil personified?

Just as the very short interlude was coming to an end, Breda slipped out of the seat and went to the back of the church, returning with a wreath of daisies. Jesus only knew where she had gotten them in January in Scotland, I thought, but then I looked, and I realized they weren't really daisies. They were just white paper, cut into the shape of a flower. Hundreds of them.

And the yellow bit, right in the center of each flower, was inscribed with the name of each and every girl he had destroyed.

Katie, Ellie, Sarah.... Every one of them remembered and mourned.

I felt the tears come to my eyes as she walked up to the top of the room. The undertaker was waiting to push the button that would start the coffin on its journey to the fire. She stopped at the side of the coffin and beckoned me up there-

"Come here Carrie"

I slipped out of the seat, my heels making a loud clicking on the tiled floor.

Looking down, I saw that the wreath was beautiful. Whoever made it must have spent hours on it.

"I made this, when you were all out the other night, I sat in and made this, because there is no one else would remember every name, every child, and even then, I forgot someone" she reached into her pocket and pulled what looked like a scrap of lavender silk.

"And when I woke up today, I remembered them Carrie, and I made this" She pressed the silk into my hand.

"Look at it Carrie, please" she whispered.

Half blinded by tears I looked at it-

"Oh Breda!" I gasped.

Five little forget me nots, the purple silk twisted round wire, and the yellow in the middle the names once more, but this time-

Doris, Robert, Phillip, Rachel, Saoirse

"Do you see them Carrie? Do you see that its time to let them go to God, and that this is the end?" She clutched my hand, and I nodded.

I kissed them and placed them, into the wreath and we laid it on the coffin and she nodded to the undertaker. The rollers moved and the curtain went back and we watched, tears falling and not another word spoken.

After that, we went back to London. The gang went back to Ireland, but I had other things to do here first.

Steven applied for an annulment of his marriage, in February, on the grounds of diminished responsibility. Colleen had tried to come back into his life but he held her off for a while. We just weren't ready to talk to her and my, weird thought this, parents yet. We had the inquest to deal with first, and we had the papers door-stepping us all the time, so life was a bit more stressful than it should normally be, and we relished the idea of being able to forget it all shortly.

David and Becky were all loved up at home and I looked forward to their wedding, which now that the decree nisi was through, should be in September or October next.

We discovered my pregnancy in late February and we resolved to keep it secret till we got back to Ireland, but like I said, Liz was a bit more astute than that!

Breda was back on the wards nursing and loving it. In fact, Geordie Patterson, the gummy warrior in the wheelchair had made a special pilgrimage to the hospital with a fine bottle of scotch, after hearing she liked whiskey from an article that appeared in one Sunday paper. He left his Vera at home with the pigeons and came to see her, in best bib and tucker and still no teeth! They both got royally drunk in the day ward and no one cared. Breda was fine now that this was all over and done with. She had her little flat and her nursing and she was happy.

Liz scattered her father's ashes somewhere. She never told us where. But she said that she wouldn't inter them, because it might make a shrine out of his grave for all sorts of weirdoes and she didn't want that. Personally I wouldn't care a jot if she'd fecked them into a litter bin. It was all that bastard deserved.

Baird Hall was deserted now, the land being excavated to find out exactly how many little souls were lost in the years the spider reigned. The basements were gone through by forensic policemen and they found so much evidence that it was lucky for

Bard that he was dead, because I think they might have brought back hanging just for him. They tried too to find the families of the dead children, tried to find some link to them and figure out how they came to be in his clutches, but it wasn't working too well. The register for missing children was checked and apart from two little girls from London, in the 1970's, none of the others could be traced through that either.

All told, seventy little children were buried in that private, and incidentally, unconsecrated graveyard in the grounds of the hall. From Katie to Ellie, all unloved and un-mourned.

"Who in their right mind would buy a house like that anyhow, or the land even?" I asked Steven one night.

. No one wanted it, the house, or to live there, certainly we didn't. What money was left was rightfully Stevens and he agonized about it.

Dirty money, Made from the life blood of children.

What luck could we have with money like that?

In the end, we decided that we would take enough, from the sale of the publishers, not the land, to buy a house in Ireland somewhere, so that Liz could come and stay with us when she wanted. We decided that the proceeds from the sale of the land would be given to Childline or one of the children's charities; maybe do something good out of all this. But Liz wasn't too keen on the idea of Ireland, and she was already making noises about getting back to the States and her work. I think part of it was not wanting to rain on David and Becky's parade, which I admired her for. But somehow, I kept getting the feeling that when she did go back to America, she would disappear as simply as she did before.

And this time I would miss her.

We all had to speak in court. I told them about Saoirse and Ma and the boys. And then Steven spoke about his side of it all, how his grandfather manipulated him and lied to him and how he very nearly killed me.

Noel had made a full and complete statement and this was read out in court. As a codicil he had added-

I know that I am not the man I should be, and I want to say this to Carol Anne, because I know she is there today. I was misguided, in my attempt to get revenge for the wrong done to my own mother, I hurt you, and you lost what you loved, and in some way I want to make you understand, and maybe one day forgive me. I can't say anything other than I am sorry. From the bottom of what heart I have left, I apologize. I will spend my life in jail, and that is fine. Because at least I know it's over now.

We listened to them going over the litany of terrible things James Bard had inflicted on so many little souls. They played the film we had seen that night in the house and even hardened reporters were overcome with sadness and fear. And shame that this could happen and so many little children could be failed by a system that was meant to be the best in the western world.

And his diary, his ledgers kept for many years, detailing the names of all the shipments, the human cargo that he had destroyed. Maybe he wasn't as clever as he thought he was to put all that in writing. How untouchable he must have felt, to write in a dozen hard back books every little thing he had done. He must have thought the police would never get him. However, it made uneasy reading now. Name after name, child after child, hundreds of them that would never be accounted for, buried in unmarked graves, or abandoned on the streets to God knew what kind of fate. The sheer un-measurable evil of it all, it seemed to be floating like mist in the courtroom. I wasn't the only one felt sick to my stomach.

There was talk of them digging again on the site of the house and dragging the lakes and the deep pond that was nearby, to see if there were more children there, because there were too many unaccounted for and there would have to be bodies, remains, the judge granted that they could and once the digging was done and the house demolished the land could then be sold and the money given to whatever charity we wished.

They showed the picture that had put the nail into his coffin once and for all and the judge remarked that he was only sorry it wasn't the man himself in the dock, but as the saying goes, he was gone before a higher court than any on earth, and they would be his judge.

By the end of the day Liz was a free woman. Free to go home, wherever home might be now.

We walked out of the court that day, 17th March 1993, and stood on the steps. The reporters took some pictures but even they were subdued.

"All we want, as a family, all of us, is to let this rest now, let it go, so please, be kind enough to let us be, please" Steven held my arm and then, when he had said what he wanted to say, we got into a taxi and went home.

Liz flew back to America the following morning. Her decree absolute in her handbag.

Like I thought she would, she faded into obscurity, and out of our lives. She had been so much a part of us for the past couple of months that I thought it odd. It was like she was leaving him all over again. Only this time, Steven wasn't a child and he understood a little more. When he tried to phone the number she gave him, she wasn't there. He tried to find her and couldn't. So he decided to leave it so. She would contact us when she needed to, or wanted to.

But she never did.

In July, a doctor from a huge hospital in Boston called us, and told us that she was dead. Cancer. She'd known all along. She had been in treatment for about a year before and the weight gain we had noticed was actually from the drugs she was taking for the pain. The funeral was over; there was nothing to be done. She had her ashes scattered over the bay in New York, some of the women from Saoirse's House did that for her.

"She asked that you not be told till she was cremated and gone, I'm sorry" he said.

For weeks, we expected a letter or something from her, maybe something to explain why she had frozen us out. But the silence was as absolute as it had been before the events in Baird Hall last Christmas.

Walking along the Embankment one evening in late summer, my bump enormous, I asked-

"Why do you think she did it?"

"Went away again? I suppose she wouldn't have come back only she had to, she had her life over there, and she knew she couldn't be part of mine any more, it was all too weird, she did right by Dad, and us, and then went home to die I think"

"It's a pity; she might have liked to have seen the baby"

He looked up at the sky, with all of London and the river in front of us-

"Wherever she is, she'll know, she'll see" He took my hand-

"Come on darlin' you look tired, let's go home to bed"

I said a prayer to her where ever she was. And I like to think she knew.

Our son, Daragh, Gaelic, meaning oak tree, for strength and courage, was born in September and his birth was mentioned in the papers. But people had moved on and thankfully we were allowed to bring him home and be peaceful for a couple of weeks. Still in the same flat we three were all we needed. This time Steven was there, one hundred per cent, with the baby and they were a joy to behold.

Becky had put her wedding on hold, and it was now set for Valentines Day 1994.

That suited us. We had already begun to make enquiries about houses in Ireland. Every day we woke up to the sound of brochures landing on the mat and spent hours comparing what each auctioneer sent us.

By December, Steven had to go to court for his annulment. This time it was in a private court hearing and I didn't go. Though my heart was in my mouth all the time he was away. Colleen was sure to be there. She had to be. I was in the process of packing up our things for the move to Ireland. In saying that, apart from baby things, there was very little, because I had initially brought a small case to that wedding, and just never went home again. I wasn't sure where the heck home was now anyhow!

I put Daragh in the cot and went to the window, looking out into the rain to see was there any sign of Steven.

He walked up the steps to the house and stopped at the door.

Something's wrong, I can feel it.

I waited till he was in, and his coat off and then asked him how it went-

"Oh God it was terrible Carrie, Colleen was there, and heres the thing, she fought the annulment, she wanted a divorce instead, because..."

Tell me. There's a baby isn't there?

There was.

Michelle Elizabeth, born in July, which was why she desperately wanted him to see her. He had thought that she was trying to make him change his mind.

"So you see now, Carrie, we can't get an annulment, because that would mean the marriage hadn't existed, and that the baby would be illegitimate and Colleen cares about that a great deal, she was married, she said, when she fell pregnant, and married when she had the baby, and she wants that recognized"

"But Steven, the marriage wasn't legal; she married Gary Bard, who doesn't exist! What the fuck does she want? Your nothing to the Bards anymore, your Steven Williams, you always have been" I cried.

"I know, I *know* but she is determined to make this stick, and she says she doesn't care how long it takes, she wants her rights!" he put his head down on the table and sighed.

"Fucking hell, Carrie, how long is it going to take before we have a life?"

My mind reeled. There had to be something we could do. Maybe she just didn't get it; maybe she was so into him that she wanted him at any price. But then again, she didn't know him, she only knew Gary, the man she married, who hadn't even known himself! And she, by the sounds of things, had been well aware that she was marrying an alter ego and not the real person, and now, she wanted that union recognized! What sort of woman *was* my sister?

I made a decision then and there-

"Listen to me Steven Williams, I'm your woman, and you are my man, and I don't give a flying fuck if I never marry you as long as you never leave me again, and Daragh is yours, and he loves you too! But I am not giving in to her, she's played the steel magnolia long enough, she has to be made to see sense, so we are packing this place up, shipping it all to Ireland next week and then, the two of us are going to Liverpool" I slapped the table so hard that the baby woke up again. Steven sat up-

"Jesus you're a terror when your angry!" he grinned.

"Well fuck it; I've had enough of my life on hold, its time to sort this once and for all.

Part Three
1970-1973

18

Valerie

Let's make the best of the situation
Before I slowly go insane
Please don't say,
We'll never find a way
Don't tell me all my loves in vain
©Eric Clapton "Layla" 1970

I was born in Liverpool.

1950 it was, my mother gave birth to me on the lino in our back kitchen in Kirby.

Apparently I was a big baby; for all that they were pretending that I was early. I wasn't you know, I was bang on time. It was them two that were early.

"Anticipating the Sacrament of Marriage" Father Kelly said. But he married them anyway on the side altar and I was born five months later.

Once they were safely married, Mam could take off the girdle she said was crippling her and get into her smocks and live a little.

They had other kids of course; there was Elizabeth, called after the Queen, and Philomena, after a saint. But I was the oldest and I was called Valerie. I haven't a clue where that name came from but it wasn't po faced like the ones they called my sisters.

Me Dad worked in the Hercy docks, down by the Mersey. He'd grafted there since he left school, and by God did he work. He'd come home filthy and Mam wouldn't let him into the house before he had a wash in the yard. Out there in all weathers under the cold tap he was. No wonder he got rheumatism later on. But Mam didn't care; he wasn't going to walk the grease and muck of the ship yard into her house.

She was a tartar my Mam. And bloody house proud too. We didn't have much in the line of luxury in the house but you could have eaten your dinner off the lino, any day.

It was nice growing up in Kirby, I made loads of friends, and by the time the sixties came, I was old enough to be allowed into town on my own at lunchtime to see the Beatles and Gerry and the Pacemakers in the Cavern Club.

Jammed to the wall it was with bodies, steam dripping down as we jostled to get near to the stage. Because it might happen to us you know, why, it was common knowledge that Ringo's girlfriend was one of us once. A Cavern girl.

I went to the convent school in the centre of the town. Most of the time I was in my uniform when I got to the Cavern, but then, the week I left school when I was sixteen, I went in my work clothes.

I got a job in Woolworth or Woolies as we used to call it. I had to dress smart in a skirt and blouse and my nylon shop coat went over that.

By this time the Beatles were world famous, 1966, it was. But there was always a buzz in the Cavern and I went in one Friday.

There was a girl group on first, I didn't pay much mind. I liked Dusty and Cilla and that was it. I had all their records and used to backcomb my hair like Dusty.

This fella sat on the edge of my table. I was annoyed because I had my sarnie on the table and my drink and there wasn't much room.

"D'ya mind?" I asked.

He grinned, and I have to admit, he had a lovely smile. Kind of gappy like, but cute in its own way.

"Not really love, do you?"

Cheeky beggar! I told him to go away, and he got off the table and held out his hand-

"I apologize for my being so cheeky, I just saw you and thought that I'd like to know you better, d'ya come here often?" he sat in the chair opposite.

"A bit" I smiled. What a cheesy chat up line!

"There's some good bands on today" We looked up at the chalk board where the list of performers was written daily or weekly-

"I used to come see the Beatles myself" I sniffed.

"Yeah?"

"Yeah, this lot today don't seem too good, I might not stay"

He looked really down when I said this. He sighed heavily.

"I mean, have *you* heard of *The Strangers?*" I asked.

He smiled again-

"Yeah, their great, you should stick around for them defo" He stayed at the table for a while and he told me he was working in a restaurant as a kitchen porter.

"But I'm going to be a chef one day, maybe when I'm forty or something"

The girl group finished and he looked at his watch.

"Valerie, will you let me take you out somewhere tonight?"

"Well, I dunno, I'm washing me hair tonight"

He grinned-

"Your hair looks fine to me, c'mon, let me take you dancing? I'll show yeh a good time you know, I got paid today"

"Maybe I have other plans" I didn't, but I didn't want him to think me too easy. Though in them days, in Liverpool, no one sat in of an evening unless they really wanted to, there was always something going on.

"Tell you what, stick around till the next band finish and I'll come back and ask you again, and maybe, just maybe, you might forget those plans and leave the shampoo till tomorrow night, yeah?" he was gone.

Of course, you guessed it. I went up to the stage to look at this band, The Strangers, who he reckoned were so hot, and there he was, the cheeky beggar, playing guitar and doing it well too!

And judging by the amount of admiring lassies around the stage, he wasn't short of company if he wanted it. But he picked me. I touched my hair, piled into its little beehive and sighed. It'd do for another day or two, I supposed.

So when he came back to the table, I told him I'd meet him in the station, under the clock at eight.

We were both kind of young, and the romance fizzled out after a couple of months. I started dating someone else and I thought that Jimmy Dalton, for that was his name, was off making millions with the band.

They made a couple of records, you'd hear them on the radio, and then seemed to vanish off the face of the planet. One of them was called "Shop Girl" and I liked to think it was about me. It was along the same lines as that song "Bus Stop", kind of like boy meets girl. I thought it was great! How did it go? Oh yeah...

She was sitting in her shop-coat, and she said her name was Sal

Eating lunch and drinking cola in the cavern
I said I'd like to see her, that I would take her dancing
But me shop girl said she had to wash her hair!
So I played a little music and I tried to win her round
And the song I played her, it went down a treat
For when I asked her out again, she forgot her other plans
And met me underneath the clock in Lime Street.

That's how it went? Wasn't it great? It was my little secret back then, I kind of hugged it to myself when people talked about Patti Boyd having songs written for her and Marianne Faithful and all that lot... I was one of them too, because apart from the name change, I knew in my heart that Shop Girl was for me.

I often thought of Jimmy back then. Not that I had any feelings for him or anything, but you know the way you think of people sometimes, and you wonder what their up to or whatever.

The sixties weren't as permissive as you'd think. Oh I know all about the Pill and free love but, let me tell you, there was none of that nonsense on my street! My mother had me terrified to let any of my boyfriends put a hand on me, so with the result, they were all dying to marry me. Philomena, my sister, reckoned I was making a collection of engagement rings. I used to laugh at her and say that none of them were up to scratch, neither the rings or the men who gave me them, and none of them were right for me, and when I met Mr. Right, well then, they'd be the first to know.

Came the seventies and things were definitely changing-

Well, for a start, the Beatles broke up. They hadn't been the same as the Cavern boys mind you, not in a long time. And when that Yoko came along, well that was the end of it for me. I liked the music still, but I loved the new rock sound that was coming out. And I liked to wear denims and leather jackets.

433

I loved Derek and the Dominos, and the Yardbirds; I played them on my little record player in my room. But my parents didn't like it one bit, telling me I was turning into a "beatnik" and that it wasn't respectable to wear jeans so tight. My mother laid the law down to me one evening-

"Valerie Mary Elaine Bradshaw" she called me, and I knew when I was getting the treble barrel that it was trouble.

"Yes Mam?"

"Come down here this minute, I want to see you" she shouted up the stairs. I got off the bed and put my slippers on over my socks. I'd been lying on the bed reading one of the new music mags that were coming out nearly weekly and contemplating going to see Status Quo during the week. I'd had a very long and tiresome day in work and I wasn't in the humour for an ear bashing, which is why I was in my bedroom in the first place.

"Comin' Mam" I called and stomped down the stairs.

She was in the kitchen with Lizzie, and Phil.

They had been doing the dishes and she shooed them upstairs. Dad was in the living room watching the telly. He had it blaring, he had a bit of a hearing loss from the work he did on the docks, the sound of the hooters and the bells did it, and the telly would be uncomfortably loud when he was watching.

"What's wrong Mam?" I sat down.

She sat at the table and folded her arms-

Phil had washed the table but hadn't dried the oilcloth properly so there were little puddles of wet on it. Mam clucked her tongue in dismay and went off to the sink for a dry cloth.

"Our Phil is one clotty cow" She rubbed at the cloth "There now, that's better"

She sat down again and looked at me.

"Your twenty one years of age next month, born in this very kitchen, right there on that floor, in 1950, you know that don't you?" She pointed at the spot on the lino, now; normally she only did that when she had her yearly sweet sherry at Christmas and got all maudlin. That was also the time when she told me I was her first born and that she loved me. But the rest of the year I was "that one" or "that beatnik I reared".

"Yes Mam" What the heck was this all about?

"Twenty one years old, and how many times have you been engaged?"

Oh for heavens sake! Not this again!

"Five times Mam"

"Five times Valerie, Five, that's ridiculous, and I want to know is there anything you want to tell me? Why is it that you can be five times engaged and you still aren't married?" She sat back and rested her bosom on her arms.

"Tell you? Tell you what? I didn't love them"

My mother had a great line in snorts-

"Humph, and presumably you knew this before you agreed to marry them, I mean, three weeks before the wedding to Michael O Dwyer and you called it off, there I was with the wedding cake made and ready for me to ice it, and you decide your not getting married...Three tiers it was, all fruit and brandy, I had to give it away for Christmas I did"

"*Mam for heavens sake,* he was an alcoholic"

"Every man drinks look at your Dad, it's the climate Val, and then there was Peter, now he was a nice lad, but what do you do? In the middle of the fitting for the dress you called it off, then David, a lovely lad, gorgeous too, best looking of the lot, with a few bob behind him... same thing again, now" She slapped the table and I jumped-

"Now, I'm no fool, there's something amiss here and I won't rest till I get to the bottom of it, that Dusty one that your so fond of, she's a bit like you, she isn't married yet either, I was in the hair dressers the other day and I was reading in a magazine that she is living with a woman in America, if that's what this is..." She was nearly purple in the face and I laughed out loud.

"You think I'm a lesbian?"

"Is that what they're called? Right, well then, are you?" She lowered her voice again; probably afraid my father would hear. Though the telly was so loud that the entire air force could land in the garden and he wouldn't know!

"Because it would break your Daddy's heart Val, he always wanted what was best for you and you can't deny it, he sent you to the nuns and you get the best we have of everything, you could have gone to college, could have been a teacher, but you left school and went working in Woolies and I didn't stop you, I didn't stop you when you started hanging round with them hippies, and I thank God and his Blessed Mother that you didn't come home ruined, but I need to know if you are queer Val, if your one of them lesbians, well then, you have to tell me, its not *natural* so it isn't, you should be married with a couple of babies by now, not flitting around in them jeans looking like a beatnik, Marie Crosby is a granny three times over already and her Annette is only married three years, I can't bear the shame of this, if your one of *them...* " She stopped and waited for my reply. Her eyes were tearing and she took a hanky out of the pocket of her smock.

"Annette Crosby was five months pregnant going up the aisle, is that what you want me to do Mam?" I snapped. Marie Crosby was the world's biggest gossip, until it came to her own family and then everything was shoved under the carpet. Even my Da said she should patent her curtains-

"They come with a built in twitcher, nosy old cow" he laughed when he saw her at the window the day we got the new sofa for the living room.

Mam was still sniffing into her hanky.

"Well anything beats being a queer" she muttered.

I couldn't help laughing. She pursed her lips together-

"Any road, its no harm having a bit of a head start on marriage, its human nature so it is" She'd certainly changed her tune. Normally it was a lecture on having respect for yourself and literally, your two legs in the one stocking till the ring was safely blessed and on your finger. But then again, maybe a shamed and pregnant daughter and a shotgun wedding were preferable to a dyke in the family.

"Well, answer me Val, are you or aren't you?"

"What?"

"Like that Dusty, you *know*?"

"No, *no Mammy* I'm not a lesbian, no way, I just, I just haven't found what I'm looking for" I said.

"Well will you for Gods sake go out and find it, and marry it, because I have three half made wedding dresses up in the wardrobe and I'd like to see you wear one of them!"

End of conversation.

She made a pot of tea for her and the old fella and I was left sitting at the table alone. Fuming.

Half past nine. To early for bed anyhow. And I was not going in to watch the telly with Mam and Dad. To sit there for a night of heavy sighs and head shaking?

Not bloody likely!

I also decided that I couldn't face going back up to my room, where the other two were probably going to be sitting on the bed agog, waiting for me to appear. I'd heard the stairs creaking and knew they'd been ear-wigging until they heard Mam's chair going across the lino. I could imagine Philomena-

"*What's* a *lesbian* our Valerie?" And let me tell you, there was very little Philomena didn't know. She'd only ask to make me squirm.

I couldn't face it. I stood at the bottom of the steps and thought for a second.

I took my jacket and my boots out of the hall press and grabbed my purse.

"I'm going to Sandra's place, be back in a bit"

I slammed the door before Mam could reply.

It was autumn. The nights were beginning to draw in and I walked in a foul temper. I didn't go to Sandra's house. Even if we had been friends since the day we started in playschool together and I tipped a bottle of red poster paint onto her head because she knocked the down the Lego tower I had spent a morning building, I didn't feel I could go round there and tell her that my mother thought I was a lesbian.

Sandra was all loved up anyhow, going with the same fella for the past three years; he was a merchant seaman, away for months at a time. She couldn't understand why he wouldn't swallow the anchor and get a job at home and marry her, move into her mothers and make babies.

But I knew why Roger wouldn't come home and work in an office or a factory and it had nothing to do with loving the sea, and everything to do with her religion mad mother! There were so many holy statues round that house it felt like the Blessed Virgin was one of the family! I swear to God, you'd nearly set another place at the table for the Child of Prague!

Sandra reckoned I should have married David, and couldn't understand my wanting something better than that for myself. I could do without a lecture from Mrs. Swan, her mother, about praying to St. Anne for a husband or something like that. Or another night looking at whatever letter Roger had sent from some far flung port, avoiding the subject of when he was coming home to make an honest woman of Sandra!

I walked down to the end of the street and hopped on a bus into town.

It was a weeknight but there was always something going on in town. I thought I'd head into the Cavern again, though I hadn't been there in a while.

Down Matthew Street there seemed to be a buzz. I met a girl I knew from work, a bit of a spacer but okay, and I called her-

"Sheena, come 'ere, what's the buzz?"

She smiled-

"All right Val, you goin' the Cavern?"

"Might do, why?"

"Fuckin' great band on tonight, Glorious... you'll love them, the guitarist is fuckin' amazing" she grinned.

It sounded better than going home and counting the woodchips on the wallpaper, so I slapped my few pence on the desk and went down the black stairs.

The place was jammers. More crowded than in the Beatles hey day. But it was with guys as well as girls, all long haired and wearing the leathers and jeans.

I could hear the band before I saw them. I thought they sounded good, hot, actually. I listened to a passable cover of a Black Sabbath song and nodded to the music appreciatively. The difference between this lot and the Beatles was that the front of the stage was jammed in equal proportions with boys and girls.

"Told yeh he was to die for" Sheena nudged me, and I turned from my lemonade on the bar to look, not expecting anything special, her version of to die for was usually gruesome.

And there he was. My Jimmy, Jimmy Dalton, all grown up and looking gorgeous. Twiddling with the string of his guitar, on a break between numbers, his jeans so tight you could see what he had for breakfast, his Yardbirds tee shirt shabby under his leather jacket.

The singer, Tony Onslow, was shouting into the mic-

"Next song is by the Stones..."

My eyes met Jimmy's over the crowd, and they locked together, and after God knew how many seconds he nodded, and tapped the singer on the shoulder.

A quick word to Tony and he gestured to me. Tony nodded-

"Eh, right, okay then, we're, eh, not doing that song yet, Jimmy here wants to play a special request, its Layla, the Eric Clapton number, all right?"

The crowd roared. Clapton was becoming a huge star lately and the lads in the audience wanted to see how good this cover would be. Anyone who could play like Clapton was a demi God. More muttering up on stage-

"An' he's doin' it for the gorgeous Valerie Bradshaw" The singer looked round the room and I shrank down in the crowd-

"Flippin' heck" I muttered

"She's over there? That her at the bar? Aw, she's a bit shy is she? Cool, right Jimmy, you're on"

And my God did he play. I swear to God I got stuck to the floor. This was no candy cane song of love and romance in the style of the strangers. This was pure lust, pure sex, and it looked very like Jimmy wanted me. I was totally awestruck, and I have to admit it, chuffed to bits with the attention. Jimmy sang the song as he played it and his voice was rough and husky, and I got the shivers all over me.

"Do you *know* him Val?" Sheena gasped.

I nodded, not able to take my eyes off him, strutting up on the stage like the man who owned the world.

"Yeah, he's an ex of mine" And he wouldn't be an ex for too much longer if I had my way. He was pure dynamite. Every girl in the place wanted him; you could see it in the air almost. But every time he took his eyes up from his guitar, they met mine over the heads below him and he smiled. It was as if he was saying "its all for you baby, all of it" and I loved it.

"Fucking hell, you jammy cow, wait till I tell the girls in work tomorrow" She sighed.

By the end of the set I was knackered. I couldn't take my eyes off him. I devoured him, the way he moved on stage, he had such presence and charisma.

Okay so he wasn't as tall as me, I remembered that, in fact, he was quite a bit smaller, and I remembered being embarrassed all those years ago when we were dating and people would laugh when they saw us together.

"Ere they come, the long and the short of it" They'd say, when we walked down the road or into the club. I am exceptionally tall for a woman I suppose. People used to tell me that I needed a red beacon on my head when I wore high heels, which I still did sometimes to annoy them. You don't get many almost six foot women in Liverpool.

But now, tonight, oh God, I couldn't have cared less. There he was, stocky and red haired with gappy teeth and unshaven, but to me he was Elvis and Clapton rolled into one gorgeous, sexy man!

And he loved rock and roll. You could see it, his hair flopping over his forehead as he became engrossed in some riff he was playing. They did the Stones "Paint it black" and the place erupted.

When the gig was over he fought his way through the crowd to me-

"Well stranger?" he smiled.

"Jimmy, oh, it's amazing to see yeh" I felt so good I thought I was going to sprout wings and fly out of there. This was it, this was love, and it was what I was waiting for all this time.

He leant against the bar and smiled, looking me up and down. I was wearing tight jeans and a black jumper that I'd changed into when I got home from work; I wished that I was wearing something nicer, though he didn't seem to mind-

"Not the Woolies uniform tonight then? You still working there?" he took a sip of the pint that someone handed him.

"Yeah, I am, in the music section would you believe" I grinned.

He didn't get much peace, people were coming up to him and talking to him and he really wasn't in the humour for them. Eventually he took my hand and nodded at the door-

"Come on, let's go and have a drink somewhere a bit more peaceful than here" And we left. It was getting late but I didn't give a damn, I'd have gone to the moon with him then and there had he wanted me to.

He took me out of the Cavern to a blues club that was open late and we sat drinking beers and chatting. I have to say I was expecting him to be into drugs or something, but he told me straight that he was a beer man and that was it. He's qualified as a chef but wasn't working at it, wanting to give the music one more go.

By the end of the night, I had missed my bus and I didn't want to leave him anyhow.

He brought me back to a flat that he shared with the singer from the group, Tony. We sat on the living room floor playing records and it took him till four in the morning to kiss me. But by six in the morning I think even my mother could put her mind at ease, because once and for all, I discovered that I wasn't a lesbian. Not that I *ever* thought that I was, not for a minute, but I hadn't felt desire like this in my life before. I wanted Jimmy and he wanted me and that was all there was to it.

I remember listening to the early morning traffic in the street below us and watching the horrible green curtain blowing back and forward in the draft from the broken window, and thinking that I had never felt so good, and that if all those girls who went up the aisle preggers felt this great, then I could quite understand it.

Needless to say I was neck deep in trouble when my mother got her hands on me next morning. But I couldn't care less. I was over the moon, head over heels in love, and so was Jimmy.

Christmas week 1971 was terrible.

I wasn't well; I had the flu and was lying in bed, miserable and not able to stomach food. I went to the doctor after a week of it and he took blood tests and told me to rest up and come back in the New Year.

Jimmy and I were mad about each other. Crazy. Every chance I got I was at his gigs and then back to the little flat, sometimes there were others there and we would sit drinking cheap Chianti or Vermouth and listening to records with whoever was there with us, and then, other times it was just me and Jimmy, lying under the blankets in his single bed, dreaming about the day when we would have the big house and millions in the bank.

I went round like someone in a daze, and more than once my supervisor reprimanded me for being lax in my work. But there were times when a song would come on in the shop and it would stop me in my tracks, and I would remember what we had been doing the night before as that song played in the flat. And then, I couldn't keep the grin off my face.

Jimmy would come and eat lunch with me in the café and then go and do sound-checks and prepare for that nights gig, often picking me up from work in the van with the gear in it. Often times I would bring my clothes to work and then have tea with the lads in some greasy spoon café on route to the gig.

I was treated like one of the lads and they accepted me as Jimmy's girl and while they went off pulling skirt at the end of the night, me and Jimmy would huddle in the van and cuddle and kiss and talk.

It was like having a gang of mischievous big brothers. I loved it.

There were pranks galore on the road. When they were playing a gig one night in a town near London, on the bill with a big act over from the states, they decided to freak out the very staid driver of the other lots bus. The other band had more money than Glorious did and had a proper bus and all that. We were all piled into Tony's van, squashed in with the amps and the drum kit. Sitting on ancient cushions from a sofa his mother had dumped years ago.

We left about an hour before the others and on a dark road, in the middle of nowhere, we stopped the van and Tony and

Kevin, climbed out and stripped to their underpants and when the other bus came round the corner, stuck out their thumbs as though they were hitching. I nearly split my sides laughing at the look on the drivers face.

I tell you what, in the months I went with them to gigs I saw more arse cheeks in that bloody van than I ever have since. I think they made a religion out of mooning people on the motorway!

My mother and father were climbing the walls.

They didn't like my late nights, they didn't like me being so day- dreamy and they definitely did not like Jimmy.

"He's a long haired lay about, with no prospects and no family to speak of, what do you mean by wasting your time with him?" My father, had turned off the telly to rant and I sat on the sofa listening.

It wasn't Jimmy's fault that he was orphaned young. Well, his mother was dead a couple of years then and his father hadn't been seen since she was pregnant on him, so he presumed that he was dead too. I argued with my father till I was blue in the face but he said he would never accept Jimmy as a son in law and I should drop the relationship now.

But on this I was firm. I loved him and wasn't dropping him for anyone.

Jimmy had come round to meet them and he had asked for my hand in marriage. Like it was done in them days. I mean, we knew we would marry come hell or high water, but he thought that my parents would appreciate him giving them the courtesy.

Like hell they did! There was World War Three in our living room when he went home.

"I'm not wasting me time with him, I love him" I said.

"He doesn't even work..." My mother sighed into her hanky.

"He does, the band…he earns great money with them, more than you do on the docks" He did, even though a lot of it went into a fund for the studio time they might need to record a single soon. And he was writing great songs, brilliant stuff, he would play it for me in the nights when I would stay, and I loved it. He had money for the rent and food and smokes and beers. What more did he or I need?

"That's not a bloody job Valerie, you know that, he's a chef he said, why isn't he doing that? At least it's steady and respectable"

My mother was heartbroken, sighing and wailing about the men I had turned down for this.

"Michael's a solicitor now, you could have had a big house, but no, that's no use to our Valerie, she wants some hippy that'll give her nothing only a life in shame and poverty"

"Oh Mam, what about love?" I asked.

"You can't eat it and it doesn't pay the bills" Dad snapped. He stared at me and then sighed-

"I'm only thinking of you, I'm for your good, you know, you need to stop seeing him, give him back his ring and forget him"

"I won't, I, I can't Dad, I love him" I sobbed.

He threw the paper onto the floor-

"It's an order Val, you stop this relationship or I will" He stormed out and into the night and my mother spent the rest of the evening, alternating between consoling and berating me.

You see, it wasn't that simple.

I was pregnant.

I knew it before the doctor ever told me. I hadn't had a period since that night in late September when I went back to his flat. And he had the same idea too.

In the New Year he rang me in work, the only place we could see or speak to each other-

"How far are you gone?" he whispered.

"Round four months I think, it was that first night in your place" I smiled despite myself and I could hear in his voice that he was smiling too. I wasn't one bit worried; I knew that Jimmy wouldn't leave me in trouble. I knew he would make things right, and how I wanted to be married to him, I couldn't wait to be Mrs. Dalton.

"Look, they'll have to let us marry now; I'll come round and tell them"

"Okay, I'll see you tonight then" I put the phone down. They'd have to let me marry him now. I was scared to death of what might be said that night, but relieved that they would have to see sense and let me be with him now.

Surely respectability mattered to them more than the length of Jimmy's hair?

Not so.

There we were, after tea, when the knock comes to the door and my sister brings him into the living room.

"Mr. Bradshaw, Mrs. Bradshaw, good night to yeh, I wanted to ask..." he began.

"I thought that I told you not to come here again" My dad folded the paper over the arm of the chair.

"Mister Bradshaw, I need to speak to you again" Jimmy had made an effort, his clothes were spotless and his hair tied back.

"I told you, Valerie, three weeks ago, not to see this lay about again, have you disobeyed me?" Dad was nearly foaming at the mouth.

"Mr. Bradshaw, there was no question of my not seeing Valerie, I love her, and she loves me and I need to tell you...." Jimmy didn't raise his voice; he was polite and trying to hold his temper.

My father slapped his hand on the coffee table-

"There is nothing I need to hear from you or say to you, now get out of my house"

"I think there is Sir, something you need to know, before you make a decision"

My father looked at me, and then him-

"Oh... indeed?" You could have heard a pin drop in the silence that followed. Truly the quiet before the storm.

My mother had the presence of mind to get the kids out of the room before all hell broke loose.

"..... You have the cheek to stand there and tell me that you made little of my daughter? You dirty, filthy beggar, how dare you come here and tell me that? Get the hell out before I call the police, you should be shot! You would have been ten year ago, shootings too good for you, the cheek of you!" My dad was furious.

"It wasn't like that Dad" I screamed. Why couldn't they let us be happy?

"Val, calm down love, the baby" Jimmy held my arm, and I could feel him shaking.

"Oh I can't believe this is happening, how will I face the neighbors?" Mam wailed into her apron.

"God Mam, make up your mind will you? A few months ago you thought I was a lesbian, I'd have thought you'd be happy to have a grandchild coming along" I snapped.

My father jumped off the chair and raised his hand to slap me-

"Don't you speak to your mother like that, I told you before, its hanging round with the likes of this scruff that has you the way you are"

Jimmy stood in front of me and grabbed my fathers hand-

"Don't you put your hand to her face, she's carrying a baby" He said.

"Aye, someone's bastard, like the whore she is" he sat down again.

"My baby, and I'm going to make it legal soon as possible"

"You are not!" my father roared.

447

"She's over twenty one now and she wants to marry me" Jimmy shouted back.

"Never, not while there's a breath in my body"

"Dad, please..."

"You won't see him again, and when that child is born it's going for adoption, that's the end of it then, and you, get out of my house and *don't come bloody back!*"

There was silence for a second.

Jimmy kissed me on the cheek-

"See you tomorrow pet, lunchtime, okay?"

I nodded and he left. I felt exhausted, drained. All I wanted to do was sleep.

I went to bed that night after a cup of tea my mother forced down my neck. It tasted vile, absolutely rotten. I thought it was because I was getting the flu again. I went into a deep sleep, so deep that it was late the next morning when I woke up.

I jumped out of bed and got dressed.

Pulling on my smock over my clothes I tried to open the bedroom door.

It wouldn't budge.

I hammered on it-

"Mam, Mam, the doors stuck!" I yelled.

I heard her coming up the stairs-

"Mam the door won't open, it's stuck!" I heard the creak as she sat on the stairs.

"Mam?" A cold fear came over me, because at that point I noticed the hole in the door, big enough to fit one of our dinner plates in, with the bit of wood slotted back in. with a bit of string tied to it so it could be pulled out.

"I'm sorry Valerie, it's for your own good, your staying in there till you see sense" she said.

I looked around the room. My posters and books were there, and a little transistor radio that belonged to Phil. They must have doped me; I remembered the sour taste from the tea.

They drugged me so that I would sleep through the noise they made.

"Your not, you couldn't be serious Mam, your not going to lock me in here till, till the baby comes, how will I go to the toilet, or wash?"

"There's a bucket under the bed Val, and a basin and jug, I'll bring you water every day and if your good you can have a bath Saturdays" Her voice was matter of fact and serious. She wasn't going to budge on this one.

"You can't do this to me, I'm twenty one, I can go if I like" I screamed.

"No Valerie, it's for your own good, we're not letting you ruin your life like this" She got up and I could hear the clicking of her wedding band on the stair rail.

For a while I railed against them. Screaming and crying and telling them I wanted out and they just looked in the hole in the door deadpan and either handed in or took the dishes. My father would come up every second day and remove the bucket and give me a fresh one, with clean water in my jug.

I decided that there was no point in screaming and yelling any more, that the way to fight them was to fool them into thinking I was remorseful and repentant.

But every single time Layla came on the radio I remembered and I cried.

I was due the baby in June and still there was no sign of Jimmy, and I suppose that my dad thought he had the message and wouldn't be back.

So at the start of the summer, when the weather turned and began to get hot, Mam decided that I could sit out for a bit in the garden. I behaved, because inside myself, I knew that this might be my only chance to escape, but for the first week, there was no sign of any white knight on a horse galloping up the road. I began to despair and sat like a big blob in the deckchair, saying nothing at all.

Mam would sit within three feet of me and if I so much as stretched my legs she would grab my hand. So I tried to sit quietly and sure enough, she actually let me make the tea or go to the bathroom alone a couple of times.

Some times she would talk and I'd half listen-

"I am so glad you saw sense over that Jimmy fellow, you'll be better when the baby comes and you can start again" Mam soothed, handing me a drink of lemonade.

I nodded sadly. It certainly seemed like he was history all right. And I was so sure he was for real. How can love fall apart like that? How can it be that everything I felt for him was nothing?

I mean, I'd slept with him. I was sure that he had plenty of the girls in the club, but I had thought he was special. At gigs he dedicated Layla to me every time. He told me I was the one for him. What had happened to all that? Was it all lies? Was he just like all the rest? I couldn't believe that of him, but it looked very likely that I was going to have to go through this pregnancy and birth and giving our baby away all on my own, and my heart wept.

I had less than two weeks left of the pregnancy and his ring was still on a string round my neck. My fingers were too swollen to wear it, but I kept it there, close to my heart. I was so sure he loved me, and would have at least tried to save me. But there was nothing, a big fat nothing. Besides, I was a big fat blob now; he probably wouldn't fancy me any more if he came to see me. That's if he ever came to see me again.

I looked out over the wall, the gardens were all empty, no one out on a weekday. I stared down the road at a man cleaning windows and wished that I could get back to normal.

He finished Mrs. Hayes windows and took his ladder and came whistling up the road.

I stared in shock-

"Want your windows done' Mrs.?' he asked. I tried not to laugh. Under the cap and the overalls, it was unmistakably Tony, the singer in the band.

"Oh aye, I think I will, go on then" She got out of the deck chair.

"How much is it, hang on till I get me purse" She turned to go inside-

As soon as her arse was in to the hallway, I was up off the chair.

"Val, come on!" Tony grabbed me and I ran as best as I could down the street to the van, the old van that the band used to lug the gear in to gigs.

My mother was screaming at me to stop and come back. But I didn't I ran for my life, not daring to say anything till I was in the back of the van, going full tilt out of the area.

Jimmy was waiting for me in the flat and I couldn't stop weeping. He had known all along because Sheena had met my sister who had filled her in, and she had told him what the score was. Tony had been round my road waiting for an opportunity for weeks now, and finally today, he had gotten it.

"Either that or we were goin' to break in and get yeh" Jimmy smiled as he kissed me.

"Eh, look at the size of her! We wouldn't ha' got that out the fuckin' window" Tony laughed. He was right; my bump was huge by now. I was dying for all the things I missed in the last few months, namely fast food and Jimmy.

I got them all. Lots of them.

I lay in the bed beside him, the joss stick we'd lit a while ago perfuming the air and the curtains blowing in the breeze-

"I thought you didn't love me anymore" I whispered.

"Me, not love you, get away out of that, I missed you every single day, every time I played Layla I thought of you, you're my girl, my two girls now" He smiled that gappy smile of his.

"I used to drive down your street every night with Tony hoping that you might be looking out the window or something, and sometimes I would sit on the wall opposite all night just looking over at your house, hoping you might know that I still loved you, poor Val, it must have been terrible for you" He whispered.

"What will we do Jimmy?" My head was on his chest and I could hear his heart beating in unison with my own. I was so happy I thought I'd explode. And my bump was so big I looked as though I really might.

"Elope, there's only thing we can do, get Tony to drop us up to the border and head to Gretna" He lit a cigarette and passed it to me.

"Its up in Scotland, near Glasgow I think, you don't need permission or a licence to marry there" he blew out a stream of smoke.

"When?" I asked. It was all so simple.

"Tomorrow maybe, you up to the traveling?"

Was I? If he asked me to crawl through hell on my hands and knees I would have done it for him. I nodded and he smiled-

"Right then, we go tomorrow, by this time on Monday, you'll be Mrs. Dalton"

I smiled and snuggled closer to him.

"And then there's nothing that anyone can say or do to us, ever again, Oh Jimmy, we are going to be so happy together" I sighed.

"You know it and so do I Mrs." he kissed me softly and held me close.

"My girls, I'm going to give you everything you ever wanted" He whispered into my hair.

"I already have everything I want; I have you, don't I Jimmy"

And it was nothing more than the truth.

Of course, my family didn't give up that easy.

I was in the flat when my father and my uncle John came to the door, demanding that I be returned to them. When Tony and Kevin, the bassist in the band, basically manhandled them away from the door, they went to the police and then three coppers came.

"Your over twenty one, its legal, nothing we can do" The policeman sniffed, trying to find traces of marijuana. But he was out of luck.

"Er, are you going to legalize your, eh, your *condition*?" He asked, blushing.

Jimmy put his arm round me and grinned-

"As soon as ever we can mate, tomorrow, if possible, we would have done it months ago only for all this malarkey"

The policeman nodded-

"Fair enough so lads" and went out to my uncle's car and spoke for a few minutes to them. They gave up eventually, and drove away. But the lads decided that at no time, till the wedding band was on my finger, was I to be left alone and vulnerable.

The last contact I had with my family was a small bag with my work uniform and a change of underwear in it. Nothing else, not a note, nothing from my mother. It was handed in by my uncle, tightlipped and silent.

Early next morning, Kevin nearly hammered the front door off the hinges-

Jimmy got out of bed and went down in his underpants to answer it.

"Keep your fucking wig on will yeh?" He fumbled for keys.

Kevin was roaring something through the letterbox at Jimmy and he was trying to open the door with fingers made of jelly.

I was listening in the bedroom and couldn't make out exactly what was being said, but the gist of it seemed to be that a talent scout, a biggie, was coming to hear the band, and that they had to be shit hot.

"I'm always shit hot!" Jimmy was brewing up the tea and waved to me to stay in bed. I was happy to oblige, I was hardly decent in the tee shirt he had loaned me to wear in bed.

"Yeah but, this weekend, you have to be hotter than shit hot, this could be the big break Jim, it could be the big time" Kevin was hopping round the kitchen like a puppet on speed.

Jimmy stretched, and I thought once again, how gorgeous he was, and how lucky I was. He grinned at me.

"Right, its Thursday now, if we go north today, we could be back and into the gig on Saturday, have to make an honest woman of her" he nodded to me. I blushed.

"Yeah, I know man, but will you get back?"

"Yeah, I think so, one night up there and drive back on the Saturday, what d'ya say Mrs. Dalton to be? Can you survive without a honeymoon till we hit the big time?"

Of course I could.

We got up and dressed, well Jimmy did. I waited for him to come back from Dickie Lewis' with an outfit for me. I had nothing but the smock, and like it or not, preggers or not, I wanted to look well on my wedding day.

He pawned his leather coat and bought me a maxi dress in a small pink print, and a floppy hat. And he bought the wedding ring.

"Its only cheap Val, but one day I'll buy you diamonds" he smiled as I tried it on.

I tried on my wedding dress and wouldn't let him into the bedroom as I did. I didn't want him to see me in it till later. It was bad luck. I thought of the three half made dresses in the wardrobe at home and sighed. Maybe Philomena or Lizzie would wear them? Who knew?

Into the van with Kevin and round to Lime Street for the train.

I was so excited at the thoughts of my new life that I was crippled with heartburn. I sucked mints and sat looking out the windows at the scenery changing. Jimmy was delighted at the thoughts of his big break so soon, and he was full of chat for ages about what we would do when he was famous as Clapton.

"You know, they say that there's graffiti on the underground about him, it says "Clapton is God" on a wall!" he was aghast, that someone could be that famous to inspire graffiti.

I drank more of the watery coffee we had bought in the buffet car-

"Well one day, it will be crossed out, and Jimmy Dalton will be there instead" I snuggled into him and fell asleep on his shoulder.

The train journey was long. And I slept for quite a while. We changed trains twice, and somewhere outside of Newcastle I started getting uncomfortable.

"You all right love?" he asked.

I smiled, even though the pain was making me very irritated and sore all over.

"Grand" I said, through gritted teeth.

But by the time we got near the border and changed again for the north, I couldn't hide it any longer. Jimmy managed to get me into the bathroom and I thought I'd wet myself. But when he asked someone to help, there was a nurse on the train, who told me that my waters were broken and I was in labour.

"But I can't be, there's two weeks to go!" I gasped.

She smiled.

"Babies don't wait to be born love, this one is on the way, we'll get an ambulance for you at the next station, where were you heading?" she patted my hand and I wanted to kill her.

"We're going to get married, up the north, in Gretna" Jimmy was trying to hold me up as I half sat on the lavatory.

"Well you won't be doing that yet love, and anyhow, your on the Glasgow train, you're miles away from Gretna, come on now, breathe, nice deep breaths" she coaxed.

The ambulance came and I was helped off the train with a crowd of onlookers gaping through the windows. Jimmy forgot the bag with my things and so I had nothing when I got to the hospital.

He told them my details and how long I had been in labour. He was frantic; his hair was literally on end he ran his fingers through it so much. He was panicking as much as I was and I was in such a state.

They told me to walk, to walk up and down the corridor to bring the baby down.

I walked for hours, most of Thursday night and into Friday morning. There were other mothers, with their husbands. Respectable married types they were, and as soon as they saw my bare ring finger they would frown and turn away.

We'd left the ring in the bag with my dress on the train. Maybe someone would hand it in.

I remember seeing one woman, with no husband. The wedding band on her hand looked expensive though, and she had her own nurse. She was in terrible pain and looked really frail. Jimmy took one look at her and told me she was on drugs. He knew her, he said, knew her to see, she was a party girl a couple of years ago, when he was in The Strangers.

I wanted to ask had he been with her. But I forgot about it when the next pain came and finally they took me into the ward.

Jimmy was left outside, walking up and down the corridor. He rang the flat and told Tony what had happened, and he was sympathetic and hoped that all would go well.

They let him in after a couple of hours when I was still waiting for the baby to come.

"I rang Tony, he's worried about tomorrow love, I told him I have to stay here" he rubbed my back.

"No, oh Jimmy you *can't*!" I cried.

He shushed me but I was adamant. This was their big chance, he just couldn't miss it. He had to go back.

"Look love, I'm going to be here for at least a week, they said so, when I have the baby like, so why don't you go? I can stay here and when you come back on Monday or Tuesday, we can carry on to Gretna and get married then, maybe the lads will sub you a few bob for a new ring, or the bag might have been handed in" I grimaced as yet another contraction came.

"Jesus Val, I can't leave you like this!" he shook his head.

"Please love, please go and do this for us, please?"

He rang Tony again and he and Kevin agreed to drive up to get him.

"They'll be here tonight, so come on my girl, lets get this baby born so I can see her!"

That was the longest day of my whole life.

Layla Dalton was born at seven o clock on the Friday night. I got a glimpse of her red hair and little chubby cheeks as she was whisked out of the room. Jimmy was jumping for joy out in the hall where he and the two lads had seen her being brought to the nursery.

"You're lucky she looks like you, not her old man!" Tony grinned, a bunch of garage flowers in his hands, and a bottle of champagne cider under his arm.

"Get away, our Layla's going to be a beauty queen, as gorgeous as her Ma" Jimmy kissed me.

"Maybe she'll be a rocker like her Daddy" I murmured sleepily.

The others left for a minute and left Jimmy to say goodbye.

"Your amazing Valerie, I love you, I really do love you, and I won't let you down, I'll play so good tomorrow that this scout won't know what hit him, and then I'm going to come back here to my girls and we're getting married" He kissed me again and again.

"I know, I love you too Jimmy, play good, play Layla for us, won't you?"

He turned at the door-

"I'll never play that song without thinking of tonight, as long as I live, it will always be the reminder of the most wonderful night of my life, the night my dreams came true, goodnight sweetheart, see you Monday" he blew me a kiss and was gone.

I was dying to see the baby properly, but they told me to rest. That she was in the nursery and was fine. I felt like someone had run me over with a steam roller and I nodded off. Every time I closed my eyes I could see her. I couldn't believe that I was a mother! That I was responsible for this little scrap of life and I swore that she would have everything and more.

Jimmy would make good. He would play tomorrow like he had never played before. Some day soon we would be rich and he would be famous and that would show my parents.

We'd have to get a new flat, but it wouldn't be long till we were in a big house, maybe with gates on it, a bungalow would be great... I fell asleep mentally decorating Layla's nursery.

I woke up a couple of hours later, in the middle of the night.

There was a nun in a white habit at the side of the bed and I smiled drowsily.

"Hullo sister"

"Hello Valerie, Doctor wants to talk to you, I'll call him now" She swished out of the room and returned a minute later with the doctor. He sat on the edge of the bed; the nun stood beside me and took my hand.

A cold feeling came over me, like someone had doused me in ice water.

"What is it?" I was imagining all sorts.

"Is it Jimmy? Have they had an accident?" I tried to sit up.

The nun put her hand on my shoulder.

"No, lie down child, its not, Jimmy" I lay back on the pillow, terrified. And I was right to be. Because he told me that Layla was dead.

I heard him and couldn't believe what he was saying.

"How? What happened?" I asked.

"She was early, and the long labour, we believe she was in distress, she passed away an hour ago, I'm sorry" he got up and nodded at the nun and left the room.

I was too stunned to cry. The nun asked me would I like them to phone the father. I told her not to, that he was possibly still driving home to Liverpool and there was no point in making him drive all the way back.

Oh she went on about the will of God and the fact that they had baptized her

"Rachel" she said.

"Her name was Layla" I finally wept.

"That's not a proper name" She sniffed "We called her after the midwife"

"It was her name, her Daddy wanted her to be called Layla, that's her name" I cried.

"Yes but it isn't a saints name, is it?"

"Well... Rachel is a Jewish name" I wept.

She shushed me and told me not to be crying and getting upset. But I couldn't help it. Five hours ago I had everything in the world; I had the beautiful daughter and my Jimmy going to set the world on fire with his guitar. And now I was going to have to tell him that Layla was gone, before I ever even held her, or gave her a bottle.

"Can I see her?"

"No, she's gone to the mortuary now, she'll be buried tomorrow"

So, on the day that Jimmy was up in Liverpool, blowing the talent scout off the planet with his guitar and finally getting the big break, I sat in a borrowed coat in the hospital chapel and saw them say a mass for our baby.

I had walked the floor of that hospital all night, until in the later hours, around five am they had sedated me and I slept again.

All around me, I saw women with babies. I saw their husbands coming to collect them and take them home, I saw happy families and grandparents cooing and squealing with joy over the little bundles.

On one of my walks to the nursery, I saw that nurse again, coming out of the room with a little bundle wrapped in a pink shawl. A man in a dark suit walked ahead of her, to a room up the hall.

So the drug addict had a daughter!

The nurse stopped in front of me and smiled.

I felt numb. I felt like I would never smile again.

"What did she call her?" I asked.

"Amber"

"Oh" I thought it was a nice name. The nurse stood there and stared at me. I wondered if she knew what had happened to me. She held the baby a little closer to her. And then she started to speak, started to say something, Maybe that she was sorry for my trouble. But down the corridor the door to an office opened and someone, the man, called her-

"Breda?" a tone of voice that brooked no argument. He was tall, in shadow but menacing just the same, I thought.

She sighed.

"I'm sorry for your trouble love" She whispered.

And then she was gone. Her heels clicking on the tiles in the corridor.

He waited till she passed into the room and then the door clicked softly shut.

I turned and went back to my room alone.

"We did it honey, we're home and dry, he loved us" Jimmy came bounding into the room with a huge bunch of roses, all pink. He planted a kiss on my cheek and sat on the bed.

"He loved it, loved the new song that Kev wrote, says we are going to be bigger than the Beatles ever were, he said..." he stopped.

I hadn't said a word. I was lying on the bed, looking out the window when he came. I rubbed my flattened stomach, wishing that I could turn the clock back and have Layla in there again, as safe as she could be.

"Val?"

I turned my head, and he saw the tears.

"Val?" he turned white.

"Oh Jimmy, I'm sorry" I gasped.

"What? What happened? Val?" he whispered. He grabbed my cold hand in his.

"Oh Jimmy our baby, our Layla died, I, I didn't ring you, I'm sorry, it happened on Saturday, when you were in the Cavern, she just..." I sobbed.

He shook his head.

"No, this has to be a mistake, she was healthy, she was fine, we saw her when we were leaving, me and the lads, we, no, NO Valerie, this isn't true!"

He grabbed me-

"Valerie, please love, tell me this is all a sick joke, please?"

I shook my head sadly and he sat on the bed and dissolved into tears. He put his head on the bed and literally sobbed. Sometimes he would speak but I couldn't make out what he was saying, except once-

"It was all for you and Layla, it's all gone now, its all for nothing now"

I don't know how long we stayed that way, crying and holding each other. But a priest came to the room and sat talking to us later and told us that the baby was buried in a numbered plot in the hospital graveyard and we could have the number to go to the grave when we felt up to it.

"Maybe it's for the best, you were not married after all" he said.

Jimmy exploded-

"How can this be for the best? Tell me? That's our child you're talking about!"

One more day and we would have been married. One more day and no one would be saying that our child dying was for the best! Jimmy was incensed with anger. Just one more day and things might have been so different.

"Jimmy, please love, leave it eh?" I sighed. The fight was totally gone out of me.

I just felt like we were cursed. I wanted to go home. Go back to Liverpool and get on with our lives, which looked as though they were going to be so different to the joyful and hopeful times we thought we were set for the previous week.

Back in the flat and back in work, Jimmy and I battled on.

The band was doing great things, gigs sold out all over the place. There were groupies and girls of course, but Jimmy came home to me most nights.

He never again played Layla on stage, and if it caught him unawares, like it did one morning on the radio, he would fill up and would have to turn it off.

I was back working on the counter in Woolies. I told some of the girls what happened and I have to say that they were sympathetic to me. At least no one said it was for the best. Mam came to see me in the café with a mass card, and she appeared to be genuinely sorry for us.

"Come home love, come on home where I can help you" She patted my hand.

"No Mam, thanks, but Jimmy is all I want at the moment, okay?"

"Look, your father will see sense now, he'll let you see Jimmy, I'm sure he will"

"Have you told him you were coming here today?" I asked.

She blushed-

"Not exactly Val, he knows your back in work though, I just didn't tell him I was coming here to see you"

I sighed-

"Mam, Dad will never ever change, and I don't want to be under his thumb any more, I'm happy with Jimmy, and we will survive this mess together, okay?"

She nodded, and I watched her walk away in her second best coat and her head scarf on, and felt really sad, because for the first time ever I realized that Mam was getting on a bit in years and she hadn't had much of a life with the oul fella.

I was off with the flu when the letter came from the solicitor.

Jimmy was hung-over again. He had been drinking a fair bit and I was worried. I knew he still loved me, and I him, but he was taking this really badly, to the point where he was fucking up on stage and the lads had to cover for him a lot.

"Jesus!" he said.

"What?" I asked mouth full of toast.

"I've been left money" He smiled.

"How much money?"

He read the letter-

"Followin' the death of Michael Parsons, we the undersigned wish to inform you that you are his sole beneficiary" He looked up.

Parsons was his mother's maiden name. She'd died a while ago, and his father was long gone too.

"I don't know any Michael Parsons" he said.

"Well, they knew you Jim, keep reading!" I smiled.

"Val, there's a house, and about four thousand pounds" he whispered.

"Holy shit!" I swallowed.

It was a simple matter; we had to go out to the Wirral to this solicitor with his birth cert, which I had in my handbag, from the time of our ill fated trip to Scotland. We were given the cheque and the keys to the house and we went out to take a look at it.

In a little terrace, it had a tiny back yard and was straight out onto the road.

It looked as though an old man lived in it, so dated was it, but the place was clean, I had to say that for it. And I wanted it so much. I was tired of clearing up after the lads and stepping over whatever chick Tony brought home to the flat after a gig, when I wanted to go to the bathroom in the night.

So we moved into it.

We had nothing at all for the while, till that cheque cleared and then we went shopping and bought a bed, and a cooker and all the paint and wallpaper. We spent a couple of weeks doing the place up and then it was really our home.

New Years Eve 1972 was spent with me at home, watching the telly while Jimmy played a gig in the centre of the town. It was a showcase, and he was warned before hand not to get pissed. But his nerves or something must have got the better of him, because Tony dumped him back at the house at four in the morning, and told me that he was fired. That I could tell him when he woke up. He wasn't going to ruin what chance they had to make it and they already had the replacement so he need not bother coming to the studio on Wednesday.

"I'm sorry Val, he'll get credits for what he did on the album, but he's finished, he's got a drink problem and he's a dead weight on us" The old van backfired into the night and Jimmy threw up into the gutter.

I was heartbroken, Jimmy and Tony had been the best of pals since they started in the same class as five year olds, and it must have been so hard for Tony to dump his best mate out of what really was his band.

I mean, it had been Jimmy who had slogged around with tapes of their own songs, hoping to land a deal, and who spent hours writing and working on lyrics and music and trying to be the best. Glorious was him and Tony's vision, and now Tony had made the decision for the greater good of the band. I just wondered how Jimmy would take the rejection.

I got him inside and he snored on the sofa.

I sat up all night long, waiting for him to wake up.

I had been trying to find a good time to tell him I was pregnant again. And this time I wanted so much for it to go right. But I wasn't bringing a child into this relationship. Not the way things were. We had no income left now; I wouldn't be able to keep working when I began to show. The way things were, one mistake was all right, but a second child out of wedlock would be really frowned upon.

Jimmy was out of the band now, and that four thousand wouldn't last forever. He had to shape the heck up!

I must have nodded off on the chair because he woke me with a kiss and a cup of coffee the next day. He was bleary eyed and looked like he'd got sick a couple more times, but he'd at least washed his face and combed his hair.

"Jim, Tony dropped you home last night in an awful state..." I began, not knowing how to tell him.

He leaned on the windowsill and looked at me.

"I know Val, I know" he said quietly.

"What will you do?"

"Dunno" he lit a cigarette.

'Jim, for heavens sake, you have to stop the drinking! It's ruined your career" I started, but he raised his hand and stopped me speaking-

"Val, love, listen to me, I've been playing in a band for the past ten years, and you know what? I've had me breaks and they never came right, and then last year, when me and you were on that train, I thought that was the biggest break of my life, and it *was* the biggest break of my life, I was never so fucking happy as I was on that train heading up to get married to you and give Layla my name, but Jesus Val, nowadays, I can't even *play* Layla anymore, I've lost it, the fires gone out, I don't want to be up there any more, don't want to be part of that scene" he sighed. I was stunned, Jimmy hadn't said so much in months. He must be really feeling it.

He looked so broken there. My heart went out to him. I suppose I had been thinking that I was the only one with a right to grieve. I mean, I'd carried Layla inside me all those months. I never thought for a moment that he might be sad for what might have been too! I never thought about what a daddy might feel, and I felt terrible.

"But, what will you do?" I asked.

"I was talking to Eddie there a while back" Eddie was a roadie for the band and he had been a voice of reason when they, the other lads were ready to kill Jimmy for his drinking and carrying on.

"Yeah?"

"He has a cousin, an old guy out in Birkenhead, runs a pub, restaurant thing, says I can have a start with him if I want" he smiled.

"But the band? You... will you stick it?" I asked.

"It's a wage, isn't it?"

Jimmy hadn't planned on being a chef till he was at least forty and got the rock and roll out of his system. But it seemed that at the age of twenty odd, he'd become tired.

"I'm sorry Val, Maybe I'm just not cut out to be a superstar any more" His shoulders drooped and I got off the chair and went over to hug him.

"Jimmy Dalton, your one in a million to me, and I love you, and if this is really and truly what you want, then I won't look back again, not ever" I held him tight and we stayed like that for ages.

It was a day for talking and putting all the wrongs, bar one, to rights.

He asked me to marry him again and I said yes, and this time I wore a proper wedding dress, and covered my swelling tummy with my bouquet. Mam and Dad still weren't all that impressed, but they seemed pleased that Jimmy was the manager and head chef of the pub and had given up his wild ways.

Mam was happy that I had the house, and when our Colleen was born in the summer, well, things couldn't have been nicer or better.

She was followed by our son, Robbie, in 1977.

Mam died a couple of months after that, of a stroke. My da worked on the docks for the rest of his working life and went in 1984 himself. He and Jimmy became mates at the end. That's the thing about my Jimmy, he's so soft hearted, and he wouldn't hold a grudge for anything. He watched the band become huge, and just smiled and wished them well. Truly, I think he was happier as he was. Least he always said so.

His guitar and all his stage gear was gathering dust in the attic and I can't remember him ever taking them out to look at them even. He has put the past to rest, really and truly. As time went on he buried the hatchet with Tony and the other lads and they often asked him to play with them, but he would smile and say no, that his rock star ways were buried in the past and that's where they were staying.

"C'mon man, it'll be worth your while" Tony would say, But Jimmy told him straight that no money could buy him happiness and that's what he had, a nice quiet happy little life, and it was more than enough.

We lived in our little terraced house and sent the kids to nice schools and I was delighted when Colleen told us she had been accepted into training in Leeds in 1990. She was just about to turn 17 and I was so proud that she would have a career. She is young to be living away from home but sure, things could be worse!

Lizzie, my sister, actually *was* a lesbian. Imagine that! Mam must be turning in her grave.

She used to camp up on Greenham Common with the rest of the CND women and the few times I saw her, she looked rough.

Jimmy used to call her Private Benjamin, cos she used to wear the combat clothes like in the army. She never told my Mam, she said it was enough the way she gave me GBH of the ear hole that night in 1971.

"I knew you pair were listening that night" I laughed.

"I wouldn't have stood for it" She said.

"Yeah? And you would have given our Mam what for I suppose, yeah right, a backhander with a wet cloth in the face is what you'd have got for looking cheeky at her never mind anything else" I smiled.

Mam was a real tartar. But sometimes I missed the oul biddy. She was nothing if not honest, I suppose. And I never forgot her defying my Dad to bring me the mass card for Layla. That was the first time I remember thinking that my Mam was getting old. She didn't live to old age though; I think that the last couple of years were her happiest ones. At least she saw grandchildren and me settled which is what she wanted all along.

So now, Lizzie lives with Stella, her black, American girlfriend. Stella is an actress and she has a singing voice that would make you shiver. She sings in a band in a blues club and honest to God she sings so like Billie Holliday that it's frightening. She's always after Jimmy to jam with him some time.

"Cos you look like you *know* the blues baby!" she drawls, cigar in hand, her lips painted a deep glossy red. God I can't imagine what she sees in Lizzie, with her army fatigues and her bitten nails. Still, takes all sorts I suppose.

But he laughs and shakes his head-

"That part of my life is over now love, get a real musician to do it" he grins.

"Ooh no, one fine day you'll be up there again, and I'm gonna be there to see it, you have it in your soul baby, you got soul, and its too in you to ever leave you, one day..." she waves her cigar and laughs when he tells her no again.

"We'll see, Jimmy Dalton, we'll see"

"No you won't Stella love, I tell ya, pigs will fly across the Mersey before I get on a stage again, your betting against the wrong man" he laughed.

Philomena, my other sister married a guy from Germany, his name is Klaus, Colleen used to call him Santa Klaus and he wouldn't even smile, would you believe? Talk about no sense of humour! And after the wedding, he and Phil moved over there. I rarely see her, she's a born again Christian or something and doesn't come here much. She and the old fella had words when she stopped going to mass and all, and married a happy clapper as he called him. I don't know what Phil sees in him either, with his close cropped hair and his stern face, he looks like a German officer in a war film, and Jimmy nicknamed him the "Sour Kraut". And Phil changed when she met him, stopped wearing mini skirts and dying her hair, and now she looks years older than I do. But still, she seems to be happy enough.

Before she went away she arrived down to the house with a load of stuff.

Mam was dead at this stage and Da was pottering around the house a bit and took it into his head to have a clean out. So up into the attic he went and hauled a load of gear down to the landing.

She had a big bin liner full of stuff and she tipped it out onto my table-

"Phil, you clotty swine, I just cleaned that!" I yelled.

"Oh shut up, look what I got for you"

I laughed.

Most of it was rubbish, old music papers and the Beatles fanzine I used to get in the sixties. Dozens of them. But underneath it all was a leather bag, battered out of shape by the years in the attic-

"Some guy brought this to the house after you'd run off, said your name was on the badge in your purse, your old Woolies badge, remember, and when he brought it there, they sent him to the house, Mam near went crazy when she realized you'd eloped with Jimmy" She smiled.

"Da must have fired it into the attic, and it lay there all this time"

I unzipped the bag and the pink and white dress fell out.

"Jesus what's that?" Phil laughed. It was voluminous, made to cover my first pregnancy bump, and the floppy hat was under it, gone yellow at this stage.

Phil snorted with laughter.

"Fucking hell sis, that's a right looking yoke!"

"That was high fashion at the time, I'll have you know Phil, and it was going to be a wedding dress" I smiled.

"Yikes, I'm glad you waited"

I rooted and found the little gold band. I slipped it onto my finger beside my other ring and it still fit. The gold was discolored

and cheap looking mind you, so I put it on the windowsill in some water and fairy liquid.

"That should bring it up a bit"

The ticket for the pawn shop, long gone now, for Jimmy's leather coat. I smiled. He'd bought another, and it was hanging in the spare room now, unused.

And finally.

I hadn't had anything much for the baby. Just a couple of baby suits and a few nappies. They were in the bag too, and I took them out and put them on the table.

But I knew there was one more thing in there, there had to be.

In the station, there was a machine, one of them things that typed into metal. Onto a little disc, so that you could put your name on your luggage. Jimmy had run off to the shop to buy the paper and came back beaming-

"Here" he smiled, holding out his hand.

I took the little disc.

He'd typed "Layla Valerie" on a disc.

"For my babies" he'd grinned "both of them"

He'd known from day one that it was a girl and we had discussed the names for boys too, Eric being the favorite, but he was sure certain it was a girl, and he had been right, hadn't he?

The bag is in the attic now. Along with all the rest of the memories.

I kept the little bit of metal and Colleen wore my wedding band the day she married Gary. She's a sentimental little kid you know, too young for marriage in my opinion, but then I think of how it was for me and her dad and I smile. I thought she was happy. I thought he would be good to her. Just goes to show you that money can't buy love, can it? The Beatles never wrote a truer word.

She always comes home for the mass for her big sister, and we have to call her Rachel because that's what she was christened. Colleen dresses nice and does her make up and always makes a big fuss of me when the mass is over.

I have it on New Year's Day, because that was the day that we changed our lives and finally got happiness of a sort. Though I wonder what might have been had Layla lived and Jim stayed with the band, I don't have any regrets.

I have two nice kids, one nursing and the other going to be a vet. Neither of them ever brought the police to the door or went on the drugs and that was a bonus.

Jim bought the pub a few years ago and we're comfortable.

I love the house in the Wirral, wouldn't move for anything. I did worry about Colleen going off with Gary and I did think it was too fast and she was saying how much she was going to miss me.

I told her to follow her heart and maybe she might like the traveling with him.

And even her aunt Phil had to say that it was the most romantic thing she ever heard of, just like a Mills and Boon novel, one of them Doctor and Nurse ones, except it was a nurse and patient who fell in love. I get the feeling that there'd sod all romance in her life now and she has to live vicariously through other people!

I liked Gary. Honest to God I did, he was a nice fella. I thought he was nervous or something when he came here to meet us that first time because, well, this sounds silly, but, I'd dressed up a bit for the occasion and had my make up on and if I say so myself, I'm not too bad for my forties, and I turned around and smiled at him and the poor lad nearly fainted!

He got all flustered and asked Colleen to go out for a walk.

"What d'ya think of him?" I asked Jimmy.

"Seems nice enough, and Colleen's mad about him" he said.

We had made a deal that even if Colleen was a lesbian and Robbie was gayer than Christmas, we would let them pick their own partners, no interfering from us!

"I don't care if Robbie walks in that door with Boy George on his arm, I'll make him tea and welcome him to the family" I said one night, and Robbie was mortified.

"Ma-am stop that" He groaned.

Colleen giggled-

"You needn't worry about Boy George robbing your make up Mam, our Rob has a little girlfriend, I saw them in the bus shelter, kissing" She ducked as the cushion he threw flew past her head.

She transferred to the hospital in London and we didn't see too much of her really for a couple of months, though she would ring us every day, Jesus knows what the phone bill was like, but then, Gary has the money. She told us about the wedding then at Christmas and she seemed very upset about it all, missing Rachel's mass and everything.

But then she arrived home from that wedding, that fancy French wedding that was in some chateaux in the south of France, a few days after the Christmas, and told us she's left him there.

Well I didn't know what to think and of course her Dad is all concern and Robbie, well he's worrying about the horses, because Gary told him he could come up and see them anytime-

"But if our Colleen isn't married anymore I won't be able to" he said. I threw him up to his room and we sat in the living room by ourselves.

"Insensitive little get!" I roared at him.

She rang her in laws and told them the deal and the grandfather told her to hold off with the divorce, that he'd speak to Gary himself.

She sat crying for hours till her dad gave up and went out to work and I made more tea and sat beside her-

She twisted the ring round and round her finger and sighed.

"Colleen, come on, tell me what really happened, I'm a woman too you know, and I loved your dad, still do, I know how hard things can be" I said.

Now, I had known that the accident had caused amnesia. I knew that he only remembered parts of his life and that was one of the things I worried about. But his grandfather seemed to be trying to make him slot back into the life he had before and there was no mention of the troubles he had before the tragedy.

I knew he had, or at least, they thought he had tried to kill himself.

So I worried, but Colleen was determined to have him and he seemed happy enough too.

But looking at my baby girl weeping like this I had to do something for her.

"Coll, what happened love?" I asked again.

Bit by bit, garbled and making no sense, it came out.

Seemingly, he had been having flashes. Sometimes a name or a memory would come to him and he would ask her what it meant. She didn't have a clue of course and would send him to the doctor in the hope that they could do something for him. There were times when he would go into a kind of trance, and be there for hours, just lost in thought. A couple of times, she caught him looking at her, like he should know her, like she should be someone else, but the memory was just out of his reach.

"But the worst time, oh mum" She blushed scarlet and I knew there was something deeply personal coming so I looked away from her.

"Go on love, I'm listening"

"Twice, he called me by another name when we were, *you know*, and then, other times, he, we, when we were making love, he would close his eyes and oh Mam, it was amazing, unbelievable, like he was really there and he *meant it*, you know what I mean?" She whispered.

I knew. I knew what it was like to see stars. I still did with Jimmy, every time.

"And then, then he would open his eyes, and the look of sadness on his face, the disappointment, oh it was terrible, and I've known that I'm not it, I've known for ages now, since we moved to London, but I thought that things would change, and I thought that telling him I wanted a divorce might frighten him into getting help, but then, when he went out for a walk, he met her, the other girl, Carrie, and his family, they were all going to that wedding too, and so now, he doesn't want to be with me any more, he wants her" she sobbed again, till I thought she would never ever stop.

"Oh shush love, maybe it's all a phase, he might realize that his life has moved on, that this *Carrie* is in the past and that she..." I said, stroking her head.

"No Mam, you see, I *saw* him with her, I followed him out into the street, and saw him, when they met again, and he, oh Mam he looked so happy, like all the pieces of the puzzle clicked together and fit, and she, she looks a lot like me, older, and a little taller, but like me, she could be my sister, and she was beautiful, like she was lit up from the inside, and so was he" She gulped back more tears.

"So what did you do?" My poor baby, I wanted to kill this Carrie person. Why couldn't she leave well enough alone?

"I followed them to the end of the street, he didn't even see me there, and then I went back to the hotel and waited for him to come and he did and he told me he was going away with her, so I packed my things and came home" she sighed.

She went to bed then, exhausted.

I had a sneaking suspicion that she was pregnant, but I kept it to myself till I knew for sure and she confided in me a few days later.

The day of the mass for Rachel the story hit the papers, and there in graphic detail were the stories of old Bard and his shenanigans. There was a picture of this Carrie person and I had to admit, she did look like Colleen, in a bad photo, mind you, but more than a passable resemblance. Dressed in a dark coat with her head down, I couldn't see her face, but the likeness was there.

I began to feel sorry for Gary, Or Steven, as the paper called him. It must have been like living in hell trying to remember something that had obviously meant so much to him before his life fell apart. But I never said that to Colleen.

I never got to read the whole story, Colleen came into the kitchen and saw the paper on the table with my mug beside it and flew into a rage.

"Don't read about him, it makes my life nothing, everything is nothing, do you understand me?" She screamed, incandescent with temper.

Colleen refused to allow the papers into the house after that first day. So I'm sure there was a lot of the story I missed.

But in hindsight I was sort of glad that she wasn't going to stay married to Gary, I mean with that type of carry on in the family, well, the baby wouldn't be safe, would it?

And then there was the fact that my little woman, she's always been a bit of a homebody, liking to be near me and her dad, loving the normal things in life. We've never had money, not really and I knew she was finding that hard, and the travel was never going to suit.

They are a different breed, the rich. Aren't they?

Certainly that Gary guy seemed to be, because the last bit of the paper I read was about him being locked up in Ireland for an incestuous relationship with his sister.

See? Told you it's in the blood! But the shock for me was that Colleen had known all along about it, that the old man had talked to her in great detail about Gary and his past and the importance of hiding that from him, because he had been half mad and mentally unstable, and the important thing was to keep him away from Carrie and all that, and that meant controlling what bits of the outside world came into their home.

I remember when she was packing her things to go to London that she was leaving her stereo and all behind her and I asked her why. I mean, Colleen was always playing her records in the bedroom, but she said that the old man told her that Gary would be very easily unbalanced and that she shouldn't play music around him.

"Just for a while, his sister was a musician I think, and he might get upset" she said.

It seemed a very tough life for a young girl to be going into, but she wanted to, she was bound and determined to marry him and so I kept my peace. I wish I'd done what I wanted to, and that's collar that old man for a chat before the wedding and get the home truths out of him. Too late now I suppose, he's dead and my baby's life is ruined.

Gary asked for an annulment and Colleen went crazy.

You see, an annulment means that the marriage was illegal or never valid. He said it was because he was not in his right mind, and that Gary Bard, or Gary Stanley, didn't exist, that he was Steven Williams and could not marry under another identity.

Jimmy went mad when he was told what Gary was at.

"I stood in that flippin' church and I heard you take them vows, and him, and he is not going to say he didn't, he is not going to say that the marriage was a figment of your imagination, and he will give that child your carrying his name, and look after it, or else he has me to deal with!"

Of course, us being Catholic, we weren't supposed to look for divorce, but in the circumstances.

So Colleen fought for the rights of the baby. Fought for the divorce. He wanted the marriage annulled and she wouldn't budge.

My granddaughter was born in July. And she named her Michelle. Michelle Elizabeth, after his mother, which seemed the only true part of the whole affair. Her aunt Lizzie was thrilled about that.

And then Colleen heard that he and Carrie were in London and she tried to go up to see them and he wouldn't have it.

Carrie apparently was due a baby herself, her son, in September and he didn't want anything coming in and interfering in that time for them.

What about my poor lassie? That's what I want to know! She has no one, other than me and her Dad. She deserves better than this carry on. It's not right.

I lie awake at night and my blood boils when I hear my little Colleen, my little chirpy baby, crying in the night. I wish there was something I could do for her and help her. But there isn't.

The hearing for the annulment came in December and she went to it with her Dad.

Jimmy kept his mouth shut, even when that Gary got up and told them that he didn't think the marriage was legal. But our way of thinking is this-

If he doesn't want to be married to her anymore, then that's fine, sad, but fine. She'll manage better because she has us to love her and the baby and we will take care of her.

But he cannot say it never happened. Because it did. Money can't buy love, and it won't buy his way out of this mess either!

It will be another year or more before this is sorted out. Now to give him his due he has sent money to her for the baby. And he sent her a note, the other day, to tell her he was coming to Liverpool and that he wanted to see the child. Colleen is made up, because she thinks that all she has to do is be cool and calm and clear in her mind and she might work all this out with him somehow.

Jimmy says that he even looks different, his accent has changed. His clothes. And yes, he looks like a whole person, not a shell, not the way he looked when he sat on our sofa that day.

"Have to admit Val, he looks a different fellah" he sighed, drinking his tea that night.

"Was she with him?" I asked.

"No, at home with the baby, he said"

"Humph"

Jimmy laughed at me-

"God you sounded just like your old dear then, snorting!"

"The cheek of you! No seriously Hun, do you think, there's any hope for her at all?" I asked. He shook his head, slowly.

"Not a bit, he's gone, as sure as if he had died in France, and he isn't coming back"

And then he said something strange, now, Jimmy, darling an' all that he is, well, as you know, he's not usually one for the profound statements, or musing about life, but he's sat there, in the armchair, the paper on the arm of it and his mug of tea and he says-

"Val, d'ya remember when I was in the band and it was all going well, before Layla and all that?" He asked. He got up and came over to the sofa and put his arm round me.

"Yeah, why? What's that got to do with this?"

"Well, its like this, I did it because that was what I thought was expected of me, you know I had played in a band for so long, and then the big break was coming, and then we lost the baby, well, one night I was down in the club, oh some club in the city, and I looked down at the groupies and the mayhem and I thought, d'ya know what, I hate this"

"Go on" I nodded.

He paused. You see I knew, call it women's intuition, or whatever you want to call it, but I knew that my Jimmy, well, he had played more than the guitar at them gigs. While I was at home playing house, he was, well, you know what I mean. It was hard to think that now, now that he was a bit thinner on top and a bit fatter on bottom, but once upon a time he was a sex god!

Still was, as far as I'm concerned. Especially when he did that thing to my neck, like he was doing now, not quite a kiss, not quite a bite, but lovely and shivery just the same.

"Val, the point is, well, no matter what I did, I couldn't run away from the fact, that was staring me in the face, which was that all I wanted, was for the fucking madness to end and to go home to you, and be a normal Joe soap, having a few bevies on a Saturday and making love to his missus, who has always been, and who will always be, his woman" He kissed me, and the old flutter in my stomach happened again.

"Jimmy... the kids" I whispered.

"There has always been only one girl for me, I never made love to anyone else bar you Valerie, I had sex all right, you know that, in the past, but it wasn't right, I would see you in every woman and know that it was wrong, and that, is what I think happened to Gary... He might have tried his best, tried to make it work, but its not going to work if there's someone else in your soul, because a woman like you, well, she's irreplaceable darlin', you just can't do it with anyone else when there's always going to be a shadow in your mind" he was unwrapping my dressing gown as he spoke-

"You got under my skin the first day I met you in the Cavern, and no one else ever did, I loved you then Val and I love you now, and I pity that poor fucker, because he lived in the dark for so long, chasing the shadow of what he thought could never be, and now, well it must feel like he's gone home, because that's what you always were to me love, you were home" he whispered, and then, like a pair of teenagers, we "did it" on the sofa, our ears cocked for the creaking of the stairs.

I thought about what he said and he's right you know.

I could never be with another man. Not ever. Not after Jimmy. And even when we broke up all those years ago, I didn't want to marry anyone else but him. Because it was always going to be Jimmy for me, he was the magic that made my life sparkle, made me complete.

I knew it that night in the cavern when he looked over the crowd and gave me that grin. My heart went into the pocket of them sprayed on jeans and stayed there forever and ever. From the opening bars of Layla I was his. End of story.

And if somehow, supposing, I lost him, suppose he had made it and me and him hadn't stayed together, I don't think I could ever be happy with someone else, and like Jimmy says, I'd have always been chasing the shadow of what might have been, or what should have been, and that's what poor Gary did, without even realizing.

You see, I'm a big believer in passion being a good indication of a relationships worth. If you have the spark, the passion, the lust, that makes a hell of a difference. I think that only for it, me and Jimmy might have floundered years ago, when things were bad and times were tough. But we could always make it up and make it right in bed.

The only thing that'll part me and him now is if one of us dies, and hopefully that's a long way away. But God I understand Colleen, and I feel for poor Gary too. Talk about being torn in two.

He's coming here; Gary is, on Thursday, at tea time. I hope he realizes that, despite Jimmy and his feelings, that I will have plenty to say to him. He needs to decide what he's going to do, and fast. Understanding aside, I need to know that my baby and little Michelle are going to be taken care of.

We deserve that much from him anyway.

Carrie

We spent the next few weeks packing the flat up and crating the things we wanted to take back to Ireland. I still didn't want to go up to Liverpool, and Christmas came and went before we made a proper start even on the packing.

I have to admit, that there wasn't all that much.

The temper that had driven me the day of the annulment hearing had deserted me and I just wanted to be left alone. I spent the days weaning Daragh, throwing books into boxes and dreaming of the time we'd have when we went home.

Three, going into four years of our lives and all we had were things belonging to Daragh and some small stuff like books and records, and a few cd's. We were on a mission to replace all our vinyl and we did have fun down the markets looking at the old albums shrunk into little silver discs. It didn't seem right that even the old Led Zeppelin albums could fit into your pocket now. But the times were changing, and then some.

David had told us to ship it over to him and he'd mind it all till we got back.

"When are you coming back to us?" He'd asked Steven, one morning in the New Year.

"Soon, dad, very soon, we just have one more thing to do and we're on the plane" Steven was trying to talk and feed Daragh his breakfast at the same time, I took the spoon and bowl from him and shoved him out of the way, honestly, men! He was wearing half the porridge on his tee shirt. He grinned at me and shrugged, then listened again.

"Are you okay dad?" He asked.

I stopped and looked over at him. His hair was growing again but he said he wouldn't ever let it get so long as it was when we met. He was in the habit of rumpling it up when he was stressed and he was doing that now, I wondered what this was all about, what new tragedy was beginning-

"Did you go to the doctor?"

Silence again.

"Does Becky know?"

I left Daragh with his bowl and spoon and came across the kitchen, and put my hand on Steven's shoulder. I leaned my head in and tried to hear David talking, but all I got was static and crackling. He was talking too low; maybe he didn't want Becky to hear him.

I felt the heavy chill of fear in my stomach. This wasn't good, by the sound of it.

"Okay Dad, next week, I promise, and Dad, listen, I love you, okay?"

Jesus it *must* be bad.

"Okay, bye" He clicked off the phone and sighed, and pulled me into him.

"What is it love?"

"I dunno Carrie, he says he wasn't feeling well for a while, and he went round to the doc and he sent him out to Vincent's for tests, he won't know anything till the middle of next week, but it doesn't sound too good" I held him tightly. His relationship with David was always good, apart from the time when we were given the birth certs and he nearly killed him in the living room. They had done a lot of healing between them since that night in Paris and I thought that Steven was coping very well with it all.

As for David he was brilliant, I mean he had to face so much that week too, his son coming back from the dead, hearing that he really *was* his all this time, and then seeing his wife too, and taking the decision to marry Becky, and then coping with the fall out of the James Bard issue. David had kept us going, kept us strong, it couldn't happen that we would lose him now,

He hadn't said a word to me about any of this, any of these health worries when he spoke to me the previous night. He had been full of chat about the book, my book, and finishing it. Seemingly someone wanted to buy it. There was a bit of a craze at the minute for the real life story and my book was going to be the tip of that iceberg.

"Carrie, you're going to be rich" he laughed.

"Jesus David, I wouldn't know what to do with it" I grinned, trying to scrape rusk stains off my trackie bottoms.

So much for the glamorous authoress eh?

"No, I mean really rich, someone wants to make a film of it, the rights will go for serious cash, maybe millions" he sighed.

"What?"

"Ah, I dunno love, sometimes I'd like to turn back the clock to when it all began and change it all, make you all happy and innocent again, and Steven too; no money can heal the scars, can it?"

"No, I suppose not Dave, but there's hope now, there's Daragh, and we are coming home soon, really soon, I want to get back and be normal again, you know?"

But even I had to ask myself, what was normal now?

There was no way we could slot back into the life we had, living in the mobile, me working with Nancy up in Grafton Street.

There was bound to be talk and Blanchardstown being the kind of place it was where everyone knew everyone, it would be like living in a goldfish bowl.

So we had to find an acceptable compromise, a kind of normal.

I thought we had a fair chance of finding it when we got home, eventually.

But still there were loose ends to tie up.

Young Peter was released from the hospital and was gone. He had been put into sheltered accommodation, but had run away and hadn't been seen for a few weeks. That was a worry, because by all accounts, well, Nancy's really, Dublin in 1994 wasn't the place it had been when me and her stomped around at all hours in our Doc Martens.

"I'll do my best kiddo, keep me ear to the ground, but its like finding a fucking needle in a haystack, finding a young lad on the streets, and things are difficult here at the minute" She'd said.

I hated myself for not asking what was wrong with her. But at times it was like an overloaded switch, you know, one more item plugged in and ka-boom, my brain would explode. I thought it was love trouble, maybe she and Denny weren't getting on and I couldn't expect her to run round looking after my brother.

I prayed a lot for him, he wasn't eighteen yet, and Dublin could be a cruel place when you're alone. I knew that well, didn't I?

So, after all the procrastinating and dallying, we finally went to Liverpool in February 1994. Steven wrote to Colleen and she told him to come.

No mention of me, though. Small wonder that. She must have hated me before she met me.

David had come to London the day before with Becky and shushed Steven when he asked about the test results.

"Time for that later son" he'd held out his arms for Daragh.

"Come on my little man, come to Granddad, and say hello to your granny" He grinned at Becky who rolled her eyes. It seemed to be business as usual there.

"Your gorgeous glamorous granny" he smiled and kissed her.

"That's better" she held her arms out for the baby.

"C'mere to me gorgeous boy" She smiled.

So it seemed that whatever the craic was, Becky didn't know.

They took Daragh back to Ireland with them. I didn't want to be landing up to see Colleen with my baby under my arm. It was going to be fraught enough.

"This is your last chance to be my bridesmaid Carrie, I'm putting the wedding on hold for one more month, so get this sorted and come the fuck home to us" Becky said as she hugged me.

"I will, I will, I promise"

"Just do it, you don't have to see them again if you don't want to"

"That's true enough" I smiled.

We went up on the train and came to the famous Lime Street station.

I loved it the minute I got there. Something about it felt right, felt like home. I dragged Steven there and then down to Matthew Street to the Cavern, which was all done up and re-opened fifty yards from the original. I could feel the atmosphere and closed my eyes trying to imagine the Beatles on that tiny little stage.

We had a drink there, just the one, because I didn't want to be half cut going to see Colleen. And my parents too.

"How d'ya feel Carrie?" Steven asked as I took pictures outside the cavern.

I must have looked like any other tourist, and I smiled-

"Apart from the fact that this is the weirdest day of my life, isn't it amazing that we're here? Where the Beatles came from? Imagine that" I got goose-bumps even thinking of that.

I'd grown up on that kind of music, the seventies rock and the sixties. Peter had played them on the radiogram in the living room and I'd loved it. I closed my eyes and wondered where my Da was now. In all of my troubles he hadn't come near me at all. I had thought when the papers came out, that he might. But he was gone for so long; maybe he wanted to stay gone.

Colleen wasn't expecting us till teatime and we spent a good few hours wandering round the city, going out on the Mersey ferry and looking at the sights.

"I never did this when I was here with Colleen, there was always work to be done somehow, grandfather never gave me a long leash, you know?" Steven said, leaning over the rail, looking down at the water.

"Well, we know why now, don't we?"

"Yeah, because anything at all could have jogged my memory and brought me back and the old fucker knew it"

At five o clock, we got into a taxi and he gave the address to the driver. It didn't take too long to get out to the house. It was like I had imagined.

Like one of the houses in Coronation Street, or in Bread. The type that face right out on the street. But there was a tarmac road not cobbles. And the houses were all decked out in frilly nets and bowls of flowers in the windows.

Colleen's house had a welcome mat and I stared down at it, my stomach turning.

"Oh God Steve, I want to go home, I can't do this" I whispered.

It was too late.

The door was opened by a man, dressed in a stripy shirt and slacks-

"Hullo, Gary" he held out his hand and Steven shook it-

"Steven, please, Mr. Dalton" he smiled.

The man, *my father?* Nodded.

"Right you be son, come in" he held the door wider.

Steven went inside and pulled me with him by the hand-

"You must be Carrie" My father said, staring at me like he'd been struck by lightening.

"I am" I whispered.

Oh God, I had his curly hair, and his build. He was stocky. A bit of middle aged spread maybe, but God he even stood like me.

He held out his hand-

"Hello, I'm, *Valerie!*" he roared, grabbing the banister for support.

I stood like I was rooted to the spot.

If I thought for one minute that I was like him, that all faded into insignificance when I saw my mother.

She came running from a room out back wiping her hands on a tea towel-

"Jesus Jimmy, what the fuck?" She stopped in the middle of the floor, dropping the cloth onto the carpet.

"Oh my God, Jimmy!" She breathed.

I stared.

I was her living image.

Her hair was tied back in a loose ponytail, little tendrils falling around her cheeks which were rosy from the heat, like mine get when I'm doing the housework. She was wearing jeans, and slippers. Her cardigan was open over an old tee shirt, which made me laugh. It had a faded picture of the Cavern on it, with the Beatles faces in black and white. She was a good bit taller than her husband, and thinner, definitely thinner.

Well that's where the height comes from.

I had purposely not dressed up for the meeting. I wore my jeans too, and my newer tee-shirt was visible under the long black cardigan I wore.

Like mirror images of each other we both put our hands up to our mouths and the tears started-

"*Jimmy*" she gasped.

He was still clutching the banister and Steven's hand.

The shape of her eyes, her face, her colouring, apart from the red tint in my hair that came from my father, her looks were all mine too.

Jimmy shook his head and kept saying-

"It can't be right, this isn't happening"

I couldn't talk for the crying and Steven let go of Jimmy and put his arm around me-

"Its okay, its okay, you know who this is don't you?" he looked at them.

"She's so like you Val, so *like* you, much more than Colleen is, Val, look at her" Jimmy was holding on for dear life now.

Then Valerie, she did a strange thing; she came over and looked straight into my eyes. She reached up and pushed some hair back off my forehead and she nodded.

"You're my Layla, aren't you?" She said, and when I nodded she grabbed me in a bear hug.

"My baby, my baby, Oh Layla, I knew it wasn't right, you're not dead, oh Layla" She wept.

Tears were tripping me too, I couldn't say a word.

So, the two of us, we just stood there and cried for ages, till the breeze coming in the door nearly froze us to death.

None of us could eat the meal she had made, and as for tea, that went out the window. Jimmy poured four massive drinks with shaking hands.

Colleen was no where to be seen. I was still on tenterhooks waiting to meet her.

My rival.

My sister.

We sat in the living room on a flowery sofa and drank brandies and tried to talk, tried to make sense of the last twenty three years.

I looked from one to the other as Valerie told me all about her and Jimmy meeting and the times they had and how they ended up in Glasgow in the first place, and how this mess began way back when.

"You're Jimmy Dalton!" I gasped "*The* Jimmy Dalton?"

"I am, well I was, now I'm just the man who owns the pub, why love, had you heard of me?" He laughed.

Jesus, had I heard of him?

"In the old days, before Da left Ma, he sometimes used to sit in the living room with his records on and a beer in his hand, and I used to sit with him on the arm of the chair. One night he was playing a record by a band called Glorious, and he told me that you were one of the greats, but that you'd gone off and left the band before they hit the big time, he said you were set to be bigger than Page or Clapton, he *loved* you!" I gasped.

"I only played on one of the songs on that album though, one called..." he was rooting in a sideboard now, looking for it.

"It was called *Where is Heaven* wasn't it?" I breathed.

I turned to Steven.

"You remember me playing that tape to you, I taped the album for you, remember, in the beginning?" he shook his head slightly.

"Not really Carrie, some of that time is still hazy"

Valerie was still looking at me amazed.

"Steven, the song, oh, it went like..." I couldn't sing for buttons, but somehow I remembered the song and I sang it-

"Where you are now, can you see me, see the mess I've made, cos all my dreams were for you, and now you're gone away" I blushed scarlet and smiled.

"You know the song, this is unreal!" Jimmy was grinning from ear to ear.

"He wrote that here, in this room, and we cried both of us, because we thought that if you were in heaven you might hear it" Valerie was crying still.

I laughed.

"Whatever you might have called the estate, it was a far cry from heaven anyhow, but I heard the song, I did, and I loved it, and now I know it's for me, it'll be all the better"

We were talking nineteen to the dozen then, old memories and reminisces, tales of the Cavern and the band were all tied up

in the story of the mess up in Baird hall and my being swapped and taken away.

"I saw her taking you out of the hospital that night, I should have looked closer" Valerie shook her head. She couldn't believe this day, any more than I could. In fairness though, I'd had more time to get used to it all.

We were three drinks in by the time Colleen's key turned in the front door and we fell silent, waiting.

I held Stevens hand tightly.

The door opened and in came Colleen, with Michelle in her arms, wrapped up like an Eskimo. She was the living image of Saoirse. I felt tears clogging my throat again and rooted for a tissue.

"Steven, she's the image of Saoirse, at that age" I whispered.

He stood up and held his hands out to the baby, and she leaned to him and smiled.

Oh she was his and no mistake. Ma always said that blood knew itself, or as she used to say it-

"Blood warms you know"

Colleen handed her over and stayed standing at the door.

"Colleen, come in love, you'll never guess" Jimmy began, all excited. His records were all out in the middle of the floor and he had some brilliant early stuff by Sabbath and Thin Lizzy. She looked over to where he was sitting and saw the guitar that he had insisted on climbing into the attic for and had been attempting to tune, in between pouring drinks and telling me tales about meditating with George Harrison and Pattie Boyd. I had been in awe and at the same time was giggling my head off. Not the way I thought that I was going to be at all.

"Why's your guitar down Dad?" She asked, coldly.

"Aw Coll, it's a celebration, you won't believe who this is" he said.

She looked at me and sniffed-

"Oh, I know all right, she's only the slut that broke up my marriage is all"

"Colleen, that's not fair, you know what happened" Steven was still holding the baby, who looked up at her mother confused.

"Yeah, I know, and let me tell you I knew all along about the affair you had with your *sister,* your grand father told me before I married you, told me it would be saving you from jail if you could prove it was all over and finished" She took the child back from him.

She laughed harshly.

"And I, the gullible fool I was, swallowed the tale and decided that I loved you so much that I'd save you, and what do you do?" She looked around the room.

"Go off and have an affair again and leave me holding the baby! That's what! So I know who this is, *this* is Carrie, the famous, untouchable Carrie, the Carrie that was in your head and in your heart and in our bed, even when I was in it and you were fucking me" She stopped.

"Colleen Dalton, I will not have that filthy language here!"

Jimmy jumped to his feet-

"You apologize this minute Colleen" He snapped.

"Oh no I won't, I'm standing here looking at the woman who ruined my fucking life and I won't apologize to her" She turned to me, eyes flashing and laid into me good and proper.

"You don't know what you've done to me, I'm not even twenty one, I have to rear this child on my own, because the person I've loved since I was eighteen years old, he's as good as dead, I have no money and no career, and you swan back into his life like it was all nothing, like *I'm* nothing and you take away my husband and my child's father and now he's gone and I don't know what I'm going to do!" she shouted.

"You *couldn't* understand it Carrie, you have *everything* you need, everything you ever wanted, but you had to take him, what do you know about *me* and what I'm going to face now? A single mother trying to get by rearing a child, when the man I loved is fucking gone, and I can't see him or be with him, he's gone, he might as well be dead" She was crying. And believe it or not it broke my heart.

I closed my eyes and remembered.

I could see the damp spot on the ceiling in the flat and hear Saoirse breathing in the cot next to me. I could remember praying for a sign, anything to show me that Steven could see us, hear me, was trying to break through.

I'd thought he was dead.

I understood Colleen better than anyone, because Gary *was* dead. He didn't exist any more. That's if he ever really had existed. But how did I say this to the weeping wreck that must have been the carbon copy of me, in the dark days after his funeral.

"Colleen, listen to me" I stood up and touched her on the arm.

She looked at me, eyes full of tears and hatred-

"Colleen, I know what its like, I swear to you I do"

"How, how could you *possibly* know?" She managed to be sarcastic through her tears.

"It's a long story, but you have to believe me, it's the same thing as your going through now, I've been there done that, I know what its like"

"But you're his *sister* that can't be right you know"

I laughed softly-

"Isn't that what all this is about, love? All this fighting and all the confusion and the years of thinking I was someone else and Steven too, and the accident, everything, our whole lives blown to shreds in it, and for what?" I looked back at him and he nodded-

"Colleen, I met him in 1990, whatever you say, whatever you think of me now, I was there first, we fell in love and we were having a baby and we wanted to marry, so much, I couldn't wait, and then when we went to sort it out, the birth-certs matched and we thought that we were related, so they arrested us and wouldn't let us be together at all, and then when the baby, a girl, Saoirse, was born they tried to arrest him in the hospital for breaking the barring order, and he ran and ended up in that lorry on the way to see his grandfather, and then it crashed, and we think what happened was that he had swapped jackets with the guy in the lorry, Gary Stanley, who's body was shipped home to us and we buried him, thinking it was Steven. Oh Colleen, that's when you met who you thought was Gary, but you have to see that he didn't exist, the only Gary that *did* exist is buried in Ladyswell Grave Yard now, in Dublin" I was crying again, but I had to keep going, she had to be made see what it had been like.

"I didn't just march in and take him, I thought he was dead, I went to France thinking that I would never lay eyes on him again, I lay awake for close to two years night after night, crying my heart out for him, wishing that things could have been different"

Valerie spoke again for the first time in ages. Since Colleen had come home.

"Hang on, Carrie love, *Saoirse*? Does this mean there's another grandchild out there?" She asked.

Colleen looked at her in amazement-

"What the heck do you mean *another grandchild?*"

Valerie stared.

I shook my head-

"Saoirse is dead, she died in the same fire that killed my mum and two of the three brothers I had, it was all part of the terrible crimes of James Bard, the things he did, to so many of us, but no Valerie, she's gone, I'm sorry, we buried her in the same grave as Gary"

"Mum, what do you mean? *Another Grandchild?*"

"We have our little Daragh though, he's one" Steven said.

"He's nothing us, sure he isn't Mam?" Colleen pulled at her mothers arm.

I turned to Colleen, and I have to say I pitied her, big time.

"You see, this is where the story ends Colleen, I was never related to Steven, or as you call him, Gary, I was never a Bard, and if old Bard hadn't been so evil this wouldn't have gone this far, cos you see, I'm not his sister at all" I looked at Steven and smiled.

"I'm *your* sister Colleen, I'm Layla"

October 1994

We flew home the following week.

I promised that I would keep in touch, but Colleen wasn't having any of it. We promised that the children would know who each other were, and that when Michelle was older we would have her over for holidays and such like. And Daragh could go to my family too. We didn't want this mess to ever happen again.

But Colleen wasn't into that at all. And sadly, neither was Valerie. I suppose she felt she was being disloyal to Colleen taking me into her life, and had gone up with Colleen to her bedroom that night and stayed there.

Somehow the air of celebration that had pervaded dissolved into the air. I didn't know if I would have a relationship with them, but at least I knew who I was.

But my Dad was a different matter. He seemed to think that all it really needed was time to heal all and he told me never to come to Liverpool without coming to see him. I adored him, still do in fact, and he keeps in touch, ringing and sending the odd letter too.

And no one was more thrilled than I when I read in the paper a few weeks later that Glorious, my dads old band, were reforming for a concert in Hyde Park in London, and that the full original line up would be there. Including the illustrious Jimmy Dalton.

"I've dusted the guitar off and I'm slimming into me old leather coat Layla, your old dad is back" He laughed over the phone about a month before the gig.

We were supposed to have gone, we had by this time moved into our new house in Summerhill, in Meath. And Daragh was busy trying to keep up with the puppy David bought him for a house warming gift. Daragh must have the rock and roll gene like his Grandfather, because nothing would do him but to call the puppy Bonzo, after John Bonham of Led Zeppelin. Jimmy near split his sides laughing when I told him.

I had finished the writing and re writing of the book and it was ready to go, and everything was looking fabulous for us finally.

We were still waiting for the wedding of the year; Becky and David were having trouble with that, since he was now a divorcee and not a widower. But we were sure that it would change in time. The law, I mean. Not them, they were still nuts about one another.

But the question of how much time it might take, now became an issue.

You see, when we came home to Ireland, we knew there was something he wasn't telling us. And we were right.

The tests had shown up cancer.

Testicular cancer. They were devastated, because it had been quite advanced by the time it was found, and he was going through hell on wheels with the chemo. And Becky was upset because it meant no children, probably. And she really *really* wanted a baby. She was living in the home house in Blanchardstown, still with our mobile out in the garden, even though we had taken the stereo and all our vinyl out to the new house.

But by the end of the summer, David was finished the chemotherapy and it was looking better and brighter all round.

He was still only in his forties, and quite fit and healthy. He had to knock the brandy on the head but he was making good progress, and he was determined that once his hair grew back and he was on the mend, the wedding would happen.

"Still and all, I can't expect a big mop of hair at my age, can I?" he laughed.

Becky would reassure him that bald was the new long haired and that men like Sean Connery were sex symbols the world over.

"Dave Bond? I can live with that, especially since my Miss Money penny is so darned gorgeous!"

Another huge shock was the fact that Nancy was pregnant.

I hadn't even known she was still seeing Denny, but she met me the week after we moved into the house with a bump that would soon be the size of Mount Rushmore and swollen ankles stuck into her ubiquitous stilettos.

"Jesus, *only you* could have a da like Jimmy Dalton and not be able to hold a note in a bucket!" She said when she heard me singing to Daragh in the bath.

She remained very tight lipped about Denny, the baby's father and I figure when she wants to tell us she will. She had a daughter in August, and true to form she called her Rain, after her favorite song. She's in a bad way though, I know her heart is broken, and she's finding it hard to cope. She tried to ring Denny and I know she wrote to him too, but there's been no reply.

"It's like he forgot me the minute he got famous" she sighs.

I wish I could do something for her and Serena is trying to help her too, especially since that mess in the flat had to go to court to be sorted. It's hard for her; being here on welfare and watching Denny get rich and famous. But knowing Nancy she will survive.

Young Peter is still out there. Word on the street is that he's using. I'm heartbroken about it all, but again, you can't find someone who doesn't want to be found.

Life has slowed to an easy pace. But I know what you're thinking, what about me and Steven? What about our wedding? Betcha you thought we'd be up that aisle like greyhounds out of the trap? A big showy day out, cocking a snook at the world?

Not us injuns!

See, the divorce came through in May and we thought about what we wanted. It was a strange situation to see Gary Bards name on the decree when we knew he never existed. This was why we hadn't the trouble with remarriage that Dave and Becky were having. Steven had never been married in the eyes of Irish law. So therefore we were free to do as we wanted.

The summer began to slip by us, we spent a lot of time in the house, decorating. Its actually a little cottage with the attic converted into two little bedrooms, I painted one white and got curtains in Chandra's, well, I bought beautiful sari material and made them, and while Steven went to work in Round Tower with his father, I stayed at home and painted and did the house up bit by bit.

I have a room here for my mum and dad, if they ever come to visit me. Dad might one day soon, because there's talk of him and the band doing Slane next year. What a buzz that's going to be!

And I love it here, Dubliner I might be, but there's something lovely about opening the window in the morning and seeing fields and sky and hearing the birds sing. And Sunday mornings are our time, lying in bed with the curtains floating in the breeze from the open windows and listening to the trees whispering while we make love. It's better than anything I could have hoped for and I know that we are so blessed to be here and be alive and together.

Steven is going mad for Daragh to be a little bigger and be able to go fishing with him in the river nearby. I don't mind him taking up fishing, but he better not take up golf, cos that's the greatest old fogey pastime there is!

I have room for writing in and it's lovely, with lots of shelves for the books I collect every time I go into town and hit Chapters Bookstore. Steven got the shelves built when the stack of books in the bathroom was so big he couldn't find his razor for three days and he was forced to go to a very important meeting looking like a pirate! Very sexy it was, him looking all dark and dangerous, but not when he was meeting the writer of a serious tome about the Irish Civil war.

Eddie Bruton, the author was an old schoolteacher and a stickler for etiquette and manners and good grooming, and hadn't been seen in public unshaven or in anything other than a three piece suit for years. I didn't like to think of his reaction to Steven in a shirt with no tie and unshaven, being the man he was entrusting his labour of love to.

As I thought, it didn't go too well and he rang on the way home.

"He hated me on sight, says that Meridan have offered him his own editor and a full team of proofreaders to get the manu looked over quick, Jesus Carrie we don't have them sort of resources in our place, I wish my Dad was in today and not me, he'd have it sorted in no time"

Meridan were a rival publishing house, and the bane of David's existence. David was in court that day, fighting for the right to publish the autobiography of a guy who'd been sacked from an up and coming rock band, and who wrote a warts and all account of their exploits and was being sued by the manager of the band, which was none other than Storm, the band that Denny Palmer fronted.

Small world huh? But it left poor Steven out of his depth when it came to a diva like Brutal Bruton. His last book was short-listed for so many awards that you could hardly make out the title on the cover. It was a ponderous, almost unreadable, in my opinion, account of the life of Charles Stewart Parnell and it was now being used as a reference text for Leaving Certificate. No wonder he was smelling himself a bit, eh?

"That's a bummer honey, maybe he's chancing his arm, you know"

"Nah, he looked at me like I was a down and out and asked did I sleep in my clothes"

He'd left that morning late and hadn't time to wait while I ironed his shirt.

"And the traffics fucking awful" he grumbled.

"It is Friday babes, to be expected isn't it?" I tried to humour him to no avail. He was in the horrors and nothing was making it better.

He came in that night in pigs humour and I left him to it and ran a bath. That's the best way to deal with a narky bugger, leave the dinner ready and then make yourself scarce. Daragh was in bed asleep by the time he came in, Nancy was out on a rare night out with Eddie, she was still expecting the baby then and didn't go out much, but Eddie insisted that she needed a bit of time away from her brooding and bump rubbing in her bedroom, so for once, the house was quiet and there was peace.

I clicked the CD player on and slipped into the bath with a book, something a bit more palatable than Brutal Bruton's efforts.

He stomped around for a while, ate the dinner that I left for him and then went mooching round the house, looking for clean jeans to change into, finally landing in to the bathroom in his shirt and boxers, where I was up to my neck in bubbles and the latest Frank Delaney.

"I'll make a deal with you baby" he said, finally finding his razor under a copy of Oscar Wilde's Reading Gaol, and my dressing gown.

"What?" I was in the bath, too engrossed in the book to look up.

"I promise never to be unfaithful or take up golf" He grinned.

"You bloody better not!" He being unfaithful was a thought I couldn't even begin to entertain, but in fairness, it was highly unlikely, after everything we had been through together. And as for Golf, if a grown man wanted to whack a ball round a field with a stick then why not play Hurling? That, at least was manly and a proper game, in my opinion!

"On two conditions" I could see the twinkle in his eye and knew he was winding me up. At least his bad mood was gone.

"Name them oh Darling one" I smiled, playing along with him. Though still looking at the book in my hand.

"That even if he asks you, down on his knees, in the nip, you will never, ever, leave me for Larry Mullen" He paused.

Larry Mullen, the sexy, blonde drummer from U2, was the one man we girls all agreed we would leave home for. He was talented, stunningly handsome and stinking rich, and to add spice to the mix he drove a Harley! A powerful aphrodisiac for any girl. Or boy for that matter.

Years ago I remembered reading about Boy George, saying to Bono that if he still hadn't found what he was looking for he should look behind the drum kit!

Have to say, I agreed wholeheartedly. Nancy and I had his picture Sellotaped to the fridge door and she would blow him a kiss every morning on route to the percolator-

"Mornin' Larry, yah big ride yeh" She'd coo, blowing him a kiss.

"Didn't think he was your type Nancy, didn't you used to like the dark haired ones? I thought Bono would be more your bag" David had laughed one morning when she waddled in to the kitchen for her usual routine.

"Bono? Nah, he wears higher heels than I do, give me Larry any day" She laughed.

She poured out the coffee and made light of the situation as always-

"The dark ones are never faithful" She said.

"Hey, Steven's dark, and he's faithful" I said, laughing at the cooker.

"He's the exception Carrie, I'm just changing me type is all, its strictly blondes and ginger boys for Nancy from now on"

"Eddie's ginger" Said David quietly.

"Yah don't say, first prize for perception to the oul fella in the corner, now, are you making the brekkie, Carrie, or have yeh gone to lay the eggs yourself?" She plonked herself at the table and said nothing more.

But I remembered how her face had paled at the mention of liking the "dark ones" and I felt sad for her.

The chances of Larry roaring up to the door on the Harley were slim to nil, but I pretended to think about it while I ran more water into the bath with my toes on the tap.

Steven was waiting for my reply, leaning against the sink-

"Hmm, that's a tough call Steve, he *is* loaded *and* gorgeous, a fierce combination for a man you know, but I think I remember hearing that Larry is happily settled himself, so you're most likely okay there, so what's the other one?"

"The other what?" he was lathering up at the sink.

"You said two conditions, so I don't give you the old heave ho for Larry, what's the other one?" I realized that it was true, that men couldn't do more than one thing at a time. Like wash their face and think! Lucky women can multi task isn't it? The world and everything in it would come to a grinding halt if we didn't!

"The second one? Oh yeah, that if I build you a study and shelve the damned thing, you'll stop turning the bathroom into a bloody library!"

I flung a handful of bubbly water at him and laughed-

"Very funny, now, come here, before you start shaving that beard off" I grinned, throwing the book into the hall.

"I'm all soaped up, ready to go" he sat on the side of the bath and I wrapped my arms round him. I'd put loads of bubbly oil into the water and it made me smell like raspberry ripple ice cream. Good enough to eat, I would have thought.

"So am I, and if I can't have my Larry Mullen fantasy, I'm gonna have my Alan Rickman in Robin Hood one, so c'mere" I pulled and he landed into the bath.

"Another shirt bites the dust, Carrie, how am I ever going to be a respected publisher when you keep drowning all my good clothes in bath oil?" He kissed me, and I wrapped my legs round him.

"Fuck the shirt babe, I'll get you new ones when I have me affair with Larry, and he lets me loose with the credit card, it's just, you look so dark and *menacing* with that beard, I thought you might like to deflower me"

He was shaking with laughter-

"Jesus, dark and menacing, that's a good one, come here wench, you never paid your tax and the sheriff demands payment, in kind"

Water sloshed all over the floor and the shirt ended up in a puddle beside the bath.

"Carrie, do you have to do this when the bath water is hot enough to light a smoke?" he reached and turned off the tap.

"They do say that there's nothing like hot sex" I giggled, as steam engulfed the bathroom.

Needless to say, the beard stayed put till Sunday night, when it was regretfully shaved off and he was back to his old self.

And I finally got my study!

So now, in between painting and cleaning and looking after Daragh and the menagerie of pets we seem to be adding to all the time, I write. I go in there whenever a story seems to play in my head for so long that I can't stop myself from getting it on paper and I peg away at my computer, until I am tired and can go to bed and sleep.

That's another reason I love Steven, he leaves me be when I want to write, not freaking out when its going on three hours and I haven't talked to him because I am stuck into something and just don't want to tear myself away. There are so many things he does that make me love him, and every week it seems I am finding more and more of them.

We go everywhere and do everything together, just as I wanted it to be.

Nancy reckons it's a bit sickening, but she says it's her hormones that have her in the horrors, plus a broken heart and a soupcon of jealousy too.

"But not the bad type Carrie, I just wish it was me and Denny too, you know?"

I know, and I feel for her and I try to understand and not be too loved up in front of her now.

&

Initially we thought we'd ask Ray to marry us, since he'd been going to all that time ago.

Ray and this came as a huge shock to me, was no longer a priest.

We found this out when we went up to see him with Daragh one afternoon and the housekeeper told us very snippily that he was left the order and was doing Celtic weddings in Galway.

"He's a pagan now" She sniffed.

We found him, God knows how, but we did, through the archive of the Galway Press, and we tracked him down. He's doing well; he's married himself now with two babies. making up for all the lost time. I always said that he was great with the local kids.

He wears a long white robe and beads and the locals there think he's as mad as a bag of badgers, but they love the tourism he brings to the area and leave him be.

One of these days we're going to go to the Aran Islands and find him and show him that we turned out okay. He was so good to us, always. He deserves his happiness in shed loads.

We were humming and hawing about the wedding ourselves, thinking that we might have to wait another year till David was on his feet, and at one stage there was talk about us having a double wedding with him and Becky.

But then, one night in the summer, when the stars were especially bright in Meath, I said to him, sitting in the garden-

"Do you remember that time we went to Connemara?"

He smiled-

"Yeah, I do, I remember what we did in that boat, you hussy!" he pulled me closer to him in the seat. I slipped my arm round his neck and sat on his lap.

I could smell the grass we'd cut earlier in the evening and the night scented stock I planted in tubs all round the patio and I sighed. I was so very happy here and I loved him so much, and he loved me. I felt really lucky.

I was glad he remembered Connemara. Things were really becoming clearer to him now, and I was so grateful to God and everyone up there that I knew for making it happen. We had seen a doctor who told us that he might have blackouts and that I shouldn't expect the old Steven to be here now. The brain is a funny thing, they said, he might lose personality or expressions, things that he used to be and do.

But so far so good, he was himself. Just as he was before. The one change was that he was a little less likely to get annoyed over little things, and if it was possible, he seemed even more loving and affectionate with me.

"That night the stars were just like that too, until it rained of course" I grinned, thinking of what happened after that myself. I had even more fondness for thunderstorms since that night under the boat. The mere sound of thunder in the distance could have me buzzing. We didn't get nearly enough of them in Ireland. I thought that I might go storm chasing in America one day, the two of us.

God only knows what would happen then mind you!

"Hmm" he nuzzled my neck and the old familiar spark took light again.

"You smell nice..." he said, and I laughed.

"Thanks"

He was easy to fall into, easy to forget myself with. But this time I really did want to say something, and I pulled away slightly.

"D'ya know what I remember thinking?"

"What?" still kissing me, down the side of my neck, I was getting shivers now and he bloody knew it too. He laughed softly and carried on-

"I remember thinking that if I could have you, I didn't need anything or anyone else, and I remember thinking that I'd be happy to run away and marry you when ever or where ever you wanted, because I love you, and I will, till the day I die"

And then he stopped kissing me and looked at me straight in the face, and we smiled.

Because we were never about big flashy weddings, or big statements to the world, Jesus we'd had enough of that. We'd loved each other for too long, it was like it was overdoing it to make a big noise about it now. We didn't need triumphant marches or anything else, except each other.

Our lives were one big celebration since the day I saw him again in Paris and he had never left me alone again. He understood me like no one else would or could. He loved what I loved and we were looking in the same direction in this life. We didn't need orchestras or moonlight and magnolias. I was happier dancing in my pajamas in the kitchen on a Sunday morning to the golden oldies on the radio than I ever would be in a white dress in some anonymous hotel with a load of people we hardly knew but were honor bound to invite to a wedding.

"So, what do you think?" He asked.

"Let's just do it" I smiled.

He nodded-

"Ring your Dad and Mum, tell them it's happening, it's up to them if they want to come and be there, I'll sort it all next week in Navan and we'll do it as soon as possible"

It happened that fast.

Six weeks and three days later, in mid September, I was standing in the hallway of the registry office in Navan, listening to the hum of voices in the room beyond and waiting for the registrar to settle them down.

My father had arrived that morning on the early plane from Liverpool.

"Is Valerie coming?" Steven had asked, phoning from his father's house. I'd kicked him out, wanting to spend my last night with Nancy and Becky. Nancy had Rain in her arms and couldn't be my witness, but Becky was happy to oblige. Up till he arrived at the door, I hadn't thought that my father would be with me to walk me down the aisle, because the wedding was clashing with a couple of gigs he was playing. David and Eddie had offered to step in, but I'd held out hope and he had come through.

But not my mother, sadly. She stayed at home and though she sent her best regards, I was sad that she couldn't be there out of loyalty to Colleen.

"No Steven, she isn't coming over, but I had to be here for my Layla" My dad smiled and I squeezed his arm.

The house was like a grotto with flowers and decorations. Everyone was coming back for a party after the ceremony and Nancy and I had put the balloons in the trees in the garden and the little lights for the barbeque later all around the patio. The weather was holding and there was still a bit of heat in the sun.

Daragh was his dad's best man. He was nearly two and as he told everyone-

"I'm daddy's best boy today" and was driving us mad showing us the little pocket in his waistcoat for the wedding ring.

"God Steve, don't let him lose that ring" Becky was a nervous wreck.

But he hadn't and was standing at the top of the very short aisle bursting with self importance, beside his daddy.

"Layla?" My dad, looking like a rocker in his Edwardian style coat and dark trousers, a purple orchid in his buttonhole, the exact colour of my dress, tipped me on the arm.

"You ready pet?" he asked.

"I am, are you?" I smiled.

A couple of years ago he had walked my little sister down a much bigger and fancier aisle to marry the same man, and today must be so strange for him.

He just looked into my eyes and smiled.

"Layla he loves you, and you love him, and its all turned out the way its meant to be, and one day the rest of the world will know that, so now, come on love, lets get you married and off my hands" he kissed me and I held him tight for a second.

"I love you Layla, I hope you are happy for the rest of your life" he said, his words muffled by my shoulder.

"Oh Dad, I love you too" I felt tears coming and prayed I wouldn't cry. I loved my Dad though and wanted him to know it.

He nodded in at the registrar and the opening beat of the music I had chosen came blaring out-

"Good choice of song Layla, c'mon, dry them eyes and smile, it's your big day" He handed me a hanky and I blotted under my eyes.

"Will I do?" I asked.

My dress was deep purple, my hair down, with tiny purple orchids in a ring on my crown. I carried lilies and orchids in my bouquet and my shoes were ballet flats. I'd chosen the Ramone's version of "Baby, I love you" to walk down the aisle to and I could see David smiling as he looked towards the door.

"Your beautiful kid, now, lets go" He took my hand and squeezed it and I waited for the right moment, so that the song would finish as I reached the top of the aisle.

And that was it. I did the little walk to the registrar's desk on my fathers arm and he gave me to Steven, and wished him luck.

"Not that your going to need it, just take care of my Layla, eh?"

"Always" Steven smiled.

Our wedding party went on all night, with music and dancing under the stars in the garden. Daragh and Rain were put to bed at all hours and the rest of us sat up drinking beer and talking till the dawn came creeping into the sky.

At some point we all changed out of wedding finery into jeans and pajamas for the girls and it was so nice lounging in the garden with all the people who meant the world and more to us for the last couple of years.

I got Steven to myself in the early hours and he asked me was I happy.

"I can't tell you how happy I am, its all over, the bad times are gone now, and there are no shadows any more, everything is as it should be, and I couldn't be any happier than I am now, not if I live to be a hundred" I smiled, looking back at the group on the patio who were listening to my father playing a guitar that they'd found somewhere.

He had an amazing repertoire of songs, and he even sang one for me, in place of making a speech. He said that he went back to the music because I was alive and it was better than a number one record to see me so happy now.

My eyes filled up with tears when he started to sing, his voice cracking a little with emotion.

"I got sunshine, on a cloudy day, oh when it's cold outside, I got the month of May..." all the time smiling at me.

"Oh Dad" I hugged him when he finished.

And he carried on playing long into the night, old songs and new ones that I didn't think he would know.

Nancy was singing along, her voice low and quiet, and I could see that her heartbreak was written on her face, but that she was trying to be brave and not let it show.

Becky was sitting at David's feet and he was stroking her hair, watching my dad as one song ended and he began another.

"Listen" Steven put his arms round me and I held him. The flowers were still in my hair, albeit a bit wilted now, and probably mismatched with my pink satin pajamas and bare feet.

My dad was playing "Layla", the slow bluesy version, and the notes wove out into the starry night like a dream.

I couldn't help myself, I sang along softly and we danced under the old apple tree, me barefoot and him in his jeans while everyone else stayed watching my father play. I rested my head against his shoulder and sighed.

"No more waiting and wishing, no more chasing shadows, Carrie, this is it forever and ever" he whispered.

"I know, oh its such a lovely night, I so don't want it to be over"

He laughed softly-

"It'll end, like the night always does, it's been a wonderful night, but Carrie..."

"What?"

"It's always going to be wonderful, every night, not just tonight, because every night from now on, I'll be here with you, won't I?"

"Yeah, you will"

He twirled me around as the last notes died and the birds started to sing in the early morning light.

"C'mon Mrs. Williams, come on home with me" I took his hand and we went back up the garden to the house.

Home.

Our home forever, to get old and grey in, to fill with babies and to live there with them. To lie together in our attic room and listen to the rain falling and the birds singing.

To laugh in and love in, till we forgot that it had ever been any other way.

I was finally at peace, finally where I was meant to be.

At last.

..........ends.

Printed in the United States
138511LV00002B/65/P